Guardians at the Wall

By Tim Walker

D1337407

Guardians at the Wall

Acknowledgements

I would like to thank the following for their invaluable input:
Proof reader and critique partner – Linda Oliver
Student lifestyle consultant – Tom Shacklady
Twelve beta readers for their vital feedback
Copyeditor – Sinéad Fitzgibbon (@sfitzgib)
Cover designer – Cathy Walker
(www.cathyscovers.wixsite.com)

Independently published by

Table of Contents

Map with Place Names

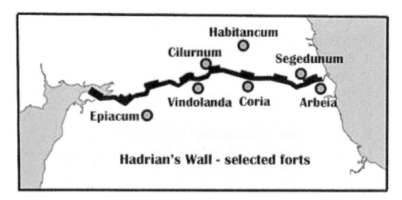

Hadrian's Wall - selected forts

Place Names

Now	Roman
Hadrian's Wall	Vallum Hadriani
Vindolanda*	Vindolanda
Corbridge*	Corioritum or 'Coria'
Wallsend*	Segedunum
South Shields*	Arbeia
Risingham*	Habitancum
Whitley Castle*	Epiacum
Chesters*	Cilurnum
Carvoran*	Magnis
York*	Eboracum

* Roman fort sites

Main Characters

Now	Roman
Noah Jessop, student	Gaius Atticianus, centurion
Maggie Wilde, professor	Aria, his wife
Mike Stone, site manager	Brutus, their son
Dave, Richard, Russ, students	Amborix, auxiliary soldier
Mavis MacDonald, PA	Paulinus Grella, optio
Sima Chaudry, archivist	Plauditus Vespasianus, centurion
Inspector Griffiths, Police	Lupus Viridio, centurion
	Helvius Pertinax, tribune
	Lucius Bebius, tribune
	Claudius Hieronymianus, legate

3

1. Hadrian's Wall, present day

Scrape, scrape, scrape. I tightened my grip on the wooden handle of the trowel, my fingers numbed by the chill breeze, submitting to the tedium of repeated but gentle scrapes at the dry, crumbly soil. Layered shades of brown to my sides spoke of the ages of Man, tantalizing my eager imagination with the possibility that the earth might yield a long-lost treasure that offered a glimpse into the lives of the people who had once lived here.

"Found anything yet?" boomed Mike Stone, site manager and keen amateur archaeologist on this combined universities dig. His dominion covered an acre where eight parallel trenches were being dug down to a depth of a metre within a pegged-out quadrant in what was otherwise coarse pastureland suited only to sheep, kept out by a rope fence on iron poles. In the corner was our headquarters, a marquee tent provided by one of the universities involved in the dig. A dozen students from four or five universities were supplemented by an equal number of community volunteers, all engaged in scraping the floor of their trench; or sieving soil at a series of trestle tables outside the marquee. Archaeology was a labour-intensive discipline.

"I've just reached the street cobbles," I replied, twisting my head to shoot him a triumphant grin. I brushed away crumbs of soil with my paintbrush to reveal a cluster of small square grey cobblestones.

"Excellent. The orientation of what looks like the main street is confirmed." He moved to stand at an angle of about forty-five degrees to my trench, scratched his red beard and then shouted the name of an occupant of the next trench. "Can you stand up, love, and stand on the edge of your cobbles. Your right edge as you face me."

I peeped over the top of my trench, stretching my back and looking at the standing woman, then down at the edge of my street. I could see the direction the street was going, and imagined it lined by circular wood and daub huts.

"Clear off your section of street, Noah, then explore the edges for any lost or discarded items. We've found all sorts of household goodies by the side of the road in the other trenches. This is a fascinating and potentially rewarding cross-section through the civilian settlement that sprung up next to Vindolanda Fort. Patience brings rewards." Mike smiled an encouraging smile and brushed soil from his old Christmas jumper before he strode over to the next student in my trench.

I forgot the cold that had numbed my fingers and set about clearing the street with renewed enthusiasm. Once the worn cobbles on my diagonal two-metre width of street were exposed, I then turned my attention to a metre-wide strip to one side of it. No pavements for the locals to walk on, just a mud or grass track that would have separated the street from the dwellings and livestock pens.

Perhaps one day I shall graduate to digging for legionary paraphernalia at the main archaeological site in the remains of the Roman fort.

Once I had established grid lines with string on either side of the street, I climbed out of the trench and wandered off to the marquee tent for the digicam so I could record my progress. I rotated my sore arms as I looked up at a clear, pale blue early November sky over a Northumberland field wedged between hills. We were a few hundred yards south of the rocky stubble of Hadrian's Wall that could be glimpsed on distant hilltops to the north.

I turned at the sound of Mike's approach, his gum boots bouncing on the wooden boards preserving the moorland grass around the outer edge of the dig. Beyond him, white woolly blobs ripped at the tough turf with teeth and jaws suited to the harsh environment.

"Once you've photographed it, make an entry in the day log," he said, before leaving me to check on the four volunteers who were sieving soil for hidden fragments of pots or small coins in a long wooden box outside the marquee.

It was the site of a settlement of wood and mud-daubed huts and their adjacent animal pens built by the Brigante people, next to what had once been the stone walls of the Roman fortress at Vindolanda. The Romans would have referred to the cluster of buildings as a 'vicus'. Every fort had one. The fortress site had been excavated almost continuously since the 1930s, and had yielded a wealth of finds that revealed a detailed picture of how successive Roman garrisons had lived their lives – including written records and correspondence that had miraculously survived for almost two thousand years entombed in layers of peat and soft clay. Now a number of archaeology undergraduates had come together to excavate and map the vicus that had once serviced the needs of the Roman occupiers.

I returned to my trench and resumed scraping the earth beside the street. After ten minutes, I stopped abruptly as my trowel blade made contact with a solid object. "Another stone," I muttered. I dug around it, slowly scraping the dark, loamy soil and patches of sticky clay, then I burrowed gently with my fingers to get underneath the object. It was no ordinary stone. I picked up my paint brush and swept away the clinging soil to reveal a carved face on a smooth, rounded stone, its form and facial features exposed to the sun and air for the first time in almost two millennia. And my eyes were the first to behold it. Time froze. The excavation didn't exist, just my breathless awe at the face that had last been touched by the hands of someone from the Roman era. I embraced our private moment and then my excitement erupted.

"Mike! I've found something!" I yelled in the direction of my crouching supervisor.

Mike stood up and strode purposefully towards me, springing on the boards like a March lamb, calling, "I'm coming!" He knelt down and stared at the stone face peering out of the soil. "Yes, you've found something alright, young Noah. Brush away the surface and then photograph in situ before easing it out."

One careful centimetre at a time, I freed the object, and I held it in my calloused hands, gently brushing away the top layer of clinging soil. I raised the carving and saw grooved swirls and inscriptions that would be revealed when it was clean, and the delicate features of the statuette. It was carved from light grey marble, had a flat base, and stood about ten inches tall. I estimated the weight to be about two pounds – a bag of sugar.

The other students and volunteers had stopped what they were doing and now gathered around, making cooing noises or remarking 'nice' and 'lovely'. I brushed some more, exposing details of the impassive face and shrouded body that suggested it was a female form, its hands cradling the mound of its belly. After admiring her for a few seconds, I handed her over to Mike, grinning like a bridegroom.

"Hmmm, it looks like a deity of the Brigante tribe, perhaps a goddess of fertility or one to ward off evil spirits. Could be carved from a lump of marble found in the quarry pits that produced the blocks used to build the fortress walls. There's a vein of quartz running through it that perhaps influenced its selection. I'll take it to Professor Wilde to get her opinion. Well done, lad. Now everyone, back to work. Noah's shown us that there are riches still to be discovered!"

I beamed with pride as if I'd uncovered the tomb of a pharaoh, and as Mike continued the process of recording and tucked up my beautiful goddess nice and safe, my eyes followed his every move, and I nodded as he talked me through it.

My friend Dave pressed a muddy hand on my shoulder. "Well done, mate," he said, smiling down at me. "That puts you one-nil up."

This was what archaeology was all about – moments of discovery that connected you to an ancient world. I knew many would dig and scrape their allotted patch for days and find nothing, so this carving – my first significant find – elevated my sagging spirits and I dug away with renewed verve, whistling a tuneless tune.

Perhaps this was the home of a quarry worker? Perhaps he or his wife had a hidden creative talent? Maybe they set up a small business and produced carvings of deities for their neighbours? Or perhaps it was made for the shrine of a mysterious druid living in the woods. Who was this enigmatic deity? My interest was piqued and I wanted to know more. I resolved to visit Professor Maggie Wilde when my shift finished.

*****

A blackbird warbled an undulating warning as I sauntered down stone steps, past a reconstruction of a Roman pottery kiln, on my way to the offices adjacent to the museum. A visiting couple, who reminded me of my parents, passed by, guidebook and camera in hand, on their way to walk around the excavated shell of the Roman fort. I smiled and wished them good morning. As part of our induction training, students and local volunteers had been told that we were, temporarily at least, members of staff, and must always be polite, friendly and helpful with visitors.

The excavation site was managed by a trust that raised money from grant-giving organisations and fundraising initiatives. It also relied on visitors paying admission fees, buying books and souvenirs, and frequenting the cafeteria that prepared excellent hot meals, cakes and sandwiches. I was staying in a dormitory block on site, sharing a room with three other male students, two of whom were studying archaeology at Newcastle University, one of the dig sponsors. My friend Dave and I were in the final year of an archaeology degree course at

Durham University. I had agreed a broad outline for my dissertation with my course tutor and hoped that inspiration for a central theme would materialise on this dig.

I skirted around the two-storey sandstone building and ducked through a doorway into a well-lit reception area and stood before Mavis, the marketing assistant.

"Hi Mavis, is Maggie in?" I chirped, picking up the latest issue of Archaeology Magazine. Professor Maggie Wilde was pictured on the cover, standing on the battlements of the reconstructed section of wall, gazing northwards towards the unconquered barbarians. She was already a celebrity archaeologist and would have made the perfect foil for Harrison Ford's movie character, Indiana Jones, with her wild, windswept strawberry blonde hair framing a striking face with cute freckles across her nose, and twinkling pale blue eyes. Her glossy lips suggested she knew the value of a warm smile or pout in a room full of men. 'It's like fancying your mum's friend', Dave had once remarked.

"She's on a conference call to the States. Wait if you like, she'll be finished soon," Mavis replied, in a cultured Edinburgh accent. Posh Scottish.

"She's the pin-up girl of British archaeology," I quipped, flashing the magazine cover.

"I don't know what she uses to keep her skin so flawless," Mavis sighed.

"Perhaps she discovered an ancient potion?" I offered, flicking through the pages to the article. I had been hovering around when the photographer had taken her photos that day – maybe I was in the background of one of the pictures? I sat and read. 'Hadrian's Wall Gives Up Its Secrets', the headline declared. The Vindolanda reading tablets were described as, 'the find of the century.' My broad idea for my dissertation was for it to be based on translations from some of the tablets – those that related to the lives and living conditions of the soldiers garrisoned at

Vindolanda and other forts in the early years of Hadrian's Wall. I had been cropped out of the photos.

"They couldn't have been more excited if they'd discovered Moses's tablets," I quipped.

"You can go in now," Mavis said, her voice dragging me away from the article. I had read half of it, and resolved to return to it when I came out.

Professor Maggie Wilde's room was bigger than the reception area, with two walls given over to floor-to-ceiling book shelves – one with books and the other with boxes of academic reports and maps. No doubt Mavis had labelled and sorted them, as Maggie gave the air of being disorganised. She was an anomaly – a successful career academic who reputedly hated being tied down to boring tasks, like report-writing, collating documents, copying and filing; a creative free-thinker who was skilled at persuading others to unburden her of boring or repetitive tasks. She held two positions – Head of Archaeology at the Trust, and part-time Archaeology Professor at Newcastle University.

"Ah, Noah, come in. Just move those over there and sit," she said, pointing to a couch piled high with maps and printouts. I moved the items and sat, twiddling my thumbs, watching the crown of her ginger head, waiting until she looked up. I had literally bumped into her at the student placement reception a few days earlier, and she had welcomed me with a firm handshake. I had blurted that I'd seen her Hadrian's Wall documentary on television, feeling like a needy fan as soon as I'd said it. She had smiled and asked me what I hoped to achieve during my placement and listened intently, planting her stylish heels as if she had nowhere else to go, a strange thing in a room where people were mingling in groups. I was grateful for her full attention and pleased when she invited me to call on her expertise any time.

"If it's a bad time I can come back?" I offered.

"There never seems to be a good time, so now will do," she said, removing her reading glasses and fixing me with a warm and welcoming smile. "I've just had a two-hour conference call with members of the US Archaeological Society, so I could do with a distraction." She leaned forward and picked up the marble figure Mike had brought to her hours earlier. He must have thoroughly cleaned and polished it before presenting it to her.

"I just wanted to hear what your thoughts are on that little lady," I said. "Do you think she's a female deity?"

She turned it over in her slender fingers and her shoulders twitched. "Ooh, I felt a slight shock, like static on a jumper," she said, placing it gently on her blotter. "Yes, most likely female, judging by the full-length robe. The slight tummy bump suggests she might be pregnant, so perhaps a fertility symbol. I'll send it to the curator at the Hancock Museum for her opinion. She'll give me a better idea of where it fits into the Brigantes' belief system. Some of their gods were twinned with Roman deities as the polytheistic Romans were keen to encourage local worship in their temples. Once we know roughly how old it is, we can look for other carvings or figures from that period and make a guess as to which deity it is. I agree with Mike; it could be a goddess whom the household would supplicate for good fortune, fertility or protection from evil spirits. Come and sit in the chair."

I nodded and moved to the visitor's chair across from her, edging it forward until my skinny jeaned knees touched her messy desk. Her chipped red nail varnish was oddly distracting.

She turned the statuette to face me, and I noticed how easily it stood upright on a flat base. "Speaking of educated guesswork, how is your dissertation coming along?" she asked.

"Well, Professor Wilde…"

"Please call me Maggie when we're one-on-one." She smiled.

"Well, Maggie, I'm working my way through photographs of the excavated and cleaned-up tablets, making my own translations and then comparing them with the official translations. There are slight differences in interpretation and meaning. I'm compiling some of the most contentious discrepancies for the classical Latin specialists. In truth, I'm still groping for a narrative – looking for a hook or a way in."

I sat back. She was scrutinising me through narrowed eyes – a look she employed to convey academic consideration. *Expect words of wisdom.*

"You're right to look for a narrative. The story of an individual soldier or officer could lead you in an unexpected direction. And an enlightening one. People see us as dusty academics, but we're much more than that. Academic practices and disciplines are a vital bedrock, but we are, in reality, storytellers. Archaeology is increasingly playing a lead role in the re-telling of ancient history. The Americans are big on that. 'You tell the story of life at Rome's most northern frontier so well, Maggie', one of the Yanks said to me." She stopped to chuckle and I willingly joined in. Her oratory could rival any politician's – it was effortless and passionate. I wanted to listen to her, and to believe.

"I'm going to recommend to your course tutor that you leave the dig at the end of this week and spend your remaining time with us in the archives, helping them translate the newest finds. Who knows, something might jump out at you that you can build your dissertation around."

She stood up and walked around the desk, sitting close to me. "You know, Noah, you are one of Durham's brightest stars, and I have high hopes for you." She leaned down with a waft of rosewater and locked her pale blue eyes onto mine, whispering conspiratorially, "I'm going to take a personal interest in your dissertation. I'd like you to join me for dinner one evening, when you can have my complete attention."

I squirmed a bit and moved my knee away from her leg. She noticed and smiled, standing up and moving to the door with a playful bounce in her step. She opened it and, after a final glance at my marble goddess, I took my cue to leave. "I'd love to," I muttered awkwardly, "please text me the where and when." We were, after all, inmates in an academic institution, with few distractions. I inched past her, flashing a grin as our eyes met for a moment, then marched straight past Mavis to the door, the magazine article forgotten. I could feel my cheeks burning as I glanced back. Maggie gave me a little wave, and I grinned again before exiting into the cool Northumbrian air.

My mind was awhirl with the day's events, and I decided to visit the re-created section of Roman fort on my way back to my room. I climbed the wooden stairs and stood on the platform, roughly where Maggie's photo had been taken, looking over stone battlements to the bleak landscape beyond. The late autumn sun was low in the west, about to touch the distant hills where outcrops of the Vallum Hadriani, the Great Wall of the Emperor Hadrian, built 1,900 years ago, could still be seen.

What would legionaries from warmer, Mediterranean countries have felt to have been posted to this wild, wet and windy northern frontier of empire? Did they hold their oaths dear and believe that the Roman Empire would never end? Did they stare out at the bleak hills and wonder if they would survive their twenty-five years of service?

Perhaps things have not changed that much for some, those who will start their working life after completing their education and commit themselves to paying off a twenty-five-year mortgage – a contract with the empire of capitalism that now rules us. Roman soldiers enjoyed wine, women and song when off duty, and conformed to the laws and rules of society, as we do. By living in an organised society, we are obliged to do service of some kind. Nothing much has changed.

A gust of cold wind on my face told me it was time to retreat to the warmth of indoors, not unlike Roman officers who would have had underfloor heating in their homes to look forward to. I followed the stony path, past the information posts that described the layout of the fort and the buildings that once stood there.

Rome demanded the loyalty of its citizens, but so do the nation states that came after. The weight of expectation that I shall attain a good honours degree and progress in academia or enter the commercial world motivates me. All societies are tiered, like the multi-coloured layers of soil we scrape in the earth, our options laid out before us, like courses at a Roman feast. But failure can easily turn you from spectator to competitor in life's arena, where you are scorned or, worse, have to fight for your life.

My grumbling stomach prompted me to shake off these ruminations and descend the steps to the dormitory block, ready for a warm shower, evening meal and banter with my mates, my onward march inexorable.

2. Vindolanda, 180 CE

Gaius Atticianus grunted and chewed a ball of phlegm before spitting over the stone battlements into the encroaching darkness. A pale crescent moon escorted by stars was rising over a line of hills that separated Vindolanda fort from the Great Wall of Hadrian. The veteran centurion of the Sixth Legion called on a young auxiliary soldier guarding this stretch of wall to bring more charcoal for their brazier. Gaius was Commander of the Watch, and would move on to the next stretch of wall after a few minutes.

"Will you tell me what 'Vindolanda' means, sir?" the youthful guard asked, swinging the brazier from its handle to encourage the glowing embers to embrace the new coals.

"Why would you want to know that?" Gaius replied, turning towards the brazier to warm his legs. The young man placed the brazier between the two of them and warmed his hands in a brazen egalitarian act.

"My mates won't tell me, as if it's their secret."

"What is your name, boy?" Gaius asked, in a voice that suggested he was irritated by the foolishness.

"I am Amborix, sir, of the Belgic people in northern Gallia." He stood to attention as he replied, sensing that he may have annoyed this commander of horses whom he had not encountered before.

"Well, Amborix of the Belgic, it means 'green sky in winter'," Gaius growled, wrapping his red cloak tightly around his leather jerkin as he shifted his gaze to the eerie green glow that now floated on the hilltops, a celestial wonder that followed dancing, twinkling stars from their daytime slumber to entertain the night watch.

"Thank you, sir – although I have been told something different," Amborix replied, also turning to watch

15

the shimmering lights. He was only a few months at the Wall, and had already spent his meagre wages on woollen socks and a thick tunic he wore day and night. He watched in silence as the mysterious wave of light added in new colours – red, blue, violet and yellow - as it climbed into the night sky. "This is a strange land," he added, throwing a stone in the direction of a hoot from an owl, "and a cursed one. Our protector, Sol Invictus, will only rise from his slumber for a few short hours."

Gaius decided to ignore his insolence and let him prattle on. His head still throbbed from the beer he had drunk with his unit at the tavern that afternoon to celebrate the start of the feast of Saturnalia. They had sacrificed a goat to Saturn and had roasted the meat on a spit beside the tavern. Now he regretted the last two toasts, but grinned at the memory of drunken tales of bravery on their last posting in the wild lands north of the Wall. A glass tankard depicting colourful gladiators fighting for their lives had been passed around his carousing mates – each making a toast and downing the contents as a serving girl stood by ready to re-fill it from a pitcher.

"It is indeed a strange and wild land, but you will see in the coming weeks that Sol Invictus will gain more hours and Artemis will sulk in her hall. The long days of summer will come to give me more time with my horses." He adjusted his shoulder guard and turned to the youth. "In Rome they say this is an empire without end, but here we are, boy, at the wild edge of Empire, hemmed in by the Wall."

"Do they even know there are distant borders to the empire in Rome?"

"They only know lust, greed and cheating each other. But there is an edge of Empire, and we are here to patrol it and keep out barbarians who now make it their ambition to get in. The lands beyond the Wall were briefly the Roman province of Valentia, where ghostly forts still stand, but it was impossible to defend and the painted people have reclaimed it. The Wall is a challenge to them, not a barrier. They think it is a gateway to untold riches, to food and horses, and so they will keep coming on."

"My people were barbarians until Caesar crushed us and burnt our villages," Amborix grumbled, poking the coals with the base of his spear.

Gaius stared at the glowing lights, knowing that the line of wall that stretched unseen beneath them was unmanned, and the guards on the mile watchtowers were most likely just as hungover as he. He took a gold coin from his pouch and held it in the palm of his hand. "I make an offering to Fortuna before I ride out on patrol, knowing that we live at the whim of the gods. This gold aureus bears the head of Julius Caesar, and I look at it and will his spirit of sound military judgement to come into me before I make a decision. He may have crushed your people, Amborix, but by doing so brought you into this empire, where there is much opportunity for a man to make something of his life beyond scratching at the soil."

Amborix grunted, unconvinced, and tugged at his grey cloak whilst glancing with envy at his officer's thicker cloak and fingerless mittens. His own ill-fitting round helmet was like a piss-pot compared to Gaius's grand centurion's plumed helmet, which bore carved inscriptions on polished bronze and had leather cheek straps to tie under the chin, unlike his canvas straps. "These are the longest hours," he moaned, reflecting on the day his father sold him into the service of Rome at their tribal meeting place in Gallia Belgica. He held out a coinless hand and a snow flake settled in his palm.

"I've served across the Empire, boy, since leaving my warm homeland in Asturia, and have seen better men than you spitted on the end of long spears, pricked by arrows or trampled under a shield press after their calves had been sliced. I'm old because I'm good at what I do. Now keep your eyes open." In truth, his own eyesight was not what it

17

once was, and the hills were but a blur to him. He would fail to see a man riding an elephant over them.

Amborix ignored his cantankerous commander and stooped to warm his hands over the glowing coals, remarking, "If I could bottle those coloured lights, I'd make a few denarii back home." He stood and glanced at the hills, then froze. "Wait! I can see movement."

Gaius leaned over a stone turret and squinted his eyes. "Where, boy?"

"Moving shapes on that hill," he replied, pointing.

"Climb up the tower and look again."

"It could be wolves," Amborix said, a note of anxiety cracking his voice.

"Still, go and look. Be sharp."

Sighing, Amborix climbed a wooden ladder to the raised platform and scanned the dark hillsides, pausing where the sickly light brought rocks and scrub into wavering relief. He shouted down, "I can't see anything moving. But it's so dark. Shall I call out the guard?"

"Are the hairs on your neck tingling, lad? Can you feel them out there watching you?"

Gaius marched along the parapet and proceeded to wind back the string on a ballista and load a wooden bolt with a sharp iron tip into the groove. He took a torch and lit it from the brazier, placing it in a cradle above the weapon. "Don't go quiet on me, boy – keep your reports coming."

"Something moved, I think but... Shall I ring the bell?"

"Trust your judgement. If you believe you saw creeping barbarians, ring the bell."

The gods were winking in mischief above the dancing, coloured lights; then one star left the others and sped across the sky. "Another bad omen," Gaius muttered under his breath as he peered into the darkness. "First owls, and now the gods are throwing fireballs." He busied himself lighting more torches, then shouted across at the next stretch of wall for the guard to be vigilant. He turned to the tower and bellowed, "Report!"

"Nothing. Maybe I saw…" Amborix's voice gave way to a groan and Gaius turned to see the young man stagger, an arrow shaft protruding from his shoulder.

"Amborix!" Gaius shouted, then ran towards the tower.

The young guard lurched towards him, dropping his spear, and fell to his knees clutching the arrow shaft, before losing his balance, breaking through the rail and tumbling from the tower. He landed on his back on the platform with a thud, his uncovered head bouncing and then lying still. Gaius knelt beside him and pushed his helmet off the walkway. Snowflakes fell on Amborix's closed eyelid and smooth, impassive cheek.

Gaius groaned and tugged at the arrow shaft, but it was too deeply embedded. He softly murmured, "I'm sorry I lied, boy. Just an old soldier's joke. Vindolanda means 'white meadow'. I meant to tell you… now lie still whilst I summon the guard…"

Gaius swivelled at a thud, to see a painted warrior plant his boots on the walkway and let out a blood-curdling cry. Jumping to his feet he drew his sword, just in time to parry a blow aimed at his head from a stone-headed axe. A desperate struggle ensued as the smaller Caledonian warrior pushed with all his strength, growling, a sour smelling foam flecking his drooping moustache. Gaius winced and drew on his reserves of strength, glancing behind him to ensure he didn't trip over the prone figure of Amborix. He growled as he grappled with his opponent, forcing him backwards towards the edge of the platform. With a cry, the warrior fell, landing on his back in a cloud of white powder, lying motionless.

Gaius shouted a warning to the other wall guards and faced another warrior who had vaulted over the parapet and now approached him. But the Asturian turned and ran from the man, leaping over his prone comrade and rushing for the bell. A war cry told him the fellow was close behind, but he knew what he must do.

Seizing the knotted rope, he rang the warning, whilst pointing his curved cavalry sword in his right hand to deflect a thrust from a long, straight sword. This intruder wore a leather thong entwined with gold thread to contain his wild hair, and a silver wolfs head brooch on his chest that glinted in the torchlight. Gaius managed three rings of the bell before giving the tribal chief his full attention. His opponent was young and strong, and drove Gaius backwards until his back was against the tower.

Their faces were close, as crossed swords separated their heaving chests, breath trails circling to the sky. Gaius was momentarily distracted by the glint of a blue gemstone in an ornate, gilded torque around the chieftain's neck. He pushed back and grinned, baring his teeth to the proud warrior as the sound of legionaries pouring from their barracks filled the cold night air. With a growl, the Caledonian chief head-butted him – connecting with the front rim of his helmet. Gaius shrugged off the blow and pushed again. But his troubles had doubled as another warrior appeared from behind the chief and took a swipe at Gaius with an ox-bone axe, catching him off balance and sending him tumbling from the platform.

With a cry, Gaius landed heavily on his side. His chin straps had worked loose in the tussle and his helmet now rolled off, his cheek resting on the settled snow. Through a hazy eye he saw a thin layer of white stretching before him, like a white meadow, pure and new. Soon, running men crossed his blurred vista and the roar of battle assailed his dimming senses. He saw Saturn, the god of hospitality, holding out a goblet of mead, smiling his approval, welcoming him to his hall. "The lads will deal with this…" he whispered before his eyes dimmed and he took the offered cup, entering between high fluted columns into the warmth and light of the divine sanctum.

*****

Figures moved across an open doorway before his bleary eye, a hazy glow came from a wall lamp to his right. Was this the fabled hall of Saturn, where nymphs frolicked in fountain pools and the gods were waited on by white-robed boys as they reclined on golden couches?

Gaius tried to call to a passing figure, but all that came from his parched throat was a croak.

"Sir! He's awake!" a ghostly figure cried.

Gaius slowly raised his right hand and felt his left arm in a sling across his chest, then further up, a bandage around his head that covered his left eye. He rubbed his right eye, blinked and opened it wide, this time seeing a bit more of his surroundings. The lime-washed walls were a disappointment, as his vision of the home of the gods dissipated before the sight of a bowl-carrying orderly.

"Lie still, sir, and I will wipe your face," a young man said, in a voice that was familiar to him. Gaius submitted, and enjoyed the sensation of being washed with cool water.

"How... long have I been here?" he asked.

"Three days sir. It is good to have you back with us."

"No nymphs frolicking naked in fountains, then?"

"What was that, sir?"

"Nothing." Gaius recognised the room as the hospital block. He was in the smaller room at one end reserved for officers, which contained four beds and had a window in the wall behind him. Above were blackened beams where sagging and mottled canvas sheets were nailed to joists to imitate a ceiling, above which were roof tiles. He heard groans coming from the other side of the partition wall.

"How many men... were injured in the attack?"

"We have seven men and yourself, sir. Now lie still whilst I fetch soup." He pressed a beaker of water into Gaius's hand and turned to leave.

"How... do I know you?" Gaius asked.

"I am Kerwyn, one of your scouts, sir."

Gaius narrowed his good eye and replied, "Of course you are. I am used to seeing you on horseback, Kerwyn, not carrying bowls and towels in the hospital."

"When I am not with a patrol, I am assigned to other duties, sir. Now I am attending the wounded." His face did not convey any emotions or give any hint as to his thoughts. His dark brown eyes held the neutral expression of a defeated people. Gaius noted his olive skin tone was similar to his own - darker than was normal with the Britons, and his features reminded him of the Hispanic people who were his tribal neighbours.

"From your looks, Kerwyn, I would guess that your father was of the Hispanic Ninth Legion that was once garrisoned here?"

At last, his eyes betrayed him, and a quick look down to the rush mat told Gaius the truth of it. It was not uncommon. He himself had taken a Briton woman as wife, but Aria was from a southern tribe and regarded as foreign by the northerners. This was his first thought for his wife, and their little son, Brutus, and he wondered why she was not there when he had regained consciousness. Aria was his second wife, and he recalled the anguish of the death of his first, and their daughter, from the winter sickness. He had mourned for a year, then, by chance he had seen a tall, elegant woman with long hair the colour of the sun as it sets, yellow tinged with orange, and followed her as she moved with a graceful swing of her hips through the market stalls in the Forum at Calleva Atrebatum. He had followed her home, and had introduced himself to her father, an elderly man who made wagon wheels for farmers and the army. He courted her for a week, and then proposed,

22

paying three cows and a horse in dowry after some hard bargaining from the wily old man.

"Please call at my house and tell my wife that I am awake, once you leave this place," Gaius asked in a tired voice. He took the beaker and sipped cold water, then lay back against the straw-stuffed pillow and carefully felt his tightly-bandaged arm in the sling across his chest. Painful to the touch. His head throbbed to a dull drum beat and he closed his eye to see if resting would ease the pain. Kerwyn returned after a short time with a bowl of soup, accompanied by a thin, silver-haired healer.

"How are you feeling, Gaius?" the grey-robed surgeon asked. Gaius had become friends with the older man, and they had often shared a gourd of watered wine whilst playing a board game at the end of the day's duties.

"Hail, Septimus," he croaked as he struggled to sit upright. "My head feels like the Furies are chasing me screaming to the gates of Hades. What has happened to my eye and shoulder? Will I get their use back?"

Kerwyn had waited for him to finish talking before stepping forward to push a spoon of meaty broth towards his mouth. Gaius waved him away impatiently. He wanted answers first.

Septimus came to his left side and lifted his eye bandage and made a humming noise. Then he prodded his shoulder until Gaius flinched. "That is good. Sensation will slowly return to your body, and your eye will regain its sight. Nothing broken, Gaius. Your shoulder joint popped out and I reset it. It will feel tender for a few more weeks. You must keep the sling on and no heavy lifting. You fell from the platform and landed on that shoulder and your head hit the ground. Perhaps before that you were struck on the side of your head. You will feel dizzy and a bit disoriented and need to rest for three more days before trying to get up."

"And miss three days of Saturnalia?" Gaius groaned. He sipped the poppy-infused draught the surgeon gave him and eased back into the pillow, his good shoulder sagging as tension was released at the favourable prognosis. He managed a crooked smile at Kerwyn and said, "Now I'm ready for your pleasant-smelling broth."

Before Septimus left, Gaius asked, "My friend, could you send a centurion to me, as I am eager to know what happened that night?" The surgeon nodded and withdrew. Gaius wondered who would come – he was one of five centurions in the cohort-strength garrison, although some units were posted at the Wall or just north of it in watchtowers and small forts.

The broth warmed his belly and, once alone, Gaius fought to remain awake to hear what had transpired four nights ago on the walls. His good eye roamed the lime-washed walls, where duelling figures slowly emerged, like those on the glass tankard. A druid emerged from between the gladiators and walked slowly towards him on a blanket of white snow, holding a dripping knife. The white-bearded holy man dissolved and was replaced by the proud, determined face of the Caledonian chief he had been battling before his fall. Hazel brown eyes had burned with hatred and battle-lust, a pin-prick tattoo of a hawk hovering over its prey stood on his left cheek; blue paint decorated other parts of his face – forehead, nose and delicate swirls on the right cheek. Perhaps his woman had carefully painted it, concern etched in every detail. His jawline and chin were shaved and a neat, trimmed moustache swung from side to side on twin silver pendulums, below which his neck was adorned with a silver torque on which the eye of a serpent winked. Gaius, aware that the poppy infusion was taking hold, marvelled at the detail his mind conjured of his enemy's features, and he longed to know if this noble leader had survived the skirmish.

"Hail, Gaius, I am glad to see you awake and sitting." A voice interrupted his visions. Gaius turned his head away from the face on the wall towards a stout frame filling the doorway, red-plumed centurion's helmet tucked under an arm.

24

"Hail, Plauditus. My thanks for your visit. Enter."
Gaius was wary of the centurion of an auxiliary infantry unit
who shared the barracks with his cavalry soldiers.

Plauditus was of noble Roman stock, and although
not a soldier by nature, he had undergone training as a
Praetorian guard with other highborn sons. He would not
wait more than a year to be promoted to tribune, then in
time, legate, he had boasted to his fellow centurions, and
could well be Gaius's commander one day. He was the
eldest son of a noble family, destined to inherit his father's
mace and seat in the Senate if he successfully navigated
the dangerous waters of Roman politics.

In contrast, Gaius was the son of a modest olive
farmer and horse trader from the Province of Asturia,
wedged in the top north-west corner of Iberia. His father
had handed him over to a Roman recruiting officer when
he was fifteen years old and marked the parchment for his
twenty-five years of service, taking their silver coins as if he
had sold a horse. Gaius had first felt disappointment, but
that soon gave way to excitement when his uniform and
weapons were issued. He had marched through Iberia and
Gaul to Germania, for his training and first posting. His
good eye and skill with horses was noticed by his
commander and he was promoted to Optio and given
charge of the officer's stable. When war flared with the
Germanic tribes, he was re-assigned to a cavalry unit. He
built a reputation as a fearless warrior and respected
leader, and when his centurion was killed in battle, he was
promoted to replace him. His cavalry cent had been
transferred to Britannia and the Sixth Legion a few years
later.

Plauditus sat on the one chair in the room and smiled
at his fellow officer. There was no malice between them,
just an unspoken understanding of a gap in social status.
"How are you feeling? Will your wounds heal quickly?"

"I am pleased at the surgeon's diagnosis. I will have
the use of my eye and arm before too long," Gaius replied,

blinking to force the coloured dots from his vision. "Pray, tell me of the events of four nights ago. I am anxious to hear the outcome of the raid."

Plauditus coughed to clear his throat. "The raiding party numbered about thirty warriors. We killed eighteen, captured two and ten escaped over the walls. It is our opinion, after questioning the captives, that they were on a mission to count our numbers and test our strength. Tribune Pertinax believes they may have their eyes on our grain stores and horses, and could mount a much bigger attack." He sniffed and sat back, looking up to the patchwork ceiling.

"What became of your auxiliary guard, Amborix? It was he who saw them coming and was about to sound the alarm when an arrow struck him."

Plauditus turned his narrow face away from the wall and looked down his hawk's beak of a nose at Gaius in mild alarm at the question. "I am not familiar with the individual status, or indeed the names of my men, only the numbers. We had five killed and a further seven in the hospital. Perhaps he survived. I will send my optio to brief you."

"My thanks, Plauditus. My memory of that night is slowly returning to me. Strange how I remembered the boy's name." There was nothing more he wanted from his visitor so he slowly shut his good eye, fluttering his eyelids for added effect.

"I can see you need rest, Gaius. I shall send word to you of the men killed and wounded, and will keep you informed of any orders. In the meantime, I am told that your optio and decurions are keeping your horses and men in good order. Sleep well." With that, Plauditus rose and left, leaving Gaius content and ready to submit to his dreams.

3. Vindolanda, present day

Golden brown leaves rustled overhead, and a gentle gust sighed, dislodging a handful that floated down to me. The forest grove had been sculpted by unknown hands, and at the centre of the space stood an altar, a flat slate on two supporting stones. The gust had summoned him, and he stepped forward, dressed in a dirty grey woven garment from neck to ankle, tied at the waist with a rope; he came crunching on twigs and leaf mulch under leather sandals, eyes of steely grey, wrinkled face and long flowing white beard, holding the stone in both hands. I was transfixed, rooted to the spot, unable to move. He stood in front of me and held up the smooth, polished effigy of a goddess holding her pregnant belly. He opened his mouth to speak but the only sound was a distorted mumble…

"Wake up, Noah! Time to embrace a new day and get out to the trenches!" It was Dave, his face close to mine, his breath minty fresh, his hand shaking my shoulder.

"Oh, man… I was in a deep dream. There was a druid holding the sacred stone…"

"No naked nymphs frolicking? I'm disappointed. Get ready and join us for breakfast."

Dave pulled the door half-closed behind him, leaving me to drag my weary body from the bottom bunkbed. I splashed cold water on my face in the corner sink and dried myself, muttering, "Of course, she's a pregnant earth mother." Dark skies outside - no rain, but the threat of it. I hurriedly dressed in light blue slim-fit jeans, oversized grey crew neck jumper and black Adidas trainers, then joined the boys in the cafeteria.

"Doesn't look promising," I remarked, taking my seat on a bench next to Russ.

"I reckon it's going to piss down, probably as soon as we get out there," he replied, between mouthfuls of mushy muesli.

Twenty minutes later we were outside, waterproof jackets and gumboots on, slogging along the muddy path to the dig.

Mike Stone was waiting to welcome us with unnatural enthusiasm. "Come on, lads. We can maybe get an hour in before the rain comes."

No sooner had I picked up my tools from the tent and jumped into my trench than spots of rain fell on my head. Big, heavy spots. The sky gods were angry. Loud peels of thunder preceded jagged shafts of lightning on the western hills. It was the overture to a storm of Wagnerian proportions. I ran for the marquee with my hood up, glancing over its roof to see if the chariots of the gods were riding the storm clouds.

"It's a soggy mess," Mike said, ushering his wet children in like a mother hen. There were about fifteen there, eight students and the rest locals who had volunteered. "Let's take the rest of the morning off to do other things. Those sifting soil can carry on in here, and those cataloguing and bagging items can continue with that at the trestle tables over there." He pointed to one end of the large indoor space. At the opposite end were sacks of soil beside a shallow sand pit on legs, waiting for willing hands to sieve the ancient soil for fragments of relics. "When the rain stops, will the rest of you please drift back from your hiding holes, and we'll crack on with the dig. I'm sure it's just a passing shower."

"Maybe they've baked some cakes," I said. "Anyone coming to the cafe?"

"Lead on MacDuff." Richard held up the tent flap.

"Mind if I join you?" Mike asked.

"Sure, you're most welcome, let's go." Dave made a run for the covered walkway that led us back to the cafeteria. Once out of boots and coats, we walked through the reception area to the cafeteria, empty apart from a disconsolate couple, hunched over mugs of coffee, who had seemingly fallen foul of the weather gamble with pre-booking tickets.

"Ah, I love the smell of coffee cake in the morning!" Dave sniffed the air as he walked in. "What lovely cakes have you been baking, Jenny?" he asked a plump, aproned caterer with perpetually rosy cheeks.

"I might have known it would be you next through that door, David," she said with a chuckle. "I've got coffee, lemon drizzle and a divine chocolate gateau, plus a tray of Bakewell tarts."

"Ooooh, you'd make someone a perfect wife, Jenny."

"I already have. What do you fancy?"

"Mmmmm, it would have to be, pot of tea for one and a slice of lemon drizzle."

We four roommates, followed by Mike, made our choices and headed for the corner table, with the firstcomers wedging themselves onto the wall bench.

Mike plonked his tray down and took the chair, facing them. "Right, how about we each share the tragic stories of our sordid little lives to this point?"

We glanced at each other and either shrugged or nodded, already distracted by the slices of cake before us. I bit into a sumptuous piece of coffee cake, savouring the flavour and light, moist texture, complemented by dark chocolate icing.

"Alright, I'll start us off," Mike replied, wiping crumbs from his bushy red beard. "I'm from Jarrow docks down the road in South Tyneside. My dad was a docker, my mam a quiet and dutiful housewife. We lived in one of those two-up-two-down terraced workers cottages, in a road that ran uphill away from the docks. I left school at sixteen with few qualifications and no idea what I wanted to do. One day, me and four mates went into town and found ourselves outside the army recruitment office. Well, three if us came out having signed on for ten years with the Grenadier Guards. When I got home and told my folks, well, Dad went mad. 'What did you do that for, soft lad. I've put your name down for an apprenticeship on the docks,' he said. Well, being a cheeky chappie, I replied in a cocksure tone, 'I just want to travel the world, like, meet interesting people and kill them.' He gave me a clip round the ear, alright."

Mike paused to sip his tea and enjoy our laughter. "I did three tours; Northern Ireland, Middle East and Afghanistan. Funny thing, though. The kids used to run after us in the dusty streets of Syria and try and sell us Roman coins. None of us were interested in history or anything like that. Who'd have thought I'd have ended up here looking to dig up Roman stuff?"

"When did you get out?" Russ asked.

"Ten years ago. I became a delivery driver at Newcastle University, fetching and delivering books and stationery, mainly. Then I met my lovely lass, Emma, who encouraged me to do a night school course in archaeology, and here I am. We're married now, with a wee lad. Still do driving jobs mind, through an agency, so I can find work when there's no digs on, although this year it's been full on. I'm now paid by various universities and trusts to organise teams of students and volunteers and supervise digs. I've worked all along the Wall, from Wallsend to Bowness." He sat back and folded his arms.

I looked at Mike with newfound respect. His route to archaeology had not been the usual academic trawl through books and lecture theatres, but was via solid and varied life experience. I resolved to curb my casual and, I had been told, almost mocking attitude, and accord him the respect he had earned. He may not be an academic, but he was a genuine, enthusiastic and knowledgeable guy.

Russ put down his cup and cleared his throat. "Well, I'm also a Geordie, although my parents moved to South Shields when I was a nipper."

"That's still technically in Geordie-land," Mike said. "We'll have yer."

Russ smiled and continued, "We also lived in a terraced cottage. I went to the appropriately-named Hadrian Primary School, directly opposite a complete block devoid of houses, but occupied by the Arbeia Roman Fort and Museum. From the playground we could see the impressive replica Roman gatehouse, standing taller than a two-storey house, looking down to the river estuary, as if standing guard over the neighbourhood. We would sneak over there after school and climb up the wooden stairs to the platform and pretend to be soldiers, but what sort of soldiers we didn't know. Pretending to shoot each other somehow didn't fit.

"In my final year, there was an organised trip to the Arbeia museum to see their new video film showing life in Roman times. I was fascinated, and ran home to tell me mam that 'Arbeia' means 'Fort of the Arab Troops', and that right on our doorstep was the remains of an eighteen-hundred-year-old fort that had been built and manned by soldiers from the Middle East. I wanted to know all about the Romans, and the people they brought to our country. She was shocked, but in a good way – I'd never shown any interest in books before then."

He broke off to bite into a Bakewell tart. After a brief munch, he continued, "It changed me, I started going to the library and reading anything on Roman Britain. When I went to the high school, I continued to follow my interest in history. I also volunteered at Arbeia on Saturdays and school holidays, cleaning and picking litter, mainly, but I also read all the reference books and memorised the explanation cards for all the exhibits."

"Remembering's your thing, Russ. That exhibition's not small." Richard sounded impressed.

"That's true. Becoming a tour guide was an easy jump, and now I'm making enough money at weekends and holidays to cover my bar bills. With the help of my history teacher, I just about got the grades to study archaeology at Newcastle Uni. I think they squeezed me in on the local quota. I took the Hadrian's Wall archaeology practical option, and here I am."

"Don't do yourself down, lad," Mike said. "There's a place for modesty, but you've done remarkably well considering your humble roots. We both have."

"The Romans will be the making of you," I joked.

"Having the Wall on your doorstep helps," Dave remarked, "for inspiration. And we live in a time of surging interest in archaeology and studying the past. That reminds me Mike, when are you letting us loose on metal detectors?"

"Ha ha ha. We're taking delivery of six units any time now, but I'll be watching closely to make sure you don't pocket any coins! It's not a training course for becoming a dirt rat detectorist. Now, who's next?"

Richard edged forward and rested his forearms on the table. "I'm local too, from Morpeth in Northumberland, north of Hadrian's Wall. My dad was a solicitor. Yes, past tense; he's passed on."

"Sorry lad," Mike murmured. Russ patted his shoulder.

"That's alright. It was five years ago. I guess my sister and me were partly kept at arm's length by being farmed out to relatives during his final months. But it cast a shadow…sorry, I shouldn't bring the mood down."

"It's your story, Richard," I said, "tell it your way." He was a couple of years older than me. He'd bridled when I'd called him 'Rich' on the day we'd moved into our dorm room, telling me firmly, 'I'm Richard, not Rich'. Although older, he was shy and rarely initiated a conversation, although his input was considered and often conclusive.

"Thanks. Yeah, I somehow got good enough grades to get a job as an office junior in an archaeological consultancy firm in Newcastle. I've been on a few digs and learned the process of logging them for client reports, and after a year I decided to scale up to get a degree. I'm now reading Archaeology at Newcastle, where I met Russ. Although a few old classmates were there, they were a year ahead and reminded me of a bad time, so to be honest, I preferred to hang out with Russ. A clean break. But sometimes… well….” Richard sat back, chin on chest, and blinked hard a couple of times.

Russ put a consoling arm around his shoulders and gave him a squeeze. Richard acknowledged the show of affection by briefly resting his head on Russ's shoulder, for a fleeting moment their eyes met, and then they both resumed their positions. This was all a revelation to me, and Dave, no doubt, as we had only known the two of them for a week, when we'd become roommates, bunking together like conscripts.

“You'll be an asset on the dig with that experience, Richard,” Mike said. “From now on, you're my number two.”

“I'll get you another cup of tea,” Russ said, getting up. “Anyone else?”

“Get a pot and five cups, here's some money,” Mike said, handing him a note. “Just take your time, lad. Dave, why don't you tell us about yourself?”

Dave's voice was gruff. “Really sorry for your loss, mate. Well, mine's an uneventful story, really. Mercifully. We're from Coventry. My dad's an architect, a designer of the glass towers of capitalism. There were still plenty of vacant plots around the city centre sixty-odd years after the Jerrys bombed it flat during the war, just waiting for a budget hotel or an army of solicitors…. oh, sorry.”

The mention of ‘solicitors', followed by Dave's awkward apology, seemed to bring Richard out from under his cloud. He laughed, and took a bite of cake, easing the atmosphere a touch. Russ returned with a tray and Mike poured the tea.

“That's OK, Dave,” Richard said, sipping the hot liquid, “Please carry on.”

"Well, we did a year of Latin as a taster subject at my high school, and that led me into A level – along with history and English lit. My interests, though, align with you guys – classical history and architecture. I met Noah during fresher's week at Durham and we became mates, and we both opted for Hadrian's Wall for our archaeology practical. I think I'd like to be a version of you, Mike, after I graduate. I love the physical side of archaeology more than the academic side – I guess I love grovelling around in the mud to see what treasures lie hidden beneath the surface!"

"Happy to be your role model, Dave," Mike said with a smile, between sips of tea. "Although you may need to take a crash course in growing a beard and wearing Christmas jumpers all year round!"

"…And don't forget the green corduroy trousers!" I added with a laugh.

"Steady on guys, don't completely stereotype me, or I'll get a complex," Mike replied, raising his out-of-control hairy eyebrows. "Young Noah, I believe it's your turn."

I coughed to clear my throat, and began. "I'm from Spennymoor in County Durham. Should I go back as far as when I was six? My mum died then."

"Go on and tell it, Noah. Now it's my turn to say 'it's your story'." Mike's bushy eyebrows rose and fell like a couple of furry caterpillars trying to escape.

"I felt a lot of resentment when my Dad re-married a few years later. Having a substitute for my mum in the house seemed to intensify my sense of loss. I would hardly ever speak to her, except to say 'thanks' or 'goodnight'. When I was about nine, Alison, my stepmum, sat me down for a clear the air talk, and after that I grudgingly agreed to call her 'mum', to everyone's relief.

"I'm one of three, and we were all given biblical names, although the church-going ended when Dad married Alison. I attended a high school in Durham, and, like Dave, chose History, English Literature and Classics for my 'A' levels."

"How do you get on with your stepmum now?" Richard asked.

"Everything's fine. She takes an interest in us and is very supportive. She's ten years younger than my dad, and quite fit, actually." I grinned when the others guffawed.

"There's nowt wrong with fancying your stepmum," Mike unexpectedly said.

"I didn't say I fancy her." I sat back and folded my arms.

"Hands up who goes to church?" Mike asked, changing the subject.

"Weddings and funerals only." Dave glanced around the table, but we all shook our heads.

"Well, on this unrepresentative sample of five, the old religions appear to be dying out with our parents' generation," Russ concluded.

Dave cleared his throat somewhat dramatically. "It's a wide field, and the sample is exceedingly small. Only a craven politician or cynical marketeer would draw conclusions..."

"Heathens aside," I interrupted, "I hope to make my parents proud by becoming the first person in our family to attain a university degree. That has become a motivator for me, a way to pay them back for all the tough times and their unwavering support, despite me being a grouchy and uncooperative teen." I sat back again, feeling like I'd been through a therapy session.

Mike stroked his beard. "I reckon they're already proud of you, lad."

"Thanks, Mike," I replied with a sheepish grin.

"We're becoming experts in pre-Christian beliefs," Richard paused to drain his tea cup. "Even our society is regressing to paganism."

"Nihilism, more likely. Except I have a moral code and don't think life is meaningless," I added.

"The wheel has come full circle," Mike said, swivelling to see what had made the room brighter. "We dig up effigies and investigate the ancient gods, fascinated by the role they played in the lives of those who lived before Christianity took root. And now we've got a sign from whichever deity you choose to believe in."

Steady drumming on the flat, asphalt roof had ceased, and a pale shaft of sunlight illuminated the room, reaching towards us across the curling carpet tiles, pointing an accusatory finger.

"Time to get back to the trenches, lads," Mike said, rousing his heavy frame from the creaking chair. "Therapy's over. Now for the practical."

Outside again, a thick bank of fog rolled towards us across the Vindolanda meadow, gobbling up sheep as it crept menacingly towards our trenches, as if the furies had come to inspect us or reclaim ancient treasures. Outside the marquee, Mike handed us buckets, plastic dishes and big carwash sponges.

"First scoop out the water with the dish, then sponge up the rest, trying your best not to disturb the surface where fragments of artefacts might be lurking," Mike explained.

We wandered over to our trenches and jumped down onto boards that were separated by inch-deep pools of muddy water.

"We're seeing some weather today," Dave groaned.

"*Quick boys, gas.*" The words popped into my head as I looked at the approaching cloud of fog. I crouched theatrically in the trench, holding the sponge to my nose like a gas mask.

"I remember that one. Wilfred Owen's War poem. We did it for English Lit."

"Yeah. I had to stand up in front of my class and recite it from memory... that old lie, dulce et decorum est pro patria mori," seeped from my lips in a whisper, like a magic spell, as I bent down to begin scooping the water at my feet.

"Ah, it is indeed sweet and proper to lay down your life for your country," Dave translated, to my back.

"You've got the hearing of a poacher," I said, laughing.

"We must have studied the same English Lit texts. I also memorised that visceral image conveyed so starkly, of Owen's experience of life in the First World War trenches. It goes like this, if memory serves me:

> *Bent double, like old beggars under sacks,*
> *Knock-kneed, coughing like hags, we cursed through sludge,*
> *Till on the haunting flares we turned our backs,*
> *And towards our distant rest began to trudge.*
> *Men marched asleep. Many had lost their boots,*
> *But limped on, blood-shod. All went lame; all blind;*
> *Drunk with fatigue; deaf even to the hoots*
> *Of gas-shells dropping softly behind."*

"*Quick boys, gas,*" I repeated, reciting the next line of the poem, as the ghostly fog billowed towards us.

Dave scooped dirty water into his bucket, then stretched. "Aye, the next bit's an horrific description of being gassed with chlorine or mustard gas. Lucky us to have been born a hundred years later."

I leant on a muddy elbow and continued in a mock-teacher's voice, "Owen ends with his own bitter conclusion on the futility of trench warfare and gives a warning to future generations not to fall for that old patriotic call to arms:

> '*My friend, you would not tell with such high zest*
> *To children ardent for some desperate glory,*
> *The old Lie: Dulce et decorum est*
> *Pro patria mori.'*"

The squelch of gum boots brought Mike to the brim of the trench.

"You'd have been shot walking on top of the trenches in the First World War." Dave waved a muddy sponge at him.

"Aye, but I wouldn't have been so daft. Keep sucking the water up so as the exposed earth isn't disturbed."

We carried on filling our buckets with sludge, like a couple of miserable Tommies.

"I once faced a cavalry charge, y'know. In Afghanistan," Mike said, gazing over our heads at the lifting fog. Behind him, others were drifting over to the marquee to get ready to continue with their tasks.

"Yeah? What happened?" I asked, genuinely interested.

"Well, the Talis rode down the mountainside towards us, on those short, stocky Asian horses, like Attila the Hun, hooting and hollering. They must've underestimated our fire power. We opened up with heavy machine gun fire and mortars."

He paused to suck in air through clenched teeth. "It was war; we had to do our duty. Shooting those men and horses was one of the toughest things I've ever done." He gazed past us at the placid sheep, a sour memory rekindled.

Mike wandered off and I was left reflecting on our lads shitting themselves as the whistle blew, a sergeant urging them out of the trench to run towards a hail of machine gun bullets to be picked off in a deadly lottery.

"Get sponging, you lazy sod," Dave moaned, flicking brown water from his boots onto mine.

Is it sweet and proper to unquestioningly lay down your life for your country? – that's what they were told. Owen was right – it was a lie from elite leaders to persuade ordinary men to fight in their wars by mobilising nationalistic feelings. Roman legionaries who had sworn an oath to Rome and Emperor, would have jogged in formation out through the fort gates, lining up behind a barrier of rectangular shields, javelins protruding like quills on a porcupine, facing an onrushing, screaming enemy... just here, close to where I'm standing, three feet below today's ground level, ready to sacrifice their lives in defence of their cause. How long does it take for the idealism indoctrinated into youths to give way to the cynicism of bitter experience? Was the Roman Empire any different from the British Empire? Somehow, I doubt it.

Mike returned to stand over us, hands on hips. "Good job, lads. Now empty the buckets and leave it to dry out for an hour. Get yourselves into the marquee where I'm about to give a fascinating talk on test pits and filling out the record log."

4. Vindolanda, 180 CE

After a week, Gaius's arm was out of the sling and, although tender, he was able to pick up and throw his two-year-old son, Brutus, into the air, filling his tiny courtyard with shrieks of pleasure. His centurion's quarters consisted of four small rooms that opened onto a covered portico around a courtyard where ducks and chickens roamed, facing a high wall separating them from the next centurion. There was always noise – if not from their fowl, then from the surrounding buildings crammed within the walls of the fort.

His wife, Aria, had chided him for his reprimand that she had not been at his bedside when he awoke in a hospital bed. She had reminded him that she had a household of three slaves to manage and a son to look after. They had visited him every day, and made offerings for his recovery at the Temple of Jupiter. She could switch from being a harsh matron to a sweet and dutiful wife in a moment, and Gaius enjoyed picking a fight with her because the making up was a pleasure that Cupid himself would have savoured.

A boy came to summon him to an officers' briefing, so he handed Brutus over to the doting house slave, Marta, and went to his room to put on his uniform. He had lost weight and his belt hung too freely around his waist. The other half of the elderly slave couple, Longinus, was sweeping dust off the stone flagstones under the covered portico. This gave onto the central space around the fountain, where the ducks and chickens roamed.

"Marta! Bring me a skewer from the kitchen," Gaius yelled.

Moments later she came, carrying Brutus on her hip, followed by Aria who had left her needlework to see what the fuss was about.

"My belt is loose and I want to make a new hole in it," Gaius explained.

"It is good you are leaner, my husband," Aria said with a smile, grabbing Brutus by the hand before he bolted in the direction of the ducks.

"I am sure Mars will thank me for it," Gaius said, meaning his stallion.

Marta took charge, holding his belt around him and making a scratch where the new hole should be. She placed the thick leather belt on the floor and drilled down on it with the foot-long skewer that was normally employed holding meat over a fire. After much exertion, a hole was finally made.

Gaius belted himself and kissed his wife and son, then tucked his helmet under his arm and followed the boy out into the crowded street. An auxiliary in green uniform stepped from the shadows in front of Gaius, causing him to halt.

"Is it you, Amborix?" Gaius asked.

"It is I, sir. Also discharged from the hospital. I wanted to thank you for your protection as I lay wounded on the battlements." He looked up through keen, green eyes.

Gaius let out a laugh and slapped the younger man on his shoulder. "I fought two of them over your body, not knowing if you were alive or dead. I am pleased to see that you live, Amborix of the Belgic. Now we have something to tell our mates over a tankard in the tavern!"

He grinned and nodded. "Is this where you live, sir?"

"Aye, with my wife and son."

"Then I shall be their guardian, should the need arise, sir."

"I am pleased to hear that, for I believe you are a man not to be messed with at close quarters," Gaius chuckled. "And now I must run to my meeting. May your gods and the Fates look over you, young Amborix." With that, Gaius was

41

gone, driving the boy in front of him, jostling past those in his way, balancing to keep his footing on wooden platforms that floated above sticky mud.

They hustled past slaves and locals carrying all manner of household goods; loaves, baskets of vegetables, jugs of olive oil or urns of beer between the stores and the barracks. The soldiers were billeted in barrack room units of eight, and would pool their weekly rations and hire a local from the village to cook and prepare their breakfast and evening meals. This included having flat loaves of bread baked in the communal ovens, and led to much to-ing and fro-ing of workers and slaves all day long, reaching a peak of activity in the late afternoon.

Gaius and the boy turned out of a narrow alleyway onto the main road and headed towards the centre of the fort and the Principium – the commander's office. Two sentries stood to attention as he bundled past them, entering the high-ceilinged room where his three fellow centurions and the bald-headed prefect, Adminius, responsible for stores and administration, sat around a long table, waiting for him. Gaius nodded in their direction and turned to his left, marching to the commander's desk where he stood to attention and saluted his commander.

"Hail Helvius Pertinax, Tribune of the Fourth Cohort, Sixth Legion," Gaius proclaimed.

"Yes, yes, Gaius. I will forgive you your tardiness as you are from the sick room. Now please join your fellow officers, we have important matters to discuss." He stood, clutching a rolled-up parchment, and edged around his desk.

Gaius took his seat as the rotund tribune pushed back the sleeves of his purple-edged toga and stood at the head of the table.

"Firstly," Pertinax began, "I must impart some ill news. In this, the year 933 since the founding of our glorious city of Rome, our much-loved emperor, Marcus Aurelius Antonius Augustus, has died."

He tapped the parchment on the table, eying his officers. Their response was groans and soft curses.

"Yes, he was popular with the legions, and we shall miss his confident and clear direction. This missive says only that he died peacefully in his bed at his camp in Germania. We shall gather as the sun goes down at our temple to Jupiter to make offerings for his peaceful passage to the afterlife."

He turned and tossed the parchment roll on his desk and then fixed his gaze on Gaius.

"Secondly, let us praise Jupiter that Gaius has been returned to us." He made a slight nod, then continued, "We believe the raiding party of last week was from the Selgovae tribe, who reside in the lands we once called Valentia. Our intelligence tells us there is a new chief in the area, a young hot-head who has been stirring up unrest. We know their harvest was not good, and they might have their eyes on our grain, horses, and weapons – anything they can get their hands on. We need to send out patrols to look for signs of a coming together of tribes."

Gaius cleared his throat and all eyes fell on him. "I may have fought with this new chief on the battlements, sir. If it was him, then I can testify he is both bold and brave to lead the raid himself."

"You mean you let him get away?" Plauditus sneered, drawing some laughs.

Gaius grinned and rubbed the scab on his temple. "Aye, I was face to face with him when another struck me and sent me tumbling."

"It is well you have survived, Gaius, and for that we are grateful," Tribune Pertinax concluded. "Are you well enough to lead a patrol northward?"

"Aye, sir. I'm ready," Gaius replied, puffing his chest and leaning forward.

"Good. I want you to lead your cavalry cent to our neighbours at Cilurnum and instruct them to patrol north and west to our outlying forts and assess the situation. You will proceed north and east to our fort at Habitancum and gather intelligence from Centurion Viridio. Take two or three scouts who can gather information from the locals. We Romans have friends enough amongst the local tribes who pass through our gates to market at month-end, from whom we collect a decima in tax, eh Adminius?" The balding prefect smiled. "And they may give us news. Centurions, use your contacts to find out what you can." His eyes moved around the table and returned to Gaius.

"Aye, sir," Gaius said, his eyes focussed and gleaming in anticipation. "Shall we act on intelligence and move further on to see for ourselves their numbers?"

Pertinax nodded. "With caution, Gaius. You are not to engage with the enemy unless attacked. Make your preparations and leave in the morning. Plauditus, you shall march your auxiliaries to the Wall to reinforce those there and double the watch at the towers and mile forts on our ten-mile stretch. The two remaining cents shall remain here and mount double guards."

The discussion moved onto stocks and resources, and it was agreed that a messenger would be sent in the morning to Legion Headquarters at Eboracum to brief their newly-appointed Legate, Claudius Hieronymianus, who was yet to tour the Wall forts. Gaius spoke with his fellow centurions outside for a while, before noticing his second-in-command, Optio Paulinus Grella hovering in the background, trying to catch his eye. He bade good day to his peers and fell into step with the dour veteran of many campaigns. Paulinus was from southern Gaul, a tough man with little compassion and a relish for battle.

"Sir, the men have been for a four-mile run and are on the parade ground awaiting your orders," he growled.

Gaius looked up a handspan at his taller deputy and replied, "You are right to sense there is something in the air, Paulinus. We shall be riding out in the morning for a patrol north of the Wall. We will need provisions for a week."

Paulinus nodded, his thin lips cracking into a smirk of approval.

They marched past the stable block and Gaius welcoming the smell of horse manure and sweat after his injury sojourn. "How is the new Sarmatian unit shaping up?"

Paulinus grunted. "They are a peculiar bunch of barbarians, sir. Hard as nails, good horsemen who can shoot arrows with uncanny accuracy from horseback at up to thirty paces. They are unfamiliar with our throwing javelins, but they will learn. I can see why our beloved Emperor, Marcus Aurelius, was keen to convert them from enemies to allies. They will come in use, but only their decurion, Meral, can understand our language, and it will take time for him to translate your orders in the heat of battle. And sir, I found them drinking pigs' blood from a human skull. They were passing it around and chanting in their language."

"Hmmm. Then we must curb some of their habits and educate them in our language and ways as quickly as possible. This patrol can help us." Gaius stopped and grabbed his deputy's arm as they passed the last stable to exit the fort through the western gatehouse to the parade ground. "Paulinus, we were given some heavy news at the briefing. Our noble Emperor, Marcus Aurelius, is dead."

Paulinus widened his eyes and stared back, open-mouthed and dumbstruck.

"I shall announce it to the men. We can only hope there is a smooth transition in power, for we can well do without the civil strife that erupted after the passing of Nero." Gaius turned and marched towards the ranks of soldiers standing at ease. His cavalry cent was now one hundred and ten men strong, with the addition of thirty Sarmatian auxiliaries added to his regulars, more than bringing them up to strength. They snapped to attention at the approach of their officers.

Gaius and Paulinus stood before the two distinct units, each with a decurion to the front. The decurions were responsible for their unit's welfare, training and discipline. They bunked with the men, and were a useful source of information for their senior officers concerning the mood and well-being of the men.

Gaius stood to attention, heels together and arms by his side, then saluted the men. They returned it, some with quizzical looks as he omitted the usual 'Hail Marcus Aurelius!' Gaius noticed the salute was a bit slow and ragged from the Sarmatian unit to his left. He began by thanking them for their votive offerings to the gods for his recovery. He was now restored and ready for the road. Paulinus led the men in a rowdy cheer for their commander.

"You may be wondering why I did not hail our glorious emperor. The sad news I have to report is that Marcus Aurelius is dead." The Gauls received this news with groans and sighs. "Yes, he was a great emperor, now a god, who led our legions to great victories in Germania, and in the Dacian Wars. Some of you are veterans of those campaigns, and will remember with fondness and pride his powerful oratory and votive thanks to our legion. We will make our offering to him this eve, but before that we must prepare to ride out on the morrow for a long patrol in the Northlands."

The men cheered at the prospect of breaking their month-long stay in barracks.

"I shall spend some hours with our new Sarmatian unit, and hand the rest of you over to Paulinus to make preparations. Hail Rome!"

Gaius clasped forearms with his new decurion. "Welcome to the Equestrian Cent of the Fourth Cohort of the Sixth Legion, Meral of Sarmatia."

Gaius stared into the dark-brown, creased face that spoke of days spent outdoors under a hot sun, with his fescue-thick black hair, crudely cropped at shoulder length. Meral remained stiffly at attention before his commanding officer, a serious expression fixed on his face. He was the same height as Gaius, but taller than most of his charges.

"I am… happy to meet you, my commander," he replied in thick, hesitant Latin.

"Walk with me," Gaius said, gesturing with his hand. He inspected the three ranks of twenty-nine men, all standing to attention in ill-fitting hand-me-downs, most likely kitted out with clothing recovered from dead soldiers. They had the older style cavalry helmets – a round polished bowl with a small spike on top, with canvas chin straps that hung down from the lining. Clearly, some of the previous owners of their helmets and clothing were bigger men, although they tended to fill out their jerkins across the chest and shoulders. They wore non-army issue leather boots that covered their calves – eminently suitable for riding in this cold climate. There was a toughness in their worn faces and oval-shaped dark eyes.

Gaius tried them out with a few basic commands – stand at ease, attention, turn to the right, the left, march, attack, retreat, and 'mount up'. Some of the commands they knew, but others had to be translated by Meral. "Alright, tell them to get their weapons and saddle their horses. We're going for a ride."

Gaius found his stableboy and was pleased to be re-acquainted with his black gelded stallion, Mars. Centurions had their pick of new strings of cavalry horses, and Mars was a big, strong horse with long mane and tail. Once saddled, he rode to the parade ground and waited as his Sarmatian unit assembled. Gaius noticed they had bigger saddles with pronounced horns at the front and dangling strips with loops for their boots. He had never seen this and gazed in surprise as the horsemen lined up before him, their knees slightly raised and their boots supported by leather hoops.

"What are they called?" he asked Meral, pointing to his boot straps.

"They are Scythian loops, sir. They... help us when we fire our arrows." Meral stood up in his loops, using his knees to grip the saddle, then twisted his torso to right and left.

Gaius raised his eyebrows in surprise at the adaptation unknown in the Roman cavalry. "That, I would like to see. Tell them to get their bows and arrow quivers and meet at the north gatehouse."

Gaius rode out at the head of his column, through the Brigante settlement that had sprung up there, and onto the wide, flat meadow after which the fort was named. It would be white under settled snow, but for now the grass shone green in the weak afternoon sun. He chuckled to himself as he recalled his exchange with Amborix on the battlements, and his regret at lying about the name of Vindolanda to the youth when he thought he was dying in his arms.

Bordering the right edge were upright wooden pallets that were used as targets for archery and javelin practice. He sat in the centre of the wide space and instructed Meral to lead his men in firing arrows at the targets. They duly lined up and rode, at a half-gallop, past the targets, at a distance of about twenty paces, standing up in their saddles and firing with unerring accuracy at the squares of wood.

"Again, but at a further distance!" Gaius shouted.

At forty paces they were less accurate as their arrows arced upwards to make the distance. Now Gaius knew their effective range. His Gallic cavalry carried quivers behind their saddles of up to eight short javelins, wooden shafts with iron tips, the length of an arm. They would ride parallel to their enemy at a distance of about twenty to thirty paces, and throw their javelins, or throw downwards or stab with them when skirmishing at close quarters.

"Draw swords and make a pass of the targets!" he shouted. They used the curved cavalry sword known as the cuirass for close combat, and would sometimes fight on foot with sword and shield. Unlike the foot soldiers' who had rectangular shields, their cavalry shields were elongated ovals, with hard steel bosses at the centre, slung on the back when riding. The commander would usually decide on the tactics in advance. In a battle, they would often harry the fringes of the enemy ranks, but sometimes they would be ordered to charge into the body of an enemy, using the horse as a weapon, hence the need for leather shin and chest pads with metal studs for their horses.

When the sun dipped behind the western hills, Gaius instructed Meral to return to barracks and prepare their meal. After that, they would meet at the Temple to Jupiter where he would make an offering of a kid on behalf of the unit to honour the memory of their departed emperor.

Gaius returned home and gave his wife, Aria, the unwelcome news that he would be riding out in the morning.

"Will we be safe here from barbarian attack?" she asked in a low, trembling voice, taking his arm and leading him to the quiet corner of their portico.

"Quite safe, my love. I have asked an auxiliary guard, Amborix, to watch over you in my absence. But I doubt the barbarians will repeat their raid."

"But are you well, my husband?" she asked, concern etched on her brow. "Only yesterday I saw you stagger and hold the wall to stop you from falling."

Gaius hugged her tight, kissing her forehead. "I admit to a moment of light-headedness, but that was lack of food. I am fit now and ready, and my tribune needs my eyes and ears as commander of horses."

"Does he know you cannot see a house lizard on the wall?" she teased.

"I have younger men around me who I rely on for long sight. Trust me, if an enemy gets close, I can see perfectly well. Now, let us go to our chamber and you can show me what I shall be missing."

She kissed him, then breathed into his neck, "We must wait until the boy is asleep and the slaves in their quarters, my love. Then I will be your Venus."

5. Vindolanda, present day

The walk to the nearest pub, The Green Man, involved gum boots, waterproofs, umbrellas and torches. The closest hamlet to Vindolanda was a good mile away, and the walk was an up-and-down-hill workout for the calves and thighs. On dark nights the return journey could be in total darkness, when we would have to link arms to keep to the lane, as if walking blindfolded, with those on the outside shouting 'left' or 'right' in a routine that would have caused much mirth on a TV game show.

"I guess Roman patrols would have hustled hard to get back to the fort before nightfall," I said, looking over the frothy head of a pint of Badger Ale to my fellow students. The four of us had gotten into the habit of the occasional jaunt to the pub.

"Easy to walk off the track and into a bog," Dave replied. We chatted for a couple of pints about my finding and some pottery ware Russ had found, comparing the ingrained dirt under our finger nails, before moving onto salacious speculation about the women on site. It was a community of about sixty, with roughly half – mainly students and some staff – living in the dormitory blocks or small houses dotted around the site.

"Professor Maggie Wilde is a looker." Dave raised his eyebrows.

"And old enough to be your mother," Richard added.

I spun a beer mat between finger and thumb. "But she's not."

"I've heard she's a lesbian," Russ chipped in.

"Oh really? Where did you hear that?" *Why was I joining in?*

Dave sat back and grinned. "I overheard the archivists gossiping over lunch."

51

"Well, they need to get their facts straight." I set my empty pint glass down. "Same again?" I'd decided not to disclose that she might have flirted with me. I still wasn't sure. Perhaps it was her way of being chummy with students. I could do without being taunted as 'Mister Lover Man'.

On my visit to the bar, I looked around the large room with low, dark beams at the dozen-or-so tables occupied by a mixture of local farming folk and Vindolanda academics. Above their bowed heads the walls appeared to be sagging under framed photographs that captured the bleak beauty of the surrounding moors. A few were shots of the crumbling Wall, including the obligatory picture of Sycamore Gap. One outcrop looked like a row of dirty grey teeth protruding from rolling green gums. The booming laugh of Mike Stone filled the room as my eyes settled on a table of female archivists, and I raised my glass to them. One returned my gesture with a smile. I completed my mission and set a tray with four pints on our table.

"I think I'll sidle over and say hello to the archivists," I said in a low voice, accompanied by a nod in their direction. I picked up my pint, and with muffled hoots at my back, walked across the sticky carpet to a table in an alcove against the far wall, where the work colleagues were clustered. "Mind if I join you?" I asked as I slid onto the bench seat.

"Sure," replied a sultry beauty of Indian heritage I had noticed before in the cafeteria. She pulled her coat towards her to make space and welcomed me with a friendly smile.

"Good evening all." I placed my pint on a stained beer mat that was curling at the corners with overuse. "How's life in the archive dungeon?"

The woman next to me took a quick sip of her tomato juice and turned to fix her dark brown eyes on me. "It's certainly not torture working there. It's as quiet as a funeral most of the time – just the way we like it. You're Noah, right? I heard from Maggie that you're going to be spending some time with us? I'm Sima." She held out a slim hand and we shook.

"Nice to meet you, Sima. Yes, I'm Noah, and I've had the OK from the prof to move indoors from next week and concentrate on translating the tablets. Besides, it's getting too wet and windy at the dig." We shared a smile and she blinked her long lashes at me, making my stomach flutter. "Are you a student or staff?"

"I'm a recent archaeology graduate and now an employee of the Trust," she replied.

She was most likely a year or two older than me, I surmised. Twenty-two was the age of responsibility – the age at which young academics were expected to wean themselves off their books and silly pranks and ease out into the real world to get a job and morph into serious problem-solvers for their employer.

"It's dry and warm for sure – twenty-two degrees to be precise. We don't want those ancient manuscripts flaking away in our hands. Do you know what you're looking for?"

A fair question. "More or less. I want to focus on the correspondence, orders, and so on, of serving officers in the post-Hadrian period. I'm hoping to stumble on an individual who I can further research and build my dissertation around. At the moment, it's just an idea. I'm hoping you can point me in the right direction."

"That sounds interesting, Noah. Of course, I can separate out the reports and correspondence from Roman officers for you to go through. Some have only had a rudimentary eye cast over them to get a broad feel of purpose, so there is virgin territory for you to plough." She finished with a coquettish giggle. Her friends had gone back to their conversation, but I was happy to talk just with Sima, flirting with her – if that's what it was. She told me she was a British-born Indian. I saw the calm and considered manner of a scientist, but her serenity was also beautiful, and I felt like a fly caught in her web – a fly that had no intention of struggling.

We chatted for a while and she went through some basic workplace rules, mentioning that she could provide a lab coat, magnifying goggles and gloves for me. Her friends all decided to go to the ladies' together and visit the bar on the way back. I wasn't sure their giggling was necessarily about me, but I feared it might be and smoothed down my hair in a nervous gesture. I glanced over at my mates, and was given a discreet thumbs-up by Dave.

"So, do you mind if I ask if you're in a relationship?" I asked, jumping in with both feet first.

She laughed and brushed her long black hair from her shoulder and fixed her dark brown eyes on mine, "You're very direct, Noah. Well, yes. My boyfriend lives in Manchester, but… I feel curiously free of his influence up here in the wild North. I feel a bit guilty about feeling unburdened – an odd sense of release. How about you?"

"I've recently split from my uni girlfriend, a couple of months ago, in fact. Apart from location, we didn't have a lot in common."

"Well, I'm the new girl here so I'm fully focussed on fitting in and doing a good job. Relationship stuff can sit on the back burner, as far as I'm concerned."

"I'm sure we'll find something to giggle about in that sterile atmosphere," I said, sitting back as the archivists returned to the table. The conversation broadened out, but before long they stood to take their leave and drive back. Sima held the car keys. Before I reached my mates, Mike Stone's loud voice stopped me in my tracks.

"Young Noah, I hear you're jumping ship, or should I say, ark?"

I hovered near his table and smiled at the upturned faces of fellow students before replying, "Yes, Mike. I've been re-assigned to the archives to work on translations for my dissertation from next week. I'll be on your team for the rest of this week, but the small idol could be my one and only find."

"But what a find!" he yelled, raising his pint glass. "Well, here's to you, I wish you success in your investigations. But if your ark founders, you'll always be welcome back to the dirt rats!" His deep, booming laugh was infectious and his minions joined in. I managed a cheesy grin as I backed away. I would not miss being a dirt rat. Perhaps my career pathway was via archives to a museum back room.

"Mike's half-cut," I commented as I re-joined my mates.

"Is she interested?" Dave asked, not prepared to be side-tracked.

Russ leaned in. "Got a date?"

I let them rib me, playing it down as expected. "Just work orientation, guys. I'll be joining with them from next week." I felt upbeat about breaking the ice with my new workmates, particularly Sima.

*****

I may have looked like a lab technician, but I felt like Marco Polo, travelling wide-eyed through new, uncharted territory. I was to work mainly from infra-red photographs that highlighted the writing on the blackened tablets. They were too fragile to handle and deteriorated with every exposure to air. The yellow-tinted magnifying goggles clarified the imprints left by the nib of an ink pen on the A5-sized birch wood tablets which had once been rubbed with a layer of beeswax to prevent the ink from spreading.

I was now studying the imprints in the wood, as the original ink had long since perished. The ones I was going over were from a batch that had been kept in a hidden compartment under the fort's office building, located by ground-scanning equipment and unearthed in wonderful condition. A combination of the peaty soil surroundings and the likelihood that the space had remained airtight for nearly two thousand years had resulted in readable items being recovered. Once removed, they were quickly re-sealed in airtight zip bags and taken indoors for storage in the dark at a cool temperature.

My studies of classical Latin script writing now came into their own, as I transcribed the inscriptions for later analysis and interpretation. I would then word process and print out my translations and give them to the archivists for their feedback.

Sima had come to stand behind me and I was keen to tell her what I had discovered. "Oh hi. I'm finding the tablets that have only been used once the most promising. Some of these tablets have been used numerous times. The layers of wax and multiple indentations render them illegible."

I paused to smile up at her. "There's a set of orders here, from Legate Claudius Hieronymianus, commander of the Sixth Legion, based at York. It's to the commander at Vindolanda, Tribune Helvius Pertinax of the Fourth Cohort, Sixth Legion. I've taken the Roman year 933 and converted it as the Year 180 CE on our modern calendar dating system. This was the last year of the reign of Emperor Marcus Aurelius."

Sima smiled at the excitement in my voice and on my face. "Is this the starting point for your investigation, Sherlock Jessop?"

"I think it might be. A toe-hold. A slight opening, perhaps. I've yet to finish reviewing the documents, so I'm hoping there will be more."

"Any idea yet what the orders were?"

"Well, fortunately the scribe had a fairly heavy hand and left a legible imprint of the letters and numerals on this tablet. It starts with salutations, then down to business with a request for more information on a recent attack by the

Caledonii – their name for the people north of Hadrian's Wall. It's fading after that, so I'll study a high res image this evening with my trusty detective's magnifying glass."

"I'm so happy for you!" Sima said, unexpectedly squeezing my shoulder.

I gave her hand a gentle tap. "I couldn't have done it without your help and guidance, Sima. Would you consider having dinner with me on Friday, to celebrate?"

"Only if we go Dutch. There's a little Italian in Corbridge we could try? I can drive us over there."

"That's great. Now I'm motivated to crack this case wide open over the next few days." I resumed my hunched position over the magnifier and she laughed and wandered back to her office. This was so promising on two fronts. Perhaps the Fates were guiding me after all.

I returned to my dorm room after five o'clock, my mood upbeat though my eyes itched from intense study. But thoughts of an upcoming evening with Sima would have to be put on hold, as I was due to have dinner with Professor Maggie in two hours at her terraced house.

"What are you smiling at?" Dave asked, swinging his backpack onto his bunk as he sauntered in.

"Oh, a breakthrough in my translations. I think I may have found a base on which to build." No mention of Sima or Maggie. I didn't want to be the source of gossip in this incestuous student environment in which everyone wanted to know everyone else's business.

"What has Mike, 'Man of Stone' got you doing?" I asked.

"I've graduated from digging to using ground penetrating radar. It's great for identifying solid objects a few feet underground, but the downside is that nearly all the objects are rocks."

"So, you're still digging in the earth then?"

"Yeah, but I'm getting to play with some expensive kit first!"

Russ and Richard reported that the main dig had stopped due to their completion of all the grids down to a depth of a metre, where they had reached street level in the settlement and in other places encountered a layer of hard rocks. Now they were sieving the topsoil for any tiny bits of pottery, items of jewellery or small coins they might have missed.

I showered and put on my favourite denim shirt and chinos, knowing this would attract comment, added to the spraying under armpits and combing of my unruly hair.

"Going somewhere nice?" Dave inquired. The other two who were lolling on their bunks with gaming consoles now leaned over, awaiting my reply.

They already knew about my dinner date with Maggie, so I owned up. "It's my meeting with Professor Maggie." Smirks and eye-rolling were the not unexpected reactions. "Yes, it's at her flat, and I don't think turning up in sweatshirt and jeans, stinking of BO, would make a favourable impression. I need to get an 'A' for my dissertation gents, or I won't get that First I'm after."

I endured a couple of ribald comments, then tried to change the subject. "What are you guys doing this evening?"

"Nothing to compare with your evening of debauched entertainment and being fed grapes on a Roman couch by a shapely Domina!" Dave exaggerated his sigh. "Just dinner in the canteen for us, then an hour of study followed by TV in the lounge. I might push the boat out and have a can of Stella."

"Well, I'm taking my research notes. As far as I'm concerned, it's an informal meet-up with an expert, so no tittle-tattle about me and the prof, please. I could do without the notoriety." I put my shoes on and made a show of sorting through my notes, waiting for them to saunter off to the canteen. Then I reached under the bed for my bag and took out the bottle of red wine I'd been saving. I packed my backpack and left via the fire escape, circling the building in the shadows and heading for the senior staff's houses.

I mused on how good things – or bad – often came together. Like three buses at once. Maybe there was something to star signs or fate. The three Fates of Greek mythology, spinning the destinies of us puny men. Now I was wondering how this eventful day was going to end.

6. Hadrian's Wall, 180 CE

Gaius led his unit out through the gatehouse in the Great Wall of Hadrian at Cilurnum fort, and across a ford through a shallow but fast-flowing river. The long column of one hundred and ten riders, two supply wagons and mules loaded with provisions and tents, followed him, as he rode beside his second-in-command, Paulinus. He felt blessed by the gods for having survived fifteen years of service with this tough and ruthless fighter by his side, mainly at the ditch and wooden barrier of Antoninus, one hundred miles to the north.

They had ridden many patrols in this bleak but alluring hill country, briefly the province of Valentia, and were familiar with the ways of the local tribespeople. They had spent nights, weeks or months in most of the dozen-or-so forts scattered across Valentia, and were now riding to Habitancum, some twelve miles distance. It was a square, timber fort that could sleep a cohort of up to five hundred men, but now had a much smaller garrison of about fifty auxiliaries. Now it was sitting in a dangerous no-man's-land, beyond the relative security of Hadrian's Wall. Two of the five cents in their cohort were at or north of the Wall, manning small forts and watchtowers.

Behind them came the vexillarius, proudly carrying the unit's banner and wearing a hollowed-out bear's head and pelt that extended down his back. The banner denoted they were the Equus Cent of the IV Cohors of the VI Legion Victrix Valorum, with a prancing horse included in the laurel leaf design. It was a prized position for a veteran member of the unit, currently a stout fellow from Gaul named Getterix, and one of danger as the banner and bearskin were trophies prized by the native tribes.

Four Brigante scouts, led by Kerwyn, rode past Gaius and galloped ahead, fanning out to the hills to his left and right.

"There will be snow," Paulinus remarked, sniffing the grey air.

"Perhaps," Gaius replied, "but with Fortuna's blessing we will reach the fort before it troubles our progress."

"Does old Blockhead know we're coming?"

Gaius laughed at Centurion Lupus Viridio's nickname. "He will have been told. Let us hope he has chased the chickens from the spare barrack blocks, expelled the damp and warmed them with braziers."

The ride through a sparsely-populated country was uneventful, the troops riding in their pairs behind their leaders at the ponderous pace of the supply wagons. Every hour or so, Kerwyn or one of his men would ride to Gaius and report.

"Still nothing, Kerwyn?" Gaius asked as they stopped at an abandoned watchtower for a midday meal. "I was expecting Selgovae scouts to be watching."

"They are there, sir, but out of sight in the woods. They have seen us, and know the presence of scouts indicates there is a body of men marching north. You shall see them before we reach the fort."

"Do you think they will try an attack?"

Kerwyn just shrugged and dismounted, leading his horse to the picket line.

"Insolent wretch," Paulinus said, spitting his disgust. "You let him get away with too much, sir."

Gaius chuckled and also dismounted. "He is a good scout and I feel I have his loyalty."

Paulinus's laugh conveyed his scepticism. He took his commander's reins and threw a comment over his shoulder. "Save me a spot by the fire, sir."

Gaius needed them all for different reasons: Paulinus for his cynical but by-the-book soldier's instincts, Kerwyn for his sharp eyes and local knowledge, and his two ranks of troops whose suspicion and distrust of each other he hoped would flower into a productive rivalry on the field of battle. He called his two decurions, Meral and a fellow Iberian named Andosini, a short, rugged type from a mountain tribe, who could put a name to all the sounds heard in this wilderness.

"We are four hours from the fort. Tell the men to be alert. From now onwards, I want four riders behind the last wagon, and ten to our left and right on the edge of the tree line. The scouts will be ahead of us…" Gaius was interrupted by a noisy dispute in the ranks. "Go and see what that's about."

Kerwyn rode into their camp and joined Gaius who was standing and looking at a scrum of men pushing and shoving.

Kerwyn laughed and said, "It is the new recruits and your older men fighting over some insult, no doubt."

"Yes. When there's no enemy to fight, they are at each other's throats. It is a soldier's way."

"It is the same with the tribes. Always watching each other and stealing the other's cattle. Your Roman discipline forges your men together, enough to drive wedges between our Briton tribes. We cannot withstand your shields in straight lines."

"It's the way of the Roman world, my friend. But without the help of some of you locals we would find it much harder in this harsh land. I have learned much from my wife about your gods and your ways. I hope once the resistance is quashed, we can all live in peace."

"Your peace, not ours," Kerwyn sneered, "and under Roman rules." Gaius ignored the slight and looked up as Paulinus returned to report.

"Sir, some of the Sarmatians took exception at being called 'flatheads', and they feel they are being served inferior rations to the Gauls. I spoke to the cook, and it seems he was intimidated by that troublemaker, Vetonrix, into serving them stale flatbread and smaller portions. I've told him to make the portions equal, sir."

"And put Vetonrix on a charge. We'll have a public flogging in the morning to focus their minds. Now, let's eat our food in peace!"

A light grey sky soon released its dubious bounty of snowflakes, which settled on the men and horses as they continued their slow progress northwards. They passed clusters of round huts within flimsy wicker palisades, smoke trails curling upwards, and sullen children minding goats or hairy cattle. The straight road followed valley floors boxed by hills, some bare but most wooded, and Gaius often craned his neck to left and right to check on the visibility of their outriders. Aside from the cawing of crows, the land was silent.

"They are watching us, sir, but keeping their distance," Kerwyn reported.

Gaius sniffed the cold air. "But will they attack before we reach the fort?"

"I think it unlikely the Selgovae will attack, sir," the scout replied, riding on the grass verge beside the officers. "We are close now."

"Then I'll send you ahead with two of my men to the fort to warn them of our approach." Gaius called up the two riders at the head of the column and sent them off. The snow flurries were becoming a nuisance, swirling in front of their faces and forming drifts on the road ahead. Mars snorted and shook his head, dislodging snow from his long mane.

Kerwyn's instinct was correct, and they reached the fort half an hour later. Gaius was greeted by old Blockhead, and after detailing his deputies to barrack the men, they retired to the commanding officer's room for a mug of warm mead.

"This is what we drink in the winter," Centurion Lupus Viridio said, warming his rear by a roaring fire. "It's honeyed ale, given the red-hot poker treatment."

Gaius was thankful of the warming drink, and cupped his hands on the pewter mug. "Then your storeman is resourceful," he replied, shaking the snow off his cloak.

"Indeed, he is. He buys from the locals, so I can treat you to a juicy beef steak this evening. But before that, join me in the baths and I will brief you on our situation."

After Gaius and Paulinus were shown to their small officer's quarters, they made their way outside a small side gate to the baths building. Slaves undressed them and guided them into the hot room, where they found their host through a steam cloud, sitting on a wooden bench.

"We have the first hour. After that, the men take their turn," Lupus explained.

"You have kept the fort well, Lupus, my congratulations," Gaius said. He was the senior officer, on years served, and Lupus knew that he would report back to Tribune Pertinax on the state of the fort and morale of the men.

"My thanks, Gaius. But let me report on what has happened. It seems there is a large influx of warriors from northern tribes beyond the Wall of Antoninus, who have been stirring up the Selgovae and Votodani. This is not good, and our relations have become somewhat strained with the local chieftains."

"Strained in what way?" Gaius queried.

"Our last patrol galloped back all in a fluster. My decurion reported that the headman he saw was edgy and clearly uncomfortable at having Romans visit his dun. When they left, they were chased by unfamiliar-looking warriors on those small shaggy ponies. There's also talk of a druid stirring the people up. It's not good, sir." He wiped the sweat from his square face and looked at his visitors, hopeful for suggestions.

"Can you estimate numbers?"

"Our scouts saw a host of over five hundred warriors training with weapons and staging mock battles. I guess there could be well over a thousand from the North. If you add in the Selgovae and Votodani, well, it could swell to four or five thousand."

"Hmmm. That all makes sense," Gaius replied. "We had a raid to test our strength at Vindolanda a week ago. That's why I've been sent here. Have you heard the news of our emperor's death?"

Lupus nodded. "It came with the last supply wagon. Sad news indeed. He was a soldier's emperor, and will be sorely missed. Who has succeeded?"

"Just as I left the fort, I intercepted a messenger. He confirmed our speculation that Marcus Aurelius's son, Commodus, was proclaimed Emperor. We must swear our loyalty to him, of course, but judging by reputation, he is not like his father."

"We can do without a period of turmoil and plots," Lupus moaned, shaking sweat from his short hair.

"Aye, but remember it's 'Hail Commodus' at tomorrow's parade. Is it worth our while talking to the chiefs of the Selgovae and Votodani? I suspect they will tell us nothing for fear of reprisals."

"My biggest fear, Gaius, is you riding away with your men and leaving us to face a siege by those northern devils."

"It is not just you. There are three more garrisons on the road between here and the Antoninus Wall. I fear for everyone's safety."

They lapsed into silence and stood to allow the slaves to scrape their sweating bodies with wooden spatulas, before entering the tepid pool. They ducked under the water and then exited to the next room to jump into a cold plunge pool. They did not tarry long, hurrying back to the relative warmth of the tepid pool.

"Ah, that has restored me from the road," Gaius said, cupping warm water over his head. "Paulinus, what are your thoughts on our mission? What can we hope to achieve here before reporting back?"

Paulinus considered the question before replying. "A warrior-chief is gathering together the northern tribes, and I fear for the safety of our small garrisons. We have an infantry cent and a handful of riders spread over four forts, and our cavalry cent. It is not enough to face down a rabble of thousands of blue noses whipped up by a prancing holy man. Their young warriors will want to blood themselves on easy prey."

"You're right. Although it's not specifically part of my orders, I feel the tribune would want me to look out for the welfare of our men. What about you, Lupus? Do you think we should pull our men out of the other forts and make an orderly retreat to the Great Wall?"

Lupus licked his lips before replying. "Traders and civilian travellers have become few. It's as if they can sense something is brewing. We cannot guard the North Road in the face of such a gathering of warriors, Gaius, and their attack on Vindolanda suggests their intention is hostile. If you decide we should all fall back, I would be extremely relieved."

"Then we will send our swiftest riders north in the morning to tell the other garrisons to abandon their forts and march back to us. I will take the blame, if there is any. But we need to distract the hostiles to give them a chance."

They were being towelled and dressed by the bath house slaves when Lupus spoke. "The Selgovae have a festival to one of their gods in these coming days. The king has invited me. Perhaps we should go and sit with him, as a courtesy. Their citadel is on top of one of the three hills for which our fort, Trimontium, is named. He will guarantee our safety whilst we are in his enclosure, but..."

"...Not after we leave," Paulinus finished.

"Yes, we'll do that, but have our cavalry close by at the ready," Gaius added.

That evening they ate a rich beef stew in the officer's mess. After the meal Lupus said, "I have arranged for the two most comely and cleanest whores to warm your beds."

Gaius smiled and replied, "Very thoughtful, but not for me, thank you. My wife is enough for me – I prefer to hold her in my dreams and know that I will look forward to my return to our bed."

"I'll take up your kind offer, sir," Paulinus said with a wolfish grin.

*****

In the half light of the grey morning, messengers were dispatched northwards, and announcements were made to the garrison parade, after which Vetonrix had his tunic removed and was given twenty lashes in front of the men. The officers departed with a guard of fifty for the Selgovae capital. Gaius matched twenty-five of his best Gauls with the same number of Sarmatians, ordering them to ride side-by-side in unfamiliar pairings. The rest remained at the fort.

Gaius rode beside Lupus and asked, "What can you tell me of the Selgovae chief?"

Lupus smiled before replying, "His name is Eildon, and he calls himself 'King of the Selgovae'. He is old, and has ruled with little trouble for twenty years. They are the largest tribe by numbers, occupying the central part of this land we once called Valentia. Some of his men are our scouts, with his blessing. They are friends of Rome, and I have carried two dozen plucked and dressed ducks, with our spices, for his table. It is his favourite. That is why he invited me."

"And what of the coming together of other tribes?"

"We have witnessed a build-up of warriors from tribes north of the Antonine line, including the Venicones and others we know only as the Caledonii. They are warlike people who hate us. They fought against Agricola at Mons Grampius, and may be responsible for greatly reducing the Ninth Hispania in numbers."

"Have your scouts seen this gathering and estimated numbers?"

"Yes. I have Brigante scouts, like your men, who were more forthcoming than our Selgovae scouts. They estimate two thousand warriors gathered in the glens to the west of the three hills."

Gaius grunted. "But am I right to suspect the tribes who neighbour the Selgovae, namely the Votodani and Damnonii, have not yet sent their warriors to the muster?"

"I would agree with that assumption. I have detailed our Brigante scouts to explore the valleys close by once we have made camp."

They followed the road north and skirted two forts on their way to Three Hills and the Selgovae capital. When they left the North Road for the track into the hills, Lupus sent a rider ahead to warn the Selgovae king of their imminent arrival.

"As you know, they prefer to live on hilltops, from where they can see us approaching and can defend themselves from attack, if necessary." Lupus appeared to be talking to the trees, perhaps informing an invisible woodland deity.

Gaius and Paulinus exchanged curious looks. "Whereas we mighty Romans build in lowlands where our roads intersect, close to a fresh water source or by a river ford," Gaius said, in a faintly mocking voice, as if educating new recruits.

They lapsed into silence as the track took them upwards, past low trees and coarse heather, separated by rocks rounded by fierce wind and rain. A hawk hovered over its victim, lowering itself in stages before plunging into the grass.

Six warriors with tattooed faces and bronze bands on their arms waited for them at the top of a ridge, turning without a word or gesture of greeting to escort them towards a palisade of wooden stakes that stood on a hilltop before them. Gaius made a show of bivouacking his men on the ridge within sight of the hillfort, and proceeded with Paulinus, Lupus, Kerwyn and two guards.

They traversed an upland glen, passing grazing livestock, and entered through a wooden gatehouse, where children leaned over the parapet to shout insults at them. Chickens scattered as they followed their escorts past round huts and animal pens to the central longhouse. Here they dismounted on a dusty, flattened area where yapping dogs circled eager boys who competed to grab their reins.

"Welcome, Romans," a grey-haired father announced from the opening to the long house. Over a full-length grey woollen gown, his cloak of red fox pelts hung from thin shoulders. He had tattoo swirls on his wrinkled cheeks, a gold torque around his mottled neck, and silver wrist bands encrusted with jewels on each forearm.

"Hail Eildon, King of the Selgovae," Lupus replied, with a slight bow of his head. "May I present Centurion Gaius Atticianus of our Sixth Legion, and his deputy, Paulinus Grella."

"You are welcome, Centurion. Please enter my hall," the elderly king said, turning to lead the way.

A rancid stench of unwashed bodies assailed Gaius's nose, and he sought to avoid stepping on dog filth amongst the reeds as his eyes adjusted to the gloom. There was a fire the length of a man burning on a raised brazier at the centre, its smoke rising to a gap in the thatched roof. Their host led them past lounging warriors to a raised dais where he sat down on a throne of carved oak, waving a thin arm at a bench. The occupants of the bench glared at the new arrivals and wandered into the shadows, and the three Romans, together with Kerwyn, took their seats.

"We have seen you before, Centurion Atticianus," Eildon said, peering at his visitor in the gloom.

Gaius had an ear for the tribal language shared across the island of Britannia, but the northern dialect was harsh and some unfamiliar terms were used. He understood bits but still glanced at Kerwyn, who would translate what he did not understand. He coughed and replied in the native tongue of his wife's people. "Yes, King Eildon, I have spent many years north of the Great Wall, and know something of this land and its people. But this is the first time I have seen the inside of your great hall."

"It is good you have learned the Briton tongue. It shows an interest in our people." This was greeted with a rumble of discontent from the onlookers.

Gaius noted that there were chiefs from at least six different tribes, judging by the difference in dress and decoration. He looked twice at one handsome young noble, who grinned at him. It was the man he had grappled with on the battlements of Vindolanda, only ten days past. Gaius recognised the glint of a blue gemstone in what he now realised was the eye of a gilded serpent entwined around the chieftain's neck. It was the most unusual and ornate torque he had ever seen, and it seemed alive as its wearer moved, ready to strike.

Eildon had noted the look of recognition between the two, and having heard of the raid on Vindolanda, grinned, showing gaps where he was missing teeth. "So, I think you have met our northern cousin, Donall, Chief of the Venicones? Step forward, Donall." He dwelt on the word 'chief' as if to assert his seniority.

Gaius did not stand, and made the decision to play down the encounter. "I believe I have fought with this chief, and felt the strength of his arm!" he said, in jest.

The hall erupted in laughter, and Gaius willingly joined in with Kerwyn.

Donall's dark eyes sparkled, and he swept his long brown hair from his face, remarking, "We grappled briefly, Roman, before I cast you from your battlements. But I see your gods have restored you!"

The laughter continued, and Gaius stood to make a brief bow and rub the healing wound on his head. "It was not you who dealt me this blow, but one of your eager warriors. One I can fight, but two is enough to test any man."

"Then let us fight now and see who is the better man!" Donall jeered, whipping up his audience into a frenzy of anti-Roman blood lust.

Gaius caught the look of concern on Lupus's face, or was it fear? The atmosphere in the hall had turned hostile, and Gaius was aware of the evil stares that burrowed into his head. He was relieved that all who entered the king's hall were required to leave their weapons with his steward at the entrance.

When Gaius hesitated to reply to the challenge, Eildon stood and raised his thin arms to quell the noise. "The centurion and his men are my guests, and he shall not be goaded into a fight. There will be time enough for that!"

A final cheer gave way to low murmurs and, finally, silence as men took their seats or stood with legs apart.

Gaius and Lupus sat on the bench as normality was restored. Gaius, although relieved to have ducked a potentially fatal duel with the younger and stronger chief, was mildly dismayed at Eildon's last comment. Was this confirmation of a gathering storm? He could stand being the butt of their jokes in order to stay true to his mission and find out what he could about the muster of tribes. Lupus nodded his understanding. Gaius turned to Eildon and said, "I apologise for visiting you unannounced when you are hosting so many tribal chiefs and your hall is full."

Eildon conferred with an aide, whilst Donall stood with arms folded, glaring at Gaius. Whispered

conversations ran around the smoky hall. Eildon faced
Gaius and replied, "We are gathered for the festival to Our
Father, great Crauchan, king of our gods. There will be
feasting tonight and games of strength and endurance over
the coming days. You are welcome to my table this eve to
share in our feast, friends."

Gaius leaned towards Lupus and whispered, "Can we
refuse?"

Lupus replied, "We risk giving offence. I advise we
remain for the feast, sleep here and leave at dawn.
Remember, we are buying time for our garrisons to march
south."

Gaius turned to Eildon and said, "Thank you, we
accept. We hope our gift of ducks prepared in our way will
be to your liking."

Lupus waved his man forward, and a hessian sack
was laid at the king's feet.

Eildon signalled to an aide to collect the offering. "I
am pleased you will join us. Let us walk now, and you can
see the preparations for our festivities."

He guided his guests out into the pale, late afternoon
light, to the cheers of his people. Gaius and Lupus filled
their lungs with fresh mountain air, happy to be outside
again if only for a while. The Romans were shown targets
set up for archery, sling shots and knife-throwing. Mock
duels with wooden swords and shields were staged for the
visitors. The thunder of hooves caught their attention as a
line of riders swung low on their unshod ponies to stab
straw figures with spears. Donall was keen to show off his
fighting skills, and easily knocked down two men, glancing
at Gaius each time.

Gaius knew they would not be shown anything the
king wanted to keep from their eyes, and was content to be
led around the wide meadow outside the enclosure where
huge barns for ponies and cattle stood at the fringes, along
with grain and vegetable stores. A cold wind buffeted them,
and dark clouds gathered to the east. Gaius asked Kerwyn

to glean as much information as he could from the other guests at the feast, once their tongues had been loosened by drink.

In the early morning, Kerwyn roused the officers who had slept where they sat, and they picked their way past snoring bodies to the hall's entrance, collecting their sword belts from a drowsy attendant. Lupus's men brought their horses and they departed in silence, riding beneath an indifferent guard on the gatehouse parapet. Their men were waiting, and they filed down the hillside path to the Roman road, turning southwards. After a mile they caught up with the garrison from Three Hills, marching four abreast, followed by three supply wagons and about thirty assorted camp followers.

Gaius asked Lupus and Kerwyn what they had found out during the evening's carousing. Lupus shook his head, his eyes red and puffed up on his pale face.

"They are gathering for war," Kerwyn simply stated. "You are wise to order your men south to the Great Wall."

7. Vindolanda, present day

She wore ornate flip flops, like something from the Arabian Nights, and a cotton tie-dye dress with purple and orange swirls, together with coloured chiffon scarves that fell from a thin leather belt. Maggie could have come straight from the Glastonbury Festival. Will you be performing the dance of the seven veils? I recalled a television production of Salome in which a bloated, lascivious King Herod hissed, "Will you *daaance* for me, Salome?" I blinked to expel the unpleasant vision and produced my bottle of wine, placing it on the table.

"Ah, a Rioja Reserva, my favourite!" she exclaimed, in girlish pleasure. "I feel like the Andalusian girl in that Kate Bush song... do you know the one?" She lifted her scarves and twisted, leaving me in no doubt that her figure-hugging dress ended mid-way up her thighs.

What factors had gone into her choosing this summer outfit in these dark days of winter? I pushed off my fleece top, suddenly noticing how warm it was in the room.

"I do – The Flower of the Mountain," I replied. Never one to miss the chance to be a know-it-all, I added, "It's her new version of Sensual World that she recorded for her Director's Cut collection."

A firm favourite of my ex-girlfriend. We had bumped and grinded to this album a few times. I was the first one to go to university in my family, and sometimes I rose to being baited by my younger siblings with stunning show-off answers to questions on University Challenge, or mocking laughter when I got it wrong. My mind was a mess of popular culture trivia mixed with the languages and customs of the ancient world.

"I have the CD somewhere. I'll put it on." She turned eagerly to her music centre in the corner.

So, no need for my notes, then. I pushed my backpack beside the armchair and smiled as music filled the room. She danced across her living room carpet with two empty wine glasses to her small table by two chairs in the alcove of a bay window. A solitary red rose stood in a crystal vase at the centre, the curtains already drawn around. Cosy.

I uncorked the wine and Maggie held out her glass to me. "Will you be my cup-bearer, Noah?" she said softly. I took it as rhetorical and made no reply, recalling from a text book that for the gods, 'cup-bearer' was often a euphemism for lover. "Let's drink to the success of your dissertation." We clinked glasses and savoured the full, dry flavour. She had re-painted her fingernails but wore no rings. We sat facing each other across the table. I felt a little uneasy and was content to let her lead the conversation.

"That Moroccan pipe music sends chills through my body," she said, with a little shiver.

"It's a very sensual and seductive song," I added, taking another sip. I wondered if she had any bottles of wine. This one would not last long.

"Yes, I've always loved Kate's music. She's such an original talent and so very in touch with her feminine nature. I love this line too, '…it slipped between my breasts'," she sang as she put her finger into her cleavage, testing the elasticity of her dress to flash the tops of her white breasts at me. Was she flirting or just being herself?

I shared her laughter. "I'm not sure what slipped there in the song. Perhaps its best left to the imagination," I said.

The song ended and we sat sipping. "Being a strapping young man, you're probably starving, so I suggest I serve our meal and then we can chat about what your latest thoughts are from your research."

I nodded and she got up and left the room. The next track, The Song of Solomon, filled the room with a soulful, melancholy vibe. It's clearly a love-gone-wrong song, and one in which Kate feels very bitter against the man who disappointed her. It's the only occurrence of bad language in any of her songs that I know of – the embittered, 'I don't want your bullshit, I just want your sensuality.' A woman who's heard enough lies and excuses and is laying out her expectations.

I could hear Maggie banging pots and pans in the kitchen next door. I stood to look around the room. There were half a dozen framed prints of French impressionist paintings – familiar, ready-made consumer art – just buy and plonk on your walls and think no more about it.

Above the fireplace on the mantelpiece stood a new acquisition – too new to have been allotted a space on the walls. It was the cover photo from the magazine, a print on canvas that was stretched onto a wooden frame. Maggie looked like a queen surveying her domain as she stared over the battlements. Above her head was an expanse of blue sky with wispy white clouds that would normally be scudding swiftly from west to east, now captured for all time in a static pose. This amazing sky had been obscured by bold lettering on the magazine cover, but now revealed it gave the picture a better sense of the place. If it wasn't for the faux fur trim on her anorak hood, it could almost be timeless. The same sky, the same bleak hills that Roman sentries once gazed upon.

"Do you like it?" she asked as she entered carrying a tray.

"Yes, it's very beautiful, particularly with the expanse of sky above you. It somehow makes the picture complete – in a natural setting."

"It's amazing what they can do these days. To put a photograph on canvas and give it texture, as if it were a painting. And all for just thirty pounds!" She put some condiments and a bread basket on the table and disappeared back to the kitchen.

I decided I would not mention the absence of any other personal photos of her with family or friends, apart from the obligatory graduation picture. I had learned in my study of research methods that photos can act as prompts to prise personal disclosures out of shy or guarded individuals. I wouldn't go there – their absence was enough to warn me off. I returned to my seat to flick through my notes to re-focus my mind on my work.

"I hope you like mushroom lasagne with salad?" she asked, as she plonked a plate in front of me and placed a salad bowl on the table.

"Yes, I love Italian food." I thought I had left vegetarian meals behind with my ex-girlfriend, but I wasn't complaining and my mouth watered.

Maggie returned with a hot dish held with an oven glove. She placed it on a picture mat and slid into her chair, throwing the oven glove on the carpet. The smell made my stomach rumble and she served me with a generous portion. "Help yourself to salad," she said, giving herself a smaller serving.

"This is delicious, Maggie," I spluttered through a hot full mouth. In her office she had told me I could drop formalities – I had called her 'professor' up till now, but she didn't correct me.

"Thanks, it's about the only thing I can cook. Cheers." She held out her wine glass and we clinked. The lighting was a bit more subdued – she had turned her dimmer switch down. She asked where I was up to with my project and I briefed her.

"I think you'll enjoy spending a week or two in the archives, translating some of our wonderful tablets," she said.

"I won't be going home for reading week, so I'll stay and work through with the staff," I replied, then asked, "Do you have plans to go home?" *She's not a student, dumbo. This might be home.*

A brief look of annoyance flashed across her face and she put her knife and fork down. "I've got plenty to do here, so I'll be staying. Besides, things are… complicated at home." She turned to face the curtain and twisted a lock of hair. Then the thought passed and she returned to her meal with a sip of wine, followed by a shy smile. "But we're celebrating your earth goddess find, and your gathering dissertation. Cheers." We polished off the wine and after she had cleared our plates she returned with a new bottle. We talked about my marble goddess and then her first find. She went back to being ebullient, entertaining Maggie, just for me.

I was fascinated and I was flattered. We laughed a lot. After more wine and a supermarket tiramisu dessert, followed by a brandy, I found myself slow dancing with her to another CD – romantic ballads by the sound of it. The smell of rosewater filled my senses and I could feel her body pressing close to mine. She was attractive, and I was aroused. She lifted her head from my shoulder and pouted her lips. I felt light-headed under the influence of the wine and responded with a kiss. She put her arms around my neck and the kiss was prolonged. It could have been fresher's week again.

"Let's continue this in my room," she breathed on my neck.

She led me by the hand up her narrow stairway and into the front bedroom, pushing me onto her bed. The smell of incense sticks still hung in the air and I saw constellations on her ceiling after she dimmed the light and slipped out of her hippy dress.

*****

I read and re-read an enlarged image of a tablet, scribbling notes in my pad. Then I read through my notes, trying to order the words into meaningful sentences.

"What have you got?" Sima asked, peering over my shoulder. She had her own work to do, but out of all the archivists, she seemed to have a sixth sense of when I felt I was invisible, puzzling away on my own, and in need of a boost.

"Oh, hi. It's a report sent by Tribune Helvius Pertinax of the fourth cohort, based here in the year 180 CE, to his commanding officer, Legate Claudius Hieronymianus, head of the Sixth Legion, based at York. This tablet must be a copy of the order, or perhaps there was a mistake or he changed his mind."

"What are the orders?" she asked, leaning in.

I caught a whiff of sweet orange scent as I turned to her. "I think it says something like, 'Salutations, etc... I am sending our cavalry to patrol north of the Wall, to seek out information of a native gathering that... may have hostile intent'. It then says, 'the cavalry commander is Gaius Atticianus, Centurion of Horses'. After that I can't make it out."

"Well done you!" she exclaimed. "That sounds like a hook to hang your hat on."

"Indeed, it is. At least worthy of further investigation. Will you keep an eye out for more from this batch of findings from the Commanding Officer's office? I'll pop over to the professor and ask her if she has any ideas on where I might find out more about Helvius Pertinax and Gaius Atticianus."

"You can tell me all about it on Friday in the Italian restaurant in Corbridge. I bet they had very different Italian cuisine here in the second century."

"I will give you a full briefing over tagliatelle." I turned off the halo neon light that surrounded a magnifying lens and carefully sealed the manuscripts pouch, handing it to her for safe storage.

"See you later, alligator." I grabbed my coat and headed for the door. It was dry but cold outside, and I hurried around the building to Professor Wilde's office. I had not seen or spoken to her since our entanglement four days ago, which loomed large in my thoughts, but remained something inexplicable to me. I didn't know what to feel.

"Hi Mavis, is she free?"

Mavis had her back to me, her head in the storeroom door. She turned abruptly and locked the door with a firm twist of a key. She wore her red and black kilt and cream chunky Aran sweater, with heavy denier tights and sensible brown brogues as if it was a guard's uniform, to make sure we students got the message that Professor Wilde's office was not a drop-in centre. "Let me check." She peered at me through round spectacles, returned to her desk and picked up the phone, spoke briefly, then nodded me through.

"Hi Maggie," I said, closing the door behind me.

"Good morning, Noah," she replied, removing her glasses as she looked up. She smiled and pointed to the chair.

I slid in and returned her smile, placing my writing pad on her desk. Best not mention the other night – I'll leave that to her. "I've part-translated a report etched onto a wooden tablet from the commander here at Vindolanda to his Legate at York. I have his name, and part of an instruction to send a named cavalry centurion north of the Wall on patrol. I think it could be an opening."

She maintained her smile and locked her pale blue eyes on mine, reaching out her hand and flicking the ears of my notepad. "That's great news, Noah. Write down the names and ranks of the officers and I'll do a search on the database." She stood and came around the desk, sitting on it and looking down to me.

"Thanks" I replied, sitting upright in the chair and scribbling a note. "I'll crack on with the translations then."

"You do that, Noah. Perhaps we can have a follow-up de-brief on Friday?"

"Oh, I'm… going out with my mates on Friday – someone's birthday."

"OK, I'm away from Saturday for three or four days so we'll catch up when I return."

"Oh, changed your plans?"

She frowned.

"I mean… you said the other evening that you were staying?"

"Yes, I did, didn't I? Well, I have matters to deal with and I've decided the phone won't do."

We exchanged looks for a brief, potentially awkward, moment. I stood. "OK, I'll look for your car for your return; otherwise, I won't bother you."

"You're no bother, Noah. By all means text me if you find something of interest. If I come up with anything, I'll send it by email. Until then, keep exploring." She stood and took my free hand in both of hers. "And Noah, I hope I can trust you to be discreet? We both overdid it with the wine, I think."

"Of course, Maggie. My lips are sealed."

I pulled my hand back from her warm grip after a few seconds, then tore the top sheet from my notepad and placed it on her desk. I smiled and backed away to the door. "I hope you get things sorted, Maggie. I look forward to hearing from you." With that I beat a retreat, passing through the domain of the unsmiling Mavis to the door.

Now I've lied to her about Friday. I hope this doesn't become complicated.

8. Vindolanda, 180 CE

A line of silent black riders sat on their mounts on the hill brow overlooking Vindolanda from the north, silhouetted against the late afternoon sky, their identity unknown to the distraught villagers below. They had their own problems to contend with, in the shape of their blue-painted and tattooed tormentors. The sullen survivors of the attack on the settlement outside the fort had been herded into cattle pens, wailing their misery as their homes were looted and torched around them.

Gaius looked down on the fort that had been his home for the past three years, and wondered if his wife and child were in there. "You know, I stood on that battlement barely two weeks past, staring up at this hill in the dead of night, watching the strange, coloured lights dance over it. That was the night of the attack – when Donall and his men came to test our strength and count our numbers."

"And now they have returned," Paulinus said. "All of them."

They looked solemnly down, across the flat meadow after which Vindolanda was named, to the stone-walled fort, now surrounded by hundreds of warriors, some riding their shaggy ponies, others looting or corralling screaming Brigante villagers into animal pens with prods from their spears. The sound of fear, desperation and anguish carried to them on the cold afternoon breeze. The soldiers on the walls of the fort looked on in silence.

Gaius squinted his eyes and leaned forward in his saddle. "How many?" he asked.

Paulinus replied readily, knowing only too well his commander's shortness of sight. "I'd say about six hundred painted warriors."

"And on the walls of the fort?"

"Roughly one hundred and fifty on the north wall and gatehouse."

"And what standards are flying above the gatehouse?"

"Now... even I have to narrow my eyes..."

"I can see, sir," Getterix the standard bearer said, eagerly moving forward to join the front line.

Gaius grinned, "So tell me – what standards fly?"

"There is the standard of our cohort, sir. Then there are the standards of the first, second and third cents, sir."

"Good lad. That tells us that Plauditus has fallen back with his men from the Wall. Chased in disarray, no doubt. If he did not lose too many, there must be roughly three hundred and fifty soldiers."

"Also, some of my people would have had helmets pushed on their heads and spears thrust in their hands," Kerwyn added.

Paulinus looked at the nonchalant scout. "Surely they can see their village burning and their women captured. Why would they not fight?"

Kerwyn glanced at him and chose not to answer.

"Aye," Gaius agreed, "Perhaps forty or fifty Brigante. That would give them around three hundred men, still less than the enemy."

"So, what is your plan?" Paulinus asked.

Gaius paused for a moment before replying, noticing that they had been spotted by the Caledonii who were being urged to form up in a defensive line by a chief. "They are obliging us by putting their warriors in a line with their puny shields and tooth-pick spears. We will ride them down; then reduce them with arrows and throwing javelins; then harry them with our swords before riding on to the north gate. That is my plan."

"But sir, what about rescuing the captured women and children?" Kerwyn asked.

83

Gaius looked at him in a sorrowful manner. "I know you fear for your family, Kerwyn, but we cannot tarry to fight, otherwise we will be dragged from our horses and slaughtered. And we would lose too many in shielding them as they run for the gate. No, we cannot. We must get to the fort and then plan an attack on these devils. I'm sorry. We must entreat our gods that they will be well treated until such a time as they can be rescued."

Kerwyn snorted, his dark looks twisted in bitter disappointment. "If it were your wife…"

"Enough!" Paulinus snapped, turning his horse. "The commander has given his orders. Let us form up in two ranks to ride down the ridge, then we fan out across the meadow ready for the order to charge!" His voice had risen to a bellow, and the men started to form up.

"But what of our supply wagons and mules?" Decurion Andosini asked.

"It is a good question," Gaius replied. "You will take eight men and escort the wagon and mule train away from here, circling around the hill behind us and heading to the west. Make for the fortlet at Owl Tree Hill – you know it?"

"Aye, sir."

"I doubt the painted people will have split their force, so if Fortuna is with us, it will be unoccupied. Wait there for two nights and I will send someone for you. If no one comes, fear the worst and continue to head west to Camboglanna. May our Father, Jupiter, watch over you." Gaius saluted the rugged Iberian, then turned his attention to organising his men.

The troop navigated their way down in two lines into a dry valley, passing its one tree bending to the east in the direction of the prevailing wind, a hardy survivor in the bleak and barren landscape. The rough track led them up a slight incline, where they filtered out to the left and right onto the flat meadow of Vindolanda. At the far side of the meadow their enemy lined up, hollering and hooting their defiance, thrusting their small, painted square cowhide shields in the air, and raising their spears and axes to the sky. Behind them, black smoke spiralled upwards to the turquoise winter sky as the settlement burned.

Gaius had Paulinus and Meral on either side in the middle of the line of ninety cavalry soldiers, their arrows nocked or javelins at the ready. He turned to Getterix and said, "Stay behind me, and follow me closely through their ranks on the road to the gatehouse. We may be slowed to fight, but we shall not stop."

The burly Gaul nodded and moved to the rear, somehow managing to hold his banner in his shield hand, and hold his sword and reins in the other.

Gaius turned to his two deputies and said, "Instruct the men to canter towards the enemy and on my command to fire or throw. They should fire or throw a second time after I give the order to charge. Then we will draw swords and ride through them. They have put about half of their force to oppose us, so let us kill as many as we can, before we all ride on to the fort. Understood?"

They nodded and rode to brief their men. Gaius then rode in front of the men and roused them for battle. "We are the Equus Cent of the Fourth Cohort of the victorious Sixth Legion of Rome! We are undefeated under my command, and it will stay that way!"

The youngest of the Gauls, Vertinax, had the task of sounding his short tin horn, and Gaius now pointed to him.

Horses pawed the ground in anticipation, their chest guards of leather, studded with metal spikes, flapping as they tossed their heads, their face and shin guards providing more protection from thrown spears or shield and sword thrusts. The men roared at the blare of the horn, and at Gaius's upraised lance as he continued, riding Mars from left to right. "Raise your weapons and make ready! Bang your shields and let them hear our war cries! Let us ride our enemy down and scatter them, let them feel the strength of our arm and taste our steel! To battle!"

Gaius returned to the centre and held up his lance once more and cried, "Forward at a canter!" gently digging his heels into Mars who tossed his great shaggy mane and trotted forward, then cantered across the meadow, gathering pace as his rider urged him on. This was what they had trained for – a full cavalry charge by an elite unit of a celebrated legion.

The drumming of four hundred hooves thundered in their ears and they closed the distance in less than a minute, reining back their mounts to a steady pace, then throwing javelins and firing arrows on command. The wide, fearful eyes of warriors, some supporting wounded comrades, filled their vision, then the cries of the dying and wounded filled their ears as they discharged their second volley, before urging their mounts forward to crash through the puny defences of their enemy with a mighty roar.

Gaius speared a determined painted warrior through his chest, dragging back the lance tip and riding on, stabbing and thrusting as he passed by others who raised their spears to him, deflecting their efforts with his oval shield and circling back to his men before reaching the burning village. Behind him was a scene of bitter fighting, with the Sarmatians riding in circles, standing up in their straps and firing arrows, keeping at a distance from their hapless prey. The Gauls were right in the thick of the enemy, slashing about them with their curved cavalry swords, some being dragged from their horses and butchered. He checked behind and was relieved to see Getterix still mounted, flaying about him with his sword, still holding the standard.

"To me!" Gaius bellowed, and Getterix responded by digging his heels into his horse's flanks and moving away from those who were jumping to grab his standard. "Let's go and find Vertinax!" he yelled, urging Mars forward into the melee of bodies.

Gaius knew they should not loiter in the midst of the enemy, as their main threat was nullified and they risked being killed. The young Gaul was nearby, fighting furiously and trying to kick away a tall warrior who had hold of his shield and was trying to drag him from his horse. Gaius spurred Mars forward and he rammed the chest guard of his stallion into the warrior, sending him to ground before the stamping hooves crushed a leg.

"Sound the recall, Vertinax!" he yelled above the din of battle.

The young man, relieved to have been helped out of a potentially fatal tugging match, put the tin horn to his lips and blew. Heads looked up and the men snapped into a response, as their training kicked in. The Gauls quickly disengaged and rode to Gaius, but the Sarmatians took some time to respond to Meral's shouts, their enthusiasm for the slaughter plain to see. Gaius grinned at the sight, knowing that he had found a very useful and deadly addition to his unit.

As Meral led his men towards him, Gaius pointed his sword to the road between burning buildings and yelled, "To the fort!"

He was loath to leave any wounded behind, knowing their fate was sealed, but they could not delay and allow the enemy to organise a counter attack. He leapt forward on Mars and cantered at a speed that would allow him to react to any obstructions, or warriors throwing themselves at him. Passing the first bellows of black smoke, he could see the gates of the fort open and a squad of soldiers jogging out to give them a protective guard on their approach. Warriors still barred his way, but only in ones and twos, and he swung his sword or punched with his shield boss at any who got too close.

Gaius slowed a bit and urged the others onwards towards the fort. He slowed to a trot and looked at the men as they passed him, waving them on. Paulinus joined him and rode at his side, also yelling to his men to continue onwards to the fort.

Gaius pointed and shouted, "Look at Kerwyn and his scouts! They have gone to their homes to search for their families, I think."

"Then may their gods go with them," Paulinus growled.

Gaius looked on with concern and met Paulinus's eyes. "We should help them make a sweep of the outlying huts and then follow our riders to the fort."

Paulinus glared his opposition to the idea at him. "Why risk your life for them?"

Gaius gritted his teeth and spurred Mars into a gallop, "Because he is my man!"

Paulinus sighed and followed. Meral was just behind, and also followed with his men, whooping at the prospect of more action. Gaius noted that his unit of Gauls had reached the safety of the fort, and the auxiliary soldiers now formed a wall of shields across the entrance to the bridge over the dry ditch, waiting for stragglers.

Gaius rode around huts and pens on the outskirts of the settlements that had yet to be burnt, kicking one warrior to the ground, before reaching a cluster of huts where four horses stood tethered. He leapt from Mars and rushed into the first hut, witnessing a bitter struggle between a scout and a painted warrior. He swiftly drew his knife and stabbed the warrior in his side repeatedly, then dropped him to the ground.

"Where is Kerwyn?" he shouted at the scout, whose wife and children now rushed to hug him.

"The next hut, sir," the man replied.

"Get everyone out of here now and back to the fort," Gaius shouted as he exited the hut.

Fights between his men and warriors were all around him now, and he barged men out of the way and entered the next hut. Kerwyn was on his back on the ground, where a bulky warrior sat on him, pushing downwards with a knife towards Kerwyn's throat. The scout was pushing back with all his might, but seemed doomed to lose the duel as the blade moved closer to his throat. Gaius sprang forward with his bloody knife, but before he reached the warrior, a woman appeared from the gloom, holding her ripped garment in one hand and a bulky object in the other. With a cry of anger, she bashed the warrior's head, sending him tumbling to the side. Gaius took two strides to the stricken warrior and finished him off by slashing his throat.

"Everyone out!" Gaius yelled. As Kerwyn was helped to his feet by his wife, Gaius ran outside and looked through the fighting for Paulinus. His deputy soon appeared, leading Mars to him. "Let's get out of here!" Gaius said as he sprung into his saddle.

The Sarmatians were slashing at the heads and necks of screaming warriors who were running towards them, buying the scouts time to jump on their horses. Gaius held out his hand to one of Kerwyn's sons, who took it and swung up behind him. Other soldiers followed suit and soon all the families were behind a rider.

"Lead us to the fort, Kerwyn!" Gaius shouted at his head scout, and followed him on a circuitous route out of the settlement towards the western gate, away from the fighting that was all around the shield wall at the north gate.

It was a clever idea that Gaius had not thought of, and soon they were clear of the settlement, riding beside the fort walls, enjoying the cheers from the battlements above. This time Gaius did not wait for his men, and rode behind the scouts, over the bridge and into the welcome sanctuary of the fortress. To his great relief, his unit followed, and after letting down the boy, he led his riders to the central square where they would do a roll call and see how many they had lost.

As his unit gathered and men dismounted to clasp each other's forearms with relief, Kerwyn and his family came to Gaius's side.

"Sir, I am indebted to you for coming to our aid, although I did not ask for it. I will await your punishment for my disobedience."

"That punishment will come, Kerwyn, but not today. Be with your family and be thankful to the gods, and your brave wife."

The scout nodded and pulled his wife forward by her hand. "This is Morwen, who put the mother of our gods to good use in my defence."

Morwen, still holding her woollen garment that was torn at the shoulder, held out a rounded stone in her other hand, and looked up sheepishly at the officer from behind an uneven fringe. In response to Gaius's puzzled expression, she lifted the rock and showed him the carved face and body on its smooth, sculptured side.

Kerwyn explained. "Brigantia is the mother of our people; she is like your goddess Minerva, and is the great protector of our children."

"Well, she certainly protected you today!" Gaius laughed.

Kerwyn nodded. "The gods were with us today." He looked shaken and ill at ease, rotating his felt riding hat through his hands.

Morwen said, "Please take the goddess to watch over your wife and family, sir." She held the stone carving out, and Gaius hesitated before accepting it.

Gaius noticed that his men had assembled and Paulinus was organising them into two ranks, whilst still holding the reins of their horses. He nodded to Kerwyn and Morwen, then turned away and went to Paulinus. "How many have we lost?"

"I make it twelve Gauls and two Sarmatians," Paulinus replied with a sigh.

Gaius flinched and took his gold coin from his pouch, burying it in his big fist. He hated the loss of any of his men, and now felt the heavy weight of his responsibility. He knew all the Gauls by name and much of their backgrounds. It was a hard loss to bear – the biggest loss in any single action since he had become cent commander.

Just then, two Gauls came into the square, leading their horses, to tired cheers from the men. It was the whipped troublemaker, Vetonrix, and another younger man with a bandaged head and bloody tunic. Some called out friendly insults in welcoming their mates.

"There is a story here," Gaius whispered to Paulinus. They grinned their shared relief that two more had survived.

"There is a story in your hand, sir," Paulinus said, nodding at the stone carving.

Gaius grinned and was about to answer when he noticed, over Paulinus's shoulder, the approach of two centurions and their tribune, Publius Helvius Pertinax. "Take this, and call the men to attention." He placed the stone carving into the puzzled Optio's hand, then turned to face his commanding officer.

"Gaius! What a marvellous action!" Pertinax gushed, holding his arms out and holding his centurion of horses by the shoulder guards. "We watched in awe as your cavalry charged those blue devils, then set about them with your many weapons. It was a sight to behold and lifted the morale of the men!"

Gaius smiled with pride. "I thank you, my tribune. Our training paid off, and the new recruits were a… revelation."

"It is for me to thank you, Gaius Atticianus, for your sound military judgement, backed up with the fearless execution of your orders by your men – it was a much welcome sight for these troubled eyes." He gasped and shook his head in sorrow. "Only yesterday our auxiliaries who were guarding the Wall came running back, wailing like children, being chased by howling savages." He turned to glare at one of the centurions behind him.

Gaius and Paulinus exchanged deadpan looks, suppressing smirks. Clearly, a swift attack on the Wall had caught out the defenders, and they had been overwhelmed.

"And what of Plauditus?" Gaius enquired.

"Well, he returned to us a day earlier with a guard." The tribune leaned in and whispered, "Between us, I am not best pleased that he abandoned his post on some trivial excuse, leaving his men with junior officers. It was a calamity."

"I am sorry our messengers did not reach you sooner," Gaius replied. "I took the decision to escort the marching legionaries to the North Road Gate before riding here, sir."

"We shall speak of that later, centurion," Pertinax said, squeezing his arm. "Let me congratulate your men before you dismiss them, and then come to my office. We need to discuss our next move."

Whilst the tribune addressed his troops, Gaius whispered to Paulinus, "After you have dismissed the men, take the stone carving to my wife. Say it is a gift from our scout's wife for saving her and her family."

9. Vindolanda, present day

I saw that it was almost seven o'clock and made my way to the car park, where I'd arranged to meet Sima. Women were definitely looming large in my horoscope.

She was waiting beside her car, quite different without her usual white coat and jeans. She looked taller in a knee-length woollen dress belted at the waist, black tights and boots, her shining hair tied in a ponytail to reveal dangling silver earrings. Her wide smile dispelled my Friday afternoon weariness, and I grinned back. She gave the impression of natural elegance, without airs, but I guessed that careful grooming was behind her smooth skin and the subtly accentuated almond allure of her eyes.

For my part, I was washed, combed and shaved, with a few dabs of last Christmas's pungent aftershave gel on my jawline. It was a dry, mild evening, so a thick jumper sufficed.

"I'm sorry I made you wait," I mumbled, approaching the passenger door.

"It's fine – I've just got here. I hope you don't mind if we pass by the Corbridge Museum first?" she asked. Then quickly added, "I just want to return some borrowed items and have a quick word with their curator."

"No, not at all. Great idea. But our reservation is for seven."

"I took the liberty of ringing the restaurant and putting it back to eight." She grinned at me with slight mischief at her fait accompli. "I hope you don't mind?"

"Then you've thought of everything," I laughed. She had her own car, a Mini Cooper, so all I had to do was get in and make light conversation. We exited the gravelled compound between sandstone gateposts and drove up a steep, single track lane, climbing above the level meadow on which the part-excavated ruins of Vindolanda fort sat.

We turned right onto a winding B road that rose and fell like a fairground ride until we topped the final hill and looked down on the street lights that lined the straight east-west main road.

"I wonder how many legionaries stopped here to take a breather and look down on the old Roman east-to-west road," I said, "most likely named after the Emperor at the time when it was built. I would guess the Via Hadrianius, then re-named the Stanegate, meaning 'stone road' or 'stone gate', by the Anglo-Saxons, now the A69." I was babbling, trying to impress her.

She indulged me with a soft giggle as we sped along beside the fast-flowing waters of the River Tyne. In barely fifteen minutes we were at Corbridge Roman Town and Museum.

"Come with me; I'll introduce you," Sima said, jumping out. She opened the boot of her car and pointed to a box. "Would you mind carrying that in for me?"

I followed her along a stone path beside a high privet hedge, then through a low, arched garden gate to be confronted with the magnificent sight of the spot-lit, part-excavated ruins of a Roman town and barracks. It covered an area roughly the size of two football pitches side-by-side. We paused for a moment to take in its silent majesty, before turning right through the unlocked door to an empty and dimly-lit shop. We walked past the guidebooks on the glass counter and through a rear door that led into the neon glow of a large room with four workstations and floor-to-ceiling shelves bulging with books and reports.

"Noah, this is Helen Rees, the curator," Sima said to me after re-acquainting herself with the plump, friendly woman who was probably in her thirties.

Helen spun on her chair to smile at me as I deposited the box on a desk. "Hi Noah. I've heard about your search for evidence of Roman soldiers in the late second century. We might be able to help." She pointed to a quilted thermal bag. "I'm signing over some of our recent finds into Sima's care. Beneath the headquarters building we excavated a strongroom where the various cohorts who were stationed here stored their valuables. There were legion and cohort standards, a chest of coins, assorted gold and silver ornaments. The most unique items were the tablets contained in that airtight bag, awaiting further translation. We believe they were placed there before the fire of 180 or 181."

"Wonderful. Thank you, Helen. But that's strange. Why didn't they come back for them after the invaders had been driven off?" I mused.

Helen looked up at me through round spectacles. "Well, that remains in the realm of speculation for now. Perhaps the Sixth Legion fell back on their base at York, and those who re-built the fort just put a new floor over it."

"Hmm. Unquestioning workers from another unit, or locals unconnected to the previous garrison who just got on with their task," Sima said.

Helen smiled. "It's a possible explanation. The stairs and doorway were full of building rubble, so perhaps the workers were driven on by an expeditious officer and just swept the rubbish into the stair well before placing wooden floorboards over it. Fabric and wood were preserved fairly well in the airtight space. We know it wasn't long before the fort and town were rebuilt."

"The Romans didn't hang about," I added, as if I knew my stuff.

"Sign here please," Helen said to Sima, who duly signed and dated the log. "Look after my tablets, please, and bring them back after you've worked your magic." Helen stood and handed the large padded bag to Sima, who held it against her chest in both arms.

I opened the doors as we headed out to the car park with our precious cargo. Sima asked me to get her keys from her pocket and open the boot. Once safely stored, we jumped in and headed off into Corbridge town to find the Italian restaurant.

*****

Sandstone terraced cottages lined the narrow main street in Corbridge. Sima slowed and found a parking space outside a commanding church with a stout, square Norman tower.

"Typical of the Normans to build their churches to look like fortresses," I muttered as I climbed out of the Mini. "The stone from the church walls and the building itself look suspiciously like cut Roman stones," I said as I rotated my neck and stretched my arms. I was not a comfortable fit in a Mini.

"I think the whole town was built from the ruins of Coria," Sima said, hoisting her shoulder bag and smiling across the roof.

I walked behind her along a narrow pavement, noting chimney smoke from some of the cottages. "There's still business for the coalman up here," I said to her swinging ponytail.

"I love that coal fire smell," she replied, half-turning. "It reminds me of my grandmother's house."

Don Giovanni's Italian Restaurant appeared at the end of a terrace to our left. It was a modern structure, a purpose-built, red-brick building with fussily engraved big glass windows on either side of a generous double door.

"I really appreciate not having to bend down to get through a door," I said, holding the inner door open for her. Inside it was a spacious open-plan room with a high ceiling above slow-twirling rattan fans, and an intimate wooden stall in front of each window held a table and chairs. In the central space there were a dozen more tables, half of them occupied.

"Welcome to Don Giovanni's," a short, Mediterranean-looking waiter said, smiling through a drooping moustache and clutching two menus to his chest. "Have you made a reservation?"

"Yes, in the name of Jessop," I replied.

He checked his book, nodded, and then led us to a side booth.

"I wonder how many legionaries posted here were short Italians," I whispered, scanning the menu.

"All shapes and sizes from all over Europe, North Africa and the Middle East," she replied. She looked up and held my gaze. "When you mentioned the Sarmatian cavalry coming here, I looked them up. It appears they were nomadic tribesmen who roamed as far east as Persia, now Iran, that borders western Pakistan – where my grandmother's from. Her family lived in the border region. They were Hindus and fled to Northern India during the partition in 1947 when the State of Pakistan was created. The British Empire was being adjusted. Counters moved on a map in London, and millions suffered upheaval or death at the hands of angry mobs."

"Wow, that's a coincidence. You being here, at Vindolanda and Corbridge, treading in the footsteps of your ancestors."

"Yes, I told my mum last night and she was thrilled to hear of the first coming of Persians and Pakistanis to Britain, a lot earlier than she had thought."

"Nearly two thousand years ago. And five thousand-odd Sarmatian soldiers would undoubtedly have contributed to the gene pool and our mongrel heritage." I laughed. "We can't escape empire-building, either at work, or discussing our own heritage. What are you having?"

The waiter returned and we ordered our meal with a bottle of wine. I would have to drink most of it, Sima said, as she would only have one glass. It was a challenge I was ready for. Carbonara sauce with freshly-made linguini is somehow suited to dark winter evenings, I mused, as I fooled around to amuse her, crossing my eyes as I sucked up the delicious threads. Our waiter was certainly treating our meal as a romantic date by lighting a solitary candle and dimming the light in our booth. O Sole Mio drifted from speakers high up in the four corners, adding to the relaxed atmosphere.

"Do you go home often?" I ventured.

"About once a month," she replied. "My old room has been re-allocated to one of my younger sisters, so I have to make do with a camp bed. Somehow, I think I'll be visiting less and less – at least to stay over. How about you?"

"The same. I feel I've left and moved on, so short visits are preferable. Did you say you have a boyfriend?"

"I do. His name is Ravi. He works in Manchester for a financial services company. I've no idea what that means!"

This casual disclosure of a name was like a stab in my heart. No vagueness today. I felt that a door I never knew was open had just closed.

A look of concern crossed her face. "Are you alright? You look like you've just bitten into a chilli."

My disappointment must have showed. "Oh… yeah, a stray bit of chilli." I drank a mouthful of water and coughed a bit to complete my act. "Yes, I recall you mentioning a boyfriend. Tell me more."

"Not much to tell, really. We're old school sweethearts. Our families know each other from the Hindu Temple. To be honest, we don't see that much of each other and he was quite bitter with me when I took this job, rather than moving to Manchester to keep house for him."

"Has he visited you since you've been here?"

"No. And I've only been to see him once. We argued before I left. Can we talk about something else? We were having such a nice time…" Her voice trailed away and she fiddled with a hair clip, frowning.

"I'm sorry, Sima," I said. "I've strayed onto something private. Please forgive me. Let's talk about Italians and Sarmatians."

This lightened the mood slightly, and we chatted about work-related things and I droned on about what I hoped to find out for my dissertation. Her mood had become subdued, though, and she turned the radio on in the car for our quiet journey home.

10. Vindolanda, 180 CE

Gaius reached for the sweet cakes that a liveried slave boy had placed on the long table in the commander's office at Vindolanda. His stomach rumbled in anticipation when he took the first bite, betraying how hungry he was. As he munched, he looked proudly at the line of standards resting upright in a custom-made wooden box against the wall behind his fellow officers. In the first slot, suspended on its crossbar, was the cohort standard, a bright red square of gold-embellished cloth, cut to an open bird's mouth at the bottom and hung with golden tassels on its edge. Inside a laurel wreath, VI Legio Victrix Pia Fidelis IV Cohors Gallic was inscribed above a charging black bull motif. Four century standards, including his own unit's, now completed the row of proud colours.

"Eat, drink, Gaius. You deserve it," Tribune Pertinax said, standing at the head of the table in a freshly-washed and pressed white toga, from where he could see over the heads of his seated officers, his shortness of stature negated. His chubby face had briefly broken into a smile, but soon the commander's wrinkled brow and pursed lips returned. "I am deeply distressed at this turn of events. Our northern patrol did indeed discover a tribal gathering with warlike intention, but the blasted savages beat them to our section of the Wall!"

Groans rippled around the gathering of five. Pertinax mopped his brow and continued. "I understand the reasons why Centurion Atticianus recalled the garrisons and escorted them to the North Road gate, but it has now given us a big problem. We are surrounded by howling savages, and one of our cents has its feet up in Coria town. What are we to do?"

Gaius carried on eating and washed down his cakes with honeyed water, knowing he would be called upon to give his briefing. The other centurions deferred to Plauditus, the Roman praetorian.

100

Plauditus sniffed down his pronounced nose and said, "Firstly, may I add my congratulations to Centurion Atticianus for his cent's devastating cavalry manoeuvre, reminding the savages that Roman skills and tactics will win out every time."

There were murmurs of assent, hand banging, and foot stamping under the table. Gaius bowed to his peers.

Plauditus continued. "Although, by delaying to send us a warning, and not returning in haste, we were unprepared for the barbarian attack and are now faced with this vexing siege." He looked down on Gaius with dead, black eyes. He was not going to take any blame for recent events.

Plauditus's rebuke met with an awkward silence. "On the question of what we do next, I'm of a mind to try a three-pronged attack, with legionaries out of one gate, cavalry out of another, and archers and ballistae firing from the battlements and towers. The cavalry has already reduced their numbers, by fifty or so, and I think we can slaughter the remainder. Then we can send out search parties to round up our auxiliaries who will be scattered in groups across the frontier." He sat back in his chair and folded his arms. He would be recalled to Rome after his one year was up, and would be greeted as a hero regardless of his performance in the field.

"An excellent plan," Pertinax agreed. "But before we discuss it, may I invite Atticianus to give us a briefing on his mission, and to share with us his thoughts."

Gaius stood and turned to an inked map on a piece of vellum. It was stretched on a wooden frame hanging on the wall by the door behind him.

"Thank you, sir, and to you all for your kind salute. We rode to Cilurnum fort, on the Wall here, where we forded the river, proceeding to the North Road and Habitancum fort where we rested and got useful intelligence from Centurion Viridio. He informed me that his scouts had reported a build-up of warriors from unfamiliar tribes. We decided to ride to the dun of King Eildon, of the Selgovae, the biggest tribe up there and one that has been friendly to Rome."

He paused to see that he had their full attention. "His dun is here, in the Three Hills, only a mile from our fort. Before we arrived there, I had sent messengers to our three forts along the road to abandon their posts and march south to the Wall, as they were sitting targets for a first wave of attacks."

He glanced at his tribune, who nodded and said, "Yes, the savages would have easily picked them off one by one and grown their confidence. You did the right thing. Proceed."

Gaius looked around the table and saw heads nodding in agreement. "We spent an uncomfortable evening and night in his hall, accepting his invitation to their feast. The king said the tribes had gathered for a festival for one of their gods, and he walked us around the meadow where warriors were displaying their skills."

"Good preparations for battle, more like," one of the centurions remarked.

"My thoughts as well," Gaius agreed. "I met the chief who led the raid on our fort, the one who knocked me from the parapet, a youthful warrior named Donall of the Venicones. Their tribal lands are here." Gaius pointed to an area above the Antonine line of defences, where the word 'Caledonii' was inked. He waited until the sniggers at his misfortune subsided. "He challenged me to combat, but the king refused the challenge as we were his invited guests." Gaius turned with a smile to the table.

"…And he is king of a client kingdom of Rome, let us not forget," Pertinax added. The room erupted in laughter and ale was poured into pewter mugs.

Plauditus couldn't resist another dig. "You've let him escape you twice, Gaius."

Gaius took a swig and continued, ignoring him. "We left them all sleeping early in the morning and returned to the road, where we found the garrison from Three Hills already marching. We gathered up the other garrisons on our march south, and once through the North Road Gate, I returned here, via Cilurnum, where I put them on full alert. Centurion Lupus Viridio carried on marching his men to Coria to report."

"Good," Pertinax said, jumping to his feet. "Then our regional headquarters has been warned. But they will not know that we have been attacked, and the savages are south of the Wall. Whilst I like the boldness of Plauditus's plan, we must also send a patrol to Coria, to ask for assistance and send our valuables for safekeeping."

"I have a feeling their numbers will swell overnight," Gaius said, returning to his seat. "May I propose we delay sending a patrol out until the morning when we will see if the situation has changed?"

It was unusual for Gaius to be so bold at meetings. He usually listened to what was said in silence and waited to be given orders. But he could see his influence had grown after recent events, and he was now at the heart of their predicament.

"Very wise, Centurion," Pertinax said, frowning. "Now, if that is all, let us see to doubling the night guard. And after our evening victuals, we shall meet at the temple to make sacrifice to Jupiter and Mars for our deliverance. May the gods preserve us."

Gaius felt an unease at the criticism he had endured, and waited outside the tribune's open door when he noticed that Plauditus and Prefect Adminius remained behind with their tribune. But he was startled when Tribune Pertinax then left in a hurry, not noticing Gaius hovering in the corner, looking through the window. Gaius returned to the open door and listened.

Plauditus spoke in a murmur to the prefect, but Gaius heard. "I know that our tribune sends you with his reports, but I will also give you a report for onward journey to our new legate, and my dear cousin, Claudius Hieronymianus. I will put the blame for this attack on Centurion Atticianus for his late return from patrol and failure to warn us in time. This will negate any criticism of me that our tribune might make. That is all you need to know. Do not betray me in this, for my promotion is assured now that my cousin commands this legion, and I may soon be your commanding officer."

"It shall be done," Adminius replied in a quiet voice. He was a gentle man, Gaius knew, content with quiet study and reflection. He would not cross the wily praetorian.

Gaius reeled at this damning turn of events and the knowledge that he would be transporting a report that may lead to his demotion at best, or at worst, execution. He hurried through the narrow streets, between lime-washed barrack blocks and a granary store, barely acknowledging the salutes of soldiers and junior officers with distracted nods, then turned at the sign of the apothecary into the Via Augustus, where ten officer's houses were grouped.

He entered his courtyard in a state of shock to be met by Aria, legs apart in her combative stance, holding the Brigantia effigy in one hand, a look of anger in her eyes.

"What do you mean by sending Paulinus to give me this carving of the local goddess, Brigantia? You know full well that we have a shrine to the water goddess of my people, Sulis, who is twinned with your goddess Minerva, and is the deity who watches over this house and our family! Have you forgotten the time our prayers and the healing waters of Sulis restored our little Brutus when he had the sweating fever?"

"Sulis be praised. But my love, it was a gift from the wife of my scout whom we saved from despoilment and murder," Gaius replied in his well-practised conciliatory tone. She had resurrected the unhappy memory of his fears that his little son would succumb to the same fever that had robbed him of his first family.

"Then you have kept your promise and delivered it to me. But it cannot remain here, or our own goddess will desert us. You shall not see it again and do not ask me about it." Gaius knew not to argue further when her temper was raised. She looked both magnificent and terrifying when her red mane was raised and her crystal eyes turned icy with rage. But like the storms of Britannia, it would soon blow out and she would be his sweet Aria again.

"You are wise, as always, my love," he whispered, now more eager than ever to soak his weary bones and clear his troubled mind. He would withhold his bad news from her and mull it over. Gaius skirted around her and went to the kitchen to seek out Longinus to make preparations for his bath. He would be up at dawn to prepare once again for battle with the Caledonii, or to lead a guard to Coria with their wives, cohort valuables, and the report blaming him for the attack. But that was tomorrow. Tonight, he would eat with his family and sleep in the arms of his beloved Aria.

*****

A cold, vicious wind drove sleet into Gaius's face as he mounted the steps to the northern corner tower. His fellow officers greeted him with nods, their eyes narrowed against the weather.

"The bastards have grown in numbers overnight," an infantry centurion grumbled, pointing needlessly at the throng clustered around fifty-or-more camp fires. "There must be close to six hundred, at least."

Tribune Pertinax moved to stand beside Gaius and said, "This changes our plans. It is far too risky to fight this army with our unequal numbers. As they are gathered at the north side, with only a handful outside our other gates, I think it best, Gaius, that you lead a guard, of say thirty, through the south gate. Take our payroll chest, cohort standard and our wives, and make a run to Coria. Then I

105

expect you to return after three days with Centurion Viridio and our men who are there, and any others that Tribune Bebius can spare, so we can slaughter these devils and reclaim our ten-mile stretch of the Wall."

Just then, they were distracted by cheers and movement on the edge of the civilian settlement, about a hundred and fifty paces from the north gatehouse. Six wooden crosses were erected and six Roman soldiers, their arms tied behind them, were led out by a shaman, an old man dressed in animal pelts and with long unkempt hair to his waist. He was waving a bleached thigh bone at them.

"The gods be praised we can't smell him," Plauditus sniffed.

The holy man cried and cursed in a loud voice, cheered on by the warriors gathered behind him, crawling in the mud and throwing handfuls of dirt into the air, oblivious to the sleet and buffeting wind. The soldiers, in tunics but stripped of armour, were lashed to the cross beams with hide ties.

"They've nicked our jars from the outlying forts," a guard commented. Pairs of men carried jars forward by their ear-like handles to where the prisoners were tied. Then they reached into the jars and began smearing the limbs and torsos of the wriggling men with black pitch.

"Oh Jupiter," Gaius groaned, "They're going to burn them in front of us to try and goad us into coming out."

Paulinus stepped forward and whispered to Gaius, "The bastards have our men from the supply convoy, sir. I can see Optio Andosini and three others amongst the captives. Andosini is second from our left, sir." He knew his commander would not be able to make out the detail of the tied men.

"May the gods grant them a quick death," Gaius breathed.

"That looks unlikely, sir. Despite the sleet, they will still burn, just more slowly," Paulinus replied.

"Are they in range of our ballistae?" Plauditus asked, leaning over the parapet, his gold-ringed fingers gripping the frozen rail. A line of snow decorated his thick, brown eyebrows as he turned his hawk eyes on his comrades.

"Yes, one hundred and fifty paces are easily within range," the centurion of the watch replied.

"Then drag two of them here!" Tribune Pertinax yelled, guessing Plauditus's plan to spoil their slow torture of the captives. "Get the engineers to rig a hoist!"

There was a flurry of activity and in a matter of minutes, two ballistae were being dragged and pushed by their runners to the gatehouse. A hoist was quickly erected and they were raised up to the platform above the gates. A third and fourth ballistae were being dragged from further away, but in the meantime, the first two were loaded with long, thick spears with sharp steel barbs at the tips.

"How quickly can you reload and fire again?" Pertinax asked the officer in charge.

"In less than a minute, sir," came the reply.

"That is my optio, second from the left, sir," Gaius said. "I ask you for a quick death for him."

The tribune nodded and said, "Start from the left."

The two weapons were aimed at their targets, and the spears were loosed. Whoosh! The twin missiles flew in arcs towards the men tied to the crossed beams. With unerring accuracy, the spears struck the chests of the first two men, the points passing through them, embedding in the wood and killing them instantly. The warriors and their shaman howled in anger as the ballistae were re-loaded. Two more ballistae were being hoisted to the platform, and Pertinax ordered all those not involved in working the machines to vacate and make space for them. The shaman howled and shook a burning brand at them, then proceeded along the line, setting fire to the screaming captives. Two more spears were sent flying through the air, killing the next two men outright.

"Hurry men!" Pertinax urged as the ballistae were re-loaded.

The third and fourth ones were also positioned and loaded. The last two Roman soldiers were now fully alight, and they writhed and screamed in pain as their bodies were slowly cooked in the pitch, its black smoke twisting to the grey sky like an evil spirit. The sleet had stopped and rows of soldiers lining the walls wailed in grief as their comrades suffered painful deaths. Two spears flew at the burning men, plunging through the fire into their bodies and finally putting an end to their torment. What the dancing shaman did not expect was two spears flying towards him so soon, and no sooner had he jigged away from the first missile than the second one struck him in the chest, flinging him backwards by two paces and pinning his lifeless body to the ground. Half-hearted cheers rang out from the walls, only in part assuaging the harrowing images that had come before.

"If they have other captives, this will continue," Gaius grimly remarked.

"You must make ready for your mission, Centurion," the tribune replied, gripping Gaius's bicep. His look was bleak. It was days like these that make the weight of command feel a heavy burden. "I will send my optio to gather the valuables and our wives and children into two carriages. Go and prepare your men and leave without further delay."

Gaius nodded and climbed down the ladder, hurrying to find Paulinus and Meral, his mind alive with thoughts. His tribune clearly felt there was a possibility that the savages might storm the fort, and he envisaged desperate fighting in the streets he now jogged through. More warriors may come in the next day or two, giving them the confidence to attack the walls, and send men through the gap where a stream ran into the fort. Vindolanda was not impregnable, as the raid had shown. They would come at night and overwhelm the watch on the walls.

He found his deputy in the barracks, cleaning his armour. "Paulinus, pick twenty of our best men, and find Meral to pick his best twenty, and make ready for a day's ride to Coria. Light rations only." He would not risk taking only fifteen or twenty. Forty would be enough to fight a determined scouting party, should they encounter one. The fate of the fort would not rest on his cavalry unit.

Gaius rushed home and told Aria to get ready to leave, with just the boy and one slave. He then jogged to the eastern gatehouse where he expected the auxiliary guard, Amborix, to be on duty. He called Amborix and the duty officer to one side and said, "I am taking this soldier and one other to guard two carriages I am escorting on an important mission for the tribune."

The optio could hardly refuse, and so he just saluted Gaius and replied, "Yes, sir!"

"Good, then pick another man to accompany us."

Amborix signalled to a friend, and the three of them hurried to the assembly point at the parade ground.

Gaius said to Amborix, "Hurry to your barracks and get your weapons and rations for one day."

Outside the stables, the tribune's two covered carriages were each being hitched to teams of four horses. Liveried house slaves carried the coin chest and the standard, wrapped in a cloak, to be placed inside the carriages on the orders of an optio. Around the carriages stood six women and a dozen children, their heads covered with hooded cloaks, holding small bags of personal items. Tribune Pertinax's wife, a bustling Roman with voluminous brown hair, named Claudia, asserted her seniority by arranging the seating plan. Aria, her friend, was to sit next to her in the first carriage with their children.

Bags and boxes were loaded onto roof racks, covered with tarpaulins and tied securely by male slaves who were to remain up there, as the grumbling passengers climbed in and arranged themselves on bench seats, their feet wedged beside the cohort's treasures. Female house slaves, including Marta, wedged themselves onto a wooden seat at the back of the carriage, under an awning to keep them dry. In the background, Paulinus oversaw the cavalry muster.

Mars was led to Gaius by his stableboy, and he slung his saddlebag behind the saddle. Gaius noticed that he now had foot slings hanging down from his saddle, and he looked around, catching Meral's eye, and nodded his approval. Gaius leant on his stableboy whilst putting his left foot in the strap, as he had seen the Sarmatians do, and swung his right leg over, sitting comfortably in the saddle, to the cheers of Meral and his men.

"We learn from each other!" Gaius shouted to them, then walked Mars over to where Aria and Brutus were waiting their turns to be seated in the first carriage. "Take courage, my love and my son. We will be going at a fast pace, and it will be a bumpy ride, so I advise folding your cloak tail under your bottoms."

Just then, the tribune's wife, Claudia, bustled beside Aria and offered her a cushion. "We'll need these," she cheerfully said, moving on to the other wives.

"Boys will have to make do with folded garments," Gaius laughed.

Kerwyn trotted to his side. "Am I needed, sir?"

"Yes, I need you and one other. Your family are as safe here as anywhere."

"I am ready. I'll fetch another." He rode away, and Gaius returned his attention to the carriage.

Gaius flinched at the sight of Prefect Adminius bustling towards the carriage, carrying a leather bag that would contain the report condemning him and putting an end to his career as an officer, or worse, his life. Once they were all seated, Gaius instructed Amborix and his

110

colleague to sit beside each driver on the platforms of the carriages, adding, "Guard the passengers with your lives."

He then led the twenty Gauls at the head of the column, with the carriages in the middle, and Meral's men bringing up the rear. At the south gate, Gaius called a halt and, with Paulinus, climbed a ladder to the battlements and then onto the platform above the gatehouse. No doubt, some of the men who had been sent to guard the south gate had crept around to the northside to see the prisoners being burnt, leaving barely twenty men gathered around two fires to the left and right of the bridge over the ditch.

"They are within an arrow's range," Gaius said, narrowing his eyes to look at whether the road was clear to the hills.

Paulinus grunted and replied, "Yes, the Sarmatians could pick off a dozen of them from here, and as for the road ahead, I can confirm it's clear of obstructions to the first bend."

Gaius chuckled. "They are not so smart, these Caledonii. If it were me, I'd have built a barrier where the road enters the hills. Run down to Meral, and ask him to send a runner to collect his remaining men with their bows and full quivers of arrows."

Paulinus was about to leave the platform when Gaius grabbed his arm. In a whisper he said, "Paulinus, as a friend, I must tell you, in confidence, that Adminius travels with a report from Centurion Plauditus to our new legate, who is his kinsman, blaming me for this unexpected attack. He covers his back in case our tribune reports that he abandoned his men at the Wall, thus offering a weak point which the barbarians exploited."

The bigger man's eyes bulged in shock at the revelation. "Sir, this is an evil action by your fellow centurion. It is unjust, as your actions and logic were flawless."

"I feel it is unjust, and know now that Plauditus is a blood relative of our new legate, and therefore a dangerous political player who may see me killed."

"Perhaps not. Let me think on it." With that, he turned and descended the ladder before a perplexed Gaius could ask him what he meant.

Gaius remained on the platform, talking to the officer in charge about the movements of their enemy. More screams of tortured prisoners carried to them on the wind, a sound that would set the men on edge and strike fear into the civilians. After twenty minutes, Meral jogged back with his remaining ten men, and they filed up the ladder to the top platform, where they joined a similar number of auxiliary archers.

"As soon as the gates open, start firing," Gaius ordered, shinning down the ladders to the ground, then running to prime his men to have a throwing javelin in hand when they rode out. He had half a dozen in his own quiver, and picked one out after he mounted Mars. The unit of Gauls were to circle around the enemy camps and keep throwing javelins at them until the carriages had passed, and then ride after them. The Sarmatian unit was to hang back until the enemy were killed, and then follow. Just to make sure, he detailed the officer in charge to prepare a squad of twenty shield men to run out behind the last rider and mop up any remaining savages.

Gaius swivelled around and got a signal from Paulinus and Meral that they were ready. Kerwyn and his man caught his eye. "Stay with the carriages, Kerwyn. Open the gates!" he yelled, and started Mars walking forward.

He spurred his frisky mount into a canter, passing out of the shadow of the gatehouse into the murky morning light, his horse's hooves rapping on the wooden bridge as a hail of arrows flew over his head. With a grating battle cry escaping from his throat, he rode close to the first man, who had barely stood to face him, spear in hand, before Gaius's javelin was buried in his chest.

Gaius rode on, making a wide circle to his left, followed closely by his men, riding in pairs and peeling to left and right. Screams from the enemy filled the air as arrows and javelins found their marks. War cries from the riders added to the noise as they circled their prey, throwing their javelins or loosing arrows. One man staggered and fell across the fire, an arrow in his neck. The carriages clattered across the bridge and were driven on at full speed along the road, followed by the scouts.

In barely three minutes, it was all over. Gaius was relieved to see that none of his men were touched in the engagement. His attention was drawn to a number of enemy riders coming their way on their small ponies, screaming and waving spears.

"How many?" he yelled at Paulinus.

"About thirty on their way, and I'm sure more will follow. Your orders?"

"Form the men up; we'll drive them onto the spears of the shield men." Gaius spurred Mars to about a hundred paces from the gate and turned to face the charging enemy, bringing his mount to a standstill. "Form up next to me!" he yelled.

The cavalry units formed up in one long line of forty, facing their soldiers who had formed a shield wall with their backs to the entrance to the gatehouse bridge, the bodies of their enemies and ruins of their camps lying between them. He glanced up at the walls to see a throng of eager faces, gathered to watch the battle.

The enemy pony riders were in a quandary between riding at the horsemen or the soldiers, and funnelled into the gap; then, as anticipated, they separated into two ragged groups.

When they were close, Gaius instructed his horn man, Vertinax, to blow and he shouted, "Charge!"

113

They sprung forward with a mighty roar and threw or fired their missiles. Then they swiftly drew swords in a training move practised a hundred times, and slashed at an enemy pony rider as they rode through them. The big cavalry horses, nostrils flared and eyes wide, bullied their smaller cousins as the Romans wheeled and set about their enemy, slicing through the puny, rectangular cowhide shields and cutting them down in short time.

Gaius was aware that more would be on their way and shouted at Vertinax to sound the recall. "Our work is done here!" he yelled at Paulinus, and spurred Mars into a gallop towards the south hills, the sombre walls of Vindolanda receding behind. His men took great delight in whooping as they drove the terrified, riderless ponies before them towards the hills, depriving their enemy of their use.

The carriage had a good head start, and the riders caught up half a mile along the road. It had slowed to negotiate a steep incline, and the driver had asked the occupants to get out and push. The house slaves who were riding on the roofs and platforms behind were pushing hard, joined by some of the older children, who thought it was a game, and the two auxiliaries. Adminius and the officers' wives walked daintily on the grass verge, holding up the hems of their garments. Straining horses finally pulled the carriages to the top where they waited for their passengers.

Gaius found them there, staring down on the beautiful vista of the River Tine valley stretching for miles to left and right. The snow clouds had scudded to the east and the late morning sky was a clear blue, dressed with high, thin white clouds. The downward slope was wooded until it reached the east to west road that ran above a riverine meadow of brilliant green, beyond which the river bubbled and raced in white patches over a stony bed between dark pools. Cows and sheep grazed peacefully in meadows beyond the river, barely two miles south of the protective arm of the Great Wall of Hadrian.

"Coria is ten miles to the east," Gaius announced, patting Mars on the neck. He dismounted and removed the leather face and metal shin guards from his sweating stallion, then stowed them in a saddle bag.

The other riders joined them, and Meral shouted in his slow, guttural Latin, "They are following, but most are on foot. Only about ten pony riders now!"

Despite the laughs from the men, Gaius knew they would have to push on to keep ahead of a determined warband of jogging warriors whose reputation preceded them for running the whole day, fuelled by leaves they chewed for energy and secret powders blown into their faces by their holy men.

"That tells me that they can spare men to chase us because they are expecting more to come and swell their numbers at Vindolanda. We must hurry onwards. Kerwyn, scout the hills to our left, for we will be turning in that direction." Gaius led the square-block wooden carriages slowly down the incline, his Gauls riding ahead and the Sarmatians keeping to the rear.

At the junction, they turned left onto an empty main road. Gaius noted the first mile stone showed thirty-three miles from the first fort at the eastern end of the Wall. He encouraged the carriage drivers to pick up speed to a brisk trot, aware that running men could keep pace with them. The road was eerily deserted in both directions, and the grazing sheep, swooping swifts and chattering meadow birds lulled the passengers into a false sense of security as children sang merry songs.

"What could possibly go wrong?" Gaius muttered to himself as he rode beside the carriages to check on the welfare of the passengers and share a warm, reassuring smile with his wife. "Only ten miles to Coria. At this speed, about an hour," he shouted, before spurring Mars forward to the head of his riders, where he fell into step beside Paulinus.

Barely fifteen minutes into their progress, Kerwyn rode up to Gaius.

"Sir, enemy riders on the ridge," he said, pointing behind him.

Gaius squinted his eyes but could see nothing beyond a blur of trees.

"I can see them, on that hill," Paulinus confirmed.

"Then they continue to run us down, like hounds on the scent of a stag," Gaius said. "Ride back, Paulinus, and urge the carriage drivers to increase their speed. There may yet be some fighting before we reach Coria."

11. Vindolanda, present day

I spent the weekend studying photographs of the Vindolanda tablets, reading the official translations and comparing them with the etchings on the tablets to test my understanding. I was certainly learning new things from the translations, and could see where assumptions had been made about missing parts. They were military orders and reports in the main, with some personal letters mixed in. Maggie sent me an email with background information on findings relating to the Sixth Legion that gave a partial list of senior officers, but with missing years where no references had been found inscribed on tablets, monuments or buildings. There were no legion records kept in any central place.

I found the Commanding Officer's quarters and office at York, where the Sixth Legion was based for most of its time in Britannia, had not yet been excavated as it lay beneath modern buildings. In fact, only two percent of Roman York has been excavated. No intact legion records have survived the ravages of time, so the main source of information remains engravings on archaeological finds. These add to accounts written by scribes such as Ennius, Suetonius and Tacitus. Most are in praise of victories and successful campaigns.

Monday morning came around and I greeted Sima with a tentative smile. "How was your weekend?"

"It was okay," she replied, yawning as she shouldered her way through her office door, briefcase in one hand and coffee in the other. The door swung shut behind her, and I returned to my workstation.

After an hour, Sima came over to me, holding the zipped pouch we had collected from Corbridge Museum on Friday evening.

"The Corbridge tablets are back from the photographer. I'm going to put them into storage. I've just emailed you the infra-red images. You'll need to play with the exposure to be able to read them."

"Thanks. They've just dropped into my inbox. I've gone as far as I can go with the Vindolanda tablets and I've given my notes on them to the experts over there." I nodded towards the two women archivists at the opposite end of the room who were the usual translators on the staff. "Now I can start on the new ones."

She nodded without any show of enthusiasm and didn't linger.

I peeked at her shapely calves as she walked away. Was I getting the cold shoulder, or was she simply preoccupied? I opened the email and saved the attachments of the images of the new tablets. I opened the first scanned image and peered at the faint lettering etched into the grainy dark wood, hoping that some meaning would emerge. I adjusted the brightness and contrast to get the best view of the nib indents, and reached for my notepad.

By lunch, I had part-translated a report from Centurion Gaius Atticianus of the fourth cohort, Legio VI Victrix. My Gaius! This was the second document I had translated that named this individual. Parts of it were illegible, but there was enough to get the gist.

Gaius was at Coria, the once-Roman town next to modern day Corbridge, to report that his unit had been attacked by barbarians on the road.

My concentration was rudely disturbed by the loud wail of a siren. Such a loud, irritating noise is specially chosen for fire alarms so that people like me, who don't like being disturbed, take notice. My fellow archivists were shutting down their computers and standing, grabbing their bags and coats.

"Come on Noah, it's the fire alarm," Sima shouted, coming out of her office.

"I can't smell any smoke," I joked as I pulled on my coat. "What about these artefacts?"

"Bring your zip bags and follow me to the safe room. It's a fire-proof vault where we keep our most precious and fragile items."

I followed her to the back of the building, to the end of a corridor lined with boxes on shelves, and she opened a door to a steel vault. Inside were more shelves, and she took the box with the tablets in polythene pouches from me and stored them.

She came out and looked at the items on the shelves with a quizzical expression, then said, "Let's put some of the rarer artefacts into there, as it's fire-proof. I'll pass them to you." She started to hand me boxes with excavated artefacts in plastic covers, and I pushed them into the vault, sliding them along the floor. I was wondering if my life was worth saving dozens of pairs of two-thousand-year-old leather shoes and assorted military gear, and glanced past her to see if there was any visible smoke. After about three minutes, and twenty-odd boxes, she stopped.

"Those are the most important ones. Let's go, in case there really is a fire in this building," she said, locking the vault door.

We retraced our steps and left through a side fire door, joining the archives team in a corner of the car park. There were about fifty people in small groups, chattering away and stamping their feet, their breath trails rising upwards. But that was all that was rising upwards. There were no visible signs of a fire.

A fire marshal came around and ticked our names on a register.

"Is there a fire?" Sima asked.

"Not that I know of. They're checking the kitchen in the cafeteria," he replied, moving onto the next group. After fifteen minutes, the marshal announced in a loud voice that the building was clear and we could return to our workplaces.

"Well, we'd better put the boxes back in their correct places," Sima said with a shrug.

"I wonder what set the alarm off?" I asked, almost rhetorically.

"Burning toast, most likely," she replied with a smile. I followed her back inside and we restored order to the precious artefacts.

"Fancy grabbing a coffee?" she asked.

"Sure, we can investigate the cafeteria kitchen as a source of the false alarm," I replied, following her out to the main corridor.

"A fire in here would destroy over three hundred artefacts, including all the displays in the museum that took years to mount and position the information cards." She said this as we passed display cases near the entrance to the museum. One of them had a partly-intact glass tankard with engraved coloured pictures of gladiators fighting in a frieze that would have encircled it. It was one of my favourite findings and I often stopped to marvel at it. I caught her up and we joined a queue of other shirkers with the same idea. I overheard Jenny answering the question that was on all our minds.

"No," she said, "nothing 'round here set the alarm off. This time we're not guilty!"

We collected our coffees and cookies, and found a table for two by the window.

"It remains a mystery," I said.

"It could have been one of the security doors being opened and wedged open for more than five minutes," Sima replied. "When I was given a set of keys and briefed, I was told that I mustn't wedge the door to the valuables cupboard open as it would set the alarms off."

"Is that the vault, or somewhere else?" I asked.

"There's a valuables cupboard where new finds are stored before they're catalogued and also things with a high value, like gold and silver coins and artefacts. It has two doors, one in my office, for which I have a key, and the other end is in Professor Maggie's outer office, for which Mavis has a key. I think Mike Stone also has a set of keys."

"I hadn't thought about this place keeping high value items. I bet the insurance premium is astronomical."

"I'm sure it is. Look, Noah, there's something on my mind and, seeing as you've shown an interest in me, and I don't really have any close friends, I wondered if I could talk to you?"

After a moment of motionless surprise, I leaned forward conspiratorially and whispered, "Of course, Sima, you can trust me with your private matters."

She leaned in and squeezed my hand. "Thanks, Noah," she smiled. "It's just, my emotions are in turmoil, and I feel guilty, as if I've done something wrong... maybe I have..."

"Just calm yourself and take a sip, then order your thoughts."

"Well, when we had dinner, I mentioned to you that my boyfriend, Ravi, is living in Manchester, and he was a bit put out when I took this job."

"Yes, I remember."

"He's been calling me to try and persuade me to leave here and go and live with him and look for a job in Manchester. He wants us to get engaged..." She sat back and took another sip of her coffee.

"Oh, and how do you feel about that?"

"I've told him that I'm not ready for commitment, and I'm really enjoying my job here and feel I'm a part of something important. We then argued, and he tried to make me feel guilty by saying it's what both our families want."

Her eyes were starting to fill with tears as she looked at me with a forlorn expression. It was my turn to squeeze her hand as she dabbed at her eye with a tissue in the other.

"You feel trapped between what he wants and what you want," I prompted, after a few seconds.

"Yes. And now my aunt and my mother have called me. They are ganging up on me." She put her hands to her face and sobbed, her shoulders gently rising and falling.

I had a sudden vision of the stony-faced Mavis, who held the position of Human Resources Officer on the staff, coldly telling her to pull herself together. "I can see this is no small matter, Sima. I've come to realise that I distanced myself from my parents before going to uni, and it's not without pain and regret. Sometimes we can't be the person our parents want us to be, and have to strike out on our own. I don't think it's unusual, what you're describing. It's hard though, following your own path."

She sniffed and wiped her eyes and nose on a tissue. "Thanks, Noah. I hoped you would understand. You know, I love Mum and Dad, and now I worry that I'm betraying them. Because they worked hard and made sacrifices for my education. That was the key to this new-found independence, miles away from them and from Ravi. But it's my life." She tried a smile but it quickly dissolved and her mascara had run down her cheeks, adding to her look of abject misery. "Will you excuse me? I must go to the ladies." She stood and shuffled away, holding the tissue to her face.

I was left feeling subdued. I didn't like to see her upset. That she had chosen me to unburden her troubles to, suggested she felt more affinity with another newcomer than with the others in the archives. Maybe there was resentment of her position of responsibility for the unit; maybe she saw them as a clique, and my clumsy prying over dinner had established a connection after all. Well, no one else was going to eat the delicious homemade cookies. When she returned, there was half a cookie left, and the dregs of our coffees.

"I saved you a piece," I said, looking at the plate.

She smiled. "That was big of you." She picked it up and nibbled at the edge. "Thanks for listening, Noah. I feel a problem shared, etcetera..."

"Not at all, I'm glad you chose me. Now that we're proper buddies, I expect regular updates."

"I know in my mind I must be strong and stand up to them. It's a form of bullying, really. You're absolutely right. It's about my choice to do what I want to do. I'll try my best to defer any firm decision until my probationary year is up, but if Ravi won't wait, then..." She popped the last bite into her mouth before we picked up our trays and left.

We wandered back to the archive dungeon for the remaining hour of the day, and I don't mind admitting, I had a slight spring in my step.

12. near Coria, 180 CE

The carriage and escort had increased their speed from trot to canter, but a determined running man would have kept up. Gaius called Meral to him and ordered four of his riders to remain behind the last carriage, and the others to ride a line on the fringe of the trees between them and the Caledonii warriors shadowing their progress on the ridge to the north.

"The crows circling above are a bad omen," Paulinus moaned, then jerked his head to the left as Meral and his men flushed out an angry thrush.

"By Jupiter, we shall make it," Gaius replied, screwing his eyes up at a blob on the road ahead. "What is that?"

"It is a farmer's wagon, pulled by a pair of oxen. He is giving way to us in a layby," Paulinus replied. Roman roads, usually built on flat ground and raised on banks to prevent flooding, had passing places every four hundred paces or so, often visible from half a mile.

"Send your fastest rider ahead to warn him of enemy in the area, and then onwards to Coria to tell them of our approach and request a mounted guard meet us on the road. He must tell the officer in charge that a tribune's wife is our precious cargo."

They rode on in pensive silence, Paulinus acknowledging the gracious bows of the farmer with a curt nod. The winter sun was above them now, casting its pale light on the tranquil landscape but offering little warmth.

"Just think of the tavern girls at Coria, Paulinus, and be contented," Gaius joked, trying to ease the tension. "There is a bigger bathhouse, and one with a hot room for officers. Once we've bathed, we shall eat in the officers' room and go out to watch a bear fight, or wrestling match, and share a drink in the taverns…" His voice trailed off as a shout from Meral, ahead to his left, grabbed his attention.

There was a break in the trees and he was pointing uphill. "Ride over and see what he's shouting about."

Paulinus kicked his horse into a trot, then urged it to jump from the road down to the soft meadow. Kicking up mud, he galloped towards the Sarmatian decurion, as Gaius fell back to the window of the first carriage.

"Is everything alright, Gaius?" Claudia Pertinax asked, leaning out of the window.

"We are being tracked by some native riders on the hill, madam. We may need to whip the horses into a gallop if we are chased. Do not be alarmed, keep hold of the children and sit back from the windows should this happen. We have enough men to protect you." Gaius smiled past her at his wife, and was gone before Claudia could ask any more questions. In truth, he was worried and now rode forward to receive the returning Paulinus.

"Meral has spotted warriors running through the woods, with hunting hounds, sir," Paulinus reported with a puff. "They made up time on us by jogging over the hills. He says there are many, and they are keeping pace with us."

"Then tell the drivers to whip their teams into a gallop, and put the men on alert."

The speed increased, but not by much, as the carriage horses could only manage a steady gallop in step with the slowest. They ambled along for a further mile before Gaius noticed the Sarmatian cavalry arcing their arrows into the trees. The cold air hummed with their shouts; then a bare-chested warrior with swirls painted on his face and body exploded from a thicket and threw an axe at a rider. The rider saw it coming and ducked, pulling hard on his rein to steer his mount away from the hollering man.

More warriors emerged from the woods, their blood-curdling war cries shattering the peace, throwing spears or axes at the riders veering away. One of the Sarmatians was pierced by a spear in his side, between front and back

125

armour, and fell with a cry to the ground. In an instant, two warriors were upon him, hacking at him with axes, and a hound seized his throat. The Sarmatian following behind felled the spearman with an arrow in his back, but did not stop for his fallen comrade, swerving as he rode away to avoid a snapping hound.

Gaius felt helpless, with no other option but to urge the carriage train onwards as fast as they could manage, but the pace could not increase above a ponderous, steady gallop. He saw Meral lead his riders towards him, then ride a line on the grass verge beside the road. Enemy pony riders were tracking them on a parallel course, and a host of warriors, some with huge hairy hounds beside them, ran silently to allow for steady breathing, adding menace to their pursuit. They were closing the gap to Meral's men, who resumed loosing arrows at them when they got too close.

"That's Kerwyn up ahead!" Paulinus shouted, pointing. The two scouts were stationary on the road, and started their horses forward to match their pace once they caught up.

"There is a turning to the right, sir, which we should take. It is a shortcut to the Roman town!" Kerwyn shouted above the drum of hooves.

"Will the carriages manage it?" Gaius shouted back.

"It is well worn, sir," Kerwyn replied. "It is our best hope to outrun these devils."

Gaius had counted six milestones, but that left them three miles short of their destination. He glanced to his left and saw the running warriors and line of pony riders playing a game of ducking arrows with the Sarmatians, all the while getting closer to the road. "Alright, we will take it!" he yelled.

Paulinus shouted to him, "Sir, is it wise to leave the road? We may find a relief column ahead."

"We will follow the guidance of our head scout. We cannot continue for much longer like this."

Kerwyn galloped ahead, and before long they saw him and his fellow scout waving for them to leave the road. Gaius fell back to tell the carriage drivers what to do, noting the looks of alarm around him. He dropped behind to lead the four rear guards. Up ahead, Paulinus was waving his arms at Meral to indicate they should leave the road in gaps before and between the two carriages.

Gaius and the rear guard were forced to slow to a trot as the carriages slowed to make inelegant exits from the stone-paved road onto a track of compacted earth. When an arrow flew past Gaius's ear, he instinctively ducked, just before the rear-most rider cried out in pain as an arrow struck his neck. Gaius glanced back and saw him remain mounted, although slumped forward, as they left the road for the track that he hoped would lead them to safety. One advantage was already apparent – the track was flanked by high bushes and trees, some overhanging, so that their pursuers would have to funnel onto the track and run no more than four-abreast.

The last thing Gaius saw before entering the tunnel of brush was Kerwyn and his companion sitting calmly on the road. Why had he not led them from the road? A cry from behind told him that the wounded rider had fallen from his horse, perhaps hit by a second arrow or spear. They were following the second carriage at a much slower pace, dust billowing in their faces. Although glad for his shield slung on his back, now peppered with arrow shafts, Gaius knew they would soon be caught and pulled from their horses by the barbarians. There was just him and three others with nowhere to go, as they were boxed in behind the second carriage. The faces of three house slaves riding on the rear platform, cowering under a blanket pulled over their knees, stared at him.

A scream from behind let Gaius know that a second rider had been felled, and ahead, the carriage bounced noisily over a branch across the road. He swivelled in his saddle to see a host of warriors, some with dogs beside them, running close to the last rider, who was desperately urging his mount forward to run beside his comrade. Gaius and the other rider were just ahead of them. They passed the gates to a farm estate and kept going, the carriage occasionally bouncing and bumping over tree roots or fallen branches. It was only a matter of time before they were picked off. They were trapped, at the mercy of the chasing pack.

Surely, they had travelled more than a mile and must be close to the walls of Coria? Gaius's mind was a whirl of thoughts. Any guards sent to meet them on the road would miss them. Above all, he was concerned for the safety of his wife and child, and the others under his charge he may not be able to protect. A spear thrown forward struck the rump of the horse behind and it whinnied in pain and fear, buckling and throwing its rider as it went down. Gaius glanced back to the dust cloud and saw the first line of runners tripping over the stricken animal. The riders had gained a few yards on their pursuers, the second rank now jumping over the horse and their fallen comrades to take up the pursuit.

After what seemed like another half a mile, the carriage began to slow, and gradually come to a halt, much to Gaius's horror. He reined Mars to a halt and swivelled to face the enemy in a cloud of dust, his two remaining Sarmatians on either side. He glanced at the two brown-skinned riders to his left as they nocked arrows in their bows.

Gaius leaned forward and shouted to the petrified slaves, "Climb over the carriage!" He then fetched a javelin from his side quiver and got ready to meet the chanting hoard of warriors bearing down on them, barely thirty paces behind.

Gaius turned to the front to see four Sarmatians on the roof of the carriage, helping the slaves climb up and get past them. Once the grateful slaves had gone, they knelt with bows at the ready.

"So, this is it – our last stand," Gaius growled between gritted teeth. Arrows flew at the onrushing enemy and he swivelled to throw his javelin, finding his mark in the chest of a man. A large hairy hound snapped at Mars, causing the stallion to buck and kick out in self-defence. Gaius leaned forward and held tightly to the reins. Mars struck the dog on its head and it whimpered as it rolled from the path in a ball of dust. Gaius drew his curved cuirass, but Mars had turned to his right, meaning Gaius was exposed on his shield side. A warrior leapt at him; axe raised ready to strike. Gaius punched his shield boss into the man's face, knocking him off his feet.

The air filled with war cries and the screams of the wounded as arrows, javelins and axes flew through the air. Gaius was relieved to see his Gallic soldiers appear on foot from either side of the carriage, punching their shields into the angry warriors and stabbing in a mechanical motion with their swords. Mars was trotting on the spot, agitated by the aggressive crowd and snapping dogs, but could see there was nowhere to go. Gaius drew another javelin from his quiver and picked out a target in the melee. The battle was intense, but confined by thick bushes on either side of the track to a width of no more than ten paces. More warriors pressed from behind, and the wall moved ever closer. Gaius nodded to the other two riders and then jumped from Mars, whispering, "Sorry, boy." They scrambled up the back of the carriage and were helped up by those on top. Two brave soldiers defended the sides of the box-shaped vehicle for as long as they could, but it did not take the enraged warriors long before they pushed past the frightened horses and started battering their shields.

Sarmatian soldiers released the last of their arrows down on the attackers, but once spent, had no choice but to draw swords to defend the top of the carriage from those who flung themselves at the back. Gaius moved to the front, jumped down and ran to Paulinus to find out what had happened.

"The road ahead is blocked with a tree, sir. A deliberate roadblock. I fear we have been betrayed by Kerwyn."

Gaius stared in shock at the suggestion. He had trusted the scout and had risked his own life only the day before to save his family from their hut. "Maybe there is another explanation," he muttered, noting the sceptical look in his deputy's face.

"There's a walled estate up ahead, sir. I've sent the civilians and men carrying our chest and standard there," Paulinus shouted against the din of battle ringing in their ears. "It has a high wall and corner towers, as if they had prepared for this moment."

"Then that must do for us to make our stand. Lead half of the men there with the horses. I will follow on foot with the remaining men, fighting a defence if necessary."

Paulinus slammed his arm across his chest and stood to attention, saluting his officer as if for the last time. He turned and jogged away to squeeze down the side of the first coach.

Gaius shouted after him, "And send a rider to the fort for help!" He was left with eight men at his back, watching with concern as the Sarmatians on the roof edged back towards him, duelling with warriors. The Gauls down the side of the carriage were also edging backwards, as fierce warriors battered their shields with repeated axe blows.

"Fall back to the first carriage!" Gaius yelled, turning to jog the short distance and clamber up onto the roof. The Sarmatians jumped down, away from onrushing warriors, and the soldiers on each side turned and ran. Two did not make it – a Sarmatian and a Gaul were struck down, one by spear, the other by axe. Gaius glanced back to see the distance to their walled sanctuary was about a hundred paces. Men were lining the eight-foot wall on either side of a corner tower, which told him there was a platform of some kind behind the lime-washed structure.

"We will hold them until our javelins and arrows are spent!" Gaius shouted. His Gaul riders still had javelins to throw, and some Sarmatians had arrows. The tattooed and painted warriors crowded the space between the two carriages, and when Gaius slammed down his raised arm, they were met with a hail of javelins and arrows, always more effective when delivered in a co-ordinated volley. Half a dozen fell with cries, as their blood-crazed brothers leapt over them and charged on.

"The last one, sir," a soldier said, handing Gaius a javelin.

Gaius picked a target, a tall, fierce man with plaited moustaches, and threw his weapon into the man's naked torso, the tip passing through his chest bone and lodging there. Groaning, he buckled to his knees. Gaius ducked as a retaliatory axe whizzed over his head. With a thud, the enraged warriors hit the back of the carriage, causing it to shudder. The soldiers at the sides held them back with shields in pairs, one low and one high, stabbing at the enemy with their swords.

Gaius could see it was hopeless without anything to throw or fire, and ordered the men to fall back. The men at the sides would be the last to make a run for it, and Gaius jumped down at the front with a sense of sadness as he yelled at them to run for their lives. He turned and ran, his shield now discarded, his sword in his right hand. Cries and screams behind told him all he needed to know, and he ran with all his might in body and shoulder armour, helmet and wrist guards, studded metal armour strips that hung from his belt flapping before his pumping thighs. Steel shin guards above leather boots also added to the weight, as a hated training routine proved its value. Encouragement was shouted from the walls as the last of the men made the gates.

A guard of shields awaited the runners as they filed through the gap into the estate, and Gaius staggered past sandstone columns to collapse in a heap beside his men on the grass, panting hard by a gravel track that led to an imposing villa. The last of the men entered and the gates were slammed shut and barred. Gaius noted that the high walls had metal spikes on the tops and grinned at his morsel of good fortune.

Paulinus rushed to his side, and helped him to his feet. "Sir! There are thirty estate workers manning the walls with our men, throwing sharp objects and rocks at the bastards!"

"Good job, Paulinus," Gaius puffed, trying to catch his breath. "Let us hide the chest and standard and join in the fight."

"Already in hand, sir. The lady of the house pointed out a grave that has been part-dug in their family plot, sir. Two of the boys are burying them. Remember the gravestone is in the name of Domina Drusilla Gabia. Her recently demised mother, apparently."

"Then we must be grateful for the gap between her mother's death and burial," Gaius replied, holding the stitch in his side. He turned at the noise of fighting beyond the wall. "And we must also be thankful for their high walls. Do they run all around the compound?"

"Aye, sir. They cannot come behind as a high thorn hedge prevents it. There is a small gate at the rear to a covered pathway that goes through an orchard to the woods, protected on each side by thick bushes, then down to the river. The owner is a magistrate, Lucius Gabia, who had made provision for an escape should the need arise. There is a path along the riverbank to the bridge at Coria. Our escape route, if these devils don't get behind us."

"Praise the gods that the magistrate had enemies or is of a nervous disposition. We should send the civilians now, with the wounded and a couple of guards," Gaius replied.

"Aye, sir," Paulinus said, shouting orders as he ran off.

Gaius looked up at the serene, beautiful villa, with red roof tiles and a grape vine climbing up a lime-washed wall, a peaceful scene at odds with their predicament. Then he saw Aria and the other wives helping the wounded with bandages and splints in the side garden through an archway. He bowed to a matronly lady who must be the magistrate's wife, standing in the shade of the patio, giving instructions to her fretting attendants.

He jogged past the stricken soldiers, asking how badly were they wounded, to Aria, who looked up with a cry of relief. "My love, I am so pleased to see you unhurt!" She dropped a bandage roll and threw her arms around him. Brutus ran to him and hugged his thigh with the grip of a bear cub.

"The gods be praised, I'm unhurt, Aria, but must return to my men. I have ordered two guards to take all the civilians and wounded out through the rear pathway to the river, and from there to the bridge at Coria, where the guards will look after you until we can follow."

Her tear-stained eyes widened in fright. "No, you must come with us! To stay here is to die at the hands of those barbarians!"

"I must stay and organise an orderly retreat…"

"Come with us, Papa!" Brutus cried, squeezing his leg tight.

"You have a strong grip, my son," Gaius said, lifting the boy. "Soon you will be the one protecting your mother. But for now, I need you both to be strong and prepare to leave. You may have to help the wounded, so do not carry anything heavy. Now pass on my instructions and organise the wounded to leave."

He kissed the boy's forehead, bent and put his son on the ground, then pulled Aria to him by her slender waist. He looked into her liquid green eyes and then kissed her

133

lips with all the passion and madness of the moment. "Go now, my love, and I promise you, I will follow."

He held her shoulders at arms-length, then she turned away with a look of sorrow, grabbed Brutus by the hand and ran to the lady of the house to inform her.

"May the divine Jupiter and all the Caesars protect you!" he shouted, then turned and jogged from the peaceful surroundings, through the archway and down the gravel drive, past men shovelling soil onto a grave, to the scene of chaos at the main gates.

13. Vindolanda, present day

On Monday morning, I picked up where I'd left off with the Corbridge tablets. From what I'd translated, added to guesswork on what was missing, I deduced that Gaius was at Coria to report that his unit had been attacked by unknown barbarians, whilst conveying a payroll chest from Vindolanda to Coria for safekeeping. The garrison at Vindolanda was under siege from a large force of Caledonian warriors. He had diverted his unit off the Via Vespasian (not Hadrian, as I'd earlier speculated with Sima) at milestone twenty-six, to the estate of *Lucius Gabia, Magistratus*, roughly a mile from the road. Here, he buried the chest of coins and the cohort standard. The rest of the report was unclear after that, but he referred to a grave marker for a *Domina Drusilla Gabia*.

"Hmmm, instructions on where to find buried treasure," I said. I looked around, but none of the half dozen academics or staff were looking in my direction. My pulse had quickened and my mind was racing. Firstly, that stretch of the Roman road from Coria to the Vindolanda turn-off was constructed in the reign of Emperor Vespasian, between 69 and 79 CE. This was a new discovery, and Maggie would be pleased to hear of it. Secondly, Gaius was reporting that he had to bury the cohort payroll chest in the grounds of a villa estate, close to a tombstone, so perhaps in a family burial enclosure. This was approximately one hundred yards along a side road marked by a milestone marking twenty Roman miles. Perhaps it had been recovered, or perhaps not, particularly if all those involved in the desperate action had not lived to return at a later date. Also, it was possible others had long since read the report and recovered the chest. It was a long shot if it was still buried.

I did some investigation and found that the milestones along what came to be called the Stanegate, in the post-Roman period, started from Segedunum Roman fort, now Wallsend in Newcastle, to the east, and increased in number as they progressed west. So, 26 Roman miles, indicated on the *miliarium* reported by Gaius, equates to 24.5 imperial miles. A check on UK driving distances showed me the distance from Wallsend Roman Fort to Corbridge Roman town to be 24.37 miles. So, the XXVI (26) milestone would have been situated roughly two hundred yards west of the track to the Roman fortified town of Coria.

I got the detailed Ordinance Survey Map of Northumberland and measured two hundred yards west of the turning to Coria, using my ruler. The road was predictably straight, apart from a few kinks that mirrored the river course. I studied the rural location for a clue to a track that might have once led to a Roman farm estate. Green fields lined both sides of the current road, and the map showed some dotted lines to farm houses. Now, if I could only get an idea if there were Roman estates on one or both sides of the road with an entrance track close to that point.

Sima came over, curious at my sudden burst of activity and my poring over a map.

"What you doing?" she asked.

"Oh hi. I think I've stumbled onto something from one of the tablets. A report from…" I checked myself, wondering if I should rush into spilling the full story whilst it was still formulating. Maybe caution and further investigation on my part was prudent before talking about it. "A report from an officer at Coria in the days or hours before the fire of 180 CE. I'm just checking on something that he referred to."

"Good for you, Sherlock. I hope it leads to something useful." She paused and leaned closer, then continued in a hushed tone. "Thanks, Noah, for not running for the hills. I'm all right now. I'm usually calm and collected."

"I know, Sima. I've noticed. I hope it all works out for you. Remember, you can grab me anytime if you want to offload."

There was relief in her smile when she turned towards her office, leaving me to get on with exploring my theory. I decided to send an email to Maggie, bringing her up to speed with my findings, and ask for ideas on how I could identify the location of a Roman estate to the east of Coria, one owned by the Gabia family in the year 180. If we could narrow down the search area, it might make a field study possible.

As I walked back to my room that evening, my mind was full of visions of a unit of Roman soldiers under attack, making a hurried exit from the main road to a walled villa estate. Perhaps the attacks continued and they decided they would have to fight their way out and therefore must bury their precious cargo, to be retrieved at a later date. So many Roman hoards, mainly of coins, often in jugs or vases, were buried in haste in the face of attack, with the owners either not surviving or unable to return to reclaim the goods for other reasons. This could be another instance.

"Want to go to the next level of Warzone?" Dave asked, looking over from the top bunk, waving his console at me.

"Not now, mate. I'm up to my eyeballs with something," I replied.

Just then, my tablet pinged, and I opened an email from Maggie. Her reply was enthusiastic, and she had attached a scan of the appropriate section of the oldest map of the area she could find. It was a three-hundred-year-old black ink on white map, showing towns, villages, hamlets, farms and parish boundaries. It clearly showed the Stanegate Road running east to west just below Hadrian's Wall. Where the excavated site of Coria now lies, there was a dotted line track going to a farm. The town of

Corbridge was just to the east of that, with a cross marking the location of the church.

I pulled my OS map from my backpack and estimated roughly one fifth of a mile distance, going west from the track to the farm lying over the remains of Coria. There was a track to the south of the Stanegate, going to a fairly large farm that had a rectangular dotted outline around the main buildings that indicated a wall. The farm was next to the farm that lay over the unmarked ruins of Coria, both of which were bordered by the River Tyne to the south. It was marked as Sawyer's Farm. I noticed there was no indication of any Roman ruins, apart from a few outcrops of Hadrian's Wall on some hilltops with the legend 'Roman Wall', nor did it show the site of the old Roman bridge. There is no bridge now, nor was there three hundred years ago.

"Eureka!" I shouted. It was the hour before dinner and Russ and Richard had wandered in and were also on their bunks, playing games on their devices, milking the wifi.

"Found what?" Dave asked, leaning his head over.

"I think I've found the estate where Gaius buried his unit's payroll chest. It's on a three-hundred-year-old map. It's a farm, called 'Sawyer's Farm' then, just west of Coria. According to the OS, there's a wall around it. Who's up for a treasure hunt?"

That got Russ and Richard's attention. They all turned to face me.

"Are you going to ask Professor Maggie for permission to start a dig?" Richard asked.

I thought for a moment. "Well, she knows what I'm looking for, so I'll ask her opinion. But I guess there'll be delays with red tape, applications, permissions, contacting the landowners, etcetera, and I need a quick result for my dissertation. What do you guys think?"

Richard cleared his throat. "Well, I've had experience of organising digs and it's no small thing. Permissions have to be obtained; there's a list of authorities that have to be informed, and then you need a lead archaeologist, equipment and a budget for having a team in the field…"

"OK, don't shoot it down just yet, Richard. We're still chucking ideas into the hat." I rolled my eyes in mock exasperation, then brightened up as a thought occurred to me. "You may have talked yourself into being our dig supervisor!"

"It's nearer Corbridge than Vindolanda," Dave said, "so why not sound out the curator at Coria?"

I turned to smile at him. "That's a good idea, Dave. Also, I need to look at the Land Registry to see who now owns Sawyer's Farm."

"I can help there," Russ replied. "I've done a Land Registry search for another project, and think I still have my login details to their website.

"That's great, Russ, if you wouldn't mind."

"I'll get on it right away. Pass the map over."

Richard was looking worried. "I'm not sure about being the lead on this. We will need to talk it through with Professor Wilde and Mike Stone and get their support."

"Yes, of course. Don't flap, Richard. Let's put a proposal together first, eh?"

Dave leaned over and said, "I don't want to pour cold water on your beautiful scheme, but how do you know the Romans didn't recover their chest of coins?"

I paused to consider this, then looked up. "I don't know, Dave, but it's more than a hunch. We know there was an attack across the frontier in the year 180, that led to the burning of Coria town. Gaius was ordered to take the payroll chest from Vindolanda to Coria for safekeeping, and we know he reached Coria and reported having to bury the chest and cohort standard. So, he must have reached the town and made his report before the town burnt down, as it fell into disuse for a number of years afterwards. Assumptions, yes, but I believe there's a strong case for it not being reclaimed, particularly if there was a battle at Coria, and Gaius's fate is unknown after that."

"Hmmm, I see you desperately want your assumptions to be true. Anyway, I'm in, as I want to get my hands on a ground penetrating radar device and a new metal detector and do a ground survey for my dissertation."

"Good. I'll fire an email back to Maggie," I said, enthused by the possibility. "Richard, do you mind if I mention your prior experience and willingness to supervise us?"

He looked at me glumly. "Yes, alright. As long as she gives her support, I'm in."

Time was against me as I would have to submit my completed dissertation in three months. I knew an officially-sanctioned archaeological dig could take a year or more to arrange, so an approach to the current owners of the farm would be the way to go.

"I'll put together a list of equipment we would need if we were to do an exploratory survey," Richard said.

"And I'll sound out Mike Stone about borrowing his Land Rover," Dave added.

"OK, but don't tell him the details of what we're planning just yet," I replied. "Thanks guys!"

*****

The following Saturday, we were in the car park loading Mike Stone's Land Rover with shovels, hessian sacks, sample bags, trowels, sieves, a metal detector and a ground-penetrating radar device that Richard had signed out for the weekend. We had identified the current owner of the farmhouse, Mrs Betty Hardcastle, a retired widow, and I'd spoken to her on the phone, introducing myself as an archaeology student who was interested in identifying sites of old Roman graveyards.

It had piqued her interest when I said I had a hunch that there might be a family graveyard plot in the corner of her house enclosure. She'd replied that she was a member of the Corbridge History Society, and was interested in the prospect of finding Roman remains on her land. I had played it down, saying that I would like to come over one Saturday with a couple of friends to have a look around. She had agreed, and proposed that we come over right away, on the forthcoming Saturday.

"What did Professor Wilde say to you, Richard?" Dave asked, placing a cool box of sandwiches and drinks in the back.

Richard carefully stored the last of the equipment in and shut the rear door. "She gave me a copy of the trust's dig rules and told me not to disturb or remove any artefacts we may uncover. We're only to photograph and record them, then come back and fetch Mike Stone."

I groaned at the thought of having to stop if we uncovered anything of interest. I held the passenger door open for Dave. Only three could squeeze into the cab, so Russ had agreed to stay behind.

"Well, I guess she could take the credit if we found anything," Dave said as he wedged himself in the centre seat by the gear stick.

"If we find anything, I was going to call the Corbridge Curator, Helen, as they're just next door," I replied, "but I suppose we should follow Richard's lead." The old 110 Defender started with a throaty roar, spewing black smoke out of the exhaust, I noted, looking in the side mirror.

Richard engaged first gear and drove out onto the steep lane. "It's like driving a tank!"

I grabbed up my writing pad as it slid off the dashboard. "The wind, the rain and the build-up of lead from vehicle exhaust fumes have blackened and corroded the surfaces of the oldest stones above ground," I said, reading my old notes aloud from the facing page, before scribbling the date at the top of a clean page. "No wonder we struggle to read the inscriptions on old milestones."

"Then it's good for our prospects that archaeology is largely concerned with digging up artefacts that have been buried in the ground for hundreds or thousands of years," Dave replied, "beneath our planet's toxic surface."

The drive time to Hardcastle Farm was only thirty minutes, and the electric gate opened for us after I waved at a CCTV camera. We rattled across a cattle grid onto the one-hundred-yard straight drive to the manor house, passing two dozen shaggy-coated Highland cattle and as many sheep chewing the thick, coarse moorland grass. Away to our left I saw the boundary fence and the buildings of the Corbridge Museum between trees, owned by the English Heritage Trust.

"To think that Gaius must have been so near and yet somehow thwarted from reaching Coria," I said as we waited for a second set of electric gates to swing open. Our approach had been tracked on a moving CCTV camera. The main house, front garden, barn and outhouses were all enclosed by an electric fence.

Richard parked next to a newer, but similar, Land Rover on the gravel driveway. "Let's hope this is the right place."

We got out to the barks of two large smooth-coated hounds with floppy ears, and the approach of our host, a stout, grey-haired woman in cream Aran jumper and corduroy trousers tucked into green gumboots. It was practically a uniform around here, and we were similarly attired.

"Good morning and welcome to Hardcastle Farm," she said.

"Hi, Mrs Hardcastle." I held out my hand. "I'm Noah. Thanks for inviting us to have a look around."

"Not at all, and please call me Betty." She gave me a firm hand shake. I could see from her ruddy cheeks and frame that she was an outdoors person, no doubt a keen hiker and dog walker on the Northumberland hills that rose from the river valley in which her property sat. "I'm so pleased you called. I'll take you to the overgrown corner which I think would be a good place to start. There's a pile of stones that may have been used as grave markers. I've put a couple of rakes over there. If you wouldn't mind clearing away the leaf mulch and twigs for me and tidying up, I'd be grateful."

She led the way across an expanse of mown lawn towards the corner of the enclosed area, past a stone border and hedgerow that marked the edge of the garden, and onto a rough track that led into an area of low-hanging trees and bushes. There was a disused wooden shed with a partially collapsed roof, then a secluded area with lumps of coarse grass where no trees grew, only a few bushes.

"This looks promising," I said.

"Yes, I've often wondered if this was an old graveyard. The nettles and brambles run riot, so it's a magnet for butterflies. You can rip up the bushes and slash back the grass, but leave the trees that border this area, please," Betty replied. The area covered roughly forty square yards.

"Have you got wheelbarrows we can use to bring our gear over and bags of green waste out?" Richard asked.

"Yes. Follow me." She led us to a large shed with corrugated iron walls and roof. "This is the gardener's shed, help yourselves, but please put everything back where you found it. You can pile the green waste next to the compost tanks around the corner. I'll leave you to it, and please come to the house before it gets dark for tea and scones. I'll be waiting to hear what you think is buried here."

She left us in the gardener's Aladdin's cave and we set about lining up a wheelbarrow each with green waste bags and placing what we needed in them. We spent the first two hours raking up twigs and leaves, strimming the grass and bushes, and then bagging the waste.

"My back's killing me!" Dave groaned when we regrouped to compare progress. We had cleared the area and had bagged up over twenty garden waste sacks with grass, twigs and branches.

"We haven't even broken ground yet," I said, toasting the pair with my flask cup as we sat to eat our packed lunch.

After a half-hour break, Richard stood and fetched the metal detector. "I'll first make a pass with the detector to see if there's any metal objects close to the surface. After that, I'll scan the ground to a greater depth and mark any promising readings with tent pegs to indicate large underground objects."

"Boys with toys, eh – you're in your element." Dave could barely contain his jealousy. He crammed the last sandwich into his mouth. "Good old Jenny. The sandwiches are the highlight so far."

"Don't worry, Dave. I'll let you have a go once I've got the basic readings." Richard was in charge of the equipment and made sure we knew it.

"While you're doing that, Dave and I'll look through the old stones that have been piled up in the far corner and see if there are any pieces of worked stone with engravings," I said.

An hour passed before Richard was through with his preliminary survey and the three of us re-grouped to stretch and compare notes.

"No metals detected, annoyingly. Found any gravestone fragments?"

I nodded. "Yes, quite a few with smooth faces, and about ten pieces that have partial lettering, but none with complete words. I'd say this is a graveyard, but how far back in time it goes we've yet to discover."

"I reckon we've got two hours before the sun sets. Shall we do a test dig on a promising location?" Dave asked, looking at Richard.

"Yes, I think so. I've identified a couple of promising sites. The radar has picked out some rectangular shapes that might be tombstone slabs about two or three feet under. We can try those first. Let's peg out a grid."

"OK, and we'll be careful not to disturb the occupants of any graves. We'll focus on cleaning and photographing any inscriptions," I said.

"We're like the gravediggers from Hamlet," Dave quipped as he got into a steady rhythm of digging and throwing out the dark brown soil from the deepening pit. "Alas, poor Yorick, what did you achieve in your life?"

"I can't see us uncovering any human skulls, but you never know. But if we find anything of significance, we just might expand some boundaries of knowledge." Dreaming of overnight success was one of my favourite pastimes.

"We can clean off, log and photograph any tombstone we uncover, but everything must remain in the ground until Mike comes to have a look, okay?" Richard stood by his cord fence, hands on hips, looking down at us.

"I'm glad you're here, Richard, otherwise we wouldn't be." I meant it, and joyfully shovelled the rich, dark soil out of the rectangular pit.

"We're lucky to have this opportunity to run our own dig, so let's get it right." Richard smiled as he moved the earth away from the edge with his shovel.

After Richard had pegged out our dig area, we fell into silence as we worked, grateful that there had not been a hard frost in the early days of winter. In half an hour, twenty centimetres down, we had reached a solid impediment, and gradually exposed a flat tombstone. Once we'd removed the stones and earth and brushed it clean, an inscription revealed itself.

"'Here lies Martha Anne Sawyer, wife to John and mother to Mabel and Jeremy, born 1689, died 1728.' A farmer's wife in the Late Stuart period," I said, taking photos with my digicam.

"I wonder what lies deeper," Dave said.

I sighed. Any Roman remains could be more than a metre deep. The late afternoon sun was turning pale orange as its weak, winter rays filtered through pine and beech trees. A row of horned cattle lined the fence beyond the trees, staring balefully at us, perhaps expecting to be taken to the barn.

Richard nodded at the lengthening shadows. "This could take weeks. Let's tidy up and report back to Betty."

The house had been built by James Sawyer, she told us, around 1660, most likely on the site of an earlier house. The current electric fence stood on the foundations of a former stone wall Betty confirmed. Possibly a Roman wall. We showed her the pictures of the tombstone and I wrote out the inscription on a sheet of paper for her. Her face lit up, and she began speculating about restoring the Sawyer family graveyard and organising a visit from her local history group. We said we would continue to dig down to expose the entire family graveyard over the coming weekends. Richard told her he would be following accepted archaeological practice in preparing and documenting the dig and that it would be good for our projects for us to employ the latest ground scanning techniques. After refreshing our palates on sweet tea and wolfing down her delicious scones with butter and homemade strawberry jam, we made our exit, saying we'd come back on Sunday morning to continue.

"We'll identify the extent of the Sawyer family plot over the next few weekends," Richard said, as we climbed into the car, "then go a bit wider to see what else is down there."

"It's certainly no quick-in-and-out job," Dave moaned, flexing his stiff shoulders.

"Now's not the time to hear about your love life, Dave," I joked.

"Shower, dinner and pub, are in order," Richard remarked in a weary drawl as he drove us to the gates, slowing occasionally to let sheep wander off. "Russ will be keen to know what we've found."

14. Coria, 180 CE

Gaius and Paulinus followed the estate workers along the pathway that led them through a copse at the rear of the farm estate. His remaining twelve men followed in silence. The battle at the front of the estate had been fierce but brief. They had killed or wounded a great many warriors, enough for them to be called back by a chief to lick their wounds and consider their options. It was then that Gaius had ordered a retreat, leaving only six volunteers, who claimed to be fast runners, to man the tower and walls in the hope that the enemy would not see that the rest had gone. Two of the volunteers were youths from the estate, who were gripped with excitement and willingly agreed to remain to the end and lead four soldiers, stripped of their armour, in a quick escape.

They came out of the woods in single file onto a riverside path, next to a small wooden pier, and turned left to follow the path to Coria. Gaius and Paulinus had discarded their shin and forearm guards, but retained their body armour, helmets and swords. The river bubbled noisily, the fast-flowing waters a barrier to anyone thinking of crossing it. On the opposite bank, curious farm workers had gathered to see what the commotion was about.

After twenty minutes, the runners ahead stopped on the top of a wooded hill. When Paulinus and Gaius caught them up, they could see, through the trees, a field of stubble running down to a road that connected a bridge to the walls of a large fortress positioned on a bluff above the river plain.

"It's the town of Coria, sir," a farm worker puffed, on Paulinus's enquiry, his eyes wide in fear and awe.

"Then we have made it," Gaius said, catching his breath with hands on knees. They waited until all the men had joined them, including the last six, who had run for their lives as the warriors had returned to continue their

assault on the estate. The two youths gleefully reported
that they had thrown branches across their path to
confound their pursuers.

Gaius nodded and rewarded them with a grin. "Even
so, they will soon follow. Now to the guard house at the
bridge to warn them of imminent attack." He led the
dishevelled group on a final jog down a well-worn path
towards the bridge, centurion's helmet tucked under one
arm. He would put it up as they approached to denote his
rank to any nervous soldiers on guard duty.

The bridge of wooden planks with hand rails had
stone bridgeheads on each bank, and was held up by
wooden beams driven into the river bed at regular
intervals. It was wide and strong enough for heavy wagons
to pass over, and legionaries to march eight abreast.
Beside the bridgeheads were modest stone barrack blocks
that could house up to a dozen guards.

It was a well-fed optio that strolled out to meet Gaius
as he approached. "Hail sir!" he bellowed, making a salute.

Gaius stopped in front of him and breathed deeply
before replying, "Hail, officer of the guard. I am Centurion
Gaius Atticianus of the fourth cohort, Sixth Legion, from
Vindolanda. We have been attacked on the road by
northern barbarians. Call out the guard, for they are
following."

The optio's eyebrows were raised and his eyes
widened by the end of his report. "Aye sir! Follow me to the
guardhouse!" He turned and trotted to the stone building,
shouting, "Sound the alarm! Enemy attack!"

A bell hanging from a bracket on the wall was rung,
and another soldier appeared from the guardhouse and put
a horn to his lips, sounding it in the direction of the walls of
Coria. Soon the alarm call was taken up in the fort.

Gaius asked about the civilians from the estate, and
was told they had gone to the fort. He gathered his men to
him and announced, "We must jog on one more time to the

fort to report to the commanding officer and find our fellows from the fourth cohort. Follow me in two ranks."

Gaius and Paulinus led them up the gentle rise to the south gate of the fort. This road that ran southwards for one hundred miles from the bridge to Eboracum, proceeded northwards through Coria to Hadrian's Wall, a mile to the north, and from there through the gates at a wall fort, northwards to the abandoned forts until it reached the Antonine barrier, a straight arrow through the heart of northern Britannia. It was a road Gaius and his men were very familiar with.

The gates were open wide, as they would be in peacetime during daylight hours, and Gaius led his dishevelled troop past the guards and curious onlookers, past stables and barrack blocks, towards the centre of the fortified town. The southern half was the military base. Experience told him the granary, along with warehouses, temples, shops, businesses and some civilian dwellings were situated in the northern quarters, and outside the east and west gates, shanty settlements had sprung up of crude huts and animal pens.

Despite the horns sounding on the gatehouses, men were idly walking out of their barrack rooms, putting on belts and adjusting their armour. A centurion stood on a street corner, staring at the mud-encrusted Gaius and his similarly filthy men.

"They are too lax for my liking, sir," Paulinus breathed in his commander's ear.

"This town has not come under attack since these walls were built, and they must think it is invulnerable behind the Wall," Gaius grumbled, increasing his pace and nodding casually to the quizzical centurion.

They reached the square at the town centre, where a fountain stood, spewing water from the mouths of four bronze dolphins into an ornate, circular stone pond. Women in togas or woollen dresses clustered around, their shrill chatter filling the air as they held jugs under the cascade of water. To the right, a proud temple stood, its high Greek columns supporting a triangular stone pediment above the entrance bearing a frieze of the gods frolicking on Mount Olympus. Suppliants bartered for fowl and captured birds from a throng of sellers on its lowest steps, then entered the temple to join a queue for a priest to hear their prayers and make their sacrifice to an appropriate god.

"Is this how Rome looks, sir?" Paulinus asked.

"Perhaps. I wouldn't know," Gaius replied, turning to his left. They passed administrative and storage blocks and headed for the commanding officer's building, denoted by a red legion banner fluttering from a pole. The Senate and People of Rome were represented and firmly in charge.

Outside, Gaius instructed Paulinus to find Centurion Lupus Viridio and brief him on recent events, then find new equipment and food for the men. Paulinus was about to leave when Gaius added, "I wonder if Adminius is inside with the report that damns me to an uncertain fate."

Paulinus grinned. "Do not worry, sir. When I was helping our noble prefect with his bag, I removed the document pouch and buried it beside our pay chest."

Gaius gawped in wonder at his audacity, unsure how to respond. "You have only delayed the inevitable, but I thank you for your good intentions. I owe you that drink more than ever, but it must wait."

Gaius climbed the steps to the building, entering past two guards to find a clerk sitting at a desk.

He introduced himself and asked for confirmation as to who the commanding officer was.

"It is His Excellency, Tribune Flavius Lucius Bebius, of the Third Cohort, Sixth Legion Victrix Valorum…"

"Yes, yes, can't you hear the horns sounding on the walls? We will soon be under attack by thousands of savages!"

The small, elderly man gulped as he looked up at Gaius who was leaning on his desk with muddy knuckles that would leave an imprint. "But the Tribune gave strict instructions he is not to be disturbed... even the wife of your tribune accompanied by a prefect were not permitted..." his thin voice tailed off under Gaius's glare.

"This is an emergency. Come on, let's go." Gaius marched him to a pair of smooth oak doors and the clerk made the faintest of knocks. Gaius pushed him aside and hammered his fist on the door.

"He is praetorian class, sir!" the clerk squeaked, backing away.

"What is it!" a voice shouted from within. "I told you, no visitors!"

Gaius shouted back, "Sir, the fort will soon be under attack. You must give the order to stand to!"

A scurrying noise led to the door being opened a crack, and a pretty young woman squeezed through, adjusting her toga at the shoulder. Gaius barged into the room, to find the tribune adjusting his own imperial, purple-lined garment.

"Who are you! What do you mean by this intrusion!" the tribune raged, pushing his fingers through thinning hair. His face had reddened and his hand shook as he clutched his robe.

Gaius's mission was too serious for him to gloat at catching his superior ignoring the alarm because he was in the act. He suppressed his disgust at the officer's negligence. "I apologise for the intrusion, sir, but it is an emergency. Do you hear the horns sounding from the south and west gatehouses? We will soon be under attack..."

"Don't be so dramatic, Centurion. We often have a drill at this time. What is your unit? I will speak to your tribune about this outrage..."

"It is no drill, sir. I am from Vindolanda Fort and was chased here on the road by hundreds of painted warriors who have crossed the Wall…"

"Crossed the Wall! I do not believe it! …It has not happened in my time." The ruffled tribune moved to stand behind his desk, before the standard of his cohort, and leaned forward on his hands to glare at Gaius with the full malice of rank and privilege. "Get out! And if you dare breathe a word of this to anyone…"

Gaius hesitated. "Sir, it is no drill, and I urge you to give the command to stand-to, as I have seen your men idling in the streets." He held his senior officer's stare until the tribune looked away. In the silence that followed, Gaius's eyes roved across the desk, noting the rolls of parchment, a snuff box and a silver statuette of the god Mercury – bringer of news, but more than that, translator or interpreter of messages. Useful for a Roman tribune or legate. Perhaps a gift from his wife?

"Alright, Centurion. Tell my clerk to assemble the officers here immediately. You may avail yourself of my private wash room to clean yourself." He pointed to a door in the corner. Gaius saluted and turned on his heels, marching rapidly to the clerk who was hovering outside.

"I am sure you heard that, but just in case you didn't, summon the officers now!" The clerk shrank from Gaius's shouted command and scurried away, detailing a number of juniors to run into the town.

*****

Gaius returned to the tribune's office and, not wishing to disturb the senior man, crept to the wash room. Tribune Bebius ignored him as he passed, shuffling his scrolls at his desk. Inside the washroom, Gaius was confronted with his dry, wind-blasted face in an oval mirror fixed to the wall, and he looked with mild distaste at the splatter of blood and mud on his chest armour, neck and arms. He filled a basin with water from a jug and scrubbed himself with a sponge, looking into his sunken, tired eyes. Flashbacks of the desperate fight on the road crowded his memory, and the looks of fear in the eyes of his men as he gave his orders to them. The screams of the dying rang in his head, and, once clean, he shook his head to try and rid it of the sights and sounds of battle. It seemed that Adminius had not yet reported to Tribune Bebius, and maybe he would not do so if it meant admitting he had lost official correspondence in the panic.

Gaius silently rehearsed the report he knew he would soon be giving, then composed himself as the voices of officers entering the commander's office filtered through the thin door.

"Ah, Centurion Atticianus, come forward and meet your fellow officers," Tribune Flavius Lucius Bebius said in a welcoming tone, his composure fully recovered.

"Yes, sir!" Gaius replied, standing to attention. "I am Gaius Vitellius Atticianus, Centurion of Horses of the Fourth Century, Fourth Cohort, Sixth Legion, Victrix Pia Fidelis. I was sent here by Tribune Helvius Pertinax from Vindolanda which is under attack from a large force of barbarians these past two days."

He paused as the officers gasped. With late arrivals, there were now two prefects and twelve centurions in the room, including Lupus, whom Gaius had recently escorted from Habitancum Fort to the Wall. He nodded to the Senior Centurion whom he knew, Julius Flavius or 'First Spear', who was above all centurions.

"It is necessary that you speak slowly, so that my clerk can record the detail of your report," Tribune Bebius said. Gaius glanced over his shoulder at the clerk sitting at a small table in the corner of the room, stylus hovering over a wax tablet.

"Certainly, sir. But before I continue, may I ask, what action was taken upon hearing the report by Centurion Lupus Viridio of the fourth cohort? He had witnessed the gathering of the Caledonii tribes at the dun of the Selgovae king."

A look of anger flashed across the tribune's face. After glaring at Gaius for his impudence, he looked at the huge man in polished, gilded armour standing before him. "Well, First Spear, did you receive a report from this centurion of a gathering of the tribes?"

"I… did, Your Excellency, but you were otherwise detained at the time, and so I thought it could wait until our weekly briefing, scheduled for tomorrow, sir."

"Fool! Do you not recognise an important piece of intelligence when you hear it?" The tribune's cheeks turned puce again, this time with rage. "You could learn much from Centurion Atticianus here, who practically battered down my door to give me his report of hostiles approaching…" He checked himself, and his storm blew over as quickly as it had started, and he continued in a calm manner. "Right, put the entire garrison on full alert and send out your cavalry on patrols. Is there anything else we should know, Centurion Atticianus?"

Gaius cleared his throat and replied, "We were forced off the road at the estate of Magistrate Lucius Gabia…"

Tribune Bebius chuckled, cutting him short. "Ah, Fortuna guided you there. He is a friend of mine and I know his estate is built like a fortress. He convinced himself that one day barbarians would attack… and now they have. He is away in Eboracum at the courts. The walls are high and he even had corner towers built."

"Yes, Fortuna be praised, sir. We made use of the walls and towers. And with the help of his estate workers, managed to keep the savages at bay long enough to bury our payroll chest and standard, before making a staggered retreat via the river path."

"You did well, Centurion. My compliments to you for your wise actions in what must have been a grim situation. Remain behind after I dismiss the others and give the location details to my clerk. They must be recovered after we see off the barbarians."

Heads turned to the window as cries and screams were heard, and the sound of hobnail boots on cobblestones echoed from the street.

"Hurry to rouse your men and set the defences. Go!" the tribune shouted, shooing his officers out of the door. "...And send a cent to the bridgehead to secure it!" he called after his first spear, the last out. He shrunk back in his chair and turned to Gaius. "Once again, my thanks, Centurion. Now go with my clerk to the outer office and give him the details, and then re-join your men. May Fortuna's grace continue to shower you."

Gaius stood to attention and saluted. "Thank you, sir. I escorted the wife of our tribune, Claudia Pertinax, my own wife and others. I hope they have found their way to your residence, sir?"

The tribune nodded and replied, "I am going there now and shall ensure their safety. You are dismissed."

Gaius spun on his heels and marched out, followed by the scurrying clerk clutching half a dozen tablets to his chest. Gaius could see soldiers and civilians rushing about through the windows, and knew that meant the warband had been spotted.

The clerk sat and looked up, expectantly.

"We buried a chest of coins and the fourth cohort standard at the estate of Magistratus Lucius Gabia, in a grave marked with a stone in the name, Domina Drusilla Gabia," he enunciated in a slow, deliberate manner, watching the bird's nest on top of the clerk's head wobble as he made deep and deliberate indents in the soft wax. "Those are the salient facts. And now, I take my leave."

15. Vindolanda, present day

"We've found a family graveyard plot," I said to Maggie in her office on Monday morning.

"That's wonderful news!" She took off her glasses and looked up at me.

"The only thing is, it's a three-hundred-and fifty-year-old graveyard of the Sawyer family, circa William of Orange and Queen Mary period."

"Well, it's a good foundation for further investigation at a greater depth," she said, smiling. "Family burial plots in private estates are often situated at the site of earlier burials. I'll ask Mike to go with you next Saturday to do an assessment and decide whether or not you should continue."

I smiled back with a mix of relief at her positive reaction, and mild dismay that Mike might curtail our adventure. "I was worried that you would tell me to wind it up," I said, sliding into a chair.

"I've recorded your dig as exploratory based on desk research, linked to your dissertation, so you are legit. However, it mustn't turn into a huge production, and must end this term. Stick to a team of three or four and follow Richard's lead. Also, you must fill in the test pits and put it back to a condition acceptable to the property owner once you've finished. What did she have to say about your discovery?"

"She was thrilled, and hopes we'll continue to expose all the Sawyer family graves. I told her that would involve digging down at least two or three feet. She's in a local history group and is interested in giving a talk on the Sawyers, who she knows built the current house in the 1660s."

"Excellent. If nothing else, we'll get a good bit of PR out of this and a couple of articles in the local papers, perhaps even another feature in The Archaeologist Magazine. I can see you handsome boys standing beside Stuart period tombstones, clutching our latest gizmos." She stood up and came around her desk to sit facing me, lifting my hand from the arm of the chair and squeezed it between hers. "I brought back some country farm shop food and real ale from my trip home. Why don't you come over this evening? After all that exercise, I think you could do with a good meal inside you."

"Erm, yes… that would be… nice," I stammered.

"I can do 'nice' very nicely, Noah," she crooned.

I squirmed, uncomfortable. The mischief and music of our boozy night was something I wouldn't forget, but in the broad daylight of her office, I was out of my depth. I felt as if I had strayed by chance into an illicit liaison from a television drama, something unreal. Though being a games consul type, I didn't even have much experience of those. But her tone had hit its mark, and I stood to put my hands on her waist and give her a gentle kiss on the lips.

Just then, the door opened and Mavis wandered in, carrying a bound report. My hands dropped to my sides and I hoped we hadn't been noticed in a clinch. Mavis sauntered to a book shelf and pushed the report in, glanced at us and left.

"Don't look so worried," Maggie whispered. "I often come around the desk to talk to visitors. She didn't notice."

"Right. I wasn't worried. I'll be off then. See you this evening, about seven?"

"That would be perfect. See you then, my lusty lover." She smiled and squeezed my bum as I turned, before returning to her chair. I crabbed through her half-opened door and said 'bye' to Mavis, who ignored me.

*****

The following Saturday, Mike Stone drove us in his Land Rover, with two squeezed in the back with the gear.

We removed the tarpaulin over our tombstone and Mike and Richard went into a huddle to discuss the dig so far, whilst Dave and I fetched the equipment.

Once we were set up and ready to start, Mike produced a new gadget we hadn't seen before. "This little beauty is a total station instrument. It's a kind of computerised theodolite that will give us a digital plan and record 3D locations of structures and layers of any rubble."

Dave gasped in awe. "So small and yet so... useful."

"It'll save us a lot of time, for sure," Richard added.

Mike got ready to start his survey. "It'll take me an hour to scan the entire plot, and I'll have to download the data to my PC this evening and then make a print out, so for today, just peg out your second-choice test site and start digging."

We dug down to expose another Sawyer family tombstone by lunchtime, then in the afternoon, working in teams of two, we exposed three more. Some were graves with headstones, others had heavy tombstone slabs, including that of the builder of the house, James Sawyer. They were all cut from local sandstone, and the writing was chiselled onto their grey faces. A few flakes of gold in the grooves told us that the lettering had been painted over. Mike forbade us from lifting any of the tombstones.

Betty Hardcastle was thrilled, and the afternoon teas became a ritual ending to each Saturday and Sunday.

"Our ground-penetrating radar has identified some solid objects at a greater depth, to one side of the Sawyer plot," Richard informed her, scone crumbs falling from the side of his mouth. "It warrants further exploration."

"They may just be rocks," I added, "but we'd like to investigate, if that's alright with you?"

"Oh, yes. By all means, but remember that you will have to 'make good' as the builder says, once you are finished," Betty replied.

"Great. We'll be back next weekend then. Thanks again, and good luck with your Stuart period research," I said.

"Oh yes. I've a number of library books and I've been on a few websites. My talk on James Sawyer and family will be flavoured with appropriate period detail and photographs of the tombstone inscriptions. You boys must come."

"We shall be delighted," Richard said, as we took our leave.

"What did you say that for? We'll be busy cramming for our finals from spring," Dave said with a snigger once outside.

"She's our client and we've got to keep her sweet," Richard replied, nudging him.

I opened the door for Dave to slide in. "I think she said it's on a Saturday evening, so let's make an effort to attend guys. Speaking of Saturday evening presentations, Professor Maggie is giving a talk this evening in the auditorium and she'd like us to attend."

Dave guffawed before replying. "You mean she wants to see you there; teacher's pet. You'd better get scrubbed up and be on your best behaviour."

I endured their ridicule as the Land Rover chugged down the gravel driveway, the hills that separated us from the Wall looming in front of us in the weakening light of late afternoon.

*****

Two hours later, I crept into the back of the packed auditorium. Once my eyes had adjusted to the gloom, I found my way to a seat a few rows down from the last row.

"... of course, the public have this romantic notion that Hadrian's Wall was something like the Great Wall of China – wide enough to drive a four-by-four along a raised stone parapet." She paused to enjoy the laughs and take a sip of water.

"Not a bit of it. The Wall was just that - a physical barrier standing fifteen feet high and no more than ten feet wide, strung across rolling hills from the Tyne estuary in the east to the Solent estuary in the west, a distance of seventy-three miles. I should add, that some of the stretches at the western end were not walled and remained an earth bank defence. There may have been some viewing platforms erected for soldiers to stand on, although this can't be verified, in addition to watchtowers and small forts roughly every mile. It was not built just to keep hostile Caledonian raiders out of the civilised south. No, it was a grand imperial statement by the Emperor Hadrian – we are Rome, we are mighty and we are here to stay!"

She declaimed this with a wide, senatorial sweep of her arm, eliciting soft laughter. "It also represents a change in policy. No more would Rome be an empire without end. It was the result of a review of military objectives. The Romans had made excursions into the northlands, but had ultimately been defeated by climate, tough warriors whose hit-and-run tactics had frustrated them, and perhaps an economic audit that was found wanting. It was a rationalisation of resources, and a consolidation of power. We think it settled into a useful way of controlling the passage of locals, and presented an opportunity to tax those travelling with goods to market."

Maggie, formally dressed in a dark jacket with matching skirt and illuminated by spotlights that accented her strawberry hair, paused to take a question.

"How did the Romans know that this was the shortest distance from east to west coast?"

"Now that is a very good question." She squinted her eyes and put a hand over her eyebrows, like a ship's captain searching for land. "Ah, one of our keenest students has just crept in at the back. Noah, perhaps you could answer this gentleman's question?"

I gulped as all eyes turned on me and I slowly got to my feet. The lights in the auditorium were marginally undimmed. I was literally put on the spot.

"Erm... certainly, Professor Wilde. The Romans had in their ranks surveyors and cartographers, and they were keen to map our island as a prized, mineral-rich province. The ancient Greeks had worked out how to measure longitude and latitude, and the Romans often employed Greek cartographers to make their maps. Britannia appears as a triangle in the earliest maps of empire, indicating that it was known to be an island. They would have sent galleys around the north of our island at some point to map it in its entirety."

I looked over the audience of about sixty, noting I had their attention. "For military and tactical reasons, they decided to establish a northern boundary and had worked out that the narrowest point from west to east coast, south of where they would later build the Antonine Wall, was between the estuaries of the Solway and Tyne."

My words were flowing surprisingly well, reflecting my enthusiasm for the subject matter. "They built an east-to-west road just south of their new defensive line and established a series of forts along it. This road linked the established supply fort of Arbeia on the Tyne estuary in the east, to the garrison fort of Luguvalium, now Carlisle, in the west. Then years later, in 122, they upgraded the ditch and wood barrier to a stone wall, commissioned by the Emperor Hadrian. Subsequent emperors, including Antonius Pius, decided to send the legions northwards to capture more territory from the Caledonian tribes. A new northern boundary was established at the actual narrowest point on our island between the Firth of Forth and the Clyde, just thirty-nine miles, to build a second barrier, the Antonine Wall…"

"Yes, thank you Noah for the brief history lesson," Maggie cut in, dragging her audience's attention back to her.

I sat down, realising I had begun to ramble, happy for the curtailment.

"Now, in conclusion, let me say that I am humbled to have inherited the vital legacy of Robin Birley, who in 1973 discovered the first writing tablet here at Vindolanda, a discovery that revolutionised our knowledge and understanding of life at this most northerly boundary of empire. We continue to make fascinating discoveries of mundane objects such as leather shoes, clothing, weapons, even boxing gloves, in addition to the letters and reports engraved onto writing tablets that have miraculously withstood the great time lag of almost two thousand years. Our minds have been opened to the way of life of this foreign civilisation, who occupied and upgraded our island over a period of almost four hundred years, so that we can understand and appreciate which elements the Romanised Britons adopted and developed over ensuing generations." She paused to sip her water.

"Ladies and gentlemen, I am proud to be an explorer, interpreter and guardian of this important part of our cultural heritage, and look forward to many more years of enlightenment, as we continue to shine a light onto our dimly-glimpsed past, and illuminate the origins of our civilisation and shared humanity for all to see and share in the wonder. Thank you."

She fully deserved the rapturous applause, with a handful moved to stand. Her eyes shone as she found me, and my heart leapt with pride, happiness and lust. I hung around for half an hour after the audience had dispersed, then cautiously made my way to her house.

16. Coria, 180 CE

Townsfolk ran crazily through the cobbled streets, bumping into each other, most clutching bundles of goods wrapped in cloaks, some followed by whimpering children. Gaius pushed his way to the other side of the road, where he found Paulinus waiting. "I take it the blue-nosed bastards have showed up?"

"Yes, sir. But there are two warbands. The one that followed us from the west, and another horde that has come down the North Road, and is now laying siege to the north gatehouse." They pushed their way to the central square, and Gaius looked northwards, seeing the blurred outline of soldiers' helmets dotting the walls and platform above the gatehouse. To his right stood three large warehouses, holding the grain, corn and other food supplies that were to see the entire legion through the winter months.

"Did you locate my wife and son?" Gaius asked.

"Yes, sir. They are with the men at the first barrack block a couple of streets up the east way."

"Good. Then let's go there first. Then we can look for Lupus and join with the other two cents from our cohort. We will not be able to break the siege of Vindolanda until this battle is won. Lead on."

Paulinus set off at a jog, weaving around frightened market traders who hugged their goods to their chests, balanced them on their heads, or dragged them behind on trolleys. One man was driving a braying donkey before him, loaded high with boxes, and Gaius had to alter his angle of run to pass them. Paulinus stopped and turned down a narrow side street, passing running legionaries, and entered by a door into a large barrack room. The familiar smell of horses hit Gaius's nostrils, and he looked up to see gaps at the top of the gabled side wall, knowing that he had entered the cavalry barracks with the stables backing onto the bunk rooms.

"Gaius!" Aria's shrill voice cut across the murmuring. She rushed to him and threw herself into his arms. Gaius grinned from ear to ear, then kissed her warmly on the lips. His men gave a loud cheer, and he peered over her shoulder at them, giving a wink. He felt a familiar bear hug on his thigh and ruffled his son's hair.

"I am so pleased at this reunion," he said, "for after the madness of our retreat, I wondered where you might be."

"We followed the farm workers here, for safety, knowing that trouble was not far behind you," Aria replied, hugging his neck.

"Well, I have made my report, and we must now try to join with Lupus and his men. Any ideas where they might be?" he asked this over Aria's head.

"They are in an infantry barracks, two streets over, sir," one of his Gauls said.

"Then we must go and join them." He looked at Aria and asked, "Where is our tribune's wife and the prefect?"

"They are with the wife of Coria's tribune, at the commander's villa. I was invited to join them, for they have a guard."

"Then we must be parted again, my love. That is where you must go."

"But Gaius, how will we find you again?"

"I will not be far. I will find you when the fighting is done. Now, can someone escort you there?"

Amborix and his fellow auxiliary soldier stepped forward. "We will take them there and stay there as their guards, sir," Amborix said, saluting him.

"Don't go, Papa!" Brutus wailed. "I want you to play with me!"

Gaius picked him up and ruffled his sandy hair. "There will be plenty of time for play when we return to our house in Vindolanda. Now be a good boy and go with your mother to the rich lady's house. I'm sure they will have treats for you." He put Brutus down and hugged Aria, kissing her again. "Go now, and rest until this is over."

Gaius smiled as their houseslave, Marta, hobbled after them, and he briefly wondered if her husband was safe at their house in Vindolanda. Another family separated by war. He turned to Paulinus and said, "Let's go, and we also need to find the armoury, otherwise we won't have any weapons with which to kill those bastards."

"After we find old Blockhead, erm, I mean Centurion Lupus, we should think about requisitioning some horses, sir," Paulinus said as they jogged through the streets, past the stables block. "After all, we are cavalry soldiers."

Gaius grinned and focussed his mind on finding their fellow cohort units. As expected, they were not where they were billeted. Paulinus found a boy who told him they had been sent to reinforce the west gatehouse and walls. They made their way back to the central square, pushing through a stream of determined civilians who were all heading south, pushing or pulling carts, and shouting at each other as a release for their fear. Away to the north, the sounds of battle floated in gusts, war cries mixed with the screams of the wounded in a familiar cacophony of death and destruction.

"The civilians are making for the bridge," Gaius said, glancing to his left.

"They are pessimistic of our chances of holding this town." Paulinus laughed.

They had reached the west gatehouse and Gaius entered the office in search of an officer. He found Lupus there, along with another centurion, the officer of the watch.

"Gaius, it is good to see you again, although under such dire circumstances," Lupus said, grasping his forearm.

"And you, Lupus. What can you tell me of the situation?"

"Firstly, our fellow centurion and officer of the watch is Julius Numisius."

Gaius nodded at the fidgeting young man with wandering eyes.

Lupus continued, "There is a gathering host outside, come from the west. As you no doubt heard, there is a battle ranging at the north gatehouse, and we have heard they have moved around the east side, where we are lightly guarded. The first spear has led the cavalry out through the south gatehouse, to cover the civilians' exodus. They are fighting skirmishes with the mounted barbarians whose ponies made a dash for the bridge."

"How many are we facing?" Gaius asked.

"About a thousand here, probably more at the north gate. Maybe four thousand in total," Julius said, worry lines across his youthful brow.

"You are the senior man, Gaius," Lupus said. "Tell us what to do."

"Let's get up to the platform and see what's out there. Are there any ballistae or catapults?"

"Yes, we have half a dozen ballistae with plenty of sharp spikes to scatter them," Julius replied. They climbed the ladders, and soldiers made way for them at the front of the platform. "We've a mix of regulars and auxiliaries, about three hundred."

"Is that all?" Gaius looked at him in disbelief.

"In addition to the men you have brought?" Julius asked, hopefully.

"That's only a dozen, I'm sorry to report, and we'll be looking for horses soon," Gaius growled in a low voice. He looked around for his eyes - Paulinus.

His deputy stepped to his side and said, "Eight hundred of them milling around, sir. Three chariots have arrived with an escort of about thirty more riders, mainly on ponies but some on horses, no doubt with imperial brands on their rumps. Away to the left, our cavalry is chasing off about forty pony riders, with quite a few of their mates dead on the pretty meadow, sir."

Julius looked quizzically at Lupus, who pointed to his eye with a snigger.

"So, the big chiefs have come," Gaius said, "and brought their regalia." He pointed to the tall horn with a dragon's head and gaping mouth that emitted a nerve-shredding battle call and was marched up and down in front of the rowdy warriors, thus hoping to counter any thoughts of blindness from his colleagues.

Paulinus nodded. "They even have banner-bearers carrying animal faces at the centre of those swirling patterns they love so much, sir. It's an imitation native legion alright."

Gaius replied, "This is no smash-and-grab raid. They've come for the grain and the horses, and perhaps to try and capture the fort and occupy it." He turned to his fellow centurions and added, "You'd better close your mouth, Julius, before the flies get in. And look like you're ready and know what you're doing in front of the men."

"But no native army has ever captured a fort this big on this island," Julius spluttered.

"Not since the Iceni uprising. We'd better do everything we can to prevent it," Gaius replied, leaning forward, hands gripping the rail. "First things first. Let's make sure the entire length of wall under our command is manned and the soldiers have plenty to throw or loose at them. We need the baskets of rocks filled up, and all the javelins you can find from the armoury."

Julius saluted and disappeared down the ladder.

"I'll put my men on the southern stretch, where there appear to be fewer guards, and you take charge of the northern stretch, Lupus. Julius can man this platform and direct the ballistae. Let's get them ready for a possible attack." Gaius would rather have been outside, fighting with the cavalry, but for now he would have to stay here, to see how it played out. The barbarians had come for a reason, and would not want to hang about. His instincts told him that an attack on the walls was imminent.

As if on cue, the chiefs took off to the north, followed by their guard.

"No doubt to ride around the fort and count the numbers on the walls," he muttered as he made his rounds. Some young men were milling around, hoping to get involved. Gaius told them to collect all the rocks they could find and fill up the baskets on the walkways. Soon, men came running from the armoury with javelins, spears, bows and arrows, long bolts for the ballistae, swords and even some helmets for the civilians who had stayed. Gaius shook his head, wondering if young Julius would have thought of making such preparations.

"We've really been caught with our trews down," Gaius commented to Paulinus as he strode along the battlements to check on how well his men were armed.

When the attack came, it was a coordinated assault form three sides. The warriors had ladders for the walls, and leapt across the dry ditch with disappointing ease. On the west wall, Gaius, Paulinus and Lupus yelled their defiance. Soon, Julius could be heard asserting himself from the platform. The first volley of javelins and arrows found about a quarter of their targets, adding the screams of the wounded to the noise of battle. By the time the second volley hit them, the warriors had reached the ditch and some bodies fell into it, but not enough to hamper the determined advance.

"Push the ladders back!" Gaius and Paulinus yelled as a dozen flimsy ladders were placed against the walls. Archers in the south-west corner tower, under another commander, loosed their arrows downwards to supplement the effort at the extremity of Gaius's command, but the warriors continued to stream across the ditch and follow the man ahead up a ladder. The civilian levy threw rocks, cheering whenever they knocked a blue painted warrior off a ladder. Gaius and Paulinus also joined in with javelin throws.

A battering ram was now being wheeled towards the gate.

Gaius yelled, "Bring pitch!" and sprinted to the ladder up to the gatehouse platform. "Julius, we must make fire balls for the ballistae and try to light-up that tree on wheels!"

They had left it late, as the ram was already within fifty paces. Ballistae released smooth birchwood shafts with barbed spikes at the end, piercing the bodies of some of the burly warriors selected for the task of pushing it, their screams serving to intensify the efforts of the enemy. In a few minutes, civilians appeared at the top of the two ladders with pots of black, sticky pitch.

"Wrap material, from ripped cloaks if necessary, around the tips of the bolts," Gaius commanded, as Julius looked on, his face a picture of the cluelessness of inexperience. There were three ballistae on the top platform, and each had burning bolts fitted. "Release all three at the log on my command."

With a whoosh, the three ballistae let loose their flaming loads, giving the men on the battlements something to cheer, as two of them buried their points in the thick wood. This had the desired effect of stopping the forward momentum, as the enemy made efforts to put out the fires with their cloaks. They were sitting targets now, within range of both archers and long javelin throws. Gaius looked on with grim satisfaction as the battering-ram pushers were ravaged by arrows and javelins, falling back behind the giant tree on enormous wooden wheels. Behind them, a shaman was leaping and dancing, shaking his fists in fury at the Romans.

With concern, Gaius looked to his left and right, as some warriors had succeeded in jumping onto the battlements, and desperate duels broke out along the narrow platform. The first casualties were suffered, as auxiliary guards, regular soldiers and the odd civilian fell to the ground, dying or maimed by sword, spear or axe blows. Where they had secured access, they defended their ladder heads fiercely, and more warriors streamed up, running to left and right in a blur of blue and red on white, tattooed flesh, along the platform.

The battering ram was once more moving, now spiked with ballistae bolts and arrows, the fires put out. With a crash it hit the double gates. Its crew turned and pushed it away, as many fell from arrows, javelins or rocks thrown down on their unprotected bodies. Where men had fallen, more came forward to take their place.

"Keep the men throwing and loosing arrows until they are spent, then form a shield unit behind the gates," Gaius shouted to Julius, then slapped his shoulder and added, "May the gods be with you."

He shinnied down the ladder to the battlements and rushed to the aid of Paulinus, who was battling an axe-wielding flame-haired fiend. The platform was wide enough for two men, and Gaius stood beside his deputy with his sword outstretched, jabbing at the warrior's unguarded side. Their furious opponent, eyes wide with battle rage, ignored the wound and brought his axe crashing into Paulinus' shield, inflicting a deep gash in the thin wood, and earned a groan from the Gaul as his arm took the force. Gaius lunged again, driving deeper between the man's ribs, causing him to buckle and groan. Paulinus tossed the damaged shield aside and drove his sword into the man's neck. He fell to his knees, and Paulinus kicked him off the platform.

"I had that," he snarled at his commander.

"I know, but we don't have all day!" Gaius grinned in return. "Let's try to clear this platform." The two veterans charged ahead, slashing and bashing warriors off the platform. Below, teams of soldiers and townsfolk were waiting with knives, spears and swords to finish off the wounded or drag their own wounded to the care of others behind. Paulinus picked up a discarded legionary shield and put it to good use, ignoring his aching and cut arm. Soon, they were the only ones left on the platform, facing a dozen angry, snarling warriors, and they found their movement going backwards, pushed by a determined press.

"I don't fancy the jump!" Gaius yelled.

"You slide down the ladder and I'll be right behind you," Paulinus replied, as the pair retreated with practised shield-punch followed by sword jab until they reached the gatehouse. With a quick glance, Gaius sheathed his sword and jumped down the ladder, sliding with his hands and feet on the outside. Paulinus pushed back with all his might against two warriors and followed the move. An axe hit his helmet a glancing blow, but he shrugged it off.

On the ground, things had deteriorated. Warriors were jumping from the platform and fighting was all around the pair. The gates had been breached, and men were squeezing through a narrow gap to throw themselves on the shield tortoise ten shields wide and deep that was waiting.

Gaius shouted to Paulinus to gather their men together. Most were still alive, including a blood-splattered Meral with half a dozen Sarmatians at his side, and an equal number of Gauls.

"Fall back and form a line between the first buildings on the main road!" Gaius yelled. His men reacted quickly, still fighting off warriors, who ran about with wide-eyed menace looking for someone to kill. Soldiers from other units followed, and soon Gaius stood behind a line thirty-wide, with a similar number beside him. In front of their shield wall, Julius and his tortoise were surrounded, with warriors bashing and hacking at the legionary shields in fury. To their left and right, warriors had won the space next to the walls, finishing off groaning wounded in the blood-stained dirt.

"Let's rescue them," Gaius shouted, to cheers. He sent Paulinus to the left edge and Meral to the right, with instructions to cover the flanks of the central unit, forming walls facing north and south. On his command, the central section moved forward in two lines, jogging towards the warriors who had their backs to them. In short time, they were killed and their bodies stepped over as the relief unit reached the tortoise.

"Julius! Fall back!" Gaius yelled. The two lines of shields parted, and the wounded and officers at the centre of the tortoise moved back along a corridor. Julius passed Gaius with a relieved nod. "Keep going to the street and re-form the wall!" Gaius yelled after him.

The soldiers melded together, forming a solid wall of shields, and slowly moved backwards. Some soldiers fell with screams, pierced by sword or spear thrusts through cracks in the shield wall, but were quickly replaced by others.

The north and south sides collapsed to the centre and soon formed a solid wall of shields, three-deep, facing the enemy. Gaius directed soldiers from the rear rank to cover the side streets, as the defensive line edged slowly backwards in the direction of the central square.

"It's hopeless, sir!" Paulinus shouted, "Like trying to hold back a ruptured dam."

More warriors had now come through the shattered gates and their numbers had swelled to a deadly host. The west side of the town was lost, but what of the north and east? Gaius bit his lip as he edged backwards, feeling helpless and concerned for the safety of his family. Half way down the street, he could see warriors running towards them along side roads. He was aware of cries and screams coming from the northern quarters to his right, and noticed curls of black smoke rising to the darkening sky. They passed the commander's office, now deserted with doors left wide open.

"Retreat to the Square!" Gaius shouted and turned to run. Two thoughts dogged his mind – he must get to the tribune's house to check if his wife and son were still there, and they must keep a corridor open to the south gates for an orderly retreat. At the square he was confronted with a scene of chaos. The north street was filled with noisy warriors, pushing against a retreating shield wall, similar to their own. Over the heads of the soldiers and warriors, he saw sacks of grain being carried on heads towards the north gate. A frightened horse bolted into the square to add to the panic. He looked around for the red plumage of centurions and saw only four. The east and south roads were still open, although there was fighting around the east gatehouse, so Gaius moved to the fountain and shouted for the centurions to join him. He ordered Julius's men to hold the west side of the square and sent Paulinus and the Gaul contingent to the tribune's house in the far south-east corner to look for the civilians.

"If you find them," he yelled, "make your way through the south gate to the bridge." The centurions were gathering around him, and Gaius noted that the first spear was not there.

"My friends, we must keep the south road open for an orderly retreat to the bridge. There are too many of them within for us to hold the town."

"Surely we cannot abandon the town to these savages!" a blood-stained centurion holding a cut-wound on his bicep said.

"They are within on three sides, with greater numbers," Gaius replied. "If we stay and fight, we will be

174

surrounded and slaughtered. Our best option is to withdraw and defend the north bridgehouse."

"You cannot know that," the wounded veteran commented through gritted teeth.

"We are five. We must decide now," Gaius said, looking into the eyes of the others. Julius and Lupus were quick to nod their assent, and the others soon gave in.

"Right," Gaius said. "We must send a squad to the east gatehouse and tell them to retreat to the south gatehouse, holding the enemy back as they go."

One of the centurions he did not know nodded.

"Good, take twenty men and go now." The man saluted and jogged off to find his men. Gaius turned to Julius and Lupus and said, "We must withdraw the western and northern units across the square and make an orderly retreat down the south road."

Gaius eyed the wounded centurion and said, "My friend, can you move to the south gatehouse and tell the commander there of our plan?"

His blood-shot eyes and weary face flinched; he understood he was being sent from the field of battle. "As you wish," he replied in a quiet voice.

"Then let us go to our positions, and may Mars watch over our retreat!" They drew swords and touched them in a circle of brotherhood, then turned and ran to their men.

The situation had deteriorated, and the plan to leave the stricken town was clearly the most sensible option. Fire now raged in the north-western quadrant, and any unfortunate soldiers or townsfolk behind enemy lines were a lost cause, as they were faced with noisy hordes to north and west, banging on their small, square shields, sounding dragon horns and chanting the names of their gods or chiefs.

Gaius waved his sword at the centurion to the north and they both ordered their men to fall back to the southside of the square. Such manoeuvres in the face of a lively, determined and blood-thirsty enemy are seldom smooth, and many soldiers went down as one-on-one fighting broke out across the square. Gaius blanched as one of his Gauls fell before him, an arrow protruding from his neck, beneath the impassive gaze of open-mouthed bronze dolphins. Warriors were running amok, and an unfortunate legionary was seized by two crazed warriors, who dragged him to the fountain pool and pushed his head under the water. Gradually, the ragged lines of shield men fell back to block the entrance to the south road, letting their comrades squeeze through gaps and turn to form a second line, with shouts of encouragement to their mates ringing in the cool evening air. Gaius grinned at three civilian youths with ill-fitting helmets on and bloody spears in hand, squeezing through the gap and joining the rear rank.

They were losing men at a steady rate as the shield wall edged backwards down the road towards the hoped-for sanctuary of the south gatehouse. One of Gaius's men met him at the south gatehouse, holding a horse for him, and telling him the civilians had been evacuated before the attack had reached the tribune's house. Paulinus had gone to look for them at the bridge. Gaius thanked him and led the horse outside, mounting it and waiting for the men to exit the fort. Torches lit the road to the bridge, as the darkening sky brooded over a day of anguish and bloodshed. Coria was lost.

17. Vindolanda, present day

After four weekends, we had fully exposed the Sawyer family plot and had moved onto the cleared area between it and the screen of trees that stood before the fence. Richard came with the print outs by Mike Stone of his 3D scan of the entire corner plot bounded on two sides by the fence, and now studied them.

I peered over his shoulder. "This is most likely our last weekend, so let's make it a productive one."

"These fainter readings are at deeper depths, and may give us our best chance of Roman remains," Dave said, pointing to shaded blobs on the paper.

"Then let's work in teams of two, and have two excavations," Richard advised. "I'll pair with Russ and start on this one nearest where the old wall would have been. We'll take a break when we reach our first split level at half a metre."

"OK," I agreed, "Dave and I will start on this one nearest the Sawyer plot."

"At half a metre, I'll run the metal detector over them and see if we get a reading." Dave had finally convinced Richard to let him use the equipment.

By lunchtime, both were down two levels to a metre depth and about four-square metres wide, but neither pit gave any reading on the metal detector. We munched our sandwiches and discussed the best use of our dwindling time.

"Let's abandon those excavations and move onto new ones," Richard suggested. "We're now focussing on finding metal readings at a metre depth."

Mattocks were needed to break up the soil and small stones, tough work for young men not used to labouring.

"My blisters have got blisters," Dave moaned, shaking his hand as if it would somehow help relieve the nagging pain.

A strangled cry went up from Richard's site, and he stood tall, shouting, "Come quick! Russ has fallen through a hole!"

Dave and I clambered out of our pit and ran across.

"It's Russ, the earth gave way under him and he's fallen through!" Richard pointed to a black hole next to him, about three feet across.

"Russ! Can you hear us?" Dave shouted into the black cavern. No reply at first, then a faint groan, echoing in the unknown space.

"I'll get the rope," I said, and ran to our supply of gear that we kept in a trailer under a tarpaulin so we didn't have to keep going back to the gardener's shed. I rummaged through it and grabbed thirty yards of rope, a ball of nylon twine and a flashlight.

"Is he talking yet?" I asked on my return, noting they had widened the hole.

Richard wrung his hands in concern. "Yes, he's conscious and can hear us. He's hurt his leg in the fall. He's about two metres down, in some sort of crypt, I think."

I lay down on the edge of the hole and had a look below with the flashlight. Russ was curled up in a foetal position about two metres down. "We've got a rope Russ, we'll have you out in no time," I shouted to him. He acknowledged by raising his arm.

I turned to the others and said, "I can see him. Yes, a crypt, with six tombs. Probably once a structure partly underground. It's lined with stone slabs. The roof's supported by wooden beams."

Dave had tied one end of the rope around the nearest tree, and the other end around his waist. "Lower me down. I'll tie the rope around him and you can haul him up."

178

"Take the camera and get some shots of the tombs before you come back up," I said, handing over my digicam. "This might be our only chance."

"Quite right, Indiana Jessop. Let's not pass up any opportunity." He shook his head, but took the camera and slung it round his neck.

As if on cue, the fragile roof started to creak. We lowered Dave down, gagging on the fetid air that escaped an age of entombment, and in a minute, Richard and I were hauling Russ to the surface. I untied him and threw the rope down to Dave. We helped a grateful Russ out of the excavation pit. He was covered in damp, dark soil, his eyes blinking at us like a coal miner who's come off shift.

How's the leg?" I asked. "Can you move it?"

"Yes," he groaned, "just a sprained ankle. Nothing broken."

"Good man. You might go down in history for this find."

"I've taken pictures of the inscriptions on the tombs," Dave called up. "Now pull me up, this thing is about to collapse!" The rest of the flimsy roof started to give way as we hauled him up, extracting him just as it gave way.

"Wow," I said as we all sat panting hard. I had to let the blood pounding in my ears settle for a minute. "Another burial from another age, I don't doubt. I can't wait to read those inscriptions this evening."

"How do you feel, Russ?" Richard asked. "Do you want to go to the hospital to have that looked at?"

"Na, it's alright, man. Don't fuss," he replied, massaging his ankle. "It's just a sprain. We're on a roll here and there's still two hours of daylight."

"I admire your explorer's spirit," I said, "but maybe we should call it a day."

Dave wiped mud from his hands. "How about a compromise. I've got a feeling in my bones. Let's level off our excavation and I'll make a sweep of it with the detector."

Richard seemed unsure. "I'll document this underground crypt find, but I see no harm in you continuing with your excavation."

I picked up my shovel and flexed my shoulders, before hunkering down and lifting the stony earth from our next site. In twenty minutes, excavation pit number four was level and ready. I climbed out to take a break, and Dave switched on the metal detector and jumped in.

It whined gently as it powered up and he put on the headphones, then gripped the handle and made slow sweeps of the base. In barely thirty seconds he pulled off the headphones and yelled, "Here! I've got something!" He pressed one cup of the headphone to my ear and made a sweep of the flat disc an inch above the soil.

I grinned and shouted over to Richard. "It's a metallic contact!"

Richard left Russ sitting on a folding chair with his report, and came over. Dave handed him the headphone and he listened, then laughed. "It's a hit alright, a very palpable hit! I think it's worth digging down to check it out."

Dave completed his sweep and clambered out, whilst Richard jumped in with the mattock and attacked the ground. I took up the shovel and threw out the soil and stones with renewed vigour.

In half an hour, Dave made another sweep with the detector and laughed as he pulled off the headphones. "There's definitely a big source of metal just another half metre down, I reckon, and I'm not talking one or two coins."

The sun had ducked behind a grey cloud and we noticed how murky it had become. "We're losing the light, lads," I said, shovelling as fast as my aching arms permitted. Can someone take over." I climbed out, no easy feat as the excavation was about two metres, and we'd had to widen it.

Russ had moved his chair to the edge and handed me a drink. "I wish I could help," he said.

"You've just had a near-death experience, mate. Enough excitement for one day, I'd say." I looked at the sinking sun. "Betty'll be sending out a search party soon."

"I've got something!" Richard shouted, tapping the end of his shovel in the soil. He got onto his knees and cleared the crumbly peat away, revealing the rotting top of a wooden box, held by two metal brackets. Dave dug away at one end, and Richard at the other, revealing a chest. "Alright, let's leave it undisturbed whilst I get some photos. We'll have to cover it with the tarpaulin and get Mike here in the morning to advise us on our next move. Noah, get the rule and measure it, please."

I groaned at the prospect of leaving it in the ground without sating my curiosity over whether or not it might be Gaius's payroll chest. I measured it to be 60cms by 40cms.

"It's a box of some sort, but the wood will quickly disintegrate in the air," Richard said. "Let's photograph it then get it covered and as airtight as possible."

A low growl announced the arrival of Betty's two hounds, who thankfully were familiar with our scent. Betty followed soon after, with a powerful flashlight in one hand and a walking stick in the other. She was agog at our news, and then disappointed to find that proceedings had to be halted, for now.

"This could just about have worked out perfect," Dave said, slapping me on the shoulder and gasping for breath in the cool night air. An owl hooted and a couple of nightjars swooped close by, as if to see what all the fuss was about.

I looked in the direction of the soft-winged raptor. "Owls may have been unlucky for the Romans, but not for us." My mind was a whirl of questions. "If they'd buried the chest in a grave that was already dug, wouldn't it be deeper?"

Richard shrugged. "Possibly, unless it was a work in progress and only a metre deep. We would expect to find Roman remains at between two to three metres. They may have been in a hurry and just covered it with a thin layer of soil."

"There may be a metal finial down there from the top of a cohort standard, whose shaft and material would have rotted," I said, watching the stars come out over the tops of the trees.

"We're not going back down there now, Noah," he replied.

"Betty's lending you her walking stick, Russ," Dave said, handing it over to his friend. "Will you be able to hobble to the house?"

"Yes, sure. I'll live to tell my tale."

After packing away the garden equipment and carrying our own back to the vehicle, we congregated under the motion spotlights in front of the house.

"From what period do you think that chest might be?" Betty asked, ushering us indoors for tea and cakes.

Dave and I exchanged looks before I replied. "We had heard a rumour that there might be Roman graves in this area, so we dug to two metres. Then we got a reading on the metal detector. We won't know what it is until it's excavated."

"And we made another discovery of a collapsed crypt. That will require further excavation," Richard added, biting into a slice of homemade fruit cake. "With your permission, we'd like to bring Mike Stone back tomorrow for his expert opinion. These look like major finds."

Betty nodded her agreement. "Of course. Major discoveries from different eras on my land. I could be writing a book soon!"

"They'll make you president of your society," Russ said, rubbing his shin.

Dave ummed with pleasure as he chewed. "They should elect you president just for this fruit cake, Betty."

"How is your leg, Russell?" Betty asked.

"It's not as bad now. Just a sprain. I'll be alright."

"Yeah, that's three discoveries over four weekends, possibly from three different time periods," I said. "We should all get distinctions for this."

*****

The following day, we took two vehicles to the Hardcastle Farm. Maggie was intrigued enough by my breathless account of our find to re-schedule her plans and both she and Mike Stone joined us. When Maggie congratulated Richard on his report, I felt a twinge of jealousy.

Betty all but curtsied when I introduced her to Maggie. "What an honour to meet you, Professor Wilde. I've seen you on television and now here you are at Hardcastle Farm!"

"It's lovely to meet you, Mrs. Hardcastle. Thank you for hosting us. I'm so excited by their finds in your tiered graveyard. Now, let's take a look at the excavation."

Maggie, Mike and Richard huddled next to the site where the chest had been exposed, pouring over the digital plan and muttering as they passed around photographs and context records. Dave, Russ and I unloaded our equipment and wheelbarrowed garden tools from the shed. After the two new sites had been excavated, we would record them before filling in the pits with layers of substrata rocks and soil.

Soon we were ready to start, working on both sites in two teams. The main excavation team would record the careful exhumation of the wooden chest and its contents, with Maggie supervising Richard, Russ and myself. Mike and Dave would focus on examining and recording the part-buried crypt. Betty and a friend from the historical society agreed to assist with photography and fetch any equipment we requested from our mobile store.

"Suits and gloves on," Maggie said, and we duly complied.

"I've always wanted to be in an episode of CSI," Dave whispered, getting into his white one piece.

Maggie talked us through the stages, and she recorded our progress in the context record. After removing the tarpaulin, we carefully dug around the chest, gradually exposing it to its base.

My mouth was dry from the point that the tarpaulin was removed. I had dreamed in the early hours that Betty's slobbering hounds had dug up a skull from the crypt, and had awoken in a sweat. I took this as a sign of my anxiety that the chest would have deteriorated further by the time we lifted it. Actually, to my great relief, it still looked the same.

Is this chest what I'm looking for? Is it evidence to support my translation of the fragmented sentences I've pored over? Did Gaius, my centurion, plant his feet where I am now?

Snapping back to practical thoughts, I measured the chest's dimensions before photographing it. I was desperate to see inside, but that wouldn't happen on site.

Mike joined Maggie and Richard to discuss the best method of extracting it. Their conclusion was to prevent the sides from collapsing by wrapping it with special thickness clingfilm, then burrowing under it to make two trenches that expandable thick plastic skis could be passed under. I had not seen this specialist lifting kit before, and marvelled at how it fitted together as it was passed under the chest.

After taking a break for snacks and drinks, we assembled a hoist that had come on a flatbed truck and was clearly Mike's pride and joy. "A team of four can lift a load weighing half a tonne with this!"

Maggie laughed. "Even if it's full of coins, as Noah hopes, it won't weigh that much."

We winched the chest to the surface, swinging it onto a sturdy trolley and securing it. Betty had reversed her mini-tractor along the path, and she towed the trolley to the truck, accompanied by an escort of two clucking students. I marvelled at how smooth the operation had been. Mike and Dave had also finished making a detailed record of the crypt, which was to be re-buried. After another tea break, we returned to fill in the pits and level off the site.

"Let the dead rest in peace," Mike said solemnly, patting down the last pit. We were leaving behind a level patch of dark brown soil slightly lower than the grass around it.

Betty stood with feet apart, hands on hips. "I'll lawn it and have a stone memorial made. That seems fitting. I'll include relevant plaques to the deceased. You'll all be invited to the unveiling." Despite her brusque, business-like front, I had seen how she was moved when we found gravestones with names on.

Once at Vindolanda, we didn't say our goodbyes and disperse until the chest had been locked away, temporarily in the equipment shed. There was something of an air of anti-climax in returning home empty handed, except one of us wasn't. Back in our room, Russ, Richard and I gathered around Dave to look at the gold coin he had found beside the chest. It was an Emperor Hadrian gold aureus and the detail was extraordinarily clear once cleaned, as if it had recently been minted.

"Do Maggie or Mike know you found it?" I asked.

Dave shook his head.

I picked it up from his palm and turned it over, revealing the goddess Disciplina on the obverse, leading a line of three soldiers, one carrying a legion standard. "One of Hadrian's priorities was to improve discipline in the ranks, so he had a number of coins minted with Disciplina to get the message across to his soldiers. It's a beautiful coin, alright."

Richard examined it. "You should really declare this to Professor Wilde. Maybe she'll let you keep it."

"Sounds like a fifty percent chance that I'll lose it."

Richard maintained a serious tone. "It's your call, Dave, but if you want to stick to best practice..."

Dave looked glum and wrapped his fingers around the coin. "Alright then. In the spirit of following laid down archaeological procedure, I'll show it to her tomorrow. But for this evening, we can gawp at it."

"We can do more than that," I said, taking it from him. "I'm going to photograph both sides of it on a sheet of white paper. It's something we can use in our presentations."

*****

Mavis was outside the office door the next morning, rummaging for her keys in her bag, when the appearance of Mike started her. She looked around in further surprise to see four young men carrying a box wrapped in polythene on a board.

"What's going on here, then?" she crooned in her soft Scottish accent, turning the key and pushing the outer office door open.

"The lads found something over the weekend. We excavated it yesterday, and now it needs to be entered into the stores log," Mike replied with a self-satisfied smile.

"The professor's not here yet, but bring it in," Mavis replied. We pushed the chest through the door on its trolley, still wrapped in clingfilm. "Off you go, she'll send for you when she's ready," she said, shooing us out of the door.

"But..." I objected.

Outside again, she closed the door on us.

186

Mike looked thoughtful, hands on hips. "I've got to start up the dig, but I think one of you should stay, despite what Mavis says, to hand it over to the prof."

"Yeah, I'll stay," I said. "See you guys later."

"Then here's the coin to give to her," Dave said glumly, placing it into my hand.

"You're doing the right thing, Dave. Fingers crossed she'll let you have it."

I stood outside, and after five minutes Maggie came, bustling towards the door.

"Hi Noah, want to see me?" she asked. She looked bleary-eyed, as if she'd just woken up and rushed in.

"Hi Maggie. We've brought the chest, but Mavis shooed me out. I wanted to hand it over."

"Come in, first thing's first – I could do with a coffee." We entered and found Mavis beside the chest with a Stanley knife in her hand, about to cut a hole in the polythene.

"Morning Mavis," Maggie said. "Please don't cut the polythene wrapping. It's an extremely fragile artefact of unknown age and must only be unpacked in a controlled laboratory environment. Can you make two coffees please. Come through, Noah."

We exchanged frowns at Mavis's enthusiasm to cut into the chest's wrappings. "Does she usually open new finds?"

"She knows she's not to disturb anything that comes in wrapped, and in any case, she should have cotton gloves on when handling any artefacts. I'll talk to her later. Sit."

She closed her door and gave me a hug. "I had to stop myself doing this when we lifted the chest out. You've had a busy and productive weekend."

"I looked at the pictures of the inscriptions on the tombs in the crypt last night and have seen enough to note they were in medieval Latin, so perhaps a Norman family vault. I've already emailed the photos to you," I added with a smile.

"Great. I'll look at those later."

"I'd love to be there when the chest is opened. Is that possible?"

She crinkled her nose. Bad news. "I have to report it to the trustees and the Chief Executive. They'll decide where and when it'll be opened. It might have to go as it is to the British Museum. I'll download and compile all the photos first, then summarise the excavation."

I groaned at this prospect. I might never see inside it. "Dave picked this up from the chest pit. He cleaned it off last night in our dorm. He wants you to know it's the only item found in the pits before they were filled in." I handed her the Hadrian Aureus.

She arched her eyebrows and examined it. "An almost perfect coin. Completely unblemished. Very nice."

"He wonders if it's inconsequential enough to let him keep it?"

"I'll hang on to it now and include it in my report. I'll also make a request to allow it to be returned to the finder. That decision can be made by a museum curator, based on whether or not they already have one in such good condition. You never know. Tell him to cross his fingers. They may keep this and give him a less perfect version."

She took off her glasses and sat back in her chair, regarding me with a smile. "I'm amazed at this find, Noah. Your desk research and hunch paid off spectacularly. This is so rare. Often it takes years to follow the clues to a location and make a find. Very often, not finding anything. Extraordinary. The gods have certainly smiled on you."

"I'm delighted with the way the excavation went, and we've all learned so much from Richard, Mike and yourself. But I'll be on tenterhooks until I know what's in that chest."

"You're such a quick learner, Noah." She stood and came around the desk. "I've had a stressful weekend and I wouldn't mind a shoulder rub this evening," she said in a husky voice, holding my limp hand. "You're cold."

"Yes, I stood outside for five minutes, waiting for you, after Mavis chased us all out."

She tutted. "That was uncharitable of her. Off you go to warm up. It seems the coffee we ordered will not be arriving."

I stood and gave her a peck on the cheek. "I'll call you this afternoon for an update on the chest and come over to your place after I've had dinner with my mates. They'll want an update as well."

"Of course. Let's speak later. We're starting the final week before the Christmas recess, so we'll need to discuss your dissertation before Friday."

"Yes. I've a lot to do this week before we all take a break. Speak later."

I edged past Mavis, who was still over the chest with a notebook and not brewing coffee. Outside, I made my way to the dorm room to get my notes, before going to the archives to tell Sima the news. I felt I was walking on clouds and now had photos of a lucky gold coin to inspire me. The chest had been the crowning glory of my six weeks practical at Vindolanda, and would make for a great centrepiece for my dissertation. I didn't mind the prospect of three weeks at home with my family. Bring on the Christmas festivities, and the opportunity for a good rest.

18. Coria, 180 CE

The River Tine Bridgehead was a scene of chaos. Civilians were corralled in a fretful crowd, made to wait their turn to cross the bridge in an orderly line by keen legionaries, who would glance up periodically at the glowing skyline above their burning town on the hill. There was no rush. The Caledonii were busy looting the town of all that had been left behind before it burnt to the ground. Some were hooting and hollering at the line of silent Roman cavalry below them, from the walls they now commanded.

The first spear, on his grey stallion, was staring up at a row of bare buttocks flaunted from the battlements, flanked by Gaius and another centurion. "You know these bastards better than us, centurion, what do you think their next move will be?" he asked Gaius.

The rugged Asturian answered in a measured tone. "They will send the grain and other foods north on wagons with an escort. The rest might want more fun and goad us to attack them." Above the gatehouse a row of severed Roman heads was now displayed on the points of spears.

"If only we had more men," the first spear groaned. "If I had two cavalry cents, I would send one north to attack their wagon train."

"You have a hundred and twenty, including my dozen, sir," Gaius replied. "It would be a bold move to send sixty to take them on, although we could at least scout them?"

The senior centurion looked down at Gaius, his square jaw set below hard, black pinpricks that had intimidated many soldiers and junior officers on parade grounds across the empire. "My place is here, centurion, guarding the bridgehead and overseeing our orderly retreat south of the river. Will you lead your men and fifty of mine to track the enemy northwards? Use your judgement on whether to engage or not."

Gaius wondered if he had ever asked, as opposed to commanded, a junior officer to take on a dangerous assignment. When lives are at stake, men naturally become cautious, some indecisive. "Aye sir, I will," Gaius replied, "but first, may I ride to the bridge and look for my wife and son? I would see them to safety first."

"Yes, go now and I will prepare my men."

Gaius rode down the road to the bridge, followed by his dozen who had managed to find mounts. They had left Vindolanda with forty, Gaius reflected, but now were reduced to twelve, although he hoped the eight wounded had been evacuated. In one day. And the day was not yet over.

Paulinus pointed to Amborix waving a white cloth on a spear. "Sir, they are by the guardhouse," he shouted to his squinting commander. Night had come down, but the scene by the bridge was well-lit with torches planted in the ground or held high by milling townsfolk. Paulinus led the riders to the guardhouse and Gaius jumped from his horse to be reunited with Aria again.

"We must stop meeting like this, my dear," he joked, squeezing her tight and kissing her upturned face.

"As long as you keep coming back to me, my love," she replied.

"How is the boy?"

"Tired. He is sleeping within with Marta. What is to happen, my love?"

"You will cross the bridge to a tented village they are erecting. Make sure the soldiers know you are the wife of a centurion, and you will be fed and accommodated. I must scout the barbarians, but I will find you soon." He smiled at her with all the confidence he could muster.

Gaius called Amborix to him. "My thanks, Amborix, for guarding my wife and son. They are my priceless treasures, and I ask you to stay with them through this vexing time."

"It is my honour to serve you, sir," Amborix replied, flicking his curling nut-brown hair away from his eyes.

"Then I must go. Cross the bridge when you can and seek out the officer in charge. Ask to be led to the tribune and use my name. Tell him I am leading a scouting party to the north and I commend my wife and child to his care."

Gaius turned to give Aria a kiss.

"Drink, my love, and take these cakes," Aria said, pressing a gourd into his hand and pushing food wrapped in torn linen into his belt pouch.

Gaius drank deeply, realising how thirsty he was, then kissed her forehead and turned to leap into his saddle. He led his men in a circle around the civilian scrum, up the hill towards the burning fort.

*****

Snow crunched under the hooves of a string of silent riders, wrapped in cloaks, following an animal track between bare branches reaching upwards in search of a warmer sun. They were tracking a slow-moving convoy of wagons escorted by forty riders on shaggy piebald ponies, and led by a solitary chariot pulled by a team of two black horses. Low, grey clouds scudded across a half-moon that gave occasional glimpses of their quarry from the high ground above the arrow-straight road.

"That traitor, Kerwyn, is scouting ahead for them," Paulinus said in puffs of breath clouds.

Gaius nodded, watching his former scout ride to the chariot and report. "We are close to the Wall now," Gaius replied. "It's there that we'll attack. Let's ride ahead and look for cover."

They steered their horses away from the road, out of sight and sound behind a row of hills that pointed the way north, rising and falling like the scaly back of a dragon, towards the Wall. The horses welcomed being kicked into a canter, tossing their heads and shaking snowflakes from their manes and tails. Soon they reached the last of the hills, and stopped, within sight of the white caps on top of the towers and turrets of the great, grey Wall of Hadrian, barely four hundred paces ahead.

"Send a scout ahead to see if they've got any men at the gate fort, but tell him he must make sure he is not seen," Gaius instructed Paulinus, rubbing his hands and then breathing into them. "When the first wagon goes past, we'll ride out and attack – tell the men to get ready for combat."

The horses stamped their feet on the cold ground as their riders bunched together for warmth, to chat and share a bite to eat. The cavalry regulars from Coria had seen little action, and were keen to find live targets for their javelins. The Gauls boasted of their attack on the barbarians at Vindolanda, making claims and counter-claims for the numbers they had killed.

"They're an untrained rabble on slow, small ponies," one said, "easy pickings, lads. Just get a couple of throws off, then draw your swords and slash at the vermin as you pass, then wheel and continue until they're all dead."

When the guffaws died, another added, "Remember your mates whose heads are decorating the walls of Coria."

After ten minutes, Paulinus spread the word to make ready. Cloaks were tucked under bums to free their arms, and shields were untied from their positions on their backs, the snow brushed off and fitted to non-throwing arms. The Sarmatians nocked their arrows and waited for the command to attack.

The command, when it came, was a silent wave of the arm, and the riders kicked their mounts into a trot, then canter, then a charge, following Gaius and Paulinus who swung out to the right. The riders fell into a line and rode swiftly over uneven tufts protruding from a light covering of snow across open ground. The clouds had moved on and Luna now bore witness to the impending slaughter. Cries went up from the pony riders, just fifty paces away, who turned to face the threat. Javelins and arrows flew, some finding their target. Gaius, Paulinus, Meral and the six Sarmatians headed for the chariot and the riders at the head of the convoy.

The chariot driver whipped his team into a gallop, and Gaius chased him. He had hoped for Donall, and he was not disappointed. The Venicones Chief, the sole passenger, turned and laughed in recognition of the centurion's helmet, his black cloak billowing behind him. Paulinus peeled off and chased after Kerwyn, who made a run for the hills. Gaius rode close beside the chariot and threw his javelin at Donall, who ducked and let it sail past. Meral, keen to show his skills to his boss, expertly fired an arrow into the driver's side, causing him to loosen the reins and drop to his knees. The team slowed, and a Sarmatian grabbed the reins and pulled the team to a halt.

Gaius fetched another javelin from his quiver and rode to Donall, who had jumped from the back of the chariot, his black cloak fluttering behind, and who now faced his challenger, spear in hand. Gaius threw first, again just missing his man who nimbly danced to one side. Donall threw his spear, aiming low, not at Gaius but at the horse, striking the animal in its side, just ahead of Gaius's thigh. With a neigh of pain, the horse buckled and went down on its front knees, throwing the centurion.

Donall laughed and approached his prey, pulling his long sword from its scabbard. Gaius rolled to his feet and drew his cuirass, its curved blade longer than a legionary's short sword, but shorter than the long straight-bladed sword he now faced. Donall growled as he ran at Gaius, raising his sword and bringing it crashing down on the flimsy cavalry shield, wedging it in its thin board. With two pulls Donall had worked his blade free and circled Gaius, looking for another opportunity to strike. Gaius regained his composure and waved away Meral who was ready to fire an arrow at the Briton chief, then threw himself onto Donall's small square shield, trying with all his might to push the Briton off balance.

Donall stood firm and laughed in Gaius's face. "So, you finally accept my challenge, Roman." He pushed back and Gaius stepped away, circling to his right where he had spotted a raised mound. Gaius launched himself from the mound, jumping downwards on the Briton who raised his shield arm and jabbed towards his opponent's side with his sword. But he was falling backwards and his jab missed. Gaius thrust his sword in the same manoeuvre and found his mark, cutting through Donall's padded jerkin and drawing blood from his side.

The Briton's dark eyes flared in pain and anger, and he swung his blade in a scything motion, aimed at Gaius's thighs. The centurion almost jumped clear, sustaining a shallow cut on his leather leggings. Gaius went on the offensive, thrusting the boss of his damaged shield into Donall's face, giving him a bloody nose. The Briton blinked his eyes repeatedly, and Gaius attacked again, seeing that his vision was blurred. This time, it was Gaius who let out a loud cry as he brought his cuirass down on Donall's sword shoulder, inflicting a deep wound.

Donall staggered backwards, his sword arm now hanging by his side. Gaius locked eyes on him and marched forward. Donall covered his chest with his shield hand and half-raised his sword with a painful grimace. Gaius moved in for the kill, swatting the stricken Briton's blade away and driving his sword into his gut. Donall's eye's bulged as he tripped backwards, falling flat on his back.

Gaius kneeled beside him and leaned in to whisper, "I will give you a quick death, Donall of the Venicones, and send you to meet your ancestors." Donall nodded to acknowledge the gesture, and his defeat, his proud, handsome face spoilt by a broken nose and blackened eyes, blood staining his silver-tipped moustache. He gripped his sword handle tight and locked eyes with his Roman tormentor. Gaius drove the point of his sword into his throat, killing him. On either side of his blade were the tail and head of the chief's distinctive serpent torque, it's blue eye seeming to wink at the Roman. Gaius pulled his blade out, then lifted Donall's head and freed his torque, placing it in his side pouch.

"Will you take his head, sir?" Meral asked, standing at his side.

"No, and you will not. Let his people find him and give him a burial befitting a noble chief. Tell your men to take other trophies and not heads."

"Sir, why did you risk him killing you? He was a big man with a big sword. I could have put two arrows into him to slow him down."

"We have history," Gaius replied wearily. "He had laid down a challenge to me the last time we met... and I was afraid then. Afraid he would kill me. But now, this time, after everything that has happened today, I was ready to fight." Gaius sat down heavily and his shoulders sagged, his body succumbing to fatigue.

"You are a great warrior, sir. You have overcome your demon. In my country, when you kill a warrior, his spirit goes into you to make you stronger."

Gaius laughed weakly and pointed to his damaged shield. "You see that. The shield boss has won me this, and many fights. The Britons only fight with a sharp weapon and a flimsy shield designed to deflect blows. They expect us to fight the same way. But for us, the shield is also a weapon. I knew his eyes would follow my sword, so when I held my sword out, he opened his body in readiness for my sword blow, but never expected me to strike with my shield boss, right into his face. That round bit of steel in the centre of your shield is a potent weapon in a fight, Meral. Remember it. Once he was off balance and falling backwards, I knew I had him."

"You are a great warrior, sir," Meral repeated, with a slight bow. "I will sing of you to my men in the barracks. But now I will find my men, and take my trophy." With that, the slim Sarmatian decurion swung easily into his saddle and trotted into the dark.

Gaius did not approve of the taking of heads, but did not deny himself or his men a trophy of battle. He took Donall's ornate scabbard from his belt, and sheathed his impressive, double-edged sword, forged to fine steel.

Paulinus rode up, holding up Kerwyn's head by his long hair, grinning from ear to ear.

Gaius sighed and said, "I would have questioned him to know the reason for his treachery."

Paulinus opened a saddlebag and held up a bag of coins. "I don't think our cohort quartermaster pays this well."

"And this is how our peace payments to Caledonii chiefs comes back to us," Gaius said with a grunt.

"I always said you can't trust them," Paulinus said, meaning all native scouts.

"Even so. He must have harboured a hatred for us, as so many natives hold in their hearts, hidden behind blank stares. But our two enemies are slain, and by the looks of things, the men have enjoyed their killing and we have recovered our grain," Gaius said, looking at the silhouettes of long-horned oxen grazing off the road, framed in moonlight and still hitched to wagons, as if nothing had happened. A cry went up from his cavalry command, and the riders swept past them, riding towards the Wall, hollering war cries. Gaius turned and screwed up his eyes, seeing nothing but blurs in the gloom.

Paulinus laughed and said, "About twenty of the blue-noses were running towards us from the gates, but now they're running away!"

Gaius and Paulinus shared a drink of sour wine from a gourd, whilst they waited for the men to return. Some lifted the bodies of the two cavalry soldiers who had died onto the chariot, and the half-dozen wounded who could not ride took their places on the driver's platforms of the wagons. One of the black horses hitched to the chariot neighed and turned to Gaius, nodding its head up and down.

"Mars!" Gaius cried, finally recognising his prized mount. A rider had brought a horse from one of the fallen for Gaius to ride. "Unhitch the black one nearest me and saddle him, then hitch the loose horse to the chariot. I'll ride my own horse back to the bridge."

Once all the giddy riders had returned and their chatter died down, they began their slow trek back towards Coria.

"We're heading back towards the enemy," Paulinus noted. "What if we run into them?"

"We'll take the left fork to the nearest fort east of here. Send a rider ahead to see if it's in our hands. If not, we'll still turn to the east, and make a loop to the south towards the bridge, avoiding the town. I reckon our lot will have set up camp on the south bank."

"Fortuna will watch over us, sir, but we better be where we want to be by first light, or we're a sitting target with these slow-moving wagons."

Gaius grunted and groped in his pouch for his gold Julius Caesar coin at the mention of Fortuna. He squeezed it and offered up a silent prayer of thanks, and patted Mars's neck. It had been a day of mixed fortunes, but one that had ended with bloody resolution and a peaceful ride back to camp. They rode on in silence, taking the left fork, happy for a dry and moonlit road and the burble of a brook to soothe their spirits.

19. Vindolanda, present day

Icicles hung from branches coated with a thin layer of snow now frozen hard in the grey morning light, a harsh landscape owned by a hardy robin with fluffed-up red breast, trilling its warning to the great, dirty yellow and blue beast now gathering pace. The beauty of County Durham held a serene calmness, as if the bloody history of the North was no more than a series of nonchalant re-adjustments, entirely justified in reaching the peace and tranquillity of this post-war period. The greatest threat now to this placid landscape was from those plotting to frack for shale gas beneath its skin, the latest menace from Man to test the resilience of nature. The Angel of the North stretched out its wings in either warning or welcome as the train conveyed me to Newcastle on a hopeful day in early January.

The white-dusted landscape encouraged reflection, and I smiled at the memory of the unexpected cluster of events that marked my six weeks practical attachment to the Vindolanda Trust. The chest was deemed too delicate to move, and had held together just long enough to be photographed in a secure room used for inspecting new finds in the Vindolanda Archives in late December, before crumbling to dust in the hands of the assembled archivists, curators and archaeologists. I now marvelled at the pictures of the chest, coins and tablets contained within on my modern tablet. I smiled at Mike's enthusiastic email and his vital piece of news – that none of the silver or gold coins from the chest were later than the Emperor Marcus Aurelius, so my theory about Gaius's payroll chest being buried in haste and not recovered still held. I couldn't wait to see the infra-red photos of the tablets that were found within the chest and have a go at translating whatever was inscribed on them. Could it possibly be a payroll record for Gaius's unit that named him?

Over the holiday, I had summarised the elements that were to feed into my degree dissertation; the archaeological techniques applied in the digs that yielded finds; the descriptions of the finds themselves; my translations of the tablets found at Vindolanda and Coria. I looked forward to adding in the details of the chest and hoped they would lead me to my desired conclusion.

It was another example of the minutiae of daily life in Roman Britain that would feed into the ongoing work of the Trust in building a detailed picture of human activity at this northern-most frontier of empire. To think, such payroll chests would have been travelling the roads of Roman Britain on a frequent basis – ten cohorts in a legion, five legions in Britain at a time, equals fifty monthly payroll chests containing gold and silver coins travelling the roads in armed convoys. What an operation. A prime example of the single-minded purpose and unshakable resolve of the Roman Empire to conquer the known world and bend it to their will.

*****

"I'm pleased your course tutors allowed you and David to return to us for two more weeks. You need that to continue analysing and gathering data for your dissertations," Maggie said, hugging me once her door was closed to Mavis.

"The newspaper articles about the discovery of a Roman 'treasure chest' helped to sell it," I replied, grinning.

"I missed you," she said, tilting her chin upwards and pouting her lips.

I planted a brief kiss and replied politely. "I missed you too. Christmas with the family dragged a bit, although I had a couple of good nights out with my brothers and my mates. How was yours?"

Maggie's face clouded and she detached herself from me. "It's been all go for me. I was at a conference for my university research, in Berlin, but I downed tools for a few days at Christmas. They were tense ones."

"Oh."

At first, she looked at me as if coolly regarding a child who's revealed they still believe in Father Christmas, half in envy of the innocence, half in pity at the ignorance. "The work of a university doesn't stop when term ends, I'm afraid." Then her pupils widened, and her voice fell. "But I'm here now."

How had this happened? I wanted her, I liked her, and I admired her professionally, but that didn't add up to anything deeper. She kept her home life, whatever that was, out of bounds to me with nebulous comments. And I wasn't that curious in any case. Riveting tales of her fieldwork were all I wanted to hear about. I felt my affair with Maggie was a flight of fancy with little prospect of becoming a serious relationship, but with the potential to shatter my dreams.

How could I extricate myself without upsetting her? If our working relationship became strained, if I lost her support, it could undermine my chances of a good grade. I felt powerless – she had started it, and only she could end it without causing shockwaves. Add to all this, Sima. She was the one I had really missed over Christmas, and I wanted to spend more time with her. But that would not be possible until the affair with Maggie was ended. I was not cut out for a life of deceit.

"Well, I didn't want to pry. Work can be a good tonic, I suppose." I stepped back and she did too.

"Yes, of course, and I've been thinking about your little lady a lot."

I gulped. Had she read my thoughts? "Oh, yes?"

"We're preparing to make her the centre-piece of Vindolanda's next exhibition. She has to earn her keep now."

Brigantia! "That's great, Maggie. I'll keep abreast of that." I was curiously relieved to hear that she would be safe and on display to the public. She would be relying on me, whom she chose to find her. *My marble goddess is so easy to know, the embodiment of stability and protection to those who once worshipped her, whilst the living one standing here is an enigma.*

Maggie returned to her chair and I took the seat opposite. Back to tutor and student.

"I'm sorry we couldn't open the chest when you were here Noah, but you'll be able to see the contents in person very soon. It was a shame the wood crumbled. Just to fill you in, I've translated the crypt tombstone engravings from David's photographs, and now have a neat second story to the Sawyers in the late Stuart period. These are the tombs of the family of a Norman knight, Sir Roger de Courtney, all interred between 1170 and 1190. I've recommended to the Trust that the site be properly excavated in a joint operation between Vindolanda and Corbridge. This historical continuum of burials from the Roman period up to the Stuart period is a beautiful addition to the story of our evolving nation. It covers a thousand years of continuous occupation. And it should give us a nice run of publicity releases over the coming months." She sat back and smiled, content again in her professional bubble.

The door opened as a knuckle rapped on it, and I turned to see Mavis standing there, her expression forlorn.

"Professor Wilde, there's police officer here to see you," she announced.

"Why? What's happened?" Maggie asked, jerking upright and looking over my shoulder.

"Some artefacts have… gone missing from the valuables cupboard," Mavis replied quietly, stepping to one side to allow a tall, balding man with a grey goatee beard and wearing a beige duffle coat to enter.

"Inspector Griffiths, Professor Wilde, from Northumberland Police. May I come in?" His soft Welsh lilt sounded out of place.

"You already are, Inspector, but please, keep on coming. And you, Mavis. Noah, would you mind decamping to the couch?"

I shuffled across and moved some reports to make space to sit. The inspector took my seat opposite Maggie. Mavis closed the door, standing with her back to it.

"What's happened, Inspector?" Maggie asked, sitting back.

"We received a call from your assistant, Mavis MacDonald, about an hour ago, stating that some of your valuable items had gone missing. I came over straight away."

Maggie looked from him to Mavis and said, "An hour ago, Mavis? Why didn't you tell me?"

"I'm sorry, Professor, but I was in a panic, and then I had to meet and greet the visiting lecturers," she replied.

Maggie frowned, not satisfied with the excuse, then returned to the inspector. "Alright, Inspector Griffiths, what exactly has been stolen?"

"That's what I'm yet to determine. I've been given this list of items from Ms. MacDonald, and wondered if you had a comprehensive inventory of all the contents of your valuables cupboard?"

"Yes, I do. There's a spreadsheet on the system that's updated once a new item is catalogued and placed there. It's a shared document on our server. I'm surprised Mavis hasn't printed one for you."

"I thought I'd wait for you to give your permission, Professor." Mavis squeezed her hands together, her knuckles white.

The inspector glanced at Maggie and then at me, possibly wondering why I was still there. "Could you and Ms. MacDonald could lead me through an inspection of your valuables cupboard?"

"Certainly," Maggie replied, pushing her chair back to stand.

The inspector pulled a notebook and pen from his coat pocket, then thumbed through until he found a blank page. "Before that, can you tell me the names of all those who have a key and regular access to the cupboard?"

Maggie leant on her desk. "There are three keys. Mine is held by my assistant, Mavis MacDonald, as she stores and fetches items for me on request; there's our field manager, Mike Stone, who spends most of his time outdoors at dig sites; and one of the archivists, Sima Chaudry, who was allocated her section's responsibility to store and remove items."

"So, are you the most senior person of the three key holders?"

"Yes," Maggie replied, coming around the desk. "May I see Mavis's list of items suspected to have… gone missing?"

The inspector pulled out a folded sheet from his other pocket and handed it to her.

Maggie scanned the items and looked across at me. "I'm sorry, Noah, but your precious find of Roman coins is at the top of this list."

I groaned and stood up. This was devastating news. I wanted to get permission to show some of the find during my dissertation presentation in April, and I had still seen only photographs of it. I could request that Dave's gold coin, now residing in the Great North Museum in Newcastle, be lent to me. My eyes had been roving around the room as my brain ticked, and when I settled on the shrewd eyes of the inspector, he was staring at me, as if peeling away the barriers to read my thoughts.

"There are eight items listed here as missing," Maggie continued. "All are coins, jewellery or ornaments made from gold or silver. Mavis, can you print out a copy for me, please?"

As we filed out of her office, the inspector said, "Hmm, that doesn't surprise me. Artefacts that have been catalogued would be difficult to sell, unless to unscrupulous private collectors, so the other possibility is that they will be melted down for their gold and silver content."

Maggie gasped in shock at the suggestion. I asked if I could leave. The inspector nodded, and so did Maggie.

I stood with my back to the wall outside, my heart beating as adrenalin surged through my body. This was a huge shock, and threw up questions as to who might be responsible. If there was no sign of a break-in, then Mavis, Mike and Sima were all in the frame. Surely not Sima. I made my way through the main entrance to Archives, and tapped lightly on Sima's door. When she opened it, my mood lifted and my heart leapt at seeing her again, cocooned in a rollneck plum-coloured sweater and pencil skirt over regulation black winter tights. As I hugged her, I noticed that her door to the valuables' cupboard, at the back of her office, was closed. I had been in it and knew that it was essentially a short corridor that connected the archives block to Maggie's outer office, with floor to ceiling shelves on either side of a narrow passage, and doors at both ends.

"Hi Sima, and happy new year!" I blurted, stepping back from the brief hug. I decided not to peck her on the cheek, in case any of her colleagues were watching.

"Noah! It's great to see you after what seems like ages!"

"Yeah, the longest and slowest three weeks of my life," I replied, closing her door behind her. We took our seats and I leaned forward to tell her the news in a conspiratorial whisper. "Look, you need to know that a police inspector is on the other side of that door with

Maggie and Mavis, looking into the disappearance of some artefacts, including the new Roman coins." I pointed to the valuables cupboard and she turned to see the light was showing under her door.

She turned back to me and whispered, wide-eyed, "Oh no! That's terrible! Who could have done such a thing?"

"That's literally the million-dollar question. I've just come from Maggie's office, and I'm afraid this gets worse. As one of three keyholders, you're one of the suspects."

Sima bridled. "I hope you know that I wouldn't be involved in such a criminal act, and I don't want to be suspected. You know I'm desperate to make a success of this, so I can make a break from my family and Ravi, and be self-supporting. Oh Noah, this is terrible!"

I wanted to embrace her, because her mind was now working in my favour, but thought better, so as not to make a spectacle in front of her co-workers who seemed to be taking turns to walk past the glass partition to her office. "Sima, of course I trust you. Perhaps someone picked the locks over the weekend and got in, or maybe Mavis or Mike are somehow involved..."

Just then a key turned in the cupboard lock and the door opened. Mavis stood there looking at us both. Had she overheard my last comment?

"May we come in?" she asked, walking forward, followed by Inspector Griffiths and Maggie.

"We meet again, young man," the inspector said to me, with a sardonic grin.

"Er, yes, this is where I've been based, in Archives," I replied, standing and backing away to make more space.

"And you're the one who discovered the chest of Roman coins?" he added, shuffling into the small room.

"Yes, with three other students, about two weeks before Christmas."

He scribbled in his notebook, revealing his bald pate. "Noah?"

"Noah Jessop," I said, clasping my hands in front of me. Was I a suspect?

"You can leave us now," he said, then turned his eyes to Sima. "Miss Sima Chaudry?"

"Yes," she replied.

"Can I have a few minutes of your time? My name's Inspector Griffiths, of Northumberland Police."

"Of course, please take a seat. Noah has just told me that some objects have gone missing."

"Indeed. Mister Jessop, you may leave us. It's a bit crowded in here."

I left the four of them and closed the door, turning to face quizzical looks from the three other archivists. I went over to them, obliged to give an explanation.

"There seems to be some issue with the valuables cupboard, and Mavis called the police," I said, trying to play down the incident. "I think it's best to keep this in-house, until the facts are established, don't you?" There were some raised eyebrows, but they returned to their stations. I went to my workplace and turned on my computer, wondering how this would play out.

*****

That evening, I went with a distraught Sima and puzzled Dave to the pub, to talk it through and try to take some of the tension out of the day over a meal and a few drinks.

"What did the inspector say to you?" I asked Sima.

"He asked me to show him my key. All three keys are the same, apparently. I guess that told him that I had it on my person and hadn't given it to anyone. Then he asked me for my movements over the weekend. I told him I had been away for two weeks and only returned to Vindolanda on Sunday afternoon, about five, and went to my room in the staff block. I had said hello to two of my work colleagues in the corridor, so they're my alibi, as I was dragging my suitcase behind me."

"But does he have any idea when the stuff was stolen?" Dave asked.

"Not really. It could have been any time from December twentieth, when Professor Wilde last asked Mavis to lock the new finds away and update the inventory," Sima replied. "Although some staff came to the archives section between Christmas and New Year, including a team who were convened to photograph and open the chest. Mike was there as he used his key to remove the chest from the cupboard. I was excused as they knew I'd travelled to the Midlands. The building was empty from the twenty-eighth until the fifth of January, when Mavis opened the office at nine o'clock, and soon after discovered things were missing."

"Hmm. Seven days. And Mike was the last one to be in the cupboard. Did the inspector ask her how she came to look into the valuables cupboard so soon after opening the office after a week's break?" I asked.

"Not in front of me. Maybe he asked her separately," Sima replied, sipping her trademark tomato juice. She had a note pad open. It looked as if she meant business, because she had skin in the game, but a disloyal little voice in my head asked why a person so harried by her family chose to go back to them for the whole of her holiday. A student might have to vacate the premises. She wasn't in the same situation, was she? I looked at her open face, and then at her chewed fingernails. Of course she was innocent.

Just then, a draught from the main door of the pub announced the entrance of Mike and Emma Stone. As soon as Mike saw us, he came straight over to our table, worry etched on his face.

"Happy New Year to you all, but not so happy, it turns out," he said.

"Oh, Mike you must be worried, as one of the key holders," Sima said.

He shifted uncomfortably from foot to foot before framing as humorous a reply as he could muster. "One of the Key Three, aye. That Inspector Griffiths looks like a bloodhound on a trail, alright. I'm sure he could read my thoughts before I opened my mouth."

"That's how he made me feel," Sima agreed.

"We don't see you as a suspect, Mike," Dave said. "But do you think there's a spare key floating around?"

"You know, there's nothing special about those locks. You could get a key cut at any shoe shop or supermarket. Mine never leaves my key ring." He jangled his keys, hanging from a loop on his faded blue jeans.

"We're racking our brains, Mike, to try and come up with a likely scenario," I offered, between sips of my ale. "But we don't suspect you," I quickly added.

Mike grinned and wandered off to the bar. They took a table on the far side of the pub.

"I hope he doesn't think I'm being sarcastic..." I muttered.

"Again," Dave added. "It wouldn't be your first offence."

"He surely can't be involved, can he?" Sima asked, leaning forward and whispering.

"He lacks the imagination," Dave replied. "Shall we order some food?"

We went to the bar and placed our food orders and bought another round.

I scanned the room, noting the empty tables. "Not many in," I stated, regarding the froth on my pint. "Perhaps it's a combination of the freezing cold weather and Dry January."

"And it's Monday, mate," Dave added. "A deadly trio of reasons."

The barman heard and grunted his agreement, wiping a glass with a damp tea towel. "We're glad you lot have returned to Vindolanda," he said. "Everything alright up there?"

"Erm, fine," I said.

"Had any suspicious strangers in over the past few days?" Dave asked, squinting at the barman whilst picking up his pint.

"Suspicious? Why, what's happened?"

"Oh, nothing. He's just fooling with you," I said, returning to our table. "I thought we agreed to keep this low key?" I said as we all sat down.

"Come on, it's exciting." Dave winked at Sima.

"Not for me!" Sima exclaimed. "I've been interrogated by Morse!"

"Morse is about right. I don't see him as a clumsy Clouseau." My laugh was hollow. "I have a feeling that Inspector Griffiths usually gets his man, or woman."

"Just one more thing, madam," Dave said to Sima. "Where were you when the cupboard was cleared out?"

And he thought I was insensitive!

"Actually, I've just had a thought," I said. "The outside doors are alarmed, right?"

"Yes, with a key pad on the inside that requires a four-digit code," Sima replied. "So?"

"Well, whoever stole the artefacts would have had to have known the key code to turn the alarm off, unless the theft was carried out during office hours."

"Well, I don't know it, and I'm not sure Mike Stone does," Sima replied. "He rarely comes into the main building unless summoned to a meeting."

Dave leaned in. "Except on the twenty-seventh of December when he went in for the examination of the chest. If he was first in or last out, he would have had to set the alarm code." He glanced behind at Mike's table.

"Don't look. He'll think we're talking about him. The finger of suspicion also points at Mavis MacDonald. A cold fish that one," I said.

"Mike lives on site and has a car," Dave pointed out. "If I were the inspector, I'd be looking for a reason to search his house. And Mavis's. And the Prof. She could be in cahoots with Mavis. By the way, where does Mavis live?"

"I doubt the professor is in the frame," I said, thinking hard about the boxes I had seen in her downstairs back room. I decided to keep this to myself. "Mavis lives on a farm not far away. Renting, I think."

"Now that's interesting," Sima said, brightening up and sitting back.

Our meals arrived and we shelved our speculation to enjoy the warming food. We concluded that Sima should stick to her normal routine and not do anything to attract unwanted attention, and if there were no breaks in the case by Friday, we would follow Mavis to her farm when she left work, and perhaps have a look around over the weekend. I had to act for Sima to be exonerated and to help recover the Roman coins. I would also have a secret look around Maggie's house, if she summoned me during the week, just to satisfy my curiosity and, as Morse would say, eliminate her from our enquiry.

20. Coria, 181 CE

Gaius's cavalry unit escorted the wagons of recovered grain and weapons to the River Tine before the first rays of dawn, about a mile east of Coria. It had been a cold but largely uneventful night, bypassing the glowing remains of another burnt-out fort. The only thing that broke the monotony of their slow progress was being surprised by a dozen sullen legionaries who walked into the road ahead of them from the place where they had been hiding in the hills. They told a tale of being overwhelmed in a surprise attack, and fighting their way out of the fort under the order of an officer.

Paulinus had wanted to question them individually, to compare their stories and uncover any possible evidence that they might be deserters, but Gaius restrained him, saying they came to them voluntarily and had been through much. Once they reached the river, Gaius sent out scouts to discover if the Caledonii army was still occupying the smouldering ruins of the town. They ate their rations and brewed up hot water with honey and herb fusion to warm them, stamping their feet on the frosty ground, happy for their woollen socks, leggings and leather boots as they waited for the scouts to return.

"It is a happy reunion," Paulinus remarked as he walked with his commander to the dewy marsh grass that formed a barrier to the river. A kingfisher darted down, entering the water with barely a ripple to catch its wriggling breakfast.

"A reunion between whom?" Gaius replied, dragged from his thoughts.

"You and Mars, sir."

"Oh yes. If it wasn't for my poor eyes, I'd have seen him sooner." Gaius chuckled at the memory. "He was trying to attract my attention by snorting, stamping his feet and flashing his eye lashes at me."

"Like a whore outside a tavern, sir," Paulinus laughed.

"You'd know more about that, my friend, but yes, it was a happy reunion. They must have had a fight trying to hitch him to that chariot!"

A shout went up and they returned to their men. The scouts came back to camp with news that the Caledonii were massed outside the west gate of Coria, where they could watch the bridge and the road.

"Do we still hold the north bridgehead?" Gaius asked.

"Aye, sir. There's a manned barricade guarding the approach to the bridge."

"And on the south side?" Paulinus asked.

"There's a big camp of tents and a few huts, sir."

"As I thought," Gaius said, turning to his deputy. "Then we must move to the bridgehead with our wagons and defend them, if necessary, as they cross the bridge."

"Perhaps they would move more swiftly with horses hitched to them, rather than those ponderous oxen, sir?" Paulinus suggested.

"That's a good idea," Gaius replied, slapping his deputy on his generous bicep. "We could even draw some of their riders away from the bridge by driving the oxen along the road towards them, under the guise of a couple of farmers in plain dress."

"I'll organise it, sir," Paulinus replied with his trademark grin.

"But not you. You will remain by my side," Gaius shouted after him.

Soon they were ready to move out, and Gaius instructed the six legionaries to sit on the tailboards of the wagons and be prepared to defend them with their spears. Once the two disguised soldiers were ready, they were told to drive the oxen northwards to the road, and then head westwards towards Coria. Enemy scouts would soon see them and raise the alarm, followed by hooting and hollering from pony riders. They were instructed to flee back the way they had come on their horses, then turn south towards the river in a wide circle towards to the bridge.

Gaius led his troop of riders and wagons along the river path, edging cautiously towards Coria. His scouts went ahead, to ensure the way was clear and the enemy were not in evidence outside the south and east sides of the town walls. They had been noticed by one of their own patrols on the south bank, who waved their shields and spears to let Gaius know they had been seen.

"That's good. They will alert our men at the bridge," Gaius said to Paulinus.

"We must be ready to charge at the speed of the wagons if our scouts report the enemy knows we are here, sir," Paulinus replied.

"Then you drop back to the first wagon, and stay with it. I will lead our riders to engage the enemy should they oppose us."

They did not have long to wait, as the scouts came charging back, their horses panting in hot breath trails. "Sir! They have seen us and sent their riders and a chariot to block our path!" a scout shouted.

"Then, Vertinax, sound your horn! We shall charge to meet them. Scouts, fall back to Paulinus and escort the wagons!" Gaius raised his arm and lowered it, leading his ten Gauls and Sarmatians and the forty of the remaining Coria cavalry soldiers at a canter. He knew they must move swiftly, now they were exposed, and as they reached the top of a grassy hill, they saw the town below to their right, grey smoke still rising from smouldering buildings, the bridge to their left, and a ragged band of Caledonii warriors clustered around a chariot and a dozen pony riders ahead.

Gaius knew the effect a cavalry charge has on foot soldiers, and waited until all his riders were with him, arranged in a long line on the hilltop. He saw the Roman barricade about twenty paces or so in front of the bridge, and the first spear in his plumed helmet on his magnificent grey, marshalling his remaining fifty riders behind them. Reinforcements were jogging across the bridge. "Good. Our coming is the prompt to sweep the barbarians off this plain!" he yelled.

Gaius briefed Meral and the Coria decurion to lead the left and right flanks, and he positioned himself in the middle, with Vertinax for company. He noted the unusual absence of Paulinus on his right. He glanced back and saw the approach of the wagon train, with a mere six outriders as escort. The wind blew in their faces, and the Coria unit's standard fluttered. Gaius wished he had brought Getterix with their century standard, but had not anticipated a moment like this. His eyesight was blurred, but he could see the first spear's cavalry arranged in a line, ready for the command to charge, and heard horns blowing at their barricade. Mars pawed the ground and tossed his shaggy mane in readiness.

"Charge!" Gaius yelled, and Vertinax blew his horn. They swept down the hill in a controlled gallop, conscious of keeping the line. Most men had throwing javelins, and the six Sarmatians had their arrows at the ready. The sound of hooves thundered in their ears, and the Sarmatians stood up on their hoops and emitted a warbling war cry. Ahead of them, the barbarians were whipped into line by a chief, yelling instructions from a chariot that patrolled laterally behind them. Their pony riders also hung back, leaving the men on foot to receive the charge with their puny cow hide shields.

But the charging Roman cavalry did not crash through the line of warriors. Gaius pointed to his left and right, and the line of riders separated into two, turning outwards at twenty paces distance, then throwing javelins or firing arrows at the screaming barbarians. Some hit their targets, and men fell to the ground, dying or wounded. The riders wheeled and made a second pass, keeping their distance and dodging spears thrown at them, sending a second volley at the enraged enemy. This was repeated a third time, before Gaius told Vertinax to sound the re-group. Now they formed a line again and drew swords. Gaius ordered the charge and they ploughed through the line of men, knocking some to the ground and slashing at the shoulders and heads of others. This put the riders in the thick of the milling barbarians, and vulnerable to being dragged off their horses.

Gaius smashed his shield boss into the face of a determined warrior, then kicked him to the ground. Vertinax rode over the man, breaking his ribs under his horse's hooves. The next man was slashed across the face with Gaius's sword. He jabbed his heels into Mars and moved through the melee, heading for the chief's chariot. His loyal men followed, and soon they were on either side of the chariot, throwing javelins at the occupants. But they in turn were being harried by warriors on ponies with long spears, prodding at the Romans.

Within a few minutes, the sound of horses, accompanied by familiar war cries, announced the arrival of the first spear with the remains of the Coria cavalry cent. Gaius laughed as the flea in his ear, who had been jabbing at his shield, was sent crashing to the ground by another rider, and he waved to the first spear and pointed to the chariot that was trying to make an escape. The two officers rode hard after it, pulling javelins from pouches and making ready to throw. They parted and rode on either side of the chief, a tall man with a golden helmet and a bronze shield, and threw at the same time. Gaius's javelin was batted away with the shield, but the one from the other side found its mark. The chief doubled over and sat down heavily, pulling the javelin from his side. The first spear drew in closer and slashed at the chariot driver with his sword. Gaius repeated the move from his side, and soon the driver was down too, the horses slowing as the reins slackened.

The officers dismounted when the chariot stopped, and moved in for the kill. Gaius finished off the driver, leaving the chief to the first spear.

"This is well met, Gaius," the senior centurion remarked, surveying the battlefield behind them.

"Aye, sir. We have the numbers on them today."

"Was your mission a success?"

"Yes, First Spear. See, our wagons are creeping along the river path towards the bridge. We killed the escort and another chief, sir." Gaius pointed at the stealthy wagon train with a smile of satisfaction.

"By Jupiter, you are a fighter and a strategist, Centurion Atticianus! We have regained some honour for our cohort!"

The Caledonii warriors had been carved up by cavalry attacks from front and rear. Few remained on their feet. Over by the barricade, fighting still raged on foot, with the legionaries behind rows of red rectangular shields, pushing forward into their enemy's disjointed attacks. With their chief dead, there was no one to call a retreat, and so the fighting continued until almost all the enemy were slaughtered, just a few throwing down their weapons and surrendering.

"Aye, we have reversed much of the evil done to us yesterday," Gaius replied.

"Take a gold wrist band," First Spear said, tossing a jewel-encrusted band to Gaius. The first spear helped himself to the other finery of the dead chief, before mounting. They rode back to their men, and, allowing a brief amount of time for killing the wounded and taking trophies, then led their riders across the bridge in triumph, to the cheers of the grateful civilian population, now camped on the south bank.

First Spear leaned across and shouted to Gaius, "We will go to the Tribune's tent and report."

On a slightly raised mound stood a grand tent, the size of a modest villa. The cohort banner and four cent banners fluttered outside in the morning breeze, next to Tribune Lucius Bebius, flanked by officers and scribes, on a purple carpet. Behind, was a rank of women and attendants. Gaius cursed his eyes for not allowing him to see if his wife, Aria, was amongst them.

"You have made a good spectacle," Tribune Bebius said, with a broad smile, his arms open in welcome.

First Spear bowed and handed the Caledonian chief's golden helmet to him, saying, "This is the helmet of their chief, sir, our tribute to you." He then stepped aside for Gaius to move forward and bow, making a salute with arm across chest.

"My brave officers, you have done well!" Bebius gushed. "Please come into my tent. I would hear of this battle and of your adventure, Centurion Atticianus. Your wife awaits you."

Gaius handed his helmet to an attendant as Aria flew into his arms. "I told you I would soon return, my love," he breathed into her strawberry, sweet-smelling hair.

"And so, you have kept your word, my husband," she replied, wiping a tear away as they joined the procession into the tent. Tapestries of classical scenes hung on side panels as they trod on richly woven carpets, the smell of incense wafting on the air in this temporary recreation of imperial splendour. They nodded to Claudia Pertinax, who was seated next to Tribune Bebius's wife, and Gaius gulped at the sight of Prefect Adminius, seated beside her. Gaius wondered if he had made a verbal report to the legate.

"Ah, reunions after victory are so sweet," the tribune said, clearly savouring this turn of fortunes. He pointed to a series of armchairs and Gaius sat next to the first spear, with Aria to his right. Liveried boys brought trays of snacks and goblets of sweet wine. Gaius forced some meat pastries into his mouth, washed down with a mouthful of wine. "It is now the month of Janus, a new beginning as we leave the worries of the old year behind. Let us take this victory as a sign of good things to come, and look to the future with a bold eye!" Bebius raised his goblet and all joined him in a toast to the god Janus and the new year.

"Eat, drink, you deserve it," Bebius added, turning to his wife with a broad smile and squeezing her hand. Gaius had not seen this side of him, having only briefly met him in the fraught hour before the barbarian attack, when he had barged into the tribune's office to catch him with his toga up.

"First Spear," Bebius continued, "am I right to think that the barbarians have been sufficiently reduced in numbers for us to reclaim our town?"

"Yes sir. Those we haven't killed have run off, and their leaders are slain."

"May Fortuna be praised! The gods have returned to us today, to shower us with their blessings. Centurion Atticianus, tell us about your mission under the watchful eye of Luna."

Gaius coughed to clear flakes from his throat. "We trailed the wagon train northwards, and ambushed them just before they reached the Wall, sir. Although our numbers were roughly a match, we took them by surprise, and our superior weapons, tactics, and heavier horses, made the difference. We had few casualties, and recovered the grain and stolen weapons. I killed one of their chiefs, also on a chariot, in single combat, sir."

"Single combat! You are a fearless warrior, for sure!" the tribune exclaimed, eliciting laughter.

Gaius regretted the last disclosure. All he could do was smile as Aria ruffled his hair.

"You are ever boastful, my husband," she whispered, "but he will remember your bravery." Gaius touched her hand as their eyes briefly met.

"So, we have recovered our grain and weapons that were looted, but we still have a razed town, although the walls still stand," Tribune Bebius summarised. "The enemy has been defeated and scattered, and now we must mop up any pockets and reclaim our Great Wall forts and towers." He looked at his officers for their comments.

First Spear glanced at Gaius before replying, "We have a hundred horsemen remaining, sir, and two hundred legionaries. It is a small force. The cavalry can do a sweep of the surrounding area, and check the other forts along the line of road."

"And what are your thoughts, Centurion Atticianus?" Bebius asked.

"Sir, I am anxious to return to Vindolanda and lift their siege, if it is still in place. I propose you march fifty men to the North Road Gate Fort to secure it, so that all know that we are back in charge. Also, there is the buried payroll chest at the estate to the west, sir, that must be recovered."

"Yes, yes. These are good proposals. The chest can wait for now. But we are short of men and horses, Centurion. You can spend the remainder of the day patrolling along the road and the surrounding area, then we can consider letting you return to Vindolanda tomorrow. Now, eat and drink, then return to your men. You shall receive commendations for your bravery, both of you, once order is restored."

Gaius and Aria ate and drank what they considered to be polite amounts, then asked permission to leave. Gaius asked Aria to wait outside with him as he wanted to speak to Adminius.

Adminius soon appeared with Claudia, and Gaius took him to one side.

"Prefect, may I know if you made your report to Tribune Bebius on our situation at Vindolanda?"

Adminius stepped back and stared at him, wondering what he knew of it. "I… was carrying a report from our tribune, but it somehow got lost in the rush from the carriage to the estate. Your optio had kindly carried my bag, but when he returned it to me, it was open and the documents gone. But I cannot blame him, as he was fighting a barbarian with his sword hand whilst we ran for our lives!"

Gaius looked into his fearful face as the memory of that desperate moment overcame the timid man. "It was a desperate battle indeed, and we were fortunate to be favoured by the gods. But did you make a verbal report?"

Adminius swallowed and wrung his hands, glancing past Gaius at the curious women. "In view of your own briefing to Tribune Bebius and his pleasure at your brave actions, Centurion Atticianus, I felt it best to remain silent on the matter. I feel that events have... moved on." He grinned and Gaius nodded.

"Then we shall return to Vindolanda in triumph and lift their siege, Prefect. Until tomorrow." Gaius turned on his heels, nodded to Claudia and took Aria by her arm, marching her behind the great tent before she could ask him a question.

She looked at him, perplexed, then led them to the tent she had made home, where their son, Brutus, and the maid, Marta, gave them a warm welcome.

"I am glad to see the tribune's wife has kept you close, my love," Gaius said, noting their position behind the main tent, in a guarded enclosure.

"She is now a dear friend, Gaius, and a useful contact should your next promotion ever be discussed," Aria replied. "But you must tell me about your talk with Adminius..."

Amborix interrupted her by putting his head in the opening and greeted Gaius. "All is well, sir," he said, needlessly.

"I am glad to hear it, Amborix. We have returned with all but ten of my command alive, only two of our men from Vindolanda perished, so I must make sacrifice when I am able, to thank the gods."

"There is a shrine to Jupiter and Aphrodite, beside the road, sir," he grinned, happy to be useful.

"Then we shall go there before the sun goes down. Here is a coin to buy a goat for our sacrifice. Ah, I look forward to sleeping here tonight, with my family, and hope that tomorrow we may all return to Vindolanda."

"I hope so too sir," Marta said. "I worry about my husband, Longinus, and the wellbeing of your house, sir."

"Aye, let us hope we return without the need to fight and find that all is well. Now, I must take my leave and re-join my men. I shall be here for supper!" Gaius kissed his son and frowning wife and left, marching through the busy camp to where a boy held the reins of Mars.

He found Paulinus supervising the handover of the recovered grain sacks to the quartermaster, his domain now a large canvas tent. "Well met, Paulinus. Our plan worked out well, but now we must go back out on patrol." He dismounted and approached the quartermaster, "But before I go out on patrol, a bucket of oats for Mars, and a well-earned drink."

"Aye, sir," Paulinus replied, "I'll round up the men, lest they get too comfortable, and see to the horses."

"Then let's meet at the north bank guardhouse. I'm going to look for First Spear for our orders."

An hour later, they were on patrol to the east of Coria. First Spear was leading his fifty riders to the west. They would make a loop to the north and meet at the north road gate, then return to Coria. In the meantime, the legionaries had been ordered to dig burial pits and bury the dead, then to enter the town and start the clean-up.

Gaius led his men over the bridge in the late afternoon, weary and ready for food and rest, after a largely uneventful patrol. The only excitement came when they flushed some loitering warriors out of a farm estate, killing them in a brief fight and freeing some grateful captives. But the Caledonii had withdrawn from the

222

immediate area, taking what booty, horses or slaves they had seized north of the Wall.

As Gaius led his men across the bridge, Paulinus told him that there was another grand, imperial tent on the hill, next to the tribune's, with more standards planted in the ground. When Gaius drew closer, he could see more soldiers in unsullied uniforms, and more activity. He dismissed the men, with orders to meet at the temporary parade ground in the legionaries' tented village after breakfast in the morning, for their orders.

Clearly, another senior official had arrived, and he was curious to find out who. An optio, in charge of the guard at the tribune's tent, informed him that their legion's legate, Claudius Hieronymianus, had arrived from Eboracum. Gaius's curiosity was piqued, but he decided that he could wait to find out in the morning why the commander-in-chief of his legion had come. He allowed his weary legs to carry him to his temporary home, knowing that a sacrifice was due to the gods before he could enjoy a family meal, followed by a lengthy visit to the realm of Somnus in the arms of his loving wife.

21. Vindolanda, present day

With the distraction of the thefts rattling in the background, it was hard for me to fully concentrate on my detailed description of the Roman chest find for my dissertation. But gradually, over several days, I typed up a three-thousand-word report, with photographs attached, working from my notes. I had been sent all the photographs of the chest and its contents, and was told by Maggie that her curator friend at the Great North Museum would attend my presentation with the Hadrian gold aureus coin. There was also video footage of the team of white coated, white gloved archivists, curators and Mike Stone, removing the coins from their rotting cloth bags and counting them, noting denominations and emperors. They were transferred to new canvas bags for storage. The inventory of the breakdown of coins was of interest to me, and it matched the amount expected for a cohort's pay for one month.

This fitted my theory that the chest of coins was a legion cohort payroll up to but no later than the year 180 CE, and therefore Centurion Gaius Atticianus may well have been the one who was transporting the chest from Vindolanda fort to Coria town in that year, and been forced to bury it in the graveyard of a Roman estate as a consequence of attack by unknown tribal warriors. I also typed up my translation of the tablets found inside the chest, detailing pay advances made to a dozen named officers of optio rank or higher. Perhaps legionaries were not entitled to advances and it was a perk of rank. Well, sadly, Centurion Gaius Atticianus was not one of the six officers listed as having had an advance, and his name was not visible on the partially legible payroll. Would those six officers have got away without having to repay their advances if the only record was on the tablet in the chest?

I then turned my attention to the details of a find sent to me by Maggie, after a database word search on 'Gaius Atticianus' matched one result:

'In the *Roman Inscriptions of Britain* archives, there is an entry for an altar pedestal stone inscription, dedicated to the god Hercules, found at the excavated site of the Roman fort of Epiacum, now known as Whitley Castle, located fifteen miles south of Hadrian's Wall. The translation reads:

'To the god Hercules

Gaius Vitellius Atticianus

centurion of the Sixth Legion Victrix Pia Fidelis'

The last line is illegible, but may have said, 'made this dedication'.

So, this is another tangible record of the existence and movements of Centurion Gaius Atticianus of the Sixth Legion. There is no date mentioned for when the dedication was made.'

What a great find by Maggie! But what was Gaius doing at Epiacum fort, forty miles from Vindolanda? Further research told me that Epiacum was situated on the western half of Hadrian's Wall, and may well have been built and garrisoned by soldiers of the Twentieth Legion. It was a puzzle, then, how a centurion of the Sixth Legion came to be stationed there long enough to dedicate an altar to a favourite god.

Inspector Griffiths had been in again, taking statements and nosing around. At five o'clock, I closed down my computer and knocked on Sima's door.

"Fancy a coffee?" I asked.

"Yes please," she replied, looking up with anxious eyes.

In the cafeteria, I asked, "Any developments on the case?"

"The inspector is circling us like a shark. He is none the wiser, and keeps repeating versions of the same questions, I guess hoping for inconsistencies. I do hope he gets a break to take the heat from me, because I'm starting to behave as if I've got something to hide," she moaned.

"I've noticed Mike Stone looking very distracted. Dave says he is falling apart under the pressure. In contrast, Mavis is as cool as a cucumber smoothie. The next time I speak to Maggie, I'll ask her about Mavis's background."

"Do you really think she could be involved?" Sima whispered, leaning forward.

"Well, someone did it. It could have been an expert artefacts thief who abseiled down through a skylight, I suppose."

"You've seen too many diamond heist movies," she replied, laughing just enough so that even I was convinced my humour had been intentional.

"I think we stick with our plan to follow Mavis after she leaves work on Friday afternoon. Are you up for driving?"

"She would recognise my car in her rear-view mirror, Noah. Can't you think of another car?"

I pondered her question and shrugged. "Only Mike's Land Rover. That might be less conspicuous as some of the local farmers drive them. I'll ask Dave to ask him."

That evening, I went to Maggie's house, as arranged, and had a snoop in her spare room when she was in the kitchen. There were boxes of old reports and bags of soil samples, but no artefacts, much to my relief.

"What are you doing, Noah?"

I turned to see Maggie standing behind me, hands on hips. "Oh, I was just curious, Maggie. Sorry to be nosy, but I thought you might have…"

"…the stolen artefacts? Unbelievable!" she said, her stern look making me squirm.

"I don't think you're involved, Maggie, honest, I was just... being nosy."

"Well, I hope you're satisfied. There are no stolen artefacts, and I'm angry that you could have..."

I had no choice but to put my arms around her and hold her tight. "Maggie, I promise you, I don't suspect you. I don't know what came over me. Just curiosity, that's all. I'm sorry." We kissed and I felt her body relax and melt into mine.

"You are a naughty man," she purred. She led me by the hand upstairs and I didn't hang back. I wondered if I'd ever summon the willpower and the courage to do what I knew I should. I needed to end our affair, but I was afraid of the possible consequences for my academic success.

*****

Friday came and the plan was set. Mike had given his keys to Dave, who had asked if he could do a shopping run to the local mini-mart. We all felt it was best to leave Mike out of our plans, seeing as he was a minor suspect in our eyes.

"He inhabits the complex world of older people, after all, and who knows how their minds work?" I said, to raised eyebrows from Sima.

Dave was behind the wheel in the lane outside the car park exit, and Sima and I were hidden in the back. We felt one driver was less conspicuous, and Dave wore a flat cap and a borrowed waxed farmer's coat. The car lurched forward and I winced at the sound of the gears scraping, then we slowly moved up the lane.

Half an hour later we came to a halt, and Dave came to the back and opened the tailgate.

"She's driven through the gates into this farm," Dave said, helping Sima out. We stood in a muddy track, looking over a stonewall fence at a field with cows grazing. A stone track led to a group of buildings, about fifty yards away. Dave retrieved a pair of binoculars that lived in the glove box. He leaned on the wall and focussed on the buildings, and Sima and I screwed up our eyes to look at them.

"She's backed her car up to a barn," Dave said. "She's opened the back of her people carrier and gone into the barn." He continued looking through the binoculars. A dog barked from somewhere in the farm compound.

We waited patiently, glad for dry skies after a week of showers. A partridge flapped indignantly across the track, flushed out by an unseen creature. After ten minutes, Dave continued his commentary. "She's carried a cardboard box and placed in the rear of the vehicle. I can't see any detail of the box." Then after thirty seconds had passed, he sounded triumphant. "She's placed another box in the back. I'm pretty sure that one had the Vindolanda Trust logo on the side."

"How sure?" Sima asked.

"You have a look. I don't think she's done yet." Dave handed the binoculars to Sima, who took up the vigil. The sun had gone for the day, and it was starting to get murky.

"Ten more minutes and it'll be dark," I said, unhelpfully.

"Yes!" Sima exclaimed. "It was definitely our logo on the next box she brought out. I think this is a definite connection. That woman's brought the finger of suspicion on us all and it was her. Well, might be her."

"OK, so what do we do now?" I asked.

Dave shrugged. "Either carry on watching her and wait for her to leave and follow, or call Inspector Griffiths."

Sima lifted the binoculars and carried on watching. "We can't stay out here all night. She's closed the barn door and the back of the car. She's starting to drive."

Dave and I waited patiently for the next report in the growing darkness.

"She's parked outside the farmhouse and gone inside. You can see the lights have come on."

"Let's wait for ten minutes to see if she's going out, or staying in. She might move the stuff in the morning," I said. I spoke as if this was the stolen property and nobody reined me in.

"Alright," Dave replied. "Let's sit in the car and wait until it gets dark, then leave. I've got to take this back to Mike soon or he'll wonder where I've gone."

We waited and Mavis did not come out, so we decided to call Inspector Griffiths and call it a night.

Sima had his card with his mobile number and dialled it. "No signal," she sighed after a few seconds. "Let's drive to where there's a signal."

Dave edged slowly down the lane without headlights, keeping the dark outline of the dry-stone wall a foot to his right. Darkness came quickly in the winter months, and he looked relieved to reach the B road and turn on the lights. "I'll stop at the top of this hill and you can check for a signal," he said, turning and allowing the cat's eyes to guide him. Black clouds had moved across the sky, reducing visibility to a few yards. He stopped in a layby at the top of the first hill and we got out. Sima tried the number again, moving about, but gave up after a minute. "Still no signal."

"Let's drive back and call him from the dorm block," I proposed, losing enthusiasm as it got noticeably colder.

"Hold on," Dave said, peering through a gap in the trees. "There are headlights coming down the track from Mavis's farm. I think she's leaving."

"Perhaps we should follow?" Sima asked, uncertainty in her voice.

"Alright, at least to see if she's going to somewhere local," I replied. "You can keep checking for a signal as we drive." We jumped in and turned the Land Rover around, as Mavis had turned in the opposite direction and was heading towards the main A road.

Rain started to fall, growing in intensity. Soon, Dave had the wipers on double speed, as we followed the red glows of Mavis's tail lights. She pulled into the petrol station and mini-mart just before the main road T-junction, and Dave followed, stopping in a parking space on the end of the row of cars in front of the mini-mart. Mavis had gone inside and was using a pay phone.

"Any signal?" I asked Sima.

"I'm trying. Yes, it's ringing… Hello? Is that Inspector Griffiths? This is Sima Chaudry from Vindolanda. Yes, I'm fine. I'm outside the mini-mart at the BP filling station where the B road meets the A road, by the T-junction. I'm with Noah and David. We followed Mavis MacDonald from Vindolanda to the farm where she is staying and saw her put some boxes with the Trust's logo on into the back of her vehicle. Yes, I know we shouldn't be doing that, but…" She rolled her eyes at us. "I couldn't get a signal earlier, so I'm calling you now. You should know that Mavis has stopped at the mini-mart and is talking on a pay phone. Yes, she is alone. Alright, goodbye."

"What did he say?" I asked.

"He told me to stop being Miss Marple, whoever she is, and go back to Vindolanda. He'll send an unmarked car to stake out her farm. I guess we're through?"

I turned to her. "Doesn't he think it odd that she's not using her mobile, perhaps for fear that the police are on to her and tracing her calls?"

Sima shook her head, helpless.

"After she's gone, I want to pop in and get some groceries, so Mike sees me with a full carrier bag when I drop the car off," Dave said.

"Get me a Mars Bar," I said. We waited fifteen minutes until our suspect also did some shopping and returned to her car. When she left the car park, she did not turn right to go back towards the farm, but turned left, and joined the main road, heading towards Newcastle.

"Should we follow?" I asked.

"I think so," Dave said. "We know she's got the boxes in her car, so she might be going to drop the stuff off." He also joined the main road, and accelerated to catch her up. Fortunately, there was very little traffic, and the street lights helped us to follow at a discreet distance. After a mile, she indicated left and turned off on a B road. We followed for half a mile until she reached a row of cottages and stopped in front of the first one. Dave pulled onto the grass verge, and we watched. The rain had reduced to a light drizzle, and the lights from the cottages illuminated her ringing the doorbell. A man came out, and she opened the back of her vehicle. Soon, the two of them had carried eight boxes into the cottage. The Vindolanda Trust logo was clearly visible.

"No signal," Sima said, "and my battery is about to run out."

"Let's drive back and make a note of the name of this lane, then call the inspector again when we get back to Vindolanda," I suggested.

"I'll edge forwards, and you can get the registration of the black van parked down the side of the first cottage," Dave said, leaning forward to peer past the hedge row. Mavis had gone inside and the front door closed. Dave edged forwards and I made a mental note of the registration. We turned around and left, having done our bit of sleuthing for the night.

"That's the handover," Dave said as we re-joined the main road. "Now for some speed shopping, then we get the car back to Mike as quickly as possible."

*****

After Sima had updated a grumpy Inspector Griffiths by pay phone, we went to the cafeteria for our evening meal. Sima excused herself after we'd eaten to retire, saying she wanted to get up early and go for a run with her dorm mates. Dave and I bought cans of beer and went to the communal lounge to watch television, before also getting an early night.

I was dragged from my sleep by my phone ringing. It was barely light in the crack between the curtains, but when I saw Sima's name I answered.

"Hi Sima, what's up?" I muttered, wiping sleep from my eyes.

"Get dressed quick. I'm outside the admin block, and guess who's just turned up and gone inside the building?"

"Who?" I asked, my brain not up to the task of thinking.

"It's Mavis. She's come in her people carrier. She's gone into her office and left the door open, and the back of the vehicle is open. I think she might have come back for more boxes. Get down here quick. I'm running to my room to get my car keys."

Dave had been wakened by my voice, and I quickly passed on what had been said. We got dressed and ran downstairs, leaving the main entrance in murky morning light to walk around the block to the admin car park.

"I don't think I've ever seen eight o'clock on a Saturday," Dave groaned.

"There she is," I said, ducking down behind a car. We peered across the car park and saw Mavis MacDonald putting a box in the back of her car. She then went in briefly and left, locking the door and getting behind her wheel.

"Damn, I wish I'd taken the inspector's number off Sima," I said. Now she's driving out."

"Here's Sima," Dave said, pulling my sleeve. We jumped up and converged at Sima's car. She turned her engine on and we got in.

"Can you give me your phone so I can call the Inspector," I asked.

She glanced at me and gave me his business card from her pocket. "I'm not telling you my pin number, so here's his number. Can you call him?" She put the car into gear and drove out of the car park and up the hill.

I dialled his number, but by the time we were over the first hill, the signal had dropped off. "I'll try again when I get a signal," I said. "I've saved his number," I added, as she sped along the lane. We caught up with her as she turned onto the main road and headed towards Newcastle. This time, she didn't take the left turn to her previous drop off point, but kept going.

"Shall we continue following?" Sima asked.

"Yes, we must," I replied. "Hello, Inspector Griffiths? This is Noah Jessop, from Vindolanda. I'm with Sima in her car, and we're following Mavis who's heading towards Newcastle in her vehicle. Yes, the blue Toyota, reg N364NYP. No, we weren't going to interfere... you see the thing is... if you'll let me finish, she came back to Vindolanda early this morning and went into the office and left with two more boxes. Sima spotted her whilst she was on her morning run. OK, goodbye." I ended the call and put my phone down, staring ahead.

"Well?" Sima asked.

"He says we are to stop following her and go home."

"No chance," Sima replied, with a determined tone. "She's most likely the artefacts thief, and I want this case solved and the monkey off my back!"

"Yeah, that's the spirit!" Dave said from the back seat. "Her contact must have told her to go back and get whatever she'd left behind. As we can't be sure the police are on top of this, I agree with Sima."

"OK, then let's carry on following," I said. "He was as grumpy as hell, as if I'd interrupted his bacon and eggs."

"Ah, breakfast!" Dave groaned, "Now you've really made me hungry. Look, there's a sign for a Little Chef on the A1, just to rub it in."

We sped along the A69 and entered the outskirts of Newcastle. Mavis followed the signs to the airport.

"I've never been to Newcastle airport," I said, as we entered the service vehicles parking area.

Dave snorted. "Well, you have now. Newcastle International Airport. Holiday flights mainly, but I bet they also do air freight."

Sima crept carefully past rows of parked vehicles, just keeping Mavis in sight. Mavis parked at the farthest end, near a chain link fence. Half a dozen private jets stood on the other side of the fence, on the edge of the runway.

"She's parked next to our old friend, the man with the back van," Dave said. Sima parked diagonally opposite, at a discreet distance, and we watched as the man she had met at the cottage got out and joined her behind her vehicle. There was a formal handshake, and Mavis lifted the rear door, showing him the boxes.

"Where are the police?" I asked.

Sima shrugged. "Maybe they're here in unmarked vehicles."

"Perhaps we should call the inspector again," Dave said.

Sima lifted her phone and found him in her contacts. "Hello, it's Sima. Yes. Look I know you told Noah that we shouldn't follow her, but we did, and we're now at Newcastle Airport." She put her phone on speaker so we all heard the inspector losing his cool and shouting at her. "Look, inspector, are your lot here? How were we to know if you had followed the man in the black van..."

"Stay in your car and keep out of sight!" he shouted, then the phone went dead.

Sima stared at the blank screen. "Charming, he hung up on me."

The man from the van, looking bulky in a puffer jacket, had walked to the fence, and I could see there was a gate. "He's fiddling with the padlock on the gate. They're going to put the boxes on a plane!"

Sure enough, once the gate was opened, he hurried to his van and opened the back, taking out a box. Mavis also lifted a box from her vehicle, and followed him to the gate. Two men appeared from one of the private jets to meet them. They were smartly dressed in dark suits and appeared very relaxed, like a couple of chauffeurs.

"If the police aren't here, they'll get away with it!" I squealed, looking at Sima and then Dave. We all wore expressions of helplessness, and just sat there, watching as boxes were carried and handed over.

Dave finally broke the silence, "We could try a citizen's arrest."

"They might have guns," Sima said. "It's far too dangerous."

I looked around at the other cars parked either side of us. "The police are not here. There's no one watch except us. This is terrible…"

I was interrupted by the distant sound of a siren, getting gradually louder. It came from within the airport, and as the men inside the fence scrambled to their jet, two yellow airport security cars with red lights spinning on top and sirens wailing, came speeding towards them. Then, from behind us, the screech of tyres announced the speedy arrival of four cars. Mavis and her contact panicked and slammed shut the backs of their vehicles and jumped into them. Mavis had backed out of her space when she was cornered by two cars, a third stopping behind the black van, and a fourth just in front of Sima's car. A combination of plain-clothed and uniformed police officers jumped out and swarmed all over Mavis and her contact's van, and soon they had been arrested.

Inspector Griffiths slowly got out of the back door of the fourth unmarked police car, and walked slowly to Sima's window. She meekly lowered it, and he leaned his flat-capped head in. "I'll spare you three the 'you're in a lot of trouble speech'. We've had a result, despite you holding up proceedings by getting in the firing line. You should have gone home, as you were strongly advised to do. So, let's leave it at that, shall we?"

"Yes, Inspector," Sima said.

"Can we wait to see what's in the boxes, just to be sure?" I asked.

The inspector shot me a filthy look, and I shrank back into the passenger's seat. Then he paused and said, "You know, Miss Chaudry is a member of staff, and as such can speed things up by identifying the items before we take them down town to book in. But you two lads can stay in the car."

Sima smiled as she got out, waving her ID lanyard at me. I saw her pull her stomach in and stand up tall.

"Do you always go running with that?" I asked, and laughed.

"Wouldn't be caught dead without it," she replied, slamming her door and following the inspector.

Dave and I watched in silence as the two men from the private jet were marched to the cars, handcuffed, and the boxes carried to the boots of the police vehicles. Sima and the inspector looked in all eight boxes and she nodded to him, then gave a verbal description as he scribbled in his notebook.

"Somehow I can't see him tapping the keyboard on a tablet," I said.

Sima returned, wearing a grin, and confirmed the bags of coins were there, in addition to other gold and silver Roman jewellery and ornaments.

"Little Chef on the way back?" Dave asked.

"I think we've earned it," Sima replied, starting the engine.

22. Coria, 181 CE

Gaius was pleased to find that Amborix had cleaned his sword and armour when he arose from a sound night's sleep. Aria helped dress him, and they ate honey cakes baked by Marta and dried fruits for breakfast, before Gaius kissed his wife and son and made his way to the senior officers' tents.

"Ah, Gaius, we have been called to a meeting by Legate Hieronymianus," First Spear boomed in his deep voice as Gaius approached. "Follow me."

The two centurions entered an even bigger tent than the tribune's and followed a red carpet into an inner space where Tribune Bebius was deep in conversation with a surprisingly young legate. First Spear introduced Gaius, and they took their seats opposite a raised dais set for their legion commander. They were offered honeyed water by attendants, and Gaius sipped whilst they waited, staring at the magnificent golden eagle standard of the Sixth Legion. After five minutes, Tribune Bebius took a seat beside another tribune, next to First Spear.

Legate Hieronymianus, a short, pale-skinned man in his mid-twenties and the youngest senior man present, dressed in a white gold-lined toga and a cloak of purple and gold, stood to welcome them with outstretched arms. "My dear brothers, I have come to you after receiving your messenger, who rode through the night, to be with you in this vexing moment and offer my assistance." His smile revealed a set of gleaming white teeth, the like of which Gaius had not seen.

"Two of my ten cohorts are represented here by Tribune Marcellus of the First Cohort, who escorted me from Eboracum, and Tribune Bebius of the Third Cohort, based here at the smoking ruins of Coria." He paused to glare at Bebius. "Also, I am pleased to welcome two centurions who have distinguished themselves in defeating the barbarians and reclaiming our property and town." He nodded at them, then added, "I should mention that Tribune Cassius from the Second Cohort, based at Arbeia supply fort in the east, will be joining us later in the day."

He returned to his ornate, golden throne, and paused to lift a fig from a tray and pop it in his mouth. Gaius noticed his shin guards each bore a gladiator engraved in gold, the left facing the right, ready to strike with trident and sword. To Gaius, he looked like a god, with a golden sash tied around his slim waist and circlet of gold and silver thread around his head.

The legate coughed, pulled his sleeve and resumed, "I had hoped for a better reason to tour the frontier forts than this invasion, but this is the very purpose of our posting to this cold and windy northern frontier. I can tell you that the eyes of our new emperor, Commodus, are on us, and my report on this incident will soon make its way to Rome." He cast his bright brown eyes over his officers, and although his mouth wore a smile, his eyes were as cold as a gladiator's when circling his prey.

"Needless to say, the main part of my report will be the swift response and expert deployment of military skills and weapons to devastating effect, and the exemplary conduct of two officers in particular." He summoned a clerk to bring a parchment and read from it. "Senior centurion Julius Flavius, of the First Century, Third Cohort, Sixth Legion Victrix Pia Fidelis, come forward."

The big man stood and marched to the edge of the dais, standing stiffly to attention.

"Your emperor salutes you for your bravery in battle, and awards you this silver arm band." Legate Hieronymianus placed the band on his wrist, and handed him a small rolled-up scroll, then stepped back to salute the burly veteran. First Spear returned the salute, spun on his heels, and marched to his chair; his square-jawed face impassive.

"Step forward Centurion Gaius Atticianus, of the Fourth Cent, Fourth Cohort, Sixth Legion Victrix Pia Fidelis."

Gaius repeated the drill, received his silver wrist band and scroll citation, saluted and returned to his seat, struggling to contain his emotions, his heart bursting with pride.

"The quick wits and bravery of these two officers have saved us from a very embarrassing defeat," Hieronymianus said from his throne, "and gives me a gloss to put on my report to our emperor. However, it will also be noted that the third cohort were taken by surprise, resulting in the destruction of our town and supply base at Coria." He looked coldly down at Tribune Bebius, who caught his eye and then hung his head in shame, expecting the criticism.

"To this end, some changes will be made. I have brought with me four hundred legionaries and two hundred Sarmatian cavalry troops to replenish the numbers both here and at Vindolanda, which I believe was under siege from barbarians at the time you left, Centurion Atticianus?"

Gaius jumped to his feet and snapped to attention, replying, "Yes sir, some three days ago. I estimated about six hundred barbarians, sir, although some did follow us to Coria."

"Then you shall lead your new command there, centurion, and relieve the fort. I will send you with some orders for Tribune Pertinax. I also have new orders and a new posting for you." He turned and called his clerk again and took a parchment from him.

Gaius gulped and stared ahead, wondering what was to come.

"Yes. I need a new regional commander at the fort of Epiacum, and am promoting you, Gaius Atticianus, to Senior Centurion and giving you one hundred Sarmatians and one hundred infantry regulars, in addition to the garrison there, to swell your command. This will be a deployment from your cohort and you will continue to report to Tribune Pertinax. Epiacum is a fort about fifty miles to the west of here, and is of strategic importance in that it guards a lead and silver mine. Such precious metals are highly prized and are a major asset of this province. It is all explained in these orders to your tribune. You will leave tomorrow morning and travel with Centurion Marcus Scapula, who is waiting for you outside. I trust I shall hear no more of barbarians raiding south of the Great Wall of Hadrian."

Gaius stepped forward and received two parchment rolls, one sealed with the legate's ring mark on red wax, saluted, turned and marched out. His award citation and promotion scrolls were tied with ribbons, and he would read them at his leisure. The sealed scroll was for his commander at Vindolanda. His head was spinning with all that had been said in such a short time. Aria would be thrilled to hear of his promotion, but they would have to leave their friends in Vindolanda and move to a new fort. He gripped the rolls tightly, and looked about.

A centurion in new, polished armour approached him. "I am Centurion Marcus Scapula, joining the Fourth Cohort at Vindolanda," he said, saluting Gaius.

"Senior Centurion Gaius Atticianus," Gaius replied. He would have to get used to his new rank that put him above other centurions. "I understand that you will accompany me to Vindolanda in the morning, with two hundred men."

"Yes, sir. Perhaps you'd like to brief me and my two optios on what to expect?"

Gaius looked at his keen black eyes and clean-shaven chin, eager for action. "Yes, but not now. Let's meet at the parade ground in one hour when I will introduce you to my optio and decurion." He turned and marched to his tent to tell Aria the good news and safely stow the parchments in his saddle bags. This was indeed a good day, blessed by the gods.

*****

Aria was indeed pleased, as was Marta, and it was a happy family that packed and made their preparations to leave. Gaius smiled at the memory of his son searching for a carved horse that Amborix had whittled for him, and hidden under a cushion. He hoped to have more time at home with his family as commander of his own fort and surrounding territory. He was flanked by Centurions Lupus Viridio and Marcus Scapula, his faithful deputy, Paulinus, now consigned to the second rank, with two other optios for company. They rode at marching pace, with wagons and two hundred and sixty legionaries bringing up the rear. The road was quiet, stretching ahead to the horizon in an unerring straight line, the unbreakable will of Rome echoed in every beat of Mars's hooves.

Gaius wrapped his cloak tighter against a chill wind. Januarius was a cold month, but one that brought the promise of warmer days to come. "Where do you hail from?" Gaius asked the new man.

"I am from Umbria in Italia, sir. My father was a tribune in the First Legion and is now retired on our family farm. It is a hill farm with sheep and goats. Beautiful, but rocky."

"Then you have travelled far. Is this your first command?"

"I was one year in Eboracum, on the staff at legion headquarters. I begged our new legate to give me a frontier fort command. I have yet to blood my sword in combat, and hope it will not be long, sir."

"It may come before this day is out. Once we turn off for Vindolanda and crest the first hill, I intend to leave the wagons there whilst we ride ahead to see if the barbarians are still around the fort. But before then, tell me about our new legate and your understanding of the politics that swirl around him?"

242

"There is a purge going on in Rome, and fear-tainted whispers haunt the porticos and bath houses. Our new emperor and his close friends are fixing their avaricious eyes on wealthy families with rich estates. Accusations of treason are finding their way to the doors of many patrician and equestrian families. Our legate's family can trace their ancestry to the patricians of the Republic and are favoured by the new emperor, so we are a favoured legion," he said with a wide grin.

"We are blessed to be spared the politics of Rome," Gaius replied, "but if the emperor trusts him, he may want him close, and our legion may be recalled to Italia."

"Perhaps, sir. But I think the eyes of Rome are on this northern frontier, and there is opportunity for him to win glory and praise. He will resist such a suggestion, if it comes, until we give him a big victory over the barbarians. Your victory before the walls of Coria is a start, sir, but he will expect more."

An hour later the wagons were on top of the hill, and Gaius ordered the legionaries to take a break with the passengers until they were summoned. He then rode ahead with his one hundred new Sarmatian troops, and his battle-hardened group of fourteen survivors from Vindolanda, swollen by two of the wounded now recovered enough to ride.

After a short time, a scout rode hard to Gaius and pulled up in a puff of dust. "Sir, the fort is free of barbarians!" he reported.

"Then ride back to the wagons and legionaries, and tell them to come," Gaius replied. He turned with a smile to his young companion and said, "It seems our father, Saturn, wants you to wait a while longer for your first taste of battle. Let's ride ahead."

Gaius's standard bearer, Getterix, and one other of his Gallic cavalry soldiers met them before they reach the gates, and Gaius was pleased to hear his excited report that the barbarians packed up and left the day before, heading north to the Wall.

"We shadowed them, sir," Getterix proudly reported, "and saw them leave through the gates of a deserted mile fort. We secured the fort and gates, sir."

"Did they try to enter our fort?" Gaius asked.

"They came the night you left, sir, with ladders, but we fought them off. They didn't try again."

Gaius led his troops through the south gatehouse, to an enthusiastic welcome from hollering soldiers and whooping townsfolk, thronging the platforms on the walls and leaning over upper balconies of townhouses. He enjoyed the welcome, waving and smiling like a returning hero to imperial Rome, as they slowly progressed to the central square. He detailed Paulinus and Meral to stable the horses and find barrack accommodation for the new men, then led Marcus and Lupus to the commander's office, clutching his scrolls.

"Ah Gaius!" Tribune Pertinax beamed, standing up behind his desk and extending his arms in welcome. "Please, come in." He sent his clerk to summon the centurions and ordered food and ale be brought from his kitchen, then guided the pair to seats at the long table. "And Lupus, it has been long, I trust you are well?"

"I am well, sir," Lupus replied, saluting. "I return with only sixty remaining of my cent, after the battle we fought against the barbarians at Coria, sir."

"I look forward to hearing of it. Gaius, is that an imperial seal I see?"

"Yes, sir, I carry orders from Legate Hieronymianus," Gaius replied, handing over the larger parchment with the red wax seal.

Pertinax grunted and took the scroll, opening it at once. He spent a minute reading, then looked up at Gaius. "So, our new legate left the comforts of Eboracum. You have met him before me, but I expect he will tour the frontier forts once the barbarian threat has gone. We've had a fraught two days, Gaius, but more on that later." He looked up and blinked his pin-prick eyes sunk in a doughy face. "I will be sad to lose you from my fort, although you will still be my fourth cent commander, with an enhanced command at another fort. We both profit from that. Congratulations." His frown gave way to a smile, and Gaius was put at ease.

"It was most unexpected, sir," Gaius replied. "Our commander sends you a new centurion, a cavalry cent and a hundred legionaries, sir."

"That is kind of him. But your promotion and new command is wholly deserved, Gaius. I have noted your clear thinking and bravery when faced with the enemy. It is by no means the norm. You are a warrior and a leader, Gaius, and I congratulate you on your promotion. The gods favour a man who comes through the ranks. This would have set you above our preening praetorian, Centurion Plauditus, but for the fact that our legate is promoting him to tribune, and he is to replace my friend, Flavius Lucius Bebius, at Coria." He roughly rolled up the scroll and tapped it on the table, turning to look through the window.

Gaius now understood his tribune's sour face. For every winner, there is a loser. "May I introduce his replacement, Centurion Marcus Scapula," Gaius said, leaning back so that his commander could see the new man.

"You are welcome, Marcus Scapula. Perhaps you can take over the opulent quarters that Plauditus will be vacating. Ah, here they come." Three centurions filed in and took their seats. Pertinax rose to his feet. "To have six centurions here at one time is something of a record. Gaius and Lupus have returned to us, and they bring reinforcements and a new centurion. This is Marcus Scapula."

Ale and cakes were served as the centurions welcomed the new arrivals. Plauditus looked down his hawk's beak at Gaius and offered dry congratulations on him surviving to return. Gaius smiled, knowing that Plauditus had as yet no idea of his promotion and new command, or of his own soon-to-be-announced promotion to tribune. Change is inexorable. Gaius recalled a year ago when Plauditus was the new centurion. He had boasted about his senatorial background and praetorian training, and his guaranteed fast-track via tribune to legate. It was happening.

"Take your seats, men," Pertinax squeaked to quell the chatter. "I am doubly pleased today, for not only have the wretched barbarians left us, but we are welcoming back Gaius and Lupus, and most of their men; although sadly, some perished in a bitter fight at Coria. I will let Gaius tell us about that, but first, some orders have come from our noble legate, Claudius Hieronymianus."

He unrolled his scroll and read: "By order of... etcetera, Centurion Plauditus Titus Vespasianus is hereby promoted to the rank of Tribune and transferred forthwith to the Third Cohort based at Coria." He lowered the scroll and looked at Plauditus, who wore an expression of feigned surprise. "Congratulations, Plauditus. We shall gather at the Jupiter's Temple when the sun goes down to offer sacrifice for a successful posting." The centurions offered polite applause and mumbled good wishes. "Plauditus will travel to Coria tomorrow with an escort to receive his purple-edged robes and orders from Legate Hieronymianus." He paused to sip ale from a silver goblet, wincing at some discomfort. He signalled to an attendant to take the offending goblet away, whispering, "Bring me milk."

He coughed and continued reading. "But that is not all. Centurion Gaius Atticianus is promoted to Senior Centurion and Regional Commander at Epiacum fort. He will leave in two days, after a handover, so we shall also make sacrifice for his success in his new posting." Warmer congratulations rippled around the room. "And we welcome a new centurion, Marcus Scapula, to replace Plauditus. We have a new cavalry cent, perhaps an addition to the fourth cent for administration purposes." He paused to look at his prefect, Adminius, "And I will need to find a new centurion to lead them." He looked at Gaius with upraised eyebrows and sat, giving him the floor.

Gaius rose to his feet, smiling. "My thanks to you, Tribune Pertinax, and my fellow officers. I will briefly tell you of events since I left here."

Gaius told of his progress to Coria, pursued by barbarians, but decided to omit the burial of the payroll chest. It was their pay, after all, and he knew they would be vexed at its possible loss. The legate had ordered him directly to Vindolanda, thinking it may still be under siege, and he did not feel it appropriate to take a detour to recover the chest. He had reported it to the tribune at Coria, and that was that.

He briefly talked of the desperate and ultimately futile defence of Coria, mentioning Lupus's part in their unit's ordered retreat. He then spoke of tracking the barbarian wagon train northwards and recovery of the looted grain and weapons. On his return to Coria, he had been unaware that his cavalry charge had been watched by Tribune Bebius from across the river, and the silver wrist band award for bravery on his recommendation came as a pleasant surprise. He had been further surprised the next day by the arrival of their legion's new legate with reinforcements, and his subsequent promotion and new posting. He sat to rapturous hand-slapping on the table and foot stamping. He caught Plauditus's jealous eye and smiled.

"You have brought honour on our cohort, Gaius, and it shall not be forgotten. My clerk has made a note and your award will be recorded in our records," Pertinax said, getting to his feet. "But I have one new centurion, and am losing two," he added, looking balefully at Gaius.

"Sir, may I recommend my optio, Paulinus Grella, be promoted to Centurion of Horses. He has been my shadow for fifteen years and I believe he is ready. I have already identified Paulinus's replacement as optio from within my ranks, sir."

"I can see you've given this some thought. What do the rest of you think?" Tribune Pertinax asked. There were shrugs and no one offered a counter proposal. "Very well, send this Paulinus Grella to my office, Gaius. That is all. Let us all meet at the temple after victuals. You are dismissed, except Plauditus and Marcus. We shall discuss arrangements for a handover." As they filed out, Gaius heard his tribune lament, "I dislike change, and this day has been one of tumult, akin to the storms of Neptune; I have felt the sharp barbs of his trident in my feet, and my stomach churns like rolls of breaking waves."

Gaius smiled with relief. His tribune was content, and the politically divisive praetorian, Plauditus, was leaving to lead his own cohort. With luck, their paths would not cross again.

*****

Longinus wept with joy, mixed with relief, and fell to kiss Gaius's boots when he walked through his door.

Gaius raised the old man to his feet. "Longinus, I am as relieved as you to find you are well and our home has been spared the ravages of blue-faced barbarians. My thanks to you for keeping the lamps burning and feeding the fowl. Now, stoke up the hypocaust for my hot bath, then select a fat duck for our table this eve."

He was pleased with how well his proposal for Paulinus's promotion had been received, and looked forward to meeting his oldest friend the next day at the tavern for a celebratory and farewell drink. But for now, he wanted to soak saddle-sore bones in his tub with his voluptuous wife Aria for company, then tease his son over their meal.

"You are very happy, my husband," Aria said, tickling his side as he picked his teeth with a duck bone, at table later that evening.

"I am four years from retiring, Aria, and a posting as commander should preserve my old bones and give me every chance of living to see Brutus blossom into a strong youth." He picked up the wriggling boy and sat him on his lap.

"We are four years from retiring, you mean," she said, correcting him. "I shall enjoy being the commander's wife and instructing the other wives to do my bidding."

That night, as Gaius snored, a dark-cloaked hooded figure left the villa and made her way past the guards at the north gate, out along the main road through the vicus, past the last revellers being thrown out of the tavern, before turning left onto a cobbled street that ran east to west through the heart of the native settlement.

She stopped before the shrine to the goddess Brigantia, and looked about to see that no one was watching. By the light of a half moon, she bent and dug a hole in the soft earth with a wooden spatula. Then she removed a wrapped stone object from her pocket and placed it in the hole, whispering a brief entreaty to the goddess as she covered it with soil. Standing, she trod on the burial site until it was flattened, then turned and retraced her steps back to the villa and bed, with the relief of a task accomplished.

23. Vindolanda, present day

"You three better come in, and I'll make a pot of coffee." Maggie was in her long silk kaftan and fluffy slippers, her strawberry blond hair untended.

I noted the time on my phone was eleven o'clock. We'd been up for four action-packed hours, whilst most were having a Saturday lie-in.

"Mavis, a member of a gang of international artefact thieves?" Maggie added, in utter disbelief, as she ushed us into her living room.

We sat on chairs at her dining table whilst she spooned filter coffee into her machine and set it percolating in the kitchen.

"My pulse is still going after watching the police arrest this morning," Sima whispered in my ear, her hand covering mine on the table.

"Yes, I'm still on an adrenalin high," I replied softly, turning to her.

Maggie walked in with a plate of croissants and a pot of jam, making fleeting eye contact with me as I pulled my hand away and turned around. "You must be starving after driving to Newcastle Airport and back. And up so early. Try these. The coffee will be about ten minutes." She sat on the fourth chair and pushed her hair back with her fingers. "What prompted you to follow Mavis so early?"

"I went for an early morning run with my dorm mates," Sima replied, "and just happened to see Mavis letting herself into your office. It was before eight o'clock, so I called Noah to keep watch whilst I went to change and get my car keys."

"So, you saw her loading more boxes into her people carrier?" Her face when she turned to me was deadly serious.

"Yeah. Dave joined me and we waited for Sima, then followed. It seemed pretty suspicious to us." I felt self-conscious with both Maggie and Sima so close to me. Fortunately, Sima had withdrawn her hand from the table.

"We're glad you and Mike aren't involved," Dave added.

"Thank you, David, for the vote of confidence," Maggie said, smiling at him as she rose to her feet. "I'll get the coffee."

Dave grinned like a puppy who'd had his head ruffled. "We should pop round to Mike's after this to share the good news." He broke off a piece of croissant and plastered it with a teaspoon of strawberry jam.

I groaned. "Yeah, then get some rest, I'm knackered."

"Let's go to the pub this evening for a celebratory meal," Sima proposed.

Maggie returned with a tray and served the coffee. None of us admitted to having had breakfast already. "Well, Sima, I could have wished you hadn't had this to contend with, but I'm glad you've settled in and made friends."

"Oh yes. Since Noah moved to the Archives, we've got to know each other a little." She smiled sweetly at me.

"He's such a charming and handsome young man," Maggie said, a little too caustically.

Maggie had picked up the signals, alright, and I squirmed uncomfortably as I sipped my coffee, trying not to make eye contact with either woman. My eyes settled on Maggie's photo, her Gertrude Bell pose, the archaeologist staring enigmatically at a new, unconquered land from the battlements of Vindolanda.

"Well, thanks for the coffee and croissants, Maggie," I said. "We're going to see Mike now and share the good news."

"Oh, of course. He'll be keen to know he's in the clear. But would you mind staying behind for a few minutes, Noah? I've got some notes for you, since you're here, and they require a bit of explaining."

Sima and Dave said their goodbyes and Maggie saw them to the door. Did Sima's parting look have a question in it? I hoped not. I heard the door close.

I steeled myself for an angry tirade at Maggie's sharp intake of breath on her return, but was surprised when it turned into a sob.

"My own assistant stealing from me! The trustees will be breathing down my neck now," she wailed. "She had very good references, and they all checked out."

Somewhere between the front door and the dining room, she'd dropped the guard that had been up since we arrived, and this was vulnerable Maggie, the one I hadn't seen until now. Well, at least this wasn't all about me.

"It wasn't your fault, Maggie." That was all I could think to say.

"I'm responsible, Noah. Like in the days of the Roman Empire, you know. When they promote you through the ranks, your job is to make them shine. I'm a woman with a queue of people, men for the most part, lining up to stab me in the back and slide into my seat. Well, I won't let everything that's important to me, that I've worked so hard to build up, be snatched away." Dismay had turned to defiance, which I understood better.

I felt braver now. "There's nothing going on with Sima."

"Not yet," she said softly, retying the belt on her kaftan. "Oh, come and sit down, Noah."

The kaftan evoked memories of her floaty dress that first evening we were together. It seemed like ages ago. I sat on the couch, but she didn't sit next to me, going to an armchair next to it instead. "I wouldn't want to hurt you, Maggie."

252

She looked at me and sighed, and I had the impression she was making a decision. "When I was a student, I lost somebody very dear to me. He drowned when we were on holiday, Noah."

"That's tragic," I said, actually quite shocked. "That must've been hard on you..."

She nodded and carried on. "I dealt with it by throwing myself into my studies afterwards, as if I was living his life for him, I suspect. But very soon, it was my own enthusiasm keeping me going. And I was less cautious, more adventurous."

"I know how addictive archaeology is." She spoke of adventure, but I could picture her trudging home from the library without him by her side.

"I never stopped being a student, always learning more. I layered the teaching and exploring on top, travelling overseas in the summer and burning the midnight oil in the winter. But I could only do it if I was free. Well, last autumn, I had almost been convinced to rescue yet another relationship that had drifted out of sight. But I got cold feet and wasn't sure I could stop being a free spirit."

"Not sure, because of me?" I didn't want to hear what I thought she was about to say.

"Not because of you, Noah. Don't lay that on yourself." She smiled at me and reached over and patted my hand.

"I held your little Brigantia statue in my hands and felt a shock of recognition. You get that with a piece sometimes. I wondered what sight had met her eyes after so long in the dark. When I lifted my head, you were looking at me, and I knew it was the same way you'd looked at her."

"And that was why you invited me for dinner."

"It was an impulse I should have resisted. I relished the chance to escape from the pressure I was feeling. I intended to spend a couple of hours stoking your passion for your work and giving you a few home comforts, because I was reminded of the boy I lost. You don't look anything like him, Noah, but you have his mental energy."

"I think we've both been living a bit of a fantasy," I said, looking at the magazine cover shot.

She nodded. "I knew I should end things, but I was afraid you'd give me away. It's not just that I shudder at the thought of your friends tittering about us, but if word of this got to the trustees, my reputation would be in shreds."

"I won't betray you, Maggie. What's between us is between us alone. I'm not a child." I hoped I didn't sound petulant.

"I know you well enough now to know I won't break your heart, and to believe I can trust you." She gave me a wry smile, and I looked at the carpet, not one I would have chosen myself.

"I think you're incredible, Maggie. And I'm disappointed if you're saying it's over." I genuinely meant it in the moment I said it, so there was no expression of relief to hide.

"As lovely as it's been, I need this to end, for both our sakes. I just hope I can stick to my resolve. Now, go and enjoy your weekend with your friends. I hate to say it, Noah, but I think your little marble goddess is nudging you in the right direction." She squeezed my hand and then let go.

I could feel her warmth when I bent to peck her cheek, because it was tearstained, and because I thought this was still allowed. As I left, feeling unexpectedly bereft and shaky, she wasn't the only one thinking this was a test of their resolve.

*****

With our dissertation reviews at an end, Dave and I left Vindolanda and returned to our shared student house in Durham. An hour away by train, but a world away in many respects. I had finally nailed down my dissertation, built around the dig for the Roman payroll chest and the clues about the life of Gaius. The fortnight had been capped by the intense rush of uncovering Mavis's stolen artefacts scandal.

Dave's dissertation was on the technical steps followed in both the main dig at Vindolanda and our investigation that revealed a tiered graveyard site, with exposed burials from three separate time periods. He helped me out by providing a grid diagram of the Hardcastle Estate family graveyard plot, showing light-grey shaded radar 'hits' and the actual sites that were dug to reveal artefacts. His detailed list and descriptions of equipment used and archaeological methods followed put me on a solid technical footing.

I had eight weeks to finalise my dissertation report and produce a PowerPoint version for my dual presentations to my tutors and course mates at Durham Uni, and to the archaeology and archives sections at Vindolanda.

I also needed to make myself an indispensable part of Sima's life, if she was to play as significant a part in my future as I hoped she would.

24. Epiacum, 183 CE

Gaius hated visiting the mining compound; a cluster of filthy wooden buildings on a sea of mud hemmed in by a semi-circular ditch and timber defence ending at a rocky outcrop, under which two mine shafts had been dug. He walked unsteadily from the lean-to stables to the main administration building, balancing on planks that were half-submerged in soft, wet, sticky, greyish-brown mud that made a sucking sound, as if something was trying to drag the walker down to a monster's underground lair.

He squeezed his lucky coin for comfort at the sound, and jumped from one board to another, muttering, "So this is my reward for scattering the enemy." The whole idea of men burrowing into the earth was anathema to him. Burrowing into another world inhabited by the greedy Gobelinus who resented men stealing his gold and silver – a story from childhood that still haunted his dreams. He would gaze in horror at the gaping black holes in the cliff-face into which near-naked slaves would crawl, knowing he could never be persuaded to enter. The slaves were criminals and defeated warriors from Caledonian and Briton tribes who lived on site in wooden barrack blocks.

"Ah, Commander Atticianus, you are most welcome," the well-fed, balding mine manager, Annius Plocamus, said, rising from his chair and rolling around his desk to make ingratiating bows to the senior centurion. He was well-insulated in a warm woollen ankle-length garment and socks to match. It hung loose, and Gaius was sure there was no belt in the entire province long enough to encircle his girth.

Gaius scowled and stamped some excess mud from his boots, making a mess of the reed mat. "As often as I've come here over this past two years, I'm no more used to it. I hate this infernal entrance to Hades."

"Please, have a seat, Commander, and we shall share a flask of finest brandy from Gaul." He clapped his hands and a female slave appeared from a shadowy corner. "To what do I owe the pleasure of this… unexpected visit?"

Gaius regarded him with mild contempt and waited to be served. He was the mine manager and agent of Ascanius Trading, who held a lucrative contract with the provincial governor's office to supply lead and silver. Gaius provided the camp guards and a mounted escort from the mine smelting plant to a jetty on the nearby River Tine. From there, the crates were transported by flat-bottomed barge to the bridge at Coria. He had previously witnessed braying donkeys carrying crates to bigger boats on the other side, for their onward journey to the sea port at Segedunum. Now he knew what was in the crates. He had been shown the molten lead being poured into moulds, and had held the cooled grey bars bearing the Ascanius brand, each weighing as much as his eight-year-old son, Brutus. The bars were then packed into stout wooden crates at the warehouse.

"I've come to establish the details of the recent theft for my report. My tribune will be most alarmed, as will Legate Hieronymianus."

Plocamus swallowed at the mention of the legate's name and wrung his hands. "There were eight riders that day, and two wagons. They left early in the morning and took the road over the hill to our port. As you know, it is only half a mile, and your watchtower on the next hill has them in sight at all times. I am told by my driver that a horde of about twenty riders fell on them just before they reached the port. Army deserters working with locals, most likely. They killed three of your men and wounded the others, then made off with the wagons and horses."

Gaius was comparing his account with that of his own men. "And in which direction did they go?"

"They went south on the Roman road, and from there, who knows?" He mopped his brow with a cloth and clapped again, shouting, "And cakes for the officer!"

Gaius recalled the time Plocamus had shown him the blobs of silver in the lead bars with a covetous grin, telling him that thieves usually gouge the silver out of the heavy bars and discard the lead. Not just thieves, but also the owners, who separated the silver to mint coins. "And you say shipments are roughly once a month and only arranged the day before, when there is a barge waiting at the jetty?"

"Yes, sir. There is one barge and it takes all day to get to Coria, where it must dock as it cannot pass under the bridge. The crew serve the needs of other customers, supplying forts or transporting farm produce. The barge returns after a month with supplies for us. Sometimes it remains here for a day or two until we are ready with a consignment."

"So, the appearance of the barge is a signal for the thieves," Gaius said. "But there could also be a man on the inside, who sends them word."

"Our security is very tight, sir. I doubt we have a spy amongst us."

"Even so, everyone must be more vigilant, and the penalty for spying for a gang of thieves will be crucifixion. I will talk to your workers before I leave."

Gaius munched a raison cake and raised his eyebrows. "You always have better wine, brandy and cakes than me, Plocamus. My wife would like these."

"Then I shall make a gift of the cakes and brandy for your table, centurion." He jumped to his feet and whispered instructions to his slave in the corner, then returned to hover next to Gaius.

"Gather your workers now, whilst I talk to the commander of the watch." Gaius slowly stood and waited for the door to be opened, then strode out and followed the boardwalk to the guardhouse by the main gates, placing his red-plumed helmet on his head as he marched.

*****

The commander's headquarter building stood in the centre of Epiacum fort, facing barrack blocks, stores and stables to one side, with officer's quarters, warehouses, workshops and a temple to the goddess Minerva and the god Hercules, to the rear. Gaius often stood on his portico, like a spider at the centre of its web, observing passing soldiers stop their chatter and speed up their walk under his watchful gaze, lest they be put on punishment duties. The shape of the fort was a diamond, to match the lie of the land, and that gave the walls and streets an odd, skewed appearance.

His territory included a vicus of roundhouses, animal pens, a tavern and a newly-built bath house outside of the stone walls, in addition to the mine. Previous garrisons had dug numerous ditches around the fort, as many as seven on the western side, perhaps hinting at previous security problems. In his first year, there had been relative peace in the district. The administrative issues he dealt with, in the main, were adjudicating in land disputes or related to the miners and their precious produce.

"Ah, my husband." Aria's voice broke his reflections and he turned to her with a smile. "I wish to show you these brooches and necklace designs my ladies have made." She held out her palm and Gaius lifted a round, bronze brooch with three engraved swirls that overlapped.

"These symbols are common with the Brigantes and other northern tribes," Gaius remarked.

"Yes, most of the wives are from such tribes. They have combined traditional Roman designs with the Briton symbols. What do you think of them?" She lifted the necklace from between her breasts to show a flat disc that had been dipped in blue woad with an intricate pattern in white swirls. The necklace chain was made of alternate bronze and wood beads.

"I like it well, the more so for being placed in such a delectable place," Gaius grinned, grabbing her waist and pulling her to him.

She shook her fiery reddish hair and pulled free. "You wear the grin of Faunus and ever have one thing on your mind," she replied, holding the disc up to his face.

"Yes, it is a thing of beauty and will have the women at the marketplace in Coria fighting over it. Have your women produced much of this wondrous jewellery?"

"We have boxes of them, and plan to go to the harvest festival in Coria to sell or trade them with the women there and bring back decorations for our homes."

"Oh, I'm not sure about allowing a gang of wives to be let loose on the harvest festival without their husbands. There will be lusty soldiers there drunk on cheap ale." He made another grab for her, but she danced nimbly away.

"You are getting old and fat, my husband, and can no longer catch me!" She giggled as she ran away, joining her two friends in the street who glanced back at Gaius as they made their way along the cobbled street to their workshop.

"Sir! The barge has arrived at the port," a scout shouted, jumping from his saddle.

Gaius put thoughts of dancing women out of his mind and regarded the dusty rider. "Good. Go and find Optio Getterix and Centurion Caeliamus and tell them to meet me at the stables."

Gaius returned to his office and shouted for his orderly, Amborix, to bring his sword belt and helmet. "I am leading my cavalry cent to the river. If I am not returned by sundown, tell my wife that I am out for the night, chasing bandits."

"Bandits, sir!" Amborix was wide-eyed with excitement as he fitted shoulder and shin armour to his commander.

"Yes, I know. There has been nothing but a few skirmishes here since we came, and we can be thankful to Jupiter for that, but we soldiers need a good fight every now and then to get the blood coursing through our bodies." He snatched his helmet from his orderly's hands and marched out. No sooner had he closed the door than he turned and opened it again, shouting, "Amborix, fill my flask with brandy and bring it!"

Gaius patted Mars's neck and spoke softly at the cocked ear, "We are both getting old, my friend. Your coat is losing its gloss and we have grey hairs in our manes. But I know you will never falter in the moment of battle." He instructed the stable boy to fit the chest pad and shin guards, smiling as his stallion danced and whinnied with pleasure at the prospect of a patrol.

"Commander, the men are assembled and ready." Gaius turned at the familiar deep tone of his former standard bearer, now his deputy, Getterix.

"Good. We may be chasing ghosts, but it will do us good to ride out on patrol. Rations for two days."

An hour later, the column of sixty horsemen climbed the hill that stood next to the mine complex and stopped beside a low stone building with a wooden tower on its flat roof. Before Gaius entered the building, he looked down the other side of the hill into the Tine river valley. The Port of Epiacum consisted of a single wooden jetty, with a river barge tied to it, beside a keeper's shack.

On entering, a soldier stood to attention and saluted. "Hail, fellow. How is the day?" Gaius said, removing his helmet.

"The barge came at midday. I sent a runner to the mine with a message for you for their dispatch rider, sir!"

"Anything else? Any riders or passing fellows on the riverside path?"

"Nothing, sir, apart from women with their washing."

"I have a feeling that our gang of thieves might send scouts to check if the barge is in, so stay alert, and maintain a watch all night."

"Yes, sir!"

He was one of four who were keeping watch day and night on this windy hill. The legionary turned to brief his comrades, whilst Gaius went outside to instruct the men to dismount.

Gaius took Getterix and Meral to one side and said, "I will send fifty of the men with Meral to the mine compound for the night, with strict instructions to have two on watch at all times with their eyes on this watch tower. I will have five Gauls and six Sarmatians, with you, Getterix, remain here with me, ready to follow any suspected scouts who may come. Young men with good vision. Getterix, instruct these guards to prepare a beacon in one of their braziers to only be lit on my command."

Night crept upwards from the lair of Nox, the low grey clouds finally giving way to a blanket of stars hosting Luna in crescent form. Gaius had not been on night patrol since the battle for Coria, now two years past, and he was reminded that his night vision was poor. With Paulinus gone, Getterix was now in his circle of confidence.

"Getterix, send a patrol of six to that hilltop opposite and instruct them to conceal themselves in the coppice. They should keep their eyes on the road northwards, and you stay close to me and watch the south." It was a mild night in the month of Mars, and woollen cloaks were sufficient to keep the men warm. Gaius prowled the watchtower gallery, hoping his hunch would pay off.

The hours passed, and Gaius was also reminded of his fear of owls. One had chosen to hunt mice in the thick grass in front of the watchtower, partly revealed by the glow from the braziers below where the men loitered.

One of the patrol cantered from the opposite hill, breaking the monotony. "Sir! Two riders are approaching the port from the north."

"Then ignore them if they ride on without stopping, and follow if they turn back, having seen the barge," Gaius shouted down from the rooftop, adding, "If you follow, send a rider to brief me on your position every hour." The soldier turned and disappeared into the night.

"Tell me when you see them, Getterix," Gaius whispered to his deputy.

"Sir, I see them," Getterix said, ten minutes later, pointing into the gloom. "They have stopped a short distance from the barge and dismounted."

The glow from the watchman's brazier at the jetty was but a distant blur to Gaius, giving him only a sense of distance.

"Ah, they thought it too easy, and have returned for more," Gaius said with a grin, punching his fist in his other hand. "I think we might be on for an ambush in the morning. But first, we must bait our trap with a Trojan Horse convoy. When the scouts have gone, I want you to ride down to instruct Meral and the commander of the watch to prepare a false shipment, a convoy of two wagons with a six-rider escort and a dozen men concealed under tarpaulins. It should leave the complex two hours after sunrise. The remaining riders are to join me here. If the nosy manager asks what is happening, tell him it is a training drill. Otherwise, say nothing."

The two suspected spies had crept towards the port, seen the barge, and then returned to their horses. They mounted and rode to the north, prompting Getterix to take his leave. Nearly two hours later, a rider came from Gaius's patrol, reporting that they had followed the scouts and seen a host of more than twenty men gathered around a campfire in a hidden valley.

"Then ride back and shadow them from a safe distance. They must not know of your presence. If we attack them, block the north road to slow down their escape. Go."

Gaius briefed the men and instructed them to eat their rations and make hot drinks. If they were to pursue a fleeing enemy, they may be in the field for days. For now, they played a waiting game. Before long, the sun blessed them with an unobstructed rise into a pale blue sky, a gentle breeze sending wispy white clouds scudding as birds fought in duelling pairs on hillside meadows that were only carpeted with yellow and blue flowers on the south-facing side.

"Mount up and stay out of sight of the road behind the building," Gaius ordered an hour later as the dummy convoy rattled its way to the port on the road between the two hills. It seemed to take an age to reach the crossroads with the north-south road, but it was there that the attack took place. Hollering warriors on a mix of horses and ponies rode from the north towards the convoy, its six riders adjusting themselves to form a line facing the threat.

"Charge!" Gaius yelled, jabbing his heels into Mars's flanks and leading his men down the hill. Ahead, the bandits were swarming around the two wagons, and the men hidden under the tarpaulins had jumped up to surprise them. Now they realised they had been tricked, and attempted to flee, some north and some south.

Gaius pointed to his right, indicating that Getterix should pursue those fleeing south, with the Gauls, and he held his course towards the wagons, not wanting any of his men to be slain if he could help it. As he got close, he pointed to his left, indicating that Meral should lead the Sarmatians in pursuit of those fleeing northwards. He reined in Mars at the wagons, relieved to see all his men were safe.

"Carry on to the port," he ordered the man holding the reins on the first wagon. He trotted beside the wagon, grinding his teeth at the sight of the four guards on duty at the port hurriedly fixing their armour as they staggered out of the guard hut into the morning light.

"So much for the ever-vigilant night watch," he growled as the line of four stood to attention and saluted. "You're all on punishment duty after your shift."

"Watch out, sir!" one of the guards shouted, pointing to Gaius's right.

Gaius heard the sound of galloping hooves as he turned to see an enraged deserter, still in cavalry helmet, charging him with spear in outstretched hand. He wheeled Mars to face the threat, but was caught at a standstill, desperately trying to swing his shield off his back as the enemy rider closed in for the kill. He jabbed his heels into Mars as he jerked his sword from his scabbard, just in time to deflect the spear thrust from his body, but not fast enough to prevent the blade slicing into his bicep.

"Aaaargh!" the ex-cavalry deserter cried and he rode past, spun his horse, and moved in to finish the job.

Gaius groaned, but Mars was now moving, and he kicked him into a gallop. Gaius had dropped his sword from his wounded arm, and now lifted his shield to defend himself from the next attack. He rode across the river plain, away from his men, pursued by his tormentor. Glancing back, he could see two Sarmatians riding after his pursuer. "Come on Mars," he urged in his stallion's ear, who responded with a full charge. His best chance was to hope the Sarmatians brought down his pursuer with their arrows, for he could not hope to fight this savage attacker with just a shield and dagger held by a limp hand on his wounded arm. He was riding south, and hoped to catch up with Getterix and his men if they had caught their prey.

The sting of the wound made Gaius feel light-headed and weak, compounded by the weariness of age, and lack of fitness. Mars was also old and unfit, and started to tire. He could hear his pursuer getting closer, and the cry of an anticipated kill chilled him. "Come on, old boy, just a bit further," he croaked. They rounded a spur and saw a fight between four of Getterix's men and three warriors on ponies. Getterix must have ridden on in pursuit of swifter riders on stolen Roman cavalry horses.

"Men, to me!" Gaius called as loud as he could to the cavalry men ahead. He could do little more than ride Mars into the heart of the skirmish, hoping his men would rid him of his tormentor. Mars was well trained in sudden halts and turns, and this is what Gaius now did, pulling the reins hard and turning to the left, behind a duelling pair. He gained some time, as it took his pursuer longer to turn. By now, the two Sarmatians had also drawn closer, and the first fired an arrow at the target now presented to him. Gaius also turned to face him, covering his body with his shield, waiting for the attack.

The arrow was batted away by the shield of the grimacing warrior, who, with little thought for his safety, jabbed his heels into his mount and charged straight at his intended victim. Gaius pulled Mars to the left and took the impact of the spear thrust on his shield, feeling shockwaves surge up his arm. His attacker reined hard and swivelled to make another pass, but his luck had run out. A Gaul cavalry man pushed past a wounded pony rider and thrust his spear at Gaius's attacker, pricking his unguarded ribs.

The warrior screamed in pain, but still urged his mount to Gaius, jabbing with his spear at the commander's helmet. Gaius raised his shield and held out his dagger, receiving a derisory laugh in return.

"I have you now, commander," he growled, moving closer until both mounts were side-by-side. Gaius could see his dark brown eyes glaring with hatred, and a stubbly beard protruding from his helmet strap. Who was this devil?

The deserter raised his spear for another strike, but was hit by an arrow in his back, just below his armour. He screamed in pain and leaned back, just as the Gaul rode in and drove his spear into the man's chest. This was a killing blow, and the man tumbled from his saddle, leaving Gaius exhaling in relief. The Sarmatian and the Gaul both jumped from their saddles, swords primed to deliver death blows to the stricken warrior.

Gaius glanced around him to check there were no more threats, then turned to the man, demanding, "Who are you, that sought my death with such relish?"

"I was one of your men, once, beaten and humiliated in front of my mates by Paulinus, over a trivial matter. I deserted soon after and joined a band of rogues. I do not ask for mercy, only for my mates to beat me to death. Finish me."

Gaius nodded, and his men quickly killed him. It was a grim business to instruct a captured deserter's bunk house mates to beat him to death with cudgels, as per army orders. He looked around and saw that the pony riders had been slain. "You shall both be rewarded when we reach the fort," he said to the two who had saved him. "Now, ride on to Getterix and see if he needs your help. I will return to the port."

Gaius waved his four Gauls and two Sarmatians along the road, whilst he sat on Mars, patting his sweaty neck and gazing mournfully at the blood dripping from his wounded arm. He shifted his shield onto his back to free his other arm and reached for his saddlebag to find a rag, then dabbed brandy on it from his flask and tied it around his wound. Slowly, his heavy breaths stilled and he regaining his composure from what he knew had been a near-death experience.

"I shall thank the gods for our deliverance, Mars. Yes, I will make sacrifice to Epona for you as well. We both might have come to a sticky end on the point of that spear."

Mars whinnied at the mention of his name, then tossed his shaggy mane and responded to Gaius's gentle urging with a steady walk.

25. Vindolanda, present day

I kept my head down for the remainder of the term, making sure I attended all lectures and tutorials, at pains to be both visible and keen to my tutors. I saw Sima on a couple of weekends, and was happy to play a waiting game as she worked through her family and relationship issues. She was making the slow adjustment to being single and independent in her mind. My communications with Maggie had been formal and brief.

April came, and I made my way to Vindolanda, with Dave for company, for the first of my two dissertation presentations. It was at midday in the lecture theatre, and the staff and trustees had kindly laid on a drinks and nibbles reception to follow. I admit to having butterflies at the prospect of addressing the staff, trustees, invited guests, fellow students, and with Professor Maggie Wilde sitting in the front row, no doubt. I certainly didn't want to fall flat on my face in front of her.

Dave and I had arranged to meet Russ and Richard in the cafeteria at eleven for coffee, cake and catch-up.

"Ah, Jenny, I'm not sure what I've missed most – you or your delicious cake," Dave said, reviving his antagonistic flirting with the mistress of the cake mix.

"Ee, David, cake sales have certainly struggled since you left us," she said, chuckling. "What can I get you?"

"It's coffee and walnut for me, Jenny, and your famous lemon drizzle for my mate, Noah. And two large coffees, please."

We settled into our favourite corner booth and lifted the moist cake to our mouths on delicately balanced forks, stimulating our taste buds with the familiar flavours.

Morning sunlight flooded the cafeteria, shining off the newly-mopped floor. "So, this is how it looks in springtime,"

Dave said, after washing his piece of cake down with a mouthful of coffee. "Why did we ever leave?"

Russ and Richard walked in, to a noisy reception. "I hope you've left some for us," Russ said, making his way to the counter. Richard settled on the bench and we began exchanging familiar tales of revision and hours spent in libraries.

"The four musketeers, together again," Russ said, buttering his scone. "I managed to persuade my course tutor to let me change my dissertation topic to the history of the three families whose graves we excavated, so I'll be paying a visit to Betty Hardcastle on the way back."

"You'll see her sooner, as she's coming today," I said. "I'm sure she'll look forward to collaborating with you, and induct you into the dusty halls of the Corbridge History Society."

Sima joined us, and I stood to hug her and peck her on the cheek, prompting unnecessary nudges and rolling of the eyes from the lads.

"I've signed out those items you requested, Noah," she said, taking a seat. "I'll bring them through to the lecture room just before you're ready to start."

"Time for a quick coffee?"

"Always. A skinny latte, please."

On my return, I asked, "So, what news of Mavis and the artefact thieves?"

As if on cue, Mike Stone put his bushy red head and beard around the corner remarking, "I see you lot have returned to your favourite table. What's this I heard about the artefacts theft?"

"Hi Mike. I've just asked Russ, our resident Geordie, if there's any news."

"I've brought a newspaper cutting from the Newcastle Chronicle," Russ said, unfolding a page of newsprint. "The headline reads, 'Priceless Treasures from Hadrian's Wall

Rescued'. The photo is of Inspector Griffiths grinning whilst pointing to a table of goodies." Russ showed the picture to raucous laughter, attracting looks from others in the now crowded cafeteria, no doubt gathering for my talk.

"'Ms Mavis MacDonald of Talent's Farm, Northumberland, and Mr Ivor Braithwaite of Wall in Northumberland, were arraigned this morning before High Court Judge, Mrs Judith Smith-Rowe at Newcastle Crown Court and charged with theft of gold and silver ornaments, jewellery and coins from the Roman era, their value as yet to be determined, that were excavated at or near Hadrian's Wall'. It goes on to say that a trial date has been set for June 13th. I might go along to that."

"I bet the trustees are relieved to be getting their 'goodies' back," Sima said. "Some of the items have already been returned, most notably the bags of coins, so we can place one of the bags on your table, Noah."

"Wow, that's great news," I said, checking the time on my phone. "Right, fifteen minutes to go. I'd better get in there and set up stall. See you all at the reception afterwards."

"Good luck mate," Dave said, a sentiment echoed by the others.

"I'll bring the box through to you in five minutes," Sima added, sipping her coffee.

"I'm off to do some meeting and greeting," Mike Stone said, accompanying Noah out into the crowded entrance area. "Big crowd, Noah. Break a leg," he added with a grin, before darting off into the museum.

In the dim corridor leading to the lecture hall, Maggie was waiting for me.

"Ah, Noah, how lovely to see you again," she chirped, hugging me and giving me a kiss on the cheek. "I know you've had a good excuse for avoiding me, so I won't give you a hard time."

"I've been burning the midnight oil with this presentation and sucking up to my course tutors who were saying they hardly ever see me. But I can't thank you enough for guiding me through my dissertation and your... erm, most welcome support."

"Support! Is that all it was to you?" she murmured, raising her eyebrows.

Was she angry or playful? It was almost as if our last encounter hadn't happened.

"Of course not, just me being clumsy. The time we spent together means... a lot to me..." I stuttered. *This is driving all my carefully rehearsed presentation out of my head.*

"I've been starved of conversation with somebody who wants to talk about Latin translations ad nauseam." Maggie narrowed her eyes in mock frustration.

Why was this woman so inconsistent? "I wanted to come up and see you but..."

Just then, Sima came up behind me, carrying a box. "Can you help me with this, Noah? It's quite heavy," she said.

I spun around and instantly clicked into a warm smile. "Certainly, Sima. Come and help me set up my table." Maggie backed away into the lecture theatre, her expression impossible to read, allowing us to enter before leaving.

The seats were starting to fill up, and I nodded and smiled at those I recognised. It was five minutes to, and I was flustered. We placed the excavated objects on the table and Sima whispered 'good luck', taking her seat in the second row with her fellow archivists. I plugged my flash stick into the overhead projector and opened my PowerPoint file. The first slide had my name and course details, with a photo of me at the Vindolanda dig, holding the muddy goddess statuette. The cleaned original now stood on the table, with a bag of coins and a replica tablet in a transparent plastic zip bag. I looked at my set of cards with bullet points and the salient statistics. They appeared unfamiliar to me and my mind could not settle no matter how hard I stared at the first card. I swallowed and poured a glass of water, sipping to assuage my dry lips and tongue. I must trust to fate that I would be able to talk naturally from the memory prompts, whilst looking at my audience.

Maggie was sitting in the front row, next to the trustees and some visitors I didn't know. She occasionally glanced at me, unsmiling now, pressing the button on her ballpoint pen. I stood next to my table as the doors closed and the auditorium lights were dimmed, leaving me in the spotlight. This was it – the moment I had been working towards for almost three years. Would I be feted by emperors as a returning hero, or dragged through the streets in chains, a slave without hope?

Then Maggie stood up. She edged past her guests to the aisle, and walked towards me, into the light. I was transfixed, rooted to the spot, not knowing what was about to happen. *What was she going to say?*

Maggie shot me a brief smile, then spun on her high heels and faced the audience. "Trustees of Vindolanda, invited guests, ladies and gentlemen. I'm delighted to introduce to you an archaeology student who I believe shows not only great promise, but a truly adventurous spirit and an enquiring mind to go with it. His name is Noah Jessop, and it has been my pleasure to mentor him this past six months on his degree dissertation. Without further ado, I'll hand you over to Noah, whose talk centres on his archaeology practical experiences both here and at a site close to Corbridge." With that, she gave me a quick wink over her shoulder, and returned to her seat.

When the polite applause subsided, I began. "Thanks for the glowing introduction, Professor Wilde. It's been the most enlightening and challenging six months of my young life, and I couldn't have reached this point without your expert guidance, or the support of the staff at Vindolanda and my friends."

I paused to click the remote control device and bring up my next slide. "Archaeology, I've discovered, is far more than the study of human history and prehistory through the excavation of sites and analysis of artefacts and other physical remains. Archaeology helps us as a society to address some of the most fundamental questions about who we are and why we are the way we are. Our culture, our history is part of who we are, and helps to shape our world. I have had cause to reflect on the lives of those who came before us. And here at the site of Vindolanda Roman Fort, close to one of the Roman Empire's most iconic and enduring remains, Hadrian's Wall, I have marvelled, through the many artefacts uncovered, at the lives, interests, lifestyles and purpose of those who occupied this space nearly two thousand years ago.

"Why archaeology? my friends and family asked. Well, I was a huge fan of the Indiana Jones films when growing up, and I'd developed a fascination for Roman Britain at school in nearby County Durham. After being entranced by a teacher's description of the life of a Roman legionary at Hadrian's Wall on a school trip, my mind was made up. I would be a new, British Indiana Jones."

Ripples of laughter allowed me to pause to take a sip of water and move to the next slide. "The title of my dissertation is, 'How archaeological techniques and analysis can illuminate the lives of those who lived at Hadrian's Wall during the Roman occupation of Britain."

"Firstly, I'll describe the digs I worked on, the methods used, and describe the artefacts that were uncovered. After that, I'll focus on specific discoveries that have given me a unique insight into the life of one particular Roman, a centurion in the Sixth Legion, Gaius Atticianus, who was posted here in the late second century. I will also share with you my thoughts and assumptions on the life of Gaius, and on the practice of informed speculation that fills in the gaps in our knowledge to develop an historical narrative."

I was rattling through the academic stuff on the methods and practices of archaeology, when the power cut and we were plunged into darkness.

26. Epiacum, 183 CE

Gaius led his men through the eastern gatehouse of Epiacum at midday, to cheers from wives, workers and off-duty soldiers lolling on the battlements. Then he had met with Aria, who took him to the surgeon to have his wound properly dressed. From there, he sought out the keeper of the temple. After a sleepless night, fatigue was slowing his progress through familiar streets, where shopkeepers greeted him and slaves carrying loads bowed as they passed at a respectable distance. He stood in front of the solitary temple that resided within the fort's walls to catch his breath, gazing at a statue of a naked Hercules, his powerful physique an example to all men. On the opposite side of the doorway stood a statue to Minerva, wearing a centurion's helmet, holding a spear and resting her hand on a shield. She was depicted here as the goddess of war, but she was also revered by Aria and her women's group as the goddess of artists and handicrafts.

Gaius walked up the four sandstone steps, past Greek-shaped columns and the two marble statues standing guard, into the inner sanctum. A patch of sunlight on the courtyard guided him to the centre of the building where he saw the tall figure of the head priest, Antoninus, a white-haired father who had perfected the art of making sacrifice. He was supervising a slave boy scrubbing animal blood off the altar to Minerva. It was his solemn duty to interpret the will of the gods, often by studying the death throes of a sacrificial animal and its blood pool, or by gazing to the skies and studying the flight of birds.

"Ah, Commander, welcome!" he called, on seeing Gaius stride into the light. "I trust you had a successful patrol? The augurs were strongly in your favour."

"Thank you, Antoninus. Yes, we were successful in catching and destroying our enemy, a wild bunch of deserters and disgruntled locals who won't bother us anymore."

"Ah, excellent! The gods favoured you, Commander."

"Except, I almost got killed. I'm getting old and slow, and allowed a warrior to catch me by surprise. Fortuna be praised, my men got me out of a bad situation."

A perturbed look flashed across the priest's face. "I'm sorry for that. Sometimes the detail eludes me…"

"Do not worry, Antoninus." Gaius smiled and squeezed the old man's arm in a friendly gesture. "I have not come to upbraid you. I wish to thank the god Hercules for watching over me, and to make a donation to the temple."

Antonius lifted his hands and hairy white eyebrows in surprise and excitement. "Ah, I believe Hercules has guided you here on this very day when I am expecting delivery of a new altar stone. It was carved by local craftsmen from the yellow-hued stone that is such an appealing building material. I believe our god of strength and virtue wants you to make a dedication to him on its pedestal. And, the craftsmen will want to be paid." He beamed his pleasure at Gaius, who chuckled.

"Then it is fate, Antoninus. How much is your debt to these craftsmen?"

"We agreed a price of seventy-five denarii," he said lightly, as if it wasn't the equivalent of three months' pay for a legionary.

Gaius puffed his cheeks out and put his hand to the leather pouch at his waist. He emptied its contents into his palm, then picked out a single gold aureus. "I have fifty silver denarii, and my lucky Julius Caesar gold aureus, which I believe is worth twenty-five denarii. Then the gods have matched the value of my coin pouch to your price." He returned the coins to the pouch and handed it over.

"It's a sign from Hercules himself!" Antoninus cried, folding his bony knuckles over the leather pouch, lest Gaius should change his mind.

"I retire in a year and if the gods are for me, I am hoping that this morning's skirmish will be my last. In which case, my lucky coin has served its purpose and can pay for my dedication on the Altar of Hercules. Make the inscription read, 'Centurion Gaius Vitellius Atticianus, VI Legio Victrix Pia Fidelis did dedicate this altar to Hercules Victorious'."

"Not 'Senior Centurion and Imperator'?"

"No, that is too fussy. Just 'centurion'. And use abbreviations where necessary. I came close to meeting the gods this morning, but I am not yet ready to meet Charon and cross the Styx in his boat."

*****

The year passed without incident. An increasingly anxious Gaius had made many visits to the temple to make sacrifice to Hercules on his dedicated altar, each time feeling a temporary calmness of spirit on returning to his home.

"Any day now, Aria, a messenger will come from the legate's office with my retirement document. Then we shall pack and make our way to legion headquarters at Eboracum to find out what is the retirement pay for a senior centurion."

"The army are clever, my husband. Your eyes are failing, you cough up blood and some days struggle to rise from our bed. They have had the best of you these past twenty-five years."

"And you have had the best of me these past fifteen years, my love." Gaius's laughter soon dissolved into a coughing fit and he gripped his armchair. "It is... my heartfelt wish to live to collect my retirement pay... and see you and Brutus settled in comfort in a townhouse or villa."

"Do not talk, Gaius, and drink this draught from the surgeon." She held a beaker to his lips and made sure he drank the bitter, foul-smelling liquid.

"That tastes fouler than the run-off from the stables," he said, screwing up his face and pushing her hand away. "Perhaps that's his secret ingredient."

"And you would know how that tastes?"

Their house slave appeared at the door, bobbing his head in a familiar sign of news.

"What is it?" Gaius demanded.

"A messenger from Eboracum with scrolls, sir."

"Show him to my office." Gaius rose from the armchair, walked out onto his portico and went next door, where he kept his desk, maps and scrolls.

"Bring the scrolls case," he demanded impatiently at the dust-covered rider. "Now go to my kitchen for food and drink." He took the cap off the leather parchment case and pulled out three scrolls. Two were official notifications, and the third was his retirement notice. Gaius let out a cry of joy and flattened it on his desk to read.

Aria came in at the noise and stood behind him. "Is it what you hoped for, my love?"

"Partly. It is a notice that I may take retirement or sign on for another year, if I wish, depending on passing a medical examination at Eboracum. There is no mention of the amount of retirement pay, only that I should first report to my tribune's office in Vindolanda to inform him of my decision, so that he can prepare my letter of discharge and arrange a temporary garrison commander. Then I should proceed to Eboracum to notify the legate of my final decision." He looked up at Aria with a wide grin. "I'm hoping he'll offer me part payment and a farm plot in the colonia there."

"Well, I can't see you passing a medical for another year of service, can you?" She arched her eyebrows and regarded her husband coolly.

Gaius chuckled. "You know my thoughts already, Aria. It is retirement and a life of relative leisure for me…"

The sound of shouting and hobnail boots rapping on cobble stones broke his train of thought.

Amborix, his orderly, appeared in the doorway. "Sir! There are warriors massed on the western hill!" he cried, eyes wide in apprehension.

Gaius and Aria exchanged horrified looks, and Gaius rose to his feet. "All right, sound the alarm and send my officers to meet me at the western gatehouse." He kissed Aria and scurried after Amborix to the headquarters building, breathing heavily. He put on his armour and sword belt, then grabbed his helmet and hurried out into a mass of rushing soldiers and civilians.

Gaius pushed his way past pensive townsfolk, crossing the main thoroughfare to the stores. Inside the cavernous oil lamp-lit building he thought twice about attempting to vault over the counter and raised the flap to enter behind. He marched past fretful assistants, passing racks of equipment, weapons and armour, to the office at the rear.

"Put away your coins, Decimus, and come to the counter," Gaius demanded of the startled one-eyed quartermaster.

The wealthiest man in the fort gulped and blinked his eye, swiping the coins from his desk into a box, then placing it at his feet and rising. "Yes Commander, how can I assist you?"

"You can assist me by doing your job and issuing weapons, helmets and armour to the line of civilian volunteers at your door. Now!"

Decimus hurried out and followed Gaius to the serving counter, followed by his six liveried workers.

"Is there a fire lit in the courtyard?" Gaius asked.

"Yes, commander," a youth replied.

"Then three of you melt the blocks of pitch in your cauldrons and issue buckets of the hot black liquid to soldiers who will soon come. The rest of you stay here and issue weapons, armour, spears, swords, javelins, shields and helmets to the volunteers until there are none left, then join your mates on the walls. No need to keep a record, Decimus. Now give me six javelins."

They scurried to their tasks and Gaius cradled his javelins in his arms as he opened the outer door to face a mob of agitated men from the vicus. "Form a line and enter one at a time!" he yelled. "You will be issued with weapons and armour. Then report to the commanders at one of four gatehouses!" They duly complied, and Gaius left them to jog to the west gatehouse to meet with his officers.

Although seven ditches and earth banks separated the western side of the fort from the gentle slope of the hill, the sight of a host of several hundred warriors, some on ponies, but most on foot, struck fear into the hearts of soldiers and officers alike. The fort may have been built to house up to five hundred men, but his garrison was only of two hundred infantry and one hundred cavalry soldiers.

"The spring has brought more than flowers and boxing hares," Gaius muttered.

Getterix appeared at his side and Gaius asked for a detailed description of the warriors on the hill, and a more accurate count of their number.

After a brief silence, Getterix replied. "Five hundred and fifty, sir, with fifty mounted on ponies. They have the look of that lot who put Vindolanda under siege, sir."

"Hmmm. We have had no warning from the Wall forts. They must have come over an unguarded section, or overpowered a mile fort, and made their way here. Perhaps they have heard of our silver."

"We cannot guess their reason, sir, but their purpose is clear," his second in command, Centurion Junius Caeliamus intoned in his other ear. He commanded the two hundred foot soldiers.

"Right. First thing we must do is block off the access roads to our four gates. Having ditches to slow down an enemy advance over open ground is all very well, but they can simply rush to our gates along those access roads. Put up barricades at the furthest ditches and have your ranks man them with javelins at the ready. Thirty men to each barricade."

"Aye sir." He saluted and moved to the ladder.

"Wait! You must also smother the barricades in pitch, and have a torch close by, as a last resort if they are overrun. Then they must set alight the barricades and retreat inside the gates." Junius nodded and was gone.

"Getterix. Get the civilians to bring stones and any heavy objects they can find to the four gatehouses, for missiles to throw down. And send a message to the mine to evacuate and head south, and one to Magnis Fort up the north road."

By now, civilians from the settlement were streaming into the fort through the east gate, many driving livestock or carrying baskets of clucking fowl. Gaius was left alone with his thoughts, wondering who this warband were and why they had come to his fort on this very day, when his retirement parchment had been delivered. The omens were not good.

Amborix appeared by his side, waiting for instruction. Gaius turned to him and muttered, "It is a cruel jape of the gods, Amborix, to tease me with this horde of warriors on the very day my retirement notice is delivered."

"Your... retirement notice?" his orderly stammered, disbelief on his face.

"Yes. But faced with this rabble, I now see this is my final test." Gaius leaned on the wooden handrail, knuckles white, staring ahead. The tonic rumbled in his belly and repeated in his mouth, leaving him to face his fate with a very bitter taste.

Gaius could hear the laughter of the gods in the cries of gulls wheeling overhead. So, this was his payment for twenty-five years of service – his wife, Aria, to be abused and murdered; his son, Brutus, taken for a slave; and his head paraded on the point of a barbarian's spear. Black ants swarmed down the hillside, their dread cries carrying in snatches on a buffeting moorland wind.

"Load your ballistae and bring pitch – and prepare for the battle of your lives!"

27. Vindolanda, present day

I stood in the windowless lecture theatre, beside the table, waiting until my eyes slowly adjusted to the gloom. A man's voice had risen above the murmuring to urge everyone to remain calm and stay in their seats until the cause of the power outage was established.

My mind was a whirl of thoughts, my concentration broken. Had the rest of the artefacts' criminal gang returned? In a movie, perhaps, but surely not in real life?

"Noah, are you alright?" Maggie was standing beside me. "I'm sure it's just an unfortunate glitch with the power supply. It sometimes happens, sorry it's happened to you."

"Let's hope there's a perfectly innocent explanation," I mumbled.

"I doubt it's a rival degree examination board sabotaging your presentation," she said with a smile. "Cheer up, and keep your mind focussed on your talk."

The gods intervened, and the lights suddenly came on. The OHP whirred into life, and the caretaker stuck his shaggy mop of a head through the double doors at the back and announced that a power surge had tripped the main switch. Power was fully restored, and he was sorry for the interruption. It's only the ghosts of Hadrian's Wall, he fails to add.

I looked at my next card and gathered my thoughts, then, once silence returned to the room, I picked up the thread of my presentation. "I've described the two archaeological digs to you, and what was found. I must emphasise that the weekend exploration dig at Hardcastle Farm was just that – an exploration dig undertaken by four students to practise their newfound archaeology methods, with the landowner's permission, and to investigate the possibility of a Roman payroll chest being buried there, based on the findings of desk research. It was not part of the Combined Universities dig, nor anything to do with the Vindolanda or Corbridge Trusts."

I made eye contact with Maggie, and she smiled and gave a faint nod. I moved to the table and picked up a stone-carved statuette of a native Briton goddess.

"This was my first find, on the Vindolanda vicus dig, that's the civilian settlement next to the fort. Professor Wilde told me it's an effigy of the goddess Brigantia, after whom the Brigante tribe from this area took their name. She is their mother and protector, and this carving, of a pregnant goddess, a fertility symbol who would have brought good fortune and protection to the household in which it resided. She revealed herself to me in the sticky clay beside a cobbled street in the vicus, and I will always remember her fondly as my first find. In a strange way, I feel I was destined to find her, and she in turn was meant to guide me to the discoveries subsequently made, and to this moment of completion. But maybe I'm just a romantic at heart."

I paused to return the statuette to the table. "After my stint on the dig, I went to the archives here and focussed on translating tablets. That is, comparing my translations and assumptions with those of the archivists', in search of army orders or itineraries, something with an officer's name so that I could investigate that individual. My breakthrough came with a partially legible translation of an order from Tribune Helvius Pertinax based at Vindolanda to Centurion Gaius Atticianus.

"Then later on a second mention of Gaius was brought to my attention on a tablet recovered from Coria, now Corbridge, concerning the burial of a payroll chest at the estate of Magistrate Lucius Gabia. A third mention, came from an altar stone uncovered in 1802 at the site of Epiacum fort, now called Whitley Castle, some twenty miles south and west of Vindolanda."

I moved to the next slide. "The inscription seen on the altar stone shown translates as, 'to the god Hercules,

Gaius Vitellius Atticianus, centurion of the Sixth Legion Victrix Pia Fidelis'. The last line was missing but most likely said 'made this dedication'. So, from three separate mentions of Centurion Gaius Atticianus, I have made certain assumptions about his life and career, to gain an insight into the life of a Roman officer stationed close to Hadrian's Wall."

I lifted the bag of coins from the table. "This is one of the bags of coins from the Roman chest excavation at Hardcastle Farm, near Corbridge. Okay, it's a replacement canvas bag, as the original bag fell to bits after a few exposures to air. It's also been on an unexpected journey, having been stolen and then recovered by the police." This got a laugh and lightened the mood after the strange interruption.

"The wood from the chest was carbon dated to be between 1,800 to 2,000 years old, so it fits with my theory about Centurion Atticianus being forced to bury it in the family graveyard of Magistrate Lucius Gabia in the year 180 CE, when his convoy came under attack by Caledonii warriors whilst transporting it from Vindolanda fort to Coria Roman town. The chest contained 12,500 silver denarii and 200 gold aurei. From this, I deduced that it held enough to pay a cohort of 480 men, plus officers, for one month. Roman legionaries were paid 300 silver denarii a year in the late second century. That equates to 25 denarii a month, or one gold aureus. The officers were most likely paid in gold aurei, depending on rank. Perhaps Gaius earned two gold aurei or 50 denarii a month, and maybe his tribune earned double that.

I picked up the gold coin discovered by Dave, lent to me by the curator at the Great North Museum for this presentation. "Gaius may have had a lucky coin, perhaps a gold aureus like this one, with the Emperor Hadrian on one side, and on the obverse, the goddess Disciplina." I paused to click to the next slide, from the goddess Brigantia, to enlarged details of the coin I was holding. "Hadrian pushed the ideals of frugality, sternness and fidelity, the virtues of

285

the Goddess Disciplina, onto his army, and many soldiers worshipped the minor deity. The cavalry base at Cilumum on the North Tyne, at Hadrian's Wall, was dedicated to Disciplina. These virtues also fitted with the honorary titles won by Gaius's regiment, the Sixth Legion, victrix pia fidelis - victorious, faithful and loyal.

"This coin shows in detail Hadrian's role as a leader of disciplined soldiers. Hadrian is depicted as being Disciplina, and appears slightly taller than the three legionaries, who follow him, each holding a military standard. Hadrian is shown leading from the front and coins of this type would surely have been popular with his army, busy at work building his wall on the northern frontier.

"The big question left unanswered is, why didn't the Romans reclaim their buried pay chest and standard? After all, they were buried less than a mile from the Roman town of Coria." I paused to let the audience ponder this and sipped my water.

"My theory is this. That the attack on Coria by Caledonii warriors from north of Hadrian's Wall was a catastrophic event for the Romans, and may have forced them to retreat from the area for a long period. The Caledonii may have stayed for weeks, picking whatever they could from the rich farms in the surrounding area, then torched the town they had captured before returning to their homes.

"Gaius Atticianus gave his report to a clerk in the headquarters building, before fighting a bloody and ultimately losing battle against a native army. I believe the chest remained lost because Gaius and his men died in that battle, and the tablet bearing his report remained buried in a room under the floor for nearly two thousand years, until discovered by archaeologists recently at Corbridge."

I paused, then clicked back to the slide of the altar stone inscription. "Therefore, it seems that Gaius was at

Epiacum fort, where he dedicated the altar to the god Hercules, before being posted to Vindolanda. What do we know of Gaius himself? His personality and the details of his life, such as if he was married, a privilege accorded to officers but not to the soldiers, remains unknown. Perhaps he remained single and enjoyed a drink with his fellow officers when off duty, in the officer's mess, or at a taverna in the vicus outside the fort's walls. Perhaps he frequented a brothel, or enjoyed gambling? We can make an informed guess at his nationality, given the previous postings of the Sixth Legion; he may have been from a Gallic or Germanic tribe. The Romans were in the habit of sending troops recruited in a province, such as Britannia, to serve in another province, to break their connection with their homeland and reduce the chances of unrest or rebellion in the ranks.

"A Roman soldier could retire after twenty-five years or sixteen campaigns and receive land and a pension. Most recruits were twenty when they joined a legion, so the most common retirement age was forty-five. Quite old in those days. But only a few would live to enjoy retirement, given that it is estimated, based on population statistics, that the average life expectancy of a soldier was mid-forties. Those who survived to retire lived in veteran communities called colonia, or colonies.

"As for Gaius Atticianus, I believe he died in the Battle for Coria in 180 or 181 CE, and his buried payroll chest remained in a grave in the corner of a walled villa complex on a farm estate until I found it, with my fellow archaeology students, David, Richard and Russell. I would like to thank Mike Stone, the site manager, and Professor Wilde for their support, guidance and encouragement; and the landowner, Mrs Betty Hardcastle. The coins have since been stolen and recovered, and most of the find now resides in the Great North Museum in Newcastle. Thank you."

*****

287

"Well done, Noah, that was excellent," Maggie said, clutching a glass of sparkling wine in one hand, with her other arm linked with that of a mystery man.

"Thanks, Professor. I couldn't have done it without your help and guidance," I replied, feeling tired, relieved and happy I'd got through it. Sima came to stand beside me, squeezing my arm, whilst Dave, Richard and Russ chatted close behind.

"Call me Maggie in informal settings, Noah. This is my husband, Brian. He managed to stay awake and looked mildly interested." She turned to kiss him briefly on the cheek. "Well done, pet."

I shared a smile with Sima, then said, "Thanks for coming, Brian. I hope it wasn't too tortuous for you?" I felt my ears burn and hoped the sign of my guilty conscience would be taken for bashfulness in his presence.

"Not at all," he replied, between sips of orange juice. "I enjoyed how you put together the story of the centurion from your findings. A great demonstration of how archaeology can breathe life into our history." He looked like he'd just come from work, wearing a dark charcoal suit with a faint blue pin strip, and polished black shoes. He was about the same age as Maggie, but his short, brown straight hair was thinning at the temples.

I suddenly felt a fool to have been worried about the consequences of my fling with Maggie – she was the one taking all the risk, and now she had patched up her differences with Brian, would most likely not give me a second thought.

"Let me get my folder from the lecture theatre," Maggie trilled, darting into the darkened room. I asked Brian about his job, and half-listened to his dry response. He worked for a firm of chartered accountants and specialised in doing audits and annual account submissions for small to medium-sized enterprises.

Maggie soon returned, accompanied by her curator friend. "May I introduce Susan Branton, Curator at the Great North Museum in Newcastle. She's got something for one of you." Maggie winked mischievously.

"Which one of you is David?" the demure curator asked.

David put his hand up and stepped forward.

She held out her hand and unfolded her fingers to reveal a gold aureus coin. "It's not the perfect specimen you found, David, but another Hadrian gold aureus the museum would like you to have from our collection, in exchange. And here's a certificate of authenticity from us." She pulled a card from her pocket and gave it to him.

"Wow, that's great. Thanks!" Dave took the coin and card, examining them with a big smile on his face before showing them to Russ and Richard.

Maggie leaned towards me and said in a low, conspiratorial tone, "If you're worried about your dissertation grade, don't be. I've spoken to your course leader and she's blown away by your work. I completely agreed with her assessment."

"That's brilliant, Maggie!" I gushed – both proud and relieved in that moment. "Thank you so much."

"You deserve it," she replied, smiling as she tapped me on the elbow. Professor to student relationship restored.

Maggie looked up at her husband. "We'd better get going or we'll miss our flight," she said, colour flushing her cheeks. She pulled Brian by his arm and, in a stage whisper, said, "We're off on a mini-break to a romantic Greek island. Goodbye and good luck, all of you." She grinned as she handed me her glass and pulled Brian towards the fire exit at the far side of the room.

Sima, the lads and I exchanged bemused looks as we were left holding their glasses.

"And good luck to her. I'd better retrieve the artefacts from the lecture room," Sima said, leaving us to idle chatter whilst looking around at the guests.

She soon returned and placed the box at her feet. Picking out the polished marble goddess, she held her up to me. "Brigantia is a marvellous artefact, and seems to change colour in differing light. As a protector and unifier, I think she's still got it." She slipped her free arm through mine and pulled me close, fixing her deep, dark eyes on mine.

"She does seem to have the effect of bringing people together," I agreed, leaning towards her and pouting my lips for a kiss. Sima responded with a light peck – our first kiss in public.

Richard held his hands up. "Woah, guys, get a room!"

Dave let out a raucous laugh. "And so, our time at Vindolanda comes to an end with the mysterious goddess still working her magic." He put his coin and card into his pocket and made a show of looking at his watch as Sima and I hugged. "Come on lovebirds and budding archaeologists, one last visit to the Green Man?"

"Was that a call-out for the pub?" Mike Stone asked, leaning in. "I suppose the first round's mine after that excellent presentation. Well done, Noah."

I waited outside with the others for Sima to lock up the artefacts, welcoming the cool Northumbrian air on my face whilst gazing at the placid blue skies over the moors. Sima appeared at my side and we set off, hand-in-hand, on a familiar trudge up the lane, our onward march inexorable.

28. Eboracum Colonia, 195 CE

Gaius wore a fixed grin as he re-read the parchment missive from his son, Brutus, informing him that he had been accepted as an imperial guard by Legate Hieronymianus, and would be stationed close by at Eboracum. Gaius's heart swelled with pride as he handed the parchment to Aria, whom he had taught to read the Roman letters as a precaution in case his dimming eyesight completely deserted him. The grey-haired couple embraced at the news their son was both well and had taken up his first position with the Sixth Legion.

Aria bustled inside, arm-in-arm with Amborix's wife, Juliana, pausing only to touch the stone goddess, Sulis, in her alcove for bringing good fortune to her family. "It's wonderful news, Juliana, and we are so proud of our dear Brutus…"

Gaius remained on his porch and looked up at a silver serpent with a crystal blue eye, hanging from the eves; a torque won in battle now employed as a wind chime. Copper rods dangled and danced in the gentle breeze, striking the scales of the serpent and making a merry tune. The boy at his feet laughed and pointed. Gaius recalled his desperate but determined duel with a younger, stronger warrior. He chuckled at the thought that he had outwitted his opponent and goaded him into making a fatal mistake.

"But I'm still here, young Artorius, a citizen of Rome since my retirement, and he has gone to the hall of his ancestors."

Artorius gurgled in response, chewing his fist.

The men and women came in from the fields as the sun touched the far hills, shedding its yellow for an orange hue, their chatter centring on the chances of a good harvest. The slave couple made their way to the tool shed and then their own quarters at the rear, but Amborix joined Gaius and picked up his wriggling son.

"I see the serpent has stirred," the former orderly remarked.

"Aye. The wind is picking up. We can expect a storm tonight. It's a bauble with a purpose." He turned to regard his trusted deputy. "I sold my collection of trophy wrist bands to pay for the cows and bull. Only this remains, and my award for bravery presented by our legate, to remind me of my narrow escapes."

"You are too modest, sir. You mean your great victories." Amborix stood beside Gaius, gazing over the farmland they had cut out of wilderness that sloped away to a wide river valley. "But your greatest victory was the last one, at Epiacum."

Gaius shot him a pensive look, as if a terrifying memory had been evoked. "Our greatest victory, Amborix. I recall you fighting like a bear surrounded by wolves. We kept them out through the long night, I don't know how." He sighed and leaned a hand on the upright porch spar.

Amborix glanced at him and chuckled. "And then in the morning, the sweet sound of a horn heralded the arrival of the cavalry from Magnis fort."

"And I rode out on Mars one last time. Hercules Victorious did not abandon me. But I heard his taunts that fearful day in the cries of the crows and gulls."

"Do you remember when I first met you on the battlements at Vindolanda?" Amborix asked, turning to face the old man.

Gaius's chest gave a rattle as he coughed. "Aye. May the gods be praised that we have both survived to be standing here, and us both to have strong wives and fine sons." He pinched Artorius' cheek, but the toddler pulled away from him.

"You told me that Vindolanda meant 'green sky in winter'."

"Yes, it was a poor lie from a grumpy centurion with a hangover on night watch," Gaius lightly punched his loyal farm worker's shoulder. "But when you lay still, and I feared you were dying, I repented and told the true meaning. Did you hear it?"

"I must have, because it came to me in a dream. A druid leading a procession across a flat, snow-covered meadow. You must have said 'white meadow'."

"And so, I did. A Caledonian shaman did return to the white meadow, to torment us and burn our comrades before our eyes to haunt our dreams. It was a vexing moment. We were the guardians of Rome, Amborix, at the Great Wall. But the gods have been kinder to us, and have guided us all safely to this wondrous place."

Yawning and stretching, Gaius peered over his shoulder as a welcome aroma wafted from the kitchen. "Sol Invictus returns to his hall and Nox will soon come sniffing from her lair." Heeding his stomach rumble, he turned and held the door open for Amborix and Artorius in the gathering gloom. "Time to light the lamps."

THE END

Author's Note

This novel is a work of fiction, inspired by an inscription on a Roman artefact discovered in 1803 at Whitley Castle in Cumbria, once the Roman fort of Epiacum. In Noah's presentation, he refers to three mentions he found of Centurion Gaius Atticianus. Of these three, two are fictious and the true one is the dedication on an altar stone. In the *Roman Inscriptions of Britain* archives, there is an entry for an altar pedestal stone inscription, dedicated to the god Hercules. The translation reads:

'To the god Hercules
Gaius Vitellius Atticianus
centurion of the Sixth Legion Victrix Pia Fidelis'

This altar stone (sketch from www.romaninscriptionsofbritain.org) now resides at the Higgins Art Gallery and Museum in Bedfordshire.

From this, I have taken my character, Gaius Vitellius Atticianus of the VI Legion Victrix Pia Fidelis ('the victorious, loyal and faithful Sixth Legion'), and imagined his story, including the made-up burial of a payroll chest. One real event is included in the narrative; the burning down of Coria town in 180 or 181, thought to have been in an attack by Caledonian raiders from north of Hadrian's Wall. 180 is also the year that Emperor Marcus Aurelius died – depicted in the opening scenes of the movie, 'Gladiator'. Two of my named Roman officers are also real figures, plucked from mentions in inscriptions on monuments or in surviving records, namely Legate of the VI Legion, Claudius Hieronymianus (between 190-212 C.E. – I like the name so I've placed him in office as a young political appointee, nine years earlier); and Tribune Helvius Pertinax (tribune in the VI Legion from the 170s, who later had a brief stint as Governor of Britannia and, when retired in Rome, was proclaimed Emperor in the confusion after Commodus's assassination, lasting barely a month before he too was disposed of by the praetorian guard). Great names with half-glimpsed stories that deserve to live on.

My story of Noah and the archaeologists is fiction, although the settings are real. Both the Vindolanda Trust and English Heritage are registered trusts under UK law, and manage functioning museums situated at the sites of part-excavated Roman ruins. English Heritage manage many sites on Hadrian's Wall, including the fascinating Corbridge Roman Town, Housesteads (near the much-photographed Sycamore Gap), and the beautifully located Chesters fort, baths and Victorian era museum in the grounds of the Clayton family estate.

The Vindolanda Trust has an ongoing archaeological dig, started in the 1930s by owner Eric Birley, and continued by his son, Robin, who in 1973 oversaw the discovery of the Vindolanda tablets. Vindolanda remained with the Birley family until 1970 when the Vindolanda Trust was founded, with Dr Andrew Birley as Chief Executive Officer. Many wonderous finds, including the tablets, can be seen in the onsite museum.

I visited these places in September 2020, between Covid-19 lockdowns, and the idea for this story came to me shortly after, whilst I was blogging about my visits. I saw for myself the Gladiator drinking bowl or tankard (passed around by Gaius and his mates in chapter two and featured in miniature on the book cover) and was awe-struck by the Vindolanda tablets and the details of the inscriptions on the information cards. The whole museum is fascinating, as are the grounds. I was extremely grateful to escape the confines of my home for three glorious days in the fresh, Northumberland air. In January 2021, whilst in the midst of writing, I enjoyed watching Robson Green's television series, Walking Hadrian's Wall. I note that Mr Green is a Patron of the Vindolanda Trust, and his visit to meet with his 'old mate', Andrew Birley, was both intriguing and timely.

There is no combined universities dig at Vindolanda (that I know of), but there are archaeology degree courses offered by Durham and Newcastle Universities.

The novel's action is set at Hadrian's Wall, one of Britain's World Heritage sites. When finished, Hadrian's wall stretched 117 km (73 imperial miles) from sea to sea. It stood about 5 metres (15 ft.) high and 3 metres (10 ft.) wide. The core consisted of packed earth and clay and the sides were faced with blocks of stone and then plastered. There may have been intermittent platforms on top of some stretches of the wall between watchtowers and mile forts, where auxiliary sentries kept watchful eyes on the north lands. The wall was a highly visible symbol of the Roman Empire's might and prodigious activity at the peak of its power and dominance. Now, barely 10% of Hadrian's Wall remains in place, and its stone blocks have been pilfered over the centuries to build dry stone walls, buildings and even an entire village of over 300 dwellings called Wall.

2022 is a big anniversary year for Hadrian's Wall, marking 1,900 years since the Emperor Hadrian ordered its construction during his visit in 122 CE. At the time of writing, the Hadrian's Wall Partnership Group were planning a number of events to mark the anniversary.

Source Material

Websites:

www.hadrianswallcountry.co.uk
www.vindolanda.com
www.english-heritage.org.uk
www.romaninscriptionsofbritain.org/sites/whitley-castle
www.romanobritain.org
www.legiovieboracum.org.uk
www.u3ahadrianswall.co.uk/wordpress
www.romanhistory.org/roman-military
www.epiacumheritage.org/history/the-romans

Reference books:

Roman Britain, A New History by Guy de la Bédoyère
(Thames and Hudson, revised edition, 2013)
Roman Britain, A New History 55BC - 450AD by
Patricia Southern Amberley, 2013)
Hadrian's Wall – English Heritage Guidebook
(English Heritage, 2017)
Vindolanda Guide by Andrew Birley (Vindolanda
Trust)

Find out more about Tim Walker:

Website: www.timwalkerwrites.co.uk
Amazon page: www.Author.to/TimWalkerWrites
Twitter: www.twitter.com/timwalker1666
Facebook page: www.facebook.com/TimWalkerWrites
Goodreads:
www.goodreads.com/author/show/678710.Tim_Walker